Bloodfeather Heartsong

BLOOD SONG TRILOGY 2

AMBER L. WERNER

Contents

NORTHERN DEPTHS
DOLN
NORWICH
MIDSPORT
GRANSEA
KINGDOM OF
DRACWOOD
MAGEHAVEN
EPRORA OCEAN
ORDDON OCEAN
GREENVALE
FLAMESMOAT
BOGSMOUTH
THE BOGLANDS
STONESHORE
RAIMIRE
SLINAS
NIDO ISLANDS
SALT CLIFF
SULAND WASTE
JORIA
SOUTHERN SEA

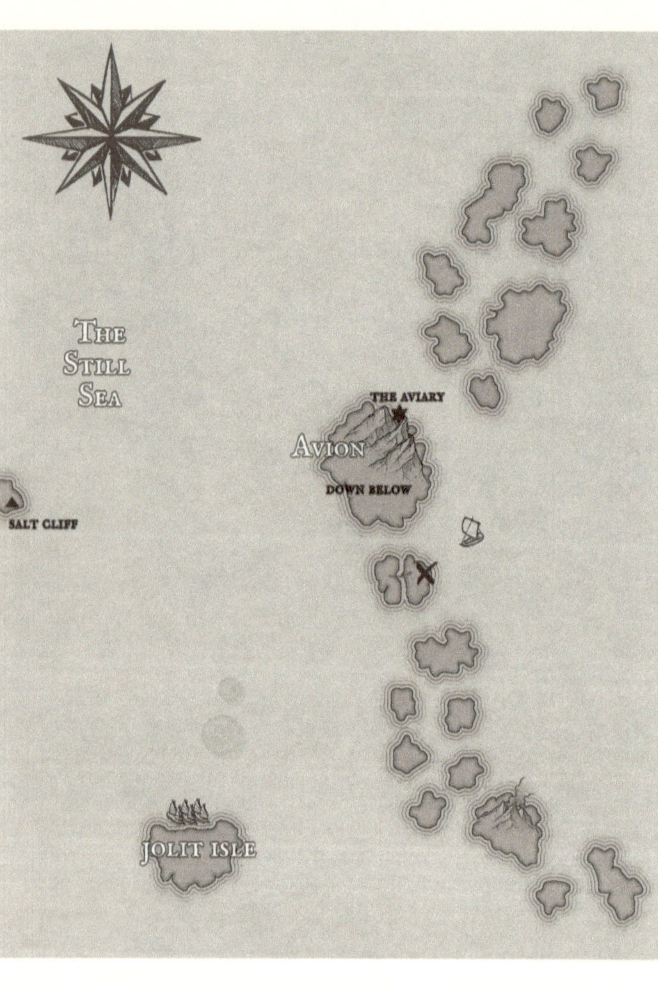

THE STILL SEA
THE AVIARY
AVION
DOWN BELOW
SALT CLIFF
JOLIT ISLE

Prologue

Spider stared at the horizon, perched atop a rickety raft out at sea. He sipped the salty air beneath his mask, and the part deep inside of him that always sang when he was on the water rejoiced.

"We're almost there," said the sunburned wretch next to him.

Spider grunted, not deigning to reply to the fool. It really was disgraceful, what he'd been party to. Bested by a few runaways, caught with his pants down.

His companion rubbed his bandaged head and winced, his skull likely still smarting from the blow he'd suffered days ago at the hands of a whore.

Now it was up to him to pick up the pieces. He was on a mission from Jurdan the Supreme. A mission he would not—could not—fail.

"Spider. We await your orders."

He whipped around, gazing back at his company. They'd crammed a half-dozen masked on the raft after the messenger crows returned with news of the embarrassing defeat at Jolit Isle.

With the entire fleet in Jolit Bay either burned or stolen, they'd been forced to use this abandoned raft. After pulling off their treacherous feat, the escapees set the hogtied wretch on it and shoved him out to sea. It was only pure luck that the idiot managed to untie himself and row to the ocean above Thalassia.

"We split up when we land. You three assess the damages at the docks. Help where needed. We need as many ships ready to sail as soon as possible. You two will come with me to debrief the men."

A chorus of nods met his orders. The men's black-and-white animal masks glittered in the midday sun.

He turned, scanning ahead. A glimmer of green hovered in the distance. The first glimpse of the island that had been his home once, long ago. Soon, they sailed past the breakers. Spider jumped off once they neared the beach to help his men tug the raft ashore.

"Spider, old friend!" A gnarled man hustled toward them, his bare feet kicking up sand. His wide smile sparkled against his deeply tanned skin, nearly all of it on display, with only a tiny pair of shorts covering him. "I'm not surprised to see you."

Spider stretched out a hand as Donalt approached and clapped the old bastard on the back. "I wish it were under better circumstances."

"Nonsense." Donalt shifted, striding back toward the wooded trail to the village. "You have a knack for showing up after a storm rolls in."

Spider fell into step beside him, a pair of men trailing in their wake. The sand crunched beneath his boots and a pleasant breeze caressed his black tunic and pants as they entered the shady trail. "How go the repairs?"

Donalt dug in one hairy ear with a wrinkled pinky. "Fair, all things considered. Those runaways certainly did a number on the docks."

"How many ships are seaworthy?"

"Only one I would trust out in the deep so far. Another pair ought to be back in order within a few days." Donalt shrugged, flicking a speck off his finger and onto a palm tree's trunk. "The rest we're looking at weeks of work to fix."

That was unfortunate. But three ships would be enough. It had to be.

"My men will speak with everyone." Spider nodded back to the pair trudging up the trail behind them. "We need to be certain nothing was missed."

"I understand." Donalt cleared his throat and leaned closer. "Is it true? Was the Supreme's heir among them?"

Spider gritted his teeth, and his chest throbbed with a ghostly prick where the dart she'd shot him with had struck. "Yes. Mariun is gone."

It was all so bizarre. Mariun had been the closest thing he'd had to a friend in Thalassia, and she'd turned on him in an instant. Even if Jurdan hadn't ordered him to follow his wayward daughter, he'd have hunted her down anyway, if only to demand an explanation.

"You'll find her." Donalt waved a hand lazily, as if success were a foregone conclusion.

Spider's reply snagged in his throat when they approached a dilapidated cabin off the path. Ivy covered the little wooden house, the roof bowed in the middle from the weight. A dirt path, absent of any leaves or palm fronds, led to the door.

"Is she...?" Spider gulped, working up the courage to ask, though he dreaded the answer.

Donalt snorted just as a black crow landed on the roof. "She's hanging in. Go on. Stop for a visit. I'll take your men the rest of the way."

Spider stood there while his men left. Once the crunch of their footsteps tapered off, he stepped down the cleanly swept path. Every day for nearly a year, he'd woken to the sound of sweeping. He should've known the stubborn old woman wouldn't have abandoned the habit, even while knocking on death's door.

"Vesie, I'm coming in." Spider brushed aside the cloth on the doorframe and ducked inside. His gaze instantly lit on the tiny woman perched in a worn rocker beside the one-room cabin's back window.

Vesie jerked awake, her rheumy gaze finding him in the doorway. "Sweets. I wasn't expecting you back so soon."

Spider frowned. She was the only one he let get away with using that nickname. He owed her that much after she'd nursed him back from the brink of death.

"Come in. And take off that silly mask while you're here. I want to see your handsome face."

A few steps brought him to her threadbare mattress—the only furniture besides her rocker. He sank down on the edge and slid the black-and-white spider mask off his face. His heart clenched. Vesie seemed so frail; the patterned floral dress she used to fill out hung lank off her reedy shoulders. "How have you been?"

"Better, now that you're here." She smiled and rocked, the bones in her ankles and knees creaking more than the old rocker.

"I wish you'd come to Thalassia. They can—"

"Now, now. Not this again. You know I won't hear of it. This is my home."

"As you wish." Her refusal to leave grated on his last nerve, but he knew it was useless to push her.

"Don't look so disappointed." Vesie chuckled. "You spend your life hiding behind a mask and you don't remember how to temper your emotion once it's off."

That statement only made his frown deepen. He felt it tugging down his cheeks before he forced his mouth into a grim line.

"But you didn't come here to be teased by an old lady." Vesie stilled her rocker, spearing him with a pointed glare. "Have you had any luck with your memories?"

Spider shook his head. "They're gone for good."

"Don't say that. You'll find them. I know it." Vesie rocked again with greater force.

His gaze trailed across the room that had been his home so long ago. No matter how hard he tried, he couldn't remember a thing before he'd awakened in this tiny cabin, half dead, his lungs burning from the seawater he'd swallowed and his head aching something awful. He'd had to relearn everything. How to walk. How to talk. If it hadn't been for Vesie's dogged determination to see him back to rights, he would've never survived.

"What of the girl? What did you call her? The singer," Vesie asked.

"The diva." He sighed. "It's almost as if I recognize her..." He could sense it when he looked at her. Even more when he heard her sing. A maddening tickle in the back of his mind that wouldn't abate no matter how hard he scratched at it. "But she didn't trigger any memories."

"Did you bother to ask her if she knew you?"

He bristled. "You know I can't do that. The Supreme would—"

"Bah! You can't let that old goat stop you. That man is not a god. No god would permit the things he does."

Spider jerked the closest shutter closed. "Vesie, you can't say that. If anyone heard..."

She waved a wrinkled hand. "My days are already numbered." Her voice softened. "Ask her. Find your people. I won't be here much longer, sweets. I don't want to come back to haunt you, only to find you alone."

"Aye, but if you haunt me, then I'll never be alone."

Vesie cackled, her glassy eyes lighting up. Then her smile dropped, and she leaned closer. "All the same, you need to ask her." Her lip curled and her gaze fell on the menacing spider mask resting in his hands. "Show her your face and learn the truth. You deserve to know who you are."

He didn't bother to tell her how impossible that would be. Even if he were willing to ignore the mask edict, the diva was gone. His stomach clenched. He wouldn't tell her about the way the diva's eyes had widened when she'd knocked his mask loose, either.

Instead, he nodded. "I promise, I will. As soon as I get the chance."

"Good." Her smile returned as the creak of bones and wood echoed in his ears. "Now how's about you scrounge up a bit of lunch for the both of us?"

He flicked a glance at the door. He really ought to be leaving, but this might be the last chance he had to spend time with the woman who was the only family he had in this harsh world. They weren't blood, but they were bonded all the same. He'd be damned if he let this chance slip out of his fingers like all the fragmented pieces of his life he couldn't remember.

"All right, Vesie. You just sit back and relax. I'll whip up something tasty."

"That's my boy. Dunno what I'd do without you, sweets."

Bright dawn sunlight spilled in the windows. Out in the yard, his wife's off-key humming whispered on the breeze. Conall cinched his pack closed and slung it over his shoulder.

"She won't like you leaving," a voice announced in his mind.

"I'm a grown man, Shadow. If I want to leave this blazing house, then I'm going to do it." Conall shook out his limbs. His leg still ached. Honestly, everything ached a bit. But that came with the territory of being stuck in a body aged far more than the years he'd lived. Gray fur flashed in the corner of his eye. Conall turned, gracing his bondmate with a crooked grin as he padded into his bedroom. *"You coming, brother?"*

"Always, little brother," Shadow answered.

Conall held back the chuckle that wanted to spill out every time Shadow called him that. The endearment was laughable now, what with him looking more like a grandpa every day.

Shadow must surely be feeling the years too, but most days he gamboled about the farm with all the pep of a young pup. While a normal wolf would surely be on death's door, after twenty long years together, Shadow still had plenty of time left.

If only wolves' boons lengthened their bondmates' lives as humans did, maybe he wouldn't be aching so much right now. Conall wrinkled his nose. Instead, he was blessed with a sense of smell that made him eager to leave this stuffy room. Weeks of lying idle in bed while his leg healed had not been a recipe for freshness.

"Where are we going?" Shadow asked.

Conall strode through the bedroom door and down the hall to the kitchen. *"How would you like to go on a long journey? I've been meaning to visit Magehaven."*

"Magehaven? This have anything to do with Violet?"

The curtains were tied back, illuminating the wooden cabinets and round table neatly laid out with a simple breakfast for two. Conall stopped beside the table and opened his pack, stuffing a half loaf of crusty bread, a hunk of cheese, and a few apples inside. He lifted a shoulder. *"She's been gone for weeks. The least I could do is be there for her when she arrives at port."*

"And that's as far as you're planning to go?"

A thread of apprehension tugged at Conall's heart. Shadow knew him too well. *"I can't just sit idly by while everyone I love is in danger."*

"And Ereni?" Shadow sat back on his haunches, head cocked. *"What will you tell her?"*

Conall nearly groaned. Ereni had been adamant that he remain on the farm with her. He'd agreed so far, but now that his leg had healed, he couldn't calm the itching desire to do *something*.

"You better figure it out fast," Shadow said. *"She's headed inside."*

The warning reached him just before the thump of footsteps pounded toward the door. Conall turned, angling his body to hide his pack.

Ereni burst into the kitchen, her cheeks flushed a rosy pink. Conall's stomach fluttered, and a smile rose unbidden. Even after all these years, the sight of her bright blue eyes and bouncy ponytail still set his heart racing. She halted in the doorway, shucking off a dirt-dusted apron and revealing a simple brown dress.

"There you are." Her gaze swept over his traveling attire, plain brown trousers and a tan tunic, and she lifted a brow. "Out of your pajamas, I see. You must be feeling better," she added brightly.

She strode over, lips pursed to kiss his cheek, as was her habit every morning, and Conall stiffened. Ereni's gaze flicked to the table, and she froze, her perfect lips morphing into a scowl. "Going somewhere?" She leaned back on her heels, hands on her hips.

He rubbed the back of his neck, grinning sheepishly.

Ereni *tsked* and shook her head. "Never mind. We'll talk about that later." Her severe expression lifted and turned positively giddy. "You won't believe who I spotted headed here off the trail."

Conall's pulse sped. "Who?"

Ereni pushed past him and threw open the window. Not a moment passed before golden-and-white-striped feathers filled the narrow space. A beautiful falcon landed on the sill.

"Muse," Conall breathed. "Does that mean—" He didn't bother with the rest of the question. He marched straight to the kitchen door and flung it open.

A warm weight collided with his chest, nearly knocking him off balance. "Brother. Blazes, I've missed you!"

"Lark." Warmth flooded him instantly, but he couldn't stop his gaze from scanning behind his sister. When he spotted only her husband's blond head disappearing into the barn, and no sign of Nox or Violet, his stomach sank. "What are you doing here? Where's Violet?"

Lark pulled back and frowned at him. "Wow. Three long years I've been gone, and *that's* the greeting you give me?" She gathered her long brown curls on one side, resting them on the shoulder of her green-and-white checkered dress.

Conall chuckled and barely avoided rolling his eyes. Lark was always one to put on a show. "My apologies." He cleared his throat and scowled at her. "You're lucky I didn't drag my broken old body halfway around the world to chase you down." He grinned. "There, how was that?"

Lark giggled. "Much better." She leaned sideways and waved at Ereni. "Aren't you two going to invite me in?"

Ereni brushed past him and grabbed Lark's hands. "Come in, sister. You must tell us all about your journey." Ereni pulled out a chair at the table, and Lark sank into it with a grateful sigh.

Conall began to close the door, but stopped when he spotted Aren exiting the barn. "Lark... what is Aren carrying?"

Lark beamed. "That would be your nephew, Dylen."

"You have a son?" Ereni breezed over to the door and tugged it out of Conall's hands, shoving it wide open again and peering outside. Then she spun to Lark, her eyes glassy. "Oh, he's gorgeous, Lark."

Soon Aren made his way to the house, bouncing the toddler in his arms. His golden curls were the perfect match for Aren's short strands, but Dylen's eyes were hazel like Lark's—and Conall's own, too.

Conall cleared his throat, blinking quickly. "Aren. I'm so glad to see you."

Lark rolled her eyes. "Saved a nice greeting for *him*, I see."

Aren chuckled, and after giving a quick hug to Ereni, he handed Dylen to her. "Meet your auntie Ereni, Dylen."

Dylen took to her instantly, cooing and wrapping his little fist around Ereni's long ponytail. Conall's heart stalled. He and Ereni had always wanted more children, but after Violet, they'd never been blessed. Seeing another babe in the house—his own nephew—warmed his soul more than he cared to admit.

"Lark has a pup." Shadow wandered over to Ereni as she sat at the table and placed Dylen in her lap. He nuzzled the boy's leg, then drew back and sneezed. *"Someone needs to change him—fast."*

Conall snorted, and everyone turned quizzical glances in his direction. "Sounds like Dylen needs a new nappy."

Aren laughed and scooped Dylen up in his arms. "Let me take care of that. Do you mind if I lay him on your bed?"

"Not at all. Make yourselves at home." Ereni smiled.

Conall sat at the table and squeezed his sister's hand. "All joking aside, I am very glad to see you. But if you don't start talking soon, I might go crazy."

Lark took pity on him and started talking. Ereni and Conall sat silently and listened, letting the wild tale sink in. She went on for so long that by the time she'd finished, Aren had returned and Dylen had fallen asleep, resting on his father's chest.

Conall leaned back as Lark finally fell silent. "So let me get this straight. You were taken to an *underwater* city"—Lark nodded, and as if that fact wasn't mind-blowing enough on its own, he continued—"where Nox was forced to battle and you were forced to sing. And Violet—*our Violet*—saved you both?"

Lark nodded more vigorously, her hazel eyes shining. "She did. That girl of yours is pretty amazing."

Conall wiped his eyes, biting back the stupid grin that wanted to stay plastered across his face.

"And you say she summoned?" Ereni turned to him, doing nothing to hold back her own luminous smile. "I knew it."

Pride swelled within Conall's chest, but another feeling was quick to douse it. His skin prickled, and his breathing kicked up as he allowed himself to linger over a particular part of his sister's story. "This man—Jurdan the Supreme—did he truly remind you of the Unseen?"

Lark bit her lip. "It was uncanny. That same feeling always washed over me when I was with him. Like my skin couldn't stop crawling and I wanted to puke."

Conall stared at the floor, his mind spinning. "It wasn't over. That's what the Unseen said before I cast that foul serpent to his death. Blazes." He rubbed a hand across his face and met Ereni's eyes.

Ereni shook her head. "I know that look. We can't go."

"She's out there with that *thing*. I don't care what your vision said. We need to help her."

Lark leaned forward. "It's been weeks since we split up. Chances are Violet and Nox already found the eggs and are on their way back as we speak."

"Well then, shouldn't someone be in Magehaven to greet them?" Conall asked.

Ereni crossed her arms. "What about your leg?"

Conall stuck it out sideways, wiggling it around. "Healed fully," he replied, stretching the truth a smidge.

"What about the farm?" Ereni countered. "And your sister's wedding? We can't just pick up and leave like when we were young and foolish, without responsibilities."

Conall grinned. "Aren and Lark can watch the farm."

Aren was quick to nod. "That we can. It's time to settle down, raise our boy right."

Lark patted her husband's arm. "Aren's right. That's what we've been planning. No reason we can't start here in Greenvale. And we'll be there for Kayda at her wedding, too."

Ereni scowled, seeming reluctant to agree even with her excuses dashed. Conall grabbed her hand. "We don't need to follow her out to sea. We'll meet her in Magehaven. Come on, love. I'm going stir-crazy cooped up in this house."

She tilted her head and rested her chin on her fist. "I suppose a bit of camping under the stars would be fun for a change."

"It'll be just like when we met." He leaned closer and whispered in her ear. "We had some good times out in those woods."

Ereni rolled her eyes, but he could see from the tiny tilt to her lips that he'd swayed her.

"Is it settled?" Lark asked.

Ereni nodded. "I suppose."

Lark clapped her hands. "Oh, it's so exciting. Let me help you pack. You can show me the changes you've made to the house while we've been out exploring." Lark grabbed Ereni's elbow and tugged her down the hall.

Aren chuckled, but his laughter faded quickly. "Thank you for offering to let us stay. I know Lark seemed agreeable earlier, but I can tell she's having trouble committing to a sedentary life. I think staying somewhere familiar will help her come to terms with the change."

Conall's heart squeezed. Aren was a good man. He could insist Lark move to his homeland of Doln, but he was putting her needs first. His sister had chosen well.

Conall met Aren's gaze. "I wouldn't dream of having you anywhere else. We're family."

Aren grinned. "Thanks, brother."

The endearment made Conall smile. And it reminded him of Shadow. He'd sat quietly while Lark spoke, patiently waiting to be filled in. He turned to Shadow. *"I haven't forgotten you, brother. I have one more matter to attend to, then I'll tell you everything."*

Shadow lifted his head lazily from where he lounged beside the open window and met Conall's eyes. *"Take your time, little brother."*

Aren watched the exchange silently, clearly used to his conversations being interrupted while Lark spoke with Muse.

Conall turned back to Aren. "I have another favor to ask."

Aren lifted a brow. "What is it?"

Conall pulled a crinkly sheet of paper out of his pocket. "I copied the map you sent with Muse. Would you mind adding the location of that underwater city, the island where the dragon eggs are, and anything else you can remember?"

Nodding, Aren took the paper and unfolded it. "Hold Dylen for me and I'll fill in what I remember."

Conall quickly agreed, and after a moment's shuffling, Aren got to work. Conall rocked his sleeping nephew, and his chest bloomed with the feel of his little body resting in his arms and the sweet scent of his hair.

"Can you believe Violet used to be this small?" He smiled indulgently at the little boy.

"I remember like it were yesterday," Shadow answered. *"Now she's big enough to whelp a pup of her own."*

Conall stilled, snapped out of his musing. *"Yeah, I guess she is."*

Aren lifted the charcoal off the page and carefully refolded the map. "Here you go." He glanced at the hall and lowered his voice. "Guess this means you're not staying in Magehaven?"

Conall accepted the paper with a shrug. "Who knows? But I'd rather be prepared. Thank you for this, Aren."

"You're welcome. Do you want me to take Dylen back now?"

Conall shook his head. "No. I'd like to hold him for a while, if you don't mind."

Aren grinned and leaned back. "I don't mind at all."

Silence settled around them like a threadbare cloak, broken with the occasional peal of laughter from Lark and Ereni touring the house. Conall held his nephew close, soaking in the quiet moment. The sad truth was, it might be the only chance he had to love on the lad.

If that fiend who'd stolen his sister really *was* connected to the Unseen... Certainty bled through his bones, chilling him to his marrow. He wouldn't rest until it was over. Really, truly over—for good.

He'd see that foul vermin destroyed, even if it was the last thing he did.

Puzzles

Nox crouched inside the stolen ship's hold, the crinkle of parchment filling the small space. He smoothed the torn map pieces flat on a rickety old desk, fitting them together like a puzzle.

If only the pieces of his shattered life fit together so easily.

"*They will in time, my friend,*" a voice whispered in his mind, making his heart clench.

"*I miss you, Flint. So much.*"

"*What's to miss? I'm right here,*" Flint replied instantly.

But he wasn't. Not really. The echo of his bondmate still existed in his mind, but it wasn't the same as having him there in the flesh. He would never pet his soft fur again. Never stare into his bright, mischievous eyes. And one day soon, another troubled animal would worm its way into his thoughts. It'd been the same story his entire life. A curse he alone seemed doomed to repeat endlessly.

"*I don't think I can do it, Flint. I don't want another bondmate.*" He sighed uneasily, twisting the final piece of parchment into place. "*Why couldn't it just be me and you till the end?*"

"Fate had other plans."

Nox twisted his lips, studying the map. *"Fate's a fickle mistress."* He'd made a promise to Kayda and Violet, but once he saw that through, he was retreating to the jungle—for good. *"I'll go home and hole up in a cabin. Maybe if I sneak there fast enough, I can avoid attracting another bondmate."*

"Time will tell." Flint's hearty chuckle spread through his mind, tipping up the corners of his mouth. *"You always were good at hide-and-find."*

A throat cleared behind him. Nox flinched and whipped around, his tenuous smile fading away to nothing.

"Do you need any help?" Mariun nodded at the desk and inched closer.

"Nah, I'm fine." Nox shifted, returning his attention to the ripped parchment.

"Really? So you read Thalassian, then?"

Nox bristled. "It's a map. I'll follow the pictures."

"Don't be silly." Mariun stopped beside him and leaned over the map. "Such a shame it's torn."

"You can blame your father for that. He's not a very gracious loser." Jurdan's cocky smirk as he'd shredded the parchment and let it flutter to the dirt floor flashed in Nox's memory.

Mariun stiffened. "Hm, maybe I can fix it." She crossed the room and opened a closet on the far wall. She bent at the waist to rummage inside. Nox gulped and tore his gaze away from her shapely rear rocking beneath her black shift dress with the motion of the boat.

"There it is." Mariun returned to the desk, a parchment and charcoal in her hands. "Thought I'd spotted some earlier." She slid atop a stool and spread the clean sheet out next to the broken pieces. "I'll trace a new one."

Nox backed away as she lifted one piece at a time, studying them carefully before inking their likeness on the fresh sheet. She worked in silence, methodical and lost in the task, the tip of her pink tongue peeking out of the corner of her full lips. She didn't pause until she lifted a piece near the middle. One stained brown with Crow's dried blood.

"Did you know him well?" Nox asked.

Mariun's cheeks drained of color. "Not really, no."

Might as well put it out there... "I'm not sorry I killed him."

Her charcoal scratched the parchment again. "I don't expect you to be. He was trying to kill you."

Nox cocked his head. Mariun was a mystery. At times she seemed so expressive. Fiery and full of passion. The kind of woman who would march through a prison cell and mend the wounded wretches within. But then there were times like these when she was closed off. Unreadable.

It shouldn't matter. *She* shouldn't matter. Not after what she'd done. But if Mariun was determined to follow them on this voyage, then didn't he owe it to Violet, to Flint, even, to discover her motivations?

She claimed to want out. But why would the daughter of a man who imagined himself a god want to leave her place at his side? What if she wasn't here to escape, but to keep tabs on them and report back to Daddy Dearest when they succeeded?

"I can feel you over there stewing." Mariun set down the bloody piece of parchment and selected the next. "Tell me, what's bothering you?" She glanced his way, then returned to her drawing. Her voice rang with command, but she didn't push further, just sat waiting. For some reason, her demand and calm demeanor rankled him.

"Why are you really here, Mare?"

She set down the charcoal and spun to face him, her brow furrowed and her gray eyes awash with sadness. "Don't call me that."

Nox crossed his arms. He wasn't sure what possessed him to shorten her name, but it had clearly struck a nerve. "Why not?"

Mariun blew out a harsh sigh and shook her head. "It doesn't matter." She twisted back to the desk. "I told you already. I wanted out. I've always wanted out."

Where did she get off, avoiding the question? After everything she'd done, all the madness she had a hand in while acting as his jailer—Flint... He sucked in a breath. "You know what? Forget it." He tugged at his sweat-soaked tunic, feeling like he was suffocating in the stifling cabin.

Air. He needed some air.

A gentle hand on his arm halted him before he mounted the stairs. "Nox, wait. I owe you a story."

He glared at her hand on his sleeve, and Mariun retracted her fingers like his gaze burned her.

"Gather the others. I don't want to tell this tale twice." She returned to the desk. "I'll join you on deck after I finish tracing the map."

Nox was tempted to argue, if only to point out that her commands held no weight. Not any longer. But he couldn't deny the burning desire to hear what she had to say.

He burst out of the tiny hold and drew a welcome breath of salty air. The sea stretched out in all directions, an unending blue carpet topped with a startling cloudless sky. The first hint of pink painted the sky to the west. Nox welcomed the arrival of dusk. He'd like to be the first to say goodbye to this wretched day.

"Uncle Nox," Violet greeted him with a grin, her ghostly pale skin shaded with a ridiculous oversized hat she'd scrounged out of the hold. "Did you get the map sorted?"

"Mariun's tracing a copy on fresh parchment." He craned his neck, searching the small deck and cocking a brow. "Where's your friend?"

"Up here," a voice called from above.

Nox shaded his eyes and spotted the dreadlocked man dangling in the rigging, muscles flexing beneath his all-black outfit. "Rot and decay. You trying to break your neck?"

The breezy sound of his chuckle preceded the thump of Ryon's boots on deck. "Don't worry. I'm a great climber." He slapped Nox's shoulder. "I was trying to see if I could catch a glimpse of land before dusk rolled in."

"Any luck?" Violet asked.

"Sorry to say not."

She shrugged, flicking her gaze away from Ryon and down at the deck. "It was worth a shot."

"It was a good idea." Ryon took a step closer to Violet, his voice gentle. "I can try again in a little while, if you'd like."

"Hold off on that," Nox said. "Mariun's agreed to tell us her story as soon as she's done with the map."

Violet smoothed her trousers and tugged down her black tunic sleeves as she settled cross-legged on the deck. "Oh good. I'm dying to learn more about Thalassia. Never in my wildest dreams did I picture myself visiting a city under the sea."

"I'll tell you about Thalassia soon." Mariun perched in the cabin's doorway. "There's something more important I need to share with you first."

"More important? What do you mean?" Violet patted the deck beside her.

Mariun paced across the deck and sank down beside Violet. She clutched her knees to her chest and sucked in a deep breath. "I know you don't trust me. I don't blame you. I wouldn't trust me, either, if I were in your shoes."

Silence stretched out after her announcement. No one rushed to disabuse Mariun of the facts. Even Violet held her tongue, though she flashed a small, encouraging smile.

Mariun stretched out her legs and stiffened her spine. "I hope the tale I tell you will change that. I know it's a lot to ask, and I plan to keep earning your trust either way, but after you hear this, you'll hold the key to my fate in your hands."

Violet scrunched her nose. "Your fate? How is that possible?"

Mariun bit her lip. "Because if Jurdan ever hears the truth, he won't hesitate to kill me."

Nox jerked where he stood, a sick feeling spreading through his veins. Would she really be that trusting of them—practical strangers—to share a secret that had the potential to destroy her own life?

"It all started when I was twelve years old," Mariun began.

The Story

"Will it hurt?" Mariun whispered. She curled her fingers through her long black hair, the silky strands fluttering like feathers across her trembling fingers.

"Of course it's gonna hurt. That's never been in question." She could picture the smirk on Whit's face, though it was far too dark to see it. "But it'll be over quick. Then we finally get to meet them."

Mariun fluffed her pillow, then rested her cheek upon it, though she was too worked up to close her eyes. All her life she'd spent waiting for this day. Twelve long years wasting away in this room with the same children. No matter what the test's outcome was tomorrow, her life would change. All of their lives would.

The quiet sounds of Mariun's roommates echoed around her. After a lifetime with them, she knew them intimately. The wheezing trill from across the room was Joben. The large shape rolling on its side restlessly would be Malik. And of course, Whit—the small boy she loved like none other, whispering beside her.

"What if they make us live on different sides of Thalassia?" Mariun's pulse pounded in her ears as she waited for Whit's response. She couldn't bear the thought of being separated from him.

"Don't worry. I'll be masked in a few years. I'll request to be stationed wherever you are."

She wrinkled her nose. "Years, Whit. What will I do without you for years?"

"It won't be so bad."

She sighed. Out of the two of them, she was usually the voice of reason. The one who would sit still and listen to their instructors, while Whit couldn't resist squirming and goofing off. But for some reason, she couldn't quiet the little voice inside whispering that something was about to go horribly, terribly wrong.

"What if they're awful?" Her voice cracked.

"Stop worrying. We'll find out soon enough."

"I don't know how you can't worry. They must be awful. They gave us away. Who does that?"

"You know that's not how they see it. We're the lucky ones."

"I don't feel lucky."

"I know. But it's almost over."

"Unless we pass."

Whit scoffed. "No one passes, Mare. Just get through tomorrow and this will all be over."

"But—"

"No more buts. I'm going to sleep. Goodnight."

"Goodnight," she whispered back.

Whit rolled over, and within moments his breathing evened. Mariun lay there in the dark, begging her mind to quiet. She tried to take comfort in Whit's assurances, but sleep was slow to find her that night.

The overhead lights kicked on. The bright glow assaulted the backs of Mariun's eyelids, making her squint and groan in her cot.

"Wake up, children. Today's the day," Seneca declared cheerily. The swish of her dress and tap of her boots rang out as she circled their little room.

Mariun resisted the urge to pull her blanket over her head and hide. She cracked open her eyes, blinking as she adjusted to the light. A fragrant bowl of spiced grain landed in her lap as she sat up. She smiled around a yawn, meeting her morning instructor's gaze. "Thank you."

"Eat up quickly now. Plenty to do before your audience with the Supreme."

Mariun shoved a spoonful of the sweet cinnamon grain into her mouth. Breakfast was usually her favorite meal of the day. Not today. The grainbowl was as tasteless as cotton, but she swallowed it down, knowing it was useless to argue.

If her instructor said eat, she ate. If they said jump, she jumped. Obedience was demanded of the Supreme's progeny. That fact had been drilled into them every day of their lives.

"One of you is going to pass. I can feel it." Seneca clutched a hand to her chest, her smile wide and radiant. "I can't wait to see the sour look on Naomi's face when she hears the news."

Mariun shared a glance with Whit. He rolled his dark-brown eyes before shoveling a spoonful of grain into his mouth.

The instructor's rivalry was heated—to say the least—each of them vying to be the one to finally present the Supreme with the perfect child. All of them were eager to earn the reward that Jurdan promised to the first instructors who were successful.

Seneca had been assigned to their class the year they were born. She was the closest thing they had to a parent, though she was careful to treat them with proper detachment. Instructors who grew too close to their charges didn't last long.

"Don't get your hopes up, Seneca." Whit scraped the bottom of his bowl. "We're much more likely to fail."

Seneca snatched the bowl out of his hands. "One of these days, someone has to pass. Why not one of you?"

Mariun allowed herself to imagine becoming the Supreme's successor. Every year, their ruler tested his children. Every year, they all failed and were returned to the women who'd birthed them. Now that it was their turn to be tested, she couldn't help but worry about the outcome. Would it be better to fail and return to the mother who had abandoned her to a loveless childhood? Or to succeed and be forever tied to the enigmatic ruler of their city?

Seneca stopped beside her cot, hand outstretched. "Hand it over, Mariun, then off to the washroom."

Mariun placed her half-eaten grainbowl in Seneca's hands and stood. Her thin nightdress fell down, swishing against her thighs as she made her way through the hall. The muffled cry of a baby pierced her ears, the wail leaking through the walls.

They lived in a suite of rooms attached to eleven other identical suites, each housing a year's worth of children. It was no secret how the rooms were run. Their instructors didn't let a day pass without reminding them of their lofty parentage. But for all the children the Supreme had fathered, he didn't lay claim to any. Once they failed the test, they were dead to him. Discarded like a piece of rubbish. And today it was her turn to be tossed aside.

Mariun sighed as she entered the washroom. Being the only girl in her class, she was allowed to wash separately from the boys. But she still wasn't alone.

"Good morning, Iona. I'm—" Mariun paused, cocking her head sideways. "You're not Iona."

The unfamiliar woman stared, her gray eyes misty. She smiled benignly and tucked a loose strand of dark-brown hair behind her ear. Then she scanned behind Mariun and quickly closed the door. "Iona was ill. I'm her replacement."

"Oh, I'm sorry to hear that. I hope she's well soon," Mariun replied. She breezed past the woman, into the toilet stall. The rush of running water sounded as her attendant filled the claw-foot tub in the outer room.

When she exited the stall, the woman was parked directly in front of it, making her gasp. Mariun raised a brow. "I'm not sure what they told you, but I can bathe myself."

A tear slid down the woman's cheek. Then another.

"Are you all right?" Mariun stepped closer, confusion and empathy warring for dominance in her belly.

The woman lifted a shaky hand and gently stroked her fingers through Mariun's hair. "I've waited so long for this day."

Mariun jerked back from the stranger's touch. *What in the—*

"Who are you?" But even as she asked, she stared at her more closely. The woman's eyes still hadn't left hers. They were red-rimmed and overflowing with tears; a familiar shade of gray.

"Mariun. I'm your mother."

"My—" She shook her head, then hissed under her breath, "What are you doing here? You're not supposed to be here."

"I-I know. I needed to see you. It might be the only chance we have to talk."

Mariun bit back a laugh. It was absurd. Her mother sneaking in to see her when they were due to meet in a few hours... It didn't make sense. No sense at all.

"I don't understand. If you had only waited—"

"I couldn't. There are things you must know before the test. I couldn't live with myself if I didn't tell you. My beautiful girl." Another tear slid down her cheek.

Mariun rubbed her chest. She didn't know what to do. Should she curl into her arms and finally experience the warmth of a mother's embrace? Should she curse and scream, demand to know why, how, the woman could abandon her to this cruel fate?

Instead of choosing either of those tempting options, she strode to the tub and removed her nightdress. "Well, *Mother*, you better talk while I bathe. We don't have much time."

Mariun sighed as she sank into the warm water. Her mother settled beside her after scrubbing her cheeks with the long sleeves of her simple cream dress.

"There's no easy way to say this." Her mother appeared to steel herself, inhaling deeply and sitting ramrod straight on the tub's edge. "I'm afraid you won't be passing the test today, Mariun."

Mariun waved a hand before grabbing a washcloth. "That's not surprising. No one ever has."

"You don't understand. You never stood a chance." She glanced nervously around as if making certain the bathroom was truly empty. "The Supreme is not your father."

Mariun scrubbed the washcloth across her face, grateful for the excuse to hide her expression. How was that possible? They were all the Supreme's children. She wouldn't be here otherwise. But this woman *was* her mother—if she could be believed. She had to hear her out.

"Why am I here, then?" she asked.

"You were supposed to be his. I-I laid with him, as was my duty. But when my courses came, I couldn't go through with it again. I hid the evidence. And your real father—the man you're meant to meet today, along with your brother and sister—he helped me fix it. To make you, before anyone noticed."

The mechanics of human mating had not been hidden from her. Their instructors sought to provide the Supreme's progeny with a well-rounded education while in their care. So even this halting confession made sense to Mariun, though she still found herself wavering between shock and disbelief.

Not only was she meant to believe that this stranger had deceived the Supreme, but Mariun was not related to him *at all*. She had an entire family out there—mother, father, brother, and sister—living together while she was stuck in here, living a lie. The abandonment she'd always struggled with rankled anew, so much that her throat tightened and the corners of her eyes stung. But she shoved the hurt aside, desperate to understand.

"Why would you do that?" She stared into gray eyes that mirrored her own. "Why tell me now and not this afternoon? You risk much by being here."

"The test. I had to see you. I had to warn you. They say none but Jurdan's true children can withstand it." Her lower lip wobbled, her voice cracking. She leaned closer and slid a wooden tube out of her dress pocket with shaky fingers. "We can escape together."

"Are you mad? No, we can't." Mariun laughed. She actually laughed at the thought.

"I know I have no right to your trust." The quiet defeat in her mother's voice stilled Mariun's laughter. "I'm so sorry, Mariun. I shouldn't have done it. I should've just suffered through my duty again. It was selfish of me to avoid it. I've regretted that mistake for twelve years, from the moment they took you from my arms."

Mariun tossed the cloth in the water. "You're right. I don't trust you. I don't *know* you. This could be a lie."

"It's not. How I wish that it were. Please, please, come with me. I can't bear to watch you tested."

"Why? Because I'm going to die?" Mariun jerked out of the warm tub, the room's cool air instantly chilling her to the bone. Was that true? Was she destined to die today, failing the test so spectacularly because she didn't *actually* have the one thing that had trapped her here?

Today was supposed to be her day to escape. Not to die.

"Come with me, Mariun. I'll—"

"And where will we go? Where will we hide that he won't find us?" she hissed.

For a heartbeat, she hoped her mother would light up at that. That she'd lay out a plan, a daring escape that she'd agonized over for years, every detail considered and every possible pitfall accounted for. But when she looked into her mother's eyes, all she saw was panic and defeat.

"You're right," Mariun declared, wrapping a towel around herself.

"I am?" Her face did light up with that statement, a stunning smile curving her lips. "Thank—"

"Selfish. You're a selfish, cruel woman to spring this on me now, when nothing can be done." Mariun blinked furiously, desperate to stem the tears spilling into her eyes. "I can't go anywhere with you."

She crossed the room and snatched up the pile of clothes laid out for her. The undergarments were new, thickly padded, and heavy in her hands. She shoved them on and threw on the plain black shirt and pants, desperate to leave.

"Mariun." Her mother's voice sounded broken, a tenuous frayed string ready to unravel. "I'm so sorry. I-I love—"

"Don't." Mariun whipped around. "Don't you dare." Then she stomped off down the hall, back to her room.

She sat on her cot and busied herself with tugging her boots out from beneath the bed as the boys rose to take their turn. Whit paused beside her. "Everything all right, Mare?"

Mariun nodded at her feet, knowing she would burst into tears if she met his gaze. "Just nervous about today. Go on, I'll be fine."

But as her friend's footsteps trailed down the hall, she only wished she could believe the lie, too. She wasn't fine. She was about to die.

The Pull

"**E**nough with the dramatics," Nox sneered, arms crossed. "It's obvious you didn't die."

"Really?" Violet barely stopped herself from leaping up and smacking the disgusted look off her uncle's face. "Blazes, have a little compassion."

Mariun sniffed and rubbed her nose on her sleeve. "He's right. Clearly I didn't die. But in that moment, I was convinced I would."

"So is it true?" Ryon asked. "Jurdan isn't really your father?"

Mariun nodded gravely. "I've never told anyone before. If Jurdan ever found out"—she gulped—"he wouldn't let me live. He has no qualms about killing those who've wronged him."

Violet shivered. She had no doubt that was true. From witnessing the cruelty of the sick games he held, she knew the ruler was no stranger to sentencing others to death.

"What about the rest?" Nox blurted. "Why did Lark think you were his daughter? How did Jurdan go so long without figuring it out?"

Mariun drew a deep breath. The sun had set while they'd listened to her tale, but the moonlight was bright enough to highlight the lone tear trailing down Mariun's cheek.

"She can tell us tomorrow," Violet insisted, her voice firm. "We're not going anywhere, and it's past time we got some sleep."

Nox fumed, pacing, his gaze flitting all over distractedly like it often did when he spoke to Flint.

Truthfully, Violet was dying to hear the rest. If Mariun didn't look like she was a heartbeat away from weeping, she'd be pressing her for more too.

Finally, Nox nodded and stalked across the deck, grumbling to himself under his breath.

"Thank you," Mariun whispered with a sigh. "I don't think I've ever been so ready to sleep."

Violet scanned Mariun closely in the moonlight. Her typical commanding presence gave her an air of maturity that belied her youth. But with her eyes shadowed by dark circles and her arms wrapped tightly around her middle, Violet could almost picture the child Mariun once was, a little girl all alone and wishing for a mother's love.

Despite her childhood struggles, that was one thing Violet had never questioned. Her mother and father were a rock-solid fixture in her life. How lonely it must have been to grow up abandoned by the people who should have loved her the most.

"I'll take first watch," Ryon offered. "You two should get some rest."

It was such a lovely night that she grabbed a bedroll instead of lying in one of the hammocks in the cabin. Violet settled down, curled up beside the center mast. The gentle lapping waves quickly lulled her to sleep.

Violet gasped, waking with the dregs of some hazy dream tickling the recesses of her mind. Stars winked down at her, begging her to return to slumber. She shivered, the cool night air chilling her skin, but not nearly as bad as the nightmare cooled her veins.

After an eternity of waiting for the motion of the boat and the gentle surf to send her back to sleep, she sighed. She wrapped a blanket around her shoulders and stood, making her way to the ship's railing.

"Would you like some company?"

Ryon turned, his dark beard and clothes shrouding his features in the moonlight. "From you? Always."

Violet's cheeks warmed. "How late is it?"

"Not very. It's only been an hour or two. Couldn't sleep?"

"Strange dreams."

"The ring again?"

She nodded, staring out at the sea. Deep below the dark waters, the massive circle waited. She could still feel its pull—a gentle tug on her heart, growing weaker the farther away they sailed. "Have you dreamed about it? Or felt drawn to the ocean, like me?"

Ryon rubbed his chin. "No. Can't say I have."

That's right. He was drawn to *her* instead.

"Do you still think it was the feathers? Their consequences?"

"Maybe not." He shrugged. "I'm not an expert."

"You know more than I do."

The bright gleam of his teeth caught on a moonbeam. "We can ask Mother Orea. She'll have an answer for you, I'd wager."

She still couldn't believe Ryon's people lived with birds they revered as gods. But then again, those orecolns could do some incredible things. "Good. I could really stand to have some of these questions answered." Violet sighed. "Feels like for every win, every little mystery we solve, a dozen more pop up in its place."

"But what wondrous mysteries they are. Can you imagine—dragons! My people have so many stories about them, but I never thought I'd see one in the flesh."

"Yeah. Me either." She curled a white strand of hair behind her ear. "What kind of stories?"

"Oh, ancient legends, mostly. Except, when I was a lad, a fellow claimed to have spotted a pair of dragons, one black and one white, posted outside the Aviary while the village was asleep. No one believed him at the time." He leaned closer and wiggled his brow. "He'd been partaking in a bit of drink, you see."

"Is that so?"

"Yeah. But now you tell me dragons were around then, fighting in that battle on your..." He squinted and elbowed her gently. "Where was it again?"

"The Abandoned Lands."

"That's right. I wonder if he had the right of it all along? Didn't Aren mention one of them having a bloodfeather?"

Violet wrinkled her nose. "He did. Huh. Another thing to ask Mother Orea, I suppose."

"Thank you again for agreeing to come with me." Ryon took her hand and squeezed. "I can't tell you what it means to me. I've been working to gain an audience with her for so long."

A question—*why?*—was on the tip of her tongue. But at that moment, Ryon yawned so loudly and widely she suppressed a giggle.

"Why don't you get some rest?" she offered. "I'll take the next watch."

"You sure?" he asked.

She nodded. Ryon gave her hand one last squeeze and wandered off to find his bedroll.

Violet spun to face the sea. If she closed her eyes, the echo of the haunting melody she'd heard in her dreams played in her ears. She stood there for a long while, bathed in moonlight and ignoring the pull on her heart.

"I'll return. One day. I promise," she whispered into the breeze.

Groping in the Dark

Fierce waves battered their little boat, and the sky split open, drenching the deck and them with it. They'd barely awoken and choked down a few bites of breakfast before the storm hit. Ryon prayed it would be a short squall, but as the day wore on, it seemed more and more likely that his prayers would remain unanswered.

Violet and Nox, being the most seasoned sailors of their quartet, rushed about, barking orders, adjusting the rigging, and doing everything in their power to keep the small craft afloat. Ryon helped where he could, but the intricacies of sailing were still a mystery to him.

Mariun had put on a brave face in the beginning, but it was soon clear she'd be no help. She'd spent half the day rushing to the railing and emptying her stomach into the sea. The other half, she'd hunkered down in the tiny cabin after Nox demanded she quit moaning before he tossed her overboard.

Ryon had nearly spoken up in her defense then. If it hadn't been for the huge swell that pummeled them immediately after, he'd have definitely done more than just scowl in Nox's general direction.

Violet appeared to trust Mariun already, but Ryon still wasn't sure what to believe. It was obvious there was some bad blood between Mariun and Nox. The others might be overeager to hear the rest of her childhood tale, but Ryon was itching for a different story. He was dying to know what exactly had happened in that underwater city before they'd showed up for their rescue.

Just before nightfall, the storm finally broke. The huge waves calmed and the heavy downpour shifted to a light sprinkle.

"I'm glad that's over." Ryon whipped his soaked dreads off his face.

Violet stared at the sky. "Sorry to disappoint but I don't think it is." She gestured at the clouds ahead, the moon's dim light hidden behind the thick layer of gray. "We've hit a lull for the moment, but it looks like more rain on the horizon."

Nox stopped beside them, scanning the cloud cover just as intensely. "I think you're right, Squirt."

Violet glared at her uncle until he flashed her a little half smile. "Sorry, Vi. Old habits." Nox sighed, scratching his chest. "You two better rest while you can. I have a feeling it's going to be a long night once we hit that second storm."

As if to give merit to his prediction, the sky pulsed with a bright flash in the distance. They all held their breath, waiting for thunder to crack. It took several heartbeats for the sound to blare through the evening air.

"Sounds like it's still a ways off." Nox hustled over to the sails. "I'll do my best to slow our approach. Give you two a chance to rest. Go on." He nudged Violet's arm with his elbow. "This might be the only chance you get to catch a few winks."

Ryon followed Violet into the tiny cabin below deck. The room was stifling but blessedly dry. Mariun was curled in the corner under a thin blanket, moaning quietly and looking utterly miserable.

She peeked up as they approached. "Is it over?"

Violet shook her head. "A temporary lull, I'm afraid."

"Wonderful," Mariun replied, her face and body language at total odds with her cheery reply.

Ryon frowned, wishing he could do something to calm Mariun's nausea. A weed grew on the mountains back home that worked wonders, but he clearly wouldn't be returning for a long while yet.

A second crack of thunder interrupted his musing. Violet flinched, but Mariun's head perked up at the sound, and her eyes widened.

"C'mon, Ryon. We need to rest." Violet flopped down on a hammock without even bothering to change out of her wet clothes.

"I hope I'm not too wound up to sleep," Ryon replied. But as he lay in the hammock beside Violet's, weariness stole over him all at once. A huge yawn split his cheeks.

Violet giggled. "Just close your eyes. I think you'll sleep just fine."

Ryon shut his eyes, the gently swaying hammock relaxing his aching muscles. "You might be right. Goodnight, Violet. Mariun."

"Goodnight," the girls repeated in a chorus, but Ryon was already drifting away.

A deafening boom woke Ryon. He gasped, jerking up so quickly he almost spilled out of the hammock. How long had he been asleep? The still-damp clothes sheathed around him suggested it hadn't been very long.

A single candle lit the little cabin, held by a shuddering Mariun. "Violet already went up. Be careful. It's pitch black except for when the lightning flashes."

Eyes narrowing, Ryon swung out of the hammock. Then he climbed the steps and stepped into a nightmarish tempest. Wind whipped rain into him, drenching him before he'd even slammed the door closed behind him. Lightning shot from cloud to cloud, painting the black sky with vivid flashes of light. Even so, he struggled to move, afraid one wrong step on the slippery boards would send him careening into the roiling sea.

Ryon forced his feet to move. He slid across the deck toward the helm, where he could just make out two shadows lit with the occasional flash.

"Hey," he called. A few more steps and he had almost reached them when the ship heaved unexpectedly. Ryon yelped, losing his center of gravity. He tumbled end over end, flying toward the railing so swiftly there was no way he wasn't about to smash through the railing and into the ocean.

Guano! This was it. This was how he was going to die.

Something clamped his ankle, stopping him a mere hairsbreadth before he slammed into the railing. He hit the deck instead with a pained groan. He looked up sheepishly and spotted Nox leaning over him. Nox dropped his ankle and stretched out a hand to help Ryon to his feet.

"Thanks," Ryon yelled, raising his voice to be heard over the surf's roar and the booming thunder.

"Don't thank me yet," Nox yelled back as he helped steady Ryon with a hand on his shoulder. "I need your help."

Ryon quirked a brow, spotting Violet grunting at the helm, her muscles quivering as she held the boat steady with all the strength she possessed. "You have it. What can I do?"

"You said you're a good climber, right?"

Ryon nodded. "I am."

Nox pointed behind them at the central mast. "Do you see that rope?"

Ryon squinted in the dark. Black soaked the sky. How Nox could see anything was a mystery to him. After a few heartbeats, another bolt of lightning flashed and Ryon spotted a long rope coiled around the top of the mast. As he watched, a short length of sail flicked out beyond it. It was clear the rope had come loose.

Ryon's stomach sank, and he suspected he knew what Nox was about to ask. "I see it."

"Good. Climb up there and tie down the top of the sail. Quickly now. I need to help Violet."

Ryon raced to comply, thankful the lightning flashes continued as he made his way across the slippery deck. He misjudged his last step, and his boots skidded. Luckily, he caught the mast before he took a second tumble.

The slick wooden mast slipped against his fingers. If not for the footholds carved in the thick wooden beam, he'd have struggled to climb. The flap of fabric above quickened his pace. He chanced a glance up in time to see a new length of the sail break free.

If the whole sail came loose... Ryon gulped, racing up the footholds. Every few heartbeats the sky blackened, making his heart still until a new bolt lit the clouds. He groped in the dark, relying on feel as much as his sight to see him safely to the top.

At last, he reached the flapping sail. It slapped him in the face, nearly knocking him off, before he caught the end and plastered the wet cloth to the mast, trapping it with his body weight. He clamped his legs and thighs tight, waiting for a flash.

There. He grabbed the rough rope in a shaking fist. Then all that was left was wrapping it back up. He tugged the soggy rope tight and knotted it like Nox had showed him on their first day out to sea.

He breathed a sigh, then nearly jumped out of his skin.

Crack.

What in the—

Ryon's gaze flitted around. That last flash of lightning and boom of thunder were so close they'd been practically on top of each other. And here he was, at the top of the mast...

Pulse pounding, he started the climb back down. But screaming below made him pause. His heart leaped into his throat as another bright strike illuminated a shadowy form standing at the very tip of the ship's bow.

Was that Violet? What was she doing away from the helm? He rushed down a few more rungs, purely by feel in the blackest darkness. Then another bolt lit the sky.

It wasn't Violet. Black hair whipped in the wind, not Violet's pale-white locks. Mariun.

And the shouting was coming from Nox. He barreled across the deck, the slick wood and shifting boat seeming no deterrent to his stride.

Ryon watched Nox's mouth drop open, and the wind whipped the single word up to Ryon's ears. "Mariun!"

Then the sky lit up. Ryon clasped the mast for dear life, his eyes forced shut instinctively. But not before a maddening glimpse burned itself on his irises.

The image of Mariun, her arms spread wide overhead as lightning crackled all around her, stayed with him. It lingered while the light burned so brightly he didn't dare open his eyes. He'd be blinded.

The air buzzed and crackled, raising the hair on his arms. Even though he couldn't see it, he knew lightning continued to rain down on them—for far longer than any strike he'd witnessed in his life. And he feared when he opened his eyes, that poor woman would be dead.

No one could survive that. No one.

No Lies

Nox sighed, his excellent night vision allowing him to watch Ryon secure the sail to the mast even when the lightning faded. The ship settled a degree without the wind whipping the cloth into a frenzy. It still wouldn't be smooth sailing until the storm ended, but at least now it wouldn't be so much of a struggle at the helm.

He cocked his head. A rhythmic thumping reached his sensitive ears even with the boom of thunder echoing around him. He turned, his gaze landing on the cabin door swinging on its hinges in the wind. "Vi, hold her steady," he shouted, relinquishing his grip on the wheel.

Violet stepped beside him and clutched the wheel with a nod.

Nox bolted across the deck, his step steady even with the pouring rain slicking everything. He reached the door and wedged it closed with a firm, "I got it."

Poor Mariun must be scared witless inside with the storm howling and the door blasting frigid water into the cabin. She really wasn't suited to this kind of travel. It was a miracle she'd even—

The thought evaporated in a cloud of smoke. Nox rubbed his tired eyes. His mind must be playing tricks on him. He could swear she stood out there, perched against the bow railing, her hands outstretched, the violent storm whipping her hair and dress wildly.

"Mariun!" he yelled, desperate for her to spin around. Or better yet, for her to fade away completely, revealed to be a figment of his overactive imagination after a sleepless night.

But then the slap of Ryon's feet on the mast halted. Nox flicked a glance upward just as a bolt of lightning illuminated his slack jaw and wide eyes.

He saw her too.

"Mariun!" Nox rushed forward in a daze. He was half the ship's length away near the mast, and with the sea rolling beneath him, every step was hard fought.

Rot and decay, what was she doing? One wrong flip of a wave would send her tumbling into the roiling waves. He had to get her back down—

Crack.

He flew backward. The strike's immense power sent him off-kilter, legs flailing. Nox's arm rose instinctively, protecting him from the blinding flash. His ears popped, and the air sizzled.

"Oof." He smacked into the mast, knocking the wind out of his chest and sending a blast of agony across his shoulder blades. But the pain barely registered. As soon as he landed, he shoved himself up, gasping. Nox forced his shaky legs to move, regaining the ground he'd lost in the blast. The crackle in the air faded, and the light snuffed out. He arrived at the bow in time to watch Mariun wobble and collapse.

He sank to his knees beside her and scooped her into his lap, his stomach sinking when she put up no resistance. "You rotting fool."

He cradled her against his chest, shoving the mop of wet black strands off her face.

"*What is it?*" Flint asked. "*I can sense something is wrong. Talk to me.*"

"*Not now,*" Nox barked. *Mother, don't take her, too.*

He vaguely registered the sound of Ryon's boots slapping the deck behind him, but he didn't turn. His heart was too busy pounding out of control, his gaze locked on the unmoving beauty clasped in his arms.

She might be all right. Just temporarily stunned.

But even as his brain fought to reassure him, his whole body thrummed with disbelief. The chances of someone surviving a direct hit by a bolt of lightning were slim. And that had been no ordinary strike. It tossed him aside without him even being close enough to be struck and lasted five times longer than it had any right to. The air still crackled faintly in the aftermath, and the hair on his skin stood on end.

It wasn't fair. He'd seen so much death. Nox clenched Mariun tightly, his chin wobbling. *Not her, too.*

"Ow." Mariun groaned. "You're hurting me."

Nox loosened his grip and stared down into gorgeous gray eyes. "Thank the Mother," he whispered. Then his voice turned stern and his hands ached. "What were you thinking?"

Mariun reached up and cradled his cheek. The tender gesture made his breath catch and the dull throb in his fingers subside.

"I had to make it stop."

His brow furrowed. "What?"

Mariun's gaze left his and swung to the night sky. "Look."

Nox tore his gaze away from her and did a double take. He'd been so consumed with worry, he hadn't noticed until now, but the lightning, the thunder, the rain—the entire storm—all of it was over. The clouds slowly receded, washing the waves in starlight.

Nox frowned. If someone had asked him a few moments ago, he would've predicted the storm would last all night. But now...

She couldn't have stopped it, could she?

He ripped his gaze off the calming sky, intent on making her explain, but Mariun's eyes were closed. Her hand slipped off his cheek and flopped against her chest. Thankfully, that rose and fell in a steady rhythm.

Violet leaned over his shoulder, curiosity shining in her gaze. "Am I going crazy, or did she—"

Nox shook his head. "I don't know. I honestly have no clue." He stood, easily hefting Mariun in his arms. "I'm going to put her in a hammock."

Violet nodded. Her brow pinched as she studied Mariun out cold in Nox's arms. "Maybe you should stay with her. Or I can—"

"I'll watch her."

"Good. You haven't slept yet. You should get some rest, too. Ryon and I will handle the sailing until morning."

Nox nudged the cabin door open with his boot. The dark interior didn't slow him in the least. He paused beside one of the hammocks. He should set her down on it and crawl into his own. But then, how would he be sure she remained breathing through the night?

With a sigh, he settled on a hammock with Mariun still cradled in his arms. She stirred as he sat, and her eyes fluttered open.

"What's going on?" she mumbled, her voice heavy with exhaustion.

"Shh. We both need to rest. And I need to watch over you. We're sharing a hammock tonight."

"Sharing?" She chuckled weakly. "You can't be serious."

Nox ground his teeth. "Fine. Guess I'll stay up instead."

"No." Mariun's eyes widened, then fluttered closed. "It's all right. We can share."

It took a bit of maneuvering, but soon they were both stretched out on the swaying ropes. Mariun snuggled against his side, and her breathing evened out quickly.

"*Can you talk to me now?*" Flint asked, his voice tinged with worry.

"*Sorry.*" Nox cringed. "*I-I, it all happened so fast. I'm not even sure what happened, exactly.*"

"*Take your time.*"

Nox frowned, his arms tensing around the sleeping woman in his arms. "*A bolt of lightning struck her.*"

"*Who? Violet?*"

"*No. Mariun.*"

"*Is she dead?*" Flint asked.

"*That's the strange thing. She should be, but she isn't. I can't see a damned thing wrong with her, except for exhaustion. And she made it stop. The storm is over.*"

"*I'm not surprised.*"

"*You're not?*"

"*I knew something was different about her the moment I saw her. You would've sensed it, too, if you weren't so busy drooling.*"

Nox scoffed. "*I was not.*"

Flint snickered. "*Admit it. You like her.*"

"*You're wrong. How could I after what she's done?*"

"*Wrong, huh? Tell me this, then. Where is she right now?*"

Nox stayed silent, clenching his jaw. Flint wasn't even present, but after nearly two decades together, clearly Flint could read him like a book.

"*Yeah, I thought so. Watching over her, hm?*"

Nox rolled his eyes. *"Did you miss the part where she was just struck by lightning? Someone needs to keep watch over her while she's sleeping."*

"Mm-hm."

"You know what? I don't need this." Nox concentrated and called on the one boon that he rarely used. He put up a mental block, snuffing out Flint's voice, his presence, like a candle doused in water.

Instantly, his stomach clenched. Though jagoths brought the skill of blocking their bondmate's thoughts, he could count on one hand the number of times he or Flint had used the rare ability. They both craved the mental connection—the closeness—that came with sharing their thoughts. But for once, Nox wanted a few moments completely alone.

Losing Flint, setting off on this journey, it was all so much. Dealing with Mariun on top of it all... It was slowly driving him insane.

Yes, he was attracted to her. Mariun was undeniably lovely. Having her curled in his arms, her sweet scent flooding his nose, those long legs tangled around his own, set off a cascade of longing inside him.

But how could he give into his feelings? She was an enigma wrapped in a web of secrets more tightly woven than the finest spider silk.

He knew he should hold her at arm's length. Yet no matter how many times he fought to distance himself, to ignore her—to climb out of the rotting hammock and leave her in peace—he just couldn't.

The physical ache he could control. It had been a long while since he'd slaked his desires with a woman, but he'd never been the kind of man who let his bodily urges drive him. Beyond that, something else drew him to her. Something that, try as he might, he couldn't define.

No matter how much he tossed it around his mind, he couldn't grasp it. And before long, the stifling weight of silence—of loneliness—became too much to bear.

With a sigh, he broke down the block in his mind. *"Flint?"* Panic bloomed, and his fingers clenched involuntarily around Mariun, making her whimper in her sleep.

"I'm here."

Nox carefully relaxed his grip. *"I-I'm sorry. I needed a moment to think."*

"I understand. You have every right to your privacy. I'm sorry I—"

"No. You were right. I don't know what I'm going to do." Nox opened his eyes in the darkened room and stared at Mariun's sleeping face. *"I shouldn't like her. She's the enemy."*

"Are you so sure about that?" Flint asked. *"She helped you escape. She left with you. Doesn't that tell you she was as much a prisoner in that strange place as we were?"*

"I—"

"Nox, I know trust is hard for you. But Mariun... I have a good feeling about her."

"A feeling? What does that even mean?"

"It means give her a chance. Listen to her story. You might have more in common than you think."

Nox sighed. *"All right. I'll try."*

"Good. Now get some sleep. I've had enough of your grumpiness in the morning to last a lifetime."

"Fine." Nox closed his eyes and embraced the weariness radiating out of his bones. But before he drifted to sleep, he whispered, *"Flint. What would I do without you?"*

"No need to worry about that. I'm right here. Always."

Dawn light spilled in the porthole window. The angle of the ship was kind enough to send a ray of sunlight shooting into the back of Nox's eyelids. He groaned, tilting his head out of the harsh beam as consciousness creeped up on him.

Why was he so—wet?

The storm. The night's events rolled over him in a flash.

Well, that explained the damp clothes. The little cabin's stifling humidity wasn't exactly helping him dry out completely. Add to that the body heat of another person draped over him... It was a wonder he'd slept as long as he had.

When he'd closed his eyes, he'd been lying next to Mariun with an arm draped gently over her waist to ensure she was still breathing steadily. In the night, she'd curled atop him. She was using his chest as a pillow, with one arm and leg wrapped tightly around him.

He slowly lifted a hand and brushed the hair off her face. Though he tried hard to choke it down, a burst of laughter exploded out of him.

Mariun's eyes popped open and darted around before connecting with his. She squeaked and her elbows and knees flailed as she tried to scramble off him.

"Hey." Nox flattened her against his chest while the hammock swayed precariously, nearly knocking them both to the floor. "Not so fast. Did you forget where you're sleeping?"

"D-did I forget? How did I get here? I don't—" She gasped.

"Remember now?" Nox chuckled.

"Why are you laughing?" She peeked at him, her brow furrowed. "What's so funny?"

"Nothing." Nox schooled his features, pushing back the grin that fought to surface at her indignant expression.

"Tell me," she insisted.

"Fine." He loosened his hold enough for her to—carefully, this time—extract herself from his arms. "I just spotted some evidence that you're not as perfect as you seem."

She propped herself on her elbows and glared at him. "Perfect? I'm not perfect."

With her long black hair draped around him in a halo and the sun washing over her lovely face, it was easy for him to disagree, until her breath blew against the soaked patch on his shirt. "Oh, I know that. You drool in your sleep."

Her mouth dropped open. "What? I do not!"

Nox didn't answer. He cocked a brow and stared down at his wet tunic. When he lifted his gaze, she was staring at his chest, her cheeks flushed a pretty pink.

"I wouldn't lie to you, Mariun," he said, laughter in his voice.

She lifted her eyes and met his gaze, and the humor drained out of him. "I won't lie to you either, Nox."

He was suddenly painfully aware of her proximity. Their lower bodies were flush, the position entirely too intimate for the seriousness of her reply. "Good." He tugged a piece of her hair, unable to keep his fingers from latching around the silky strands. "I have a lot of questions."

He waited for her to move. To roll off the hammock and make some excuse to leave. But the moment stretched out with only the sound of their breathing to punctuate the silence. When Mariun finally moved, it wasn't away. She swayed closer, her gaze flicking away from his eyes and to his mouth.

Nox's heart hammered. He licked his lips.

Bang, bang, bang.

Mariun jolted, whipping her head to the door before it swung open.

"Oh good. You're awake." Violet breezed inside, a wide smile on her face, seeming to take no notice of the bubbling tension in the cabin. "C'mon, you guys need to see this. We made it!"

To Hatch a Dragon

V iolet burst out of the cabin, leaving the door wide open. A fine cloud of mist shimmered over the ocean, quickly evaporating in the dawn sunlight. On the horizon, the first hint of land peeked out of the dark waves. Standing beside the bow railing, Ryon waited. He turned at the sound of her footsteps and graced her with a tired grin.

Ryon tilted his head in the cabin's direction. "How's Mariun?"

Violet stopped beside him. "She's awake. She was up, moving, and talking. I offered to help her climb the stairs, but she said she was fine."

"That's good." He shook his head. "I still can't believe it. I didn't think anyone could survive that."

Violet's skin prickled as the memory of that gargantuan strike washed over her. It seemed unbelievable that anyone could survive such a powerful explosion. If not for the downpour, the ship would have surely burst into flames from proximity alone. Maybe the lightning hit the ocean and not them directly? "I couldn't see much from the helm last night. Are you sure it even struck her?"

"The light was so bright I had to shield my eyes." Ryon shuddered. "But she was there... I think."

"Well, if she was, she's better now." Violet shrugged and leaned closer, lowering her voice. "She recovered enough to cuddle up with Nox."

Ryon whipped around to stare at the cabin doorway. "You're kidding."

"Looks like they slept in the same hammock last night." She waggled her eyebrows.

Nox chose that moment to mount the stairs and caught them staring as he emerged from below deck. He curled a hand through his wild brown locks, lifted a brow, and barked, "What's with the staring?"

Violet cleared her throat. "We've been waiting for you to join us."

Ryon nodded vigorously and pointed ahead. "Yep. We think that's where we're headed. Unless the storm knocked us off course."

Footsteps tapped behind them. They all turned and watched Mariun emerge from the cabin. She winced and squinted as if the sun was a touch too bright, but quickly forced a smile. "Good morning."

"Good morning," Violet and Ryon replied at the same time.

Nox only stared at her flatly, but Mariun didn't seem to mind his silence. She strode straight to his side and peered over the railing. "That's it."

"How can you tell from so far away?" Violet asked.

"Do you see how black it is? The beaches on the island we're looking for are covered with black sand. There's an active volcano in the center."

"An active volcano?" Violet's heart stuttered. "There wasn't anything about that on the map."

Mariun examined Violet's face and twisted her lips. "I heard them talking about it back in Thalassia. It's perfectly safe. The lava flow is slow moving. Easy to avoid."

"It makes sense," Nox said. "Lark said dragon eggs need a lot of heat to develop properly."

Mariun nodded. "It's true. We'll find them close to the lava flow."

Ryon's brow furrowed. "Isn't that dangerous? What if the flow changes direction? How long did you say those eggs have been missing?"

"Twenty years," Nox answered.

Violet frowned. "When they were laid, I don't think the parents had much of a choice."

"It doesn't matter." Mariun's lips thinned. "The eggs are still there or else my people wouldn't have found them."

"Are your people still there?" Nox asked. "You said you knew what we'd face. Time to share."

Mariun crossed her arms and sent Nox a crooked smile. "Finally happy you let me tag along, I see."

Nox rolled his eyes. "We can change that at any moment if you're not willing to cooperate."

Violet nearly jumped to Mariun's defense. In her experience, kindness garnered help much faster than whatever was happening between those two. But Mariun spoke before she could plan a reply.

"Relax. I'll tell you what I know." Mariun swiveled back to the railing. "A few ships' worth of masked there will be keeping watch over the bay. When the eggs were discovered, they built a port on the northeastern coast. We should swing around to the island's southwestern edge so no one spots us."

"Sounds like a smart idea," Violet said.

"Yes and no." Mariun bit her lip. "It will be a challenge to make landfall there. Where they built the docks, it's all low-lying beaches. When we head to the southern side, the mountain will hide us from their view, but from what I understand, we'll need to climb some steep terrain."

Nox nudged Ryon with his elbow. "Good thing we have an expert climber with us."

Ryon puffed out his chest and grinned. "I can go first. Set up a guide rope."

Ryon was certainly confident in his skills, but an unwelcome sensation swelled in Violet's chest. She cocked her head at Mariun. "And we'll be able to reach the eggs from where we land?"

Mariun leaned against the railing. "We'll reach them. But moving them will be a different story."

"What do you mean?" Violet asked.

"According to the reports, the eggs are enormous. As big as a boulder and just as heavy. That's why we never attempted to move them."

Violet's stomach sank. That didn't sound good. What were they going to do?

Mariun spun sideways, her gaze flicking between Nox and Violet. "Can I ask you something?"

"What is it?" Nox's brow furrowed.

"Your sister Lark has a bondmate. And you had Flint." Mariun turned to Violet. "Have you had a bondmate as well?"

Violet shook her head. "Not yet, but the talent runs in my family." She sighed. "Truthfully, I'm not sure if I'll bond one or not. Used to be it skipped a generation, but magic in my mother's family doesn't skip. My parents were always so certain I'd inherit bonding magic too." She shrugged. "For now, I'm just waiting until I meet the right animal, I guess. Why do you ask?"

"How much do you know about dragons? Do you know what happens when they hatch?" Mariun asked.

Violet rubbed her chin. "No. I can't say that I do." She glanced at Ryon and Nox, who looked as dumbfounded as she was about the topic.

Mariun drew in a deep breath and straightened her spine. "There are stories from my people about the lucky few who shared a bond with dragons. As far as I know, they're just that—stories. But one story in particular comes to mind."

Violet's eyes widened, and she leaned closer, determined to not miss a word. It was beyond time Mariun started sharing some of her people's history.

"It happened in a land far different from this one. Full of endless dangers and terrifying beasts. Even the weather was unpredictable, with storms so violent lightning tore through the sky every day and the clouds rarely broke."

"Wait, what land?" Violet interrupted.

Mariun waved a hand. "That's not important for now. Like I said, it's just a story."

Violet frowned but nodded for Mariun to continue.

"Dragons were there. Not one or two, but hundreds. Thousands, maybe. They worked side by side with bonded people to protect the small pockets of humans who somehow managed to survive against all odds. That's how they learned so much about dragons." Mariun shrugged. "If the stories can be believed."

"All right. But what does that have to do with us now?" Ryon asked.

"Normally the baby dragon's parents would come back to find their clutch when it was ready to hatch. They communicate with the hatchlings, encourage them to break free from their shell. Without them there to coax the baby dragons out, most clutches would wither away without hatching."

Violet gasped. "Is that going to happen to Dru's eggs?"

"Maybe not," Mariun continued. "I recall a tale about a hatchling whose parents died while it was still in its egg, like the clutch we're going to find. But instead of withering away, the babies were saved by a human who bonded with one of the dragons before it hatched."

Nox stiffened. "Rot and decay."

Violet leaned back. "So, you think one of us can make the eggs hatch?"

Mariun nodded. "I do. In fact, I'm willing to bet Jurdan is counting on it. That's why it was so easy for us to escape from Thalassia. And why he let Nox have the map."

Nox blanched. "Why he killed Flint." He gripped the railing tightly, and the piercing scratch of claws on wood cut through the peaceful sound of lapping waves. "Iggy. I told that rotting bastard about my previous bonds. How much do you want to bet he filled Jurdan in on how I can bond any species?"

Tears pricked the corners of Violet's eyes. "You're right. Jurdan didn't even know I existed, and I doubt Lark ever told him about Muse, but Flint was right there with you..." She gulped and turned to her uncle. "Blazes, I'm so sorry."

"I knew it was too easy." Ryon stared down at his boots. "We didn't escape. He let us go. That man is devious."

"You have no idea." Mariun shuffled and let out a deep sigh. "I'm guessing we won't have any resistance from the men keeping watch. Not until after the eggs hatch. But once they do, they'll come for us."

"If that's the case, then why don't we just pull up to the docks?" Ryon waved and mimed a few jaunty steps. "Hey, masked guys, we're here to wake the dragons." He halted and crossed his arms. "We still have the gear we found in Thalassia. We could disguise ourselves with the masks and act like Mariun's escort."

Mariun shook her head. "It won't work. Remember the crows?"

"What about them?" Ryon asked.

"The crows are Jurdan's messengers," Mariun explained. "Every ship and outpost have a few with them. Even if we could convince the men that Jurdan sent me, there's no way we can stop them from communicating back to him. Our only chance is to sneak in and hope we can find the eggs before they notice us."

"What if they're right there watching the eggs the whole time?" Nox's voice was deathly calm, but he clasped his fists around the railing, the sharp claws he'd used in the ring gouging holes into the wood.

Violet cocked a brow. What was happening to Nox? Why were those claws emerging now?

Before she could voice the question, Mariun said, "They won't be. The heat is too draining to keep a constant watch. They send regular patrols instead. If we can sneak in and out while they're between shifts—"

"It's a good plan," Violet admitted. "I think it will work."

A tingle spread up her spine. This *had* to work. If Jurdan was calculating enough to let them go, and evil enough to kill Flint for the chance of hatching these dragons, then she knew he had some greater plan in store for them. Did he want to force those innocent creatures to fight in his sick games? Or worse, was he bent on taking over the world with them at his side?

Whatever he had planned, they couldn't let him win. Those dragons didn't deserve to be imprisoned by that villain. They had to save them.

It seemed the others had the same thought. Ryon took off, mumbling something about finding rope, and Nox stepped away from the railing, his hands finally back to their human shape.

"The southwestern coast it is. I'll handle the sailing." Nox headed for the helm and called over his shoulder, "You two, help Ryon gather supplies."

Violet turned to Mariun in time to spot her wobbling slightly. "You sure you're all right?"

"I-I'm fine." Mariun stabilized her stance and sent Violet a lopsided grin. "Just not used to all this sun."

"If you say so," Violet replied. "Come on. There's water down below. We can grab a drink while we get the supplies." And maybe Mariun could be made to answer a few more questions.

"Violet," Nox called from the helm. "Forget the supplies. I need you to adjust the rigging."

Violet sighed and spun around. Guess those questions would have to wait for later.

Climbing

The sun hung directly overhead as they approached the south-western coast. After gathering the supplies he'd need for the climb, Ryon joined Nox at the helm. Together they scanned the sheer cliffside, searching for the easiest place to scale.

"How about here?" Nox's hand shot out for what might've been the tenth time. "It's the smallest cliff we've passed so far."

"No. Too much of an overhang in the middle. I wager you and I could handle it, but the girls..."

Nox scrubbed a hand across his face. "We need to try somewhere."

"We will." Ryon clapped a hand on Nox's shoulder and smiled. "We just haven't found it yet. Keep sailing."

Nox turned back to the helm, and a brooding silence fell over him. Ryon couldn't blame him for being out of sorts. Learning that his bondmate was deliberately murdered had to be hard news to stomach. Nox's suffering made his chest ache.

He still didn't know what to make of Mariun's revelations. That Violet or Nox had to be here to save those dragons—two people out of only a small handful who could accomplish such a task—and they actually were, seemed fated in itself. But if it wasn't fate, and Jurdan truly was pulling the strings all along, then what else did that foul villain have in store for them? How had Jurdan known it would come to that? Was he truly that calculating?

Ryon lifted his gaze from the cliffside and studied Nox's hunched shoulders. Could he handle the task? Violet's confidence in her uncle appeared unwavering, but Nox's moods were mercurial at best. Perhaps it would be better for Violet to bond one of the dragons. He could sense the longing in her voice when she'd spoken about her own bonding magic. At least she could be counted on to be willing.

Ryon returned his gaze to the shore, and his heart leaped. "This is it. Drop anchor."

"Here? Are you certain? It's twice the height of the last spot." Nox's brow wrinkled.

"Yes, but the incline is much more forgiving." Ryon smiled, tingles spreading through his fingers as he surveyed the black rocks stacked higher than their center mast. "This is our best option."

Nox eyed the climb warily. "Are you sure?"

Ryon nodded. "Yes. Trust me. We'll make it."

"If you say so." Nox frowned but hollered, "Vi, drop anchor."

Violet tied the rope she'd been adjusting into place and hurried to comply. Water splashed before Violet and Mariun joined them at the helm. Then the sailboat slowly halted in the clear blue water.

Ryon gulped as he gazed into the surf. The black rock forming the cliffsides peppered the seafloor. The jagged hunks of stone would provide a terrible cushion to any falls.

He just needed to make sure that no falls happened.

"You sure about this?" Violet appeared at his elbow, her lovely eyes glued to the cliffside. "I know you said you're a good climber, but—"

"I'm not just a good climber. I'm the best."

Violet crossed her arms. "Is that so?"

"Yep. Been climbing since I was a lad. It's a bit of a tradition where I come from." He shrugged and bent down, gathering the rope and the sack of supplies he'd scrounged out of the hold.

Violet leaned closer and lowered her voice. "While I'm sure that's true, perhaps you could use a wish to make sure you don't fail."

"Pfft. And waste a feather for that little anthill?" He sent her a grin full of confidence and jammed his thumb at the rocky cliff. "Trust me, Violet. I could scale that in my sleep."

The corners of her mouth tipped up, but wariness clung to her like morning dew on a leaf. "If you're sure."

"I am."

It was sweet she was so worried. Maybe there was hope for the two of them after all. Ryon pushed the thought from his mind. He had to concentrate on the climb and nothing else. Everyone was counting on him. Violet was counting on him.

"All right, everyone into the dinghy," Nox said.

Ryon led the way to the tiny craft strapped to the side of their sailboat. It was lucky they'd brought Violet's little boat along with them. Even luckier that it hadn't been lost in the mad wind and rain of that storm. Now the dinghy would see them close enough to the shore that he could begin his climb. The larger sailboat would have surely been impaled on those stones in the shallow waters close to the cliffside.

It was a tight squeeze to fit all four of them in the little craft. Violet scooched in with him on the back bench, so tightly wedged she was pressed flush against his side.

She smiled sheepishly. "Sorry. There's not much space."

"Here, let me make more room for you." Ryon lifted the arm wedged between them and wrapped it around her shoulders, his pulse racing. "How's that?"

Violet's cheeks flushed prettily. "That's better."

"Watch your elbows," Nox barked across the boat.

"You watch your own," Mariun snapped back.

Nox and Mariun were crammed just as closely in the front seat. Ryon stifled a laugh as he watched their attempts to row in tandem. The dinghy wobbled, spinning ineffectively in a circle. Finally, Nox grunted and lifted Mariun off the bench. He plopped her atop his lap, wresting the oar from her grip.

"Are you insane?" Mariun squeaked.

Nox stiffened before slicing the oars in the water. "Just sit still and let me row. Or feel free to have a seat on the floorboards."

"You'd like that, wouldn't you?" Mariun crossed her arms but settled firmly on Nox's lap. "I'm not soaking myself in a puddle because you can't be bothered to share the rowing."

Violet lifted a hand and giggled quietly behind it, her eyes twinkling. Ryon's heart stalled as she met his gaze. When she looked at him like that, wrapped in his arms, he couldn't help but feel like she was meant to be there. Never in his life had anything felt so right as her slender frame under his arm, her sweet curves pressed against him. Even with the pair's constant bickering flooding his ears, he couldn't shake the sense of belonging that struck him.

"Finally," Nox exclaimed as they pulled alongside the cliff.

Ryon sucked in a breath. The wall loomed above them, seeming far larger from directly below. But it was still nothing compared to the rock wall he'd spent years scaling.

"Are you sure—" Violet started.

Ryon squeezed her shoulder firmly. "In my sleep, Violet." He winked, then carefully retracted his arm from her shoulders and scooped up his gear. He stood, balancing on the wobbly boat. Scanning carefully, he located a rock outcropping that looked like a decent handhold and pointed. "Get me a little closer to there."

Nox nodded. A few more strokes with the oars and he was in position. The handhold he'd spotted hovered at eye level, bouncing down to chin level with the surf's constant motion. Ryon gripped the handhold and bounced gently, testing it with some of his weight. It didn't budge.

Waves crashed against the dinghy. Nox stuck out the oar, keeping them from slamming into the cliffside. "I don't mean to rush you, but we can't stay this close for long."

Ryon got ready and jumped for it.

"Oof." Hard rock bit into his chest and stomach, but his fingers held fast. After a quick glance down, he'd secured two footholds as well.

"Ryon!" Violet's panicked voice filled his ears. "Are you all right?"

Ryon tilted his head and grinned over his shoulder. "Yep. Not to worry." The one thing he hadn't counted on was the rocks being so slippery. Suppose it made sense, with the ocean slamming against them. Still, nothing he couldn't handle.

"Like scaling rocks in a rainstorm," he muttered to himself as he scaled the wet cliff. He moved one limb at a time, testing his weight on unfamiliar handholds and footholds. Luckily, the rocks here were sound, with only a handful of wobbly perches he was forced to ignore.

He paused a quarter of the way up. A wide outcropping jutted out from the rock wall, allowing him to wrap his legs around it like a seat. He took the opportunity to pull out his supplies from the sack around his back.

There hadn't been much to work with within the hold of their stolen sailboat, but he'd secured a few long nails and a painted stone paperweight to use as a hammer. Eyeing the cliffside, he searched for a likely spot to secure the rope.

The *clang* of the weight on the nail rang out. Ryon held his breath, praying nothing went wrong. There were only a handful of nails. He didn't have too many tries to secure the rope. Luckily, the nail took. He knotted the rope around it, leaving a length to dangle, then tugged hard.

He grinned at the finished product, then spared a glance below. Mariun and Violet were seated together now, hands raised to shade their eyes as they watched his progress. Nox maneuvered the dinghy to collect the end of the rope and pluck it out of the water.

Ryon waved and smiled down at them. "Easy climbing so far."

"Get on with it, then," Nox urged.

Ryon secured his supplies. Nox was likely struggling to keep the dinghy steady in the surf. He had to hurry.

As he gained height, the rocks became progressively drier, which made the climb even easier. Unfortunately, there were no outcroppings for resting at the halfway mark. He found two solid footholds and leaned against the wall instead, carefully pulling out a nail and the hammer.

Sweat pooled on his forehead as he walloped the nail. "Guano." The hole he'd chosen to wedge the nail in crumbled to dust, and he nearly lost the nail. He scanned the wall for a more stable spot.

He spotted another crack a little to the left. He leaned over, shifting his weight to one foot, heart pounding louder than the hammer.

Success! With the new guideline in place, he continued upward. The rest of the climb went smoothly, and before he knew it, he was wrapping the end of the rope over a huge boulder at the top of the cliffside.

He leaned over the edge and beamed down at the dinghy. His three companions looked so small from his new vantage point. He waved them up, deciding to keep silent in case any masked men lurked nearby.

As Mariun grabbed the rope, Ryon gazed around the clifftop. It was heavily forested, with thick underbrush and countless tree trunks blocking his view further inland. If it weren't for the black rock and slight hint of smoke lingering in the air, he wouldn't have guessed an active volcano lay nearby.

Insects chirped nosily, and the familiar whispers of birds echoed in his ears. He didn't sense any people around, but with the thick foliage, it wouldn't be hard to hide. Hopefully that would work to their advantage once they began searching.

Ryon returned his attention to the cliffside. Mariun appeared to be faring well. Her long limbs were a boon, allowing her to stretch and access the best footholds and handholds. She kept an arm wrapped around the rope but seemed to have little need for it.

Soon she'd climbed high enough Ryon clasped her hand and helped her up the last short stretch.

"That wasn't so bad," Mariun exclaimed, her cheeks rosy and her breath coming in pants.

Ryon grinned as she settled beside him to watch below. Violet was the next to take a turn. His stomach twinged when she stood.

Violet couldn't reach the same handhold he and Mariun had used to mount the cliff. She balanced with her arms extended, examining the wall, until Nox set down the oars and kneeled beside her. They talked quietly, and then Violet clambered atop her uncle's knee and leaped without warning.

Ryon gasped, heart thudding madly. For a moment she looked like she would slip, but Nox came to the rescue once again. Somehow, he balanced within the shaking dinghy and shoved Violet upward. She clung to the wall and wrapped her arm around the guide rope.

Ryon's pulse didn't slow much. Violet had a long climb ahead of her, and with her short limbs, she was at a disadvantage. It took her nearly twice as long to cover the same distance Mariun had. When she reached the halfway mark, he could sense her strength fading.

Maybe I should've given her a feather? Ryon couldn't keep his eyes off Violet, the insistent thought ringing in his ears like the worst regret. If she fell when he could've prevented it, he'd never forgive himself. She was glue holding them together. Without Violet, he wasn't sure if he could go on with this strange quest. And of course, her blood pooling on those sharp rocks would mean the end to his dreams of earning a golden feather. Of finally setting things right with his brother, Rovan, like he'd worked so hard for.

"Hey." Mariun squeezed his forearm. "She's going to make it. Relax."

Perhaps the wind carried the sound of their voices, for Violet peered up at them. Her gaze connected with his from below, and she forced a smile.

Ryon's heart squeezed as he returned her grin. He shoved his doubt aside. She would make it. The determination in her eyes left no question.

Violet climbed the second half of the cliff with renewed vigor. She panted hard, her skin coated with sweat, but her smile was radiant as he grasped her hand and tugged her to the top.

"Are you all right?" he asked.

Violet pushed damp tendrils of sweat-slicked white hair off her forehead. "Yeah. But I hope that's it for the climbing today."

They arranged themselves on the cliff edge to watch Nox climb. He tied the dinghy to the end of the guide rope, then jumped for the wall.

Ryon quickly brushed aside any misgivings about Nox's climbing abilities. Nox had no problems navigating the cliff—in fact, he might have finally met his match as far as strength and speed went.

The problem didn't appear until Nox reached the overhang, where he'd secured the first piece of rope, and stopped for a rest. Nox glanced down, and his olive skin turned a sickly shade of white.

Was he afraid of heights? That might explain why Nox seemed so shocked to see him climbing the ship's mast. And so quick to send him to fix the rigging during the storm, rather than handle the task himself.

A sick sensation spread through Ryon's gut. Long ago, he'd sworn to never insist anyone face their fears if they weren't ready. Had he just broken his promise by urging Nox make this climb?

Nox stalled there for quite a while, muttering to himself and looking queasy.

"Do you think I should climb down there and help him?" Shudders wracked Ryon's body as a memory assailed him. One he was quick to shove aside.

Violet pursed her lips. "Give him a moment. He'll start moving again."

Ryon sucked in a shaky breath. She was right. Nox would be fine. He had to be.

Mariun snickered quietly, her face shining with amusement. "If you'd asked me before now, I would have told you that man was fearless. It's a relief to see he's flawed like the rest of us."

Violet frowned. "What happened between you two?"

That cut off Mariun's laughter. She shrugged and sighed. "I don't want to talk about it."

He thought Violet might press the issue, but Nox started climbing again, drawing their attention. Ryon kept quiet, tamping down the urge to cheer him on. Nox climbed like a man on the run, scaling the cliff so quickly, he slipped in his haste at the halfway mark.

Violet cringed and Mariun gasped, clamping a hand over her mouth. And Ryon froze, praying history didn't repeat itself. Nox dangled on the guide rope, his feet scrambling for purchase.

Luckily, he was nothing if not resilient. Within a heartbeat, he'd regained his hold and clambered up the cliff again—at a slightly slower pace. Finally, he reached the clifftop, and Ryon helped him hurdle over the edge. Nox collapsed on the ground, his eyes screwed shut and his chest heaving.

Ryon laughed shakily and pressed a palm to his heart. "We all made it, just like I said we would. Now, how about we find some dragon eggs?"

The Fox

Sweat soaked Violet's tunic. Her aching arms and legs wobbled like jelly after that climb and long hours spent traipsing through the stifling underbrush. The island was clearly uninhabited, with none of the foot trails carved into the brush like in the forested countryside of her homeland. It made every step a struggle.

Ryon and Nox took turns hacking at the brush with the lone blade they'd located in their stolen ship's hold. They strolled a few paces ahead, murmuring among themselves, leaving Violet and Mariun to trail behind.

Violet's stomach rumbled. They'd stopped for a lunch of hard biscuits and salted fish at midday, but that had barely taken the edge off her hunger with all the activity they'd suffered through so far. She wasn't sure what was worse, the ache in her belly or the light sheen of sweat dampening her clothes and making her skin constantly itch.

"I would kill for a soak in a cool lake right now," Violet said.

Mariun smiled beside her. "I've never seen a lake, aside from pictures in books. Do you have many where you're from?"

Violet shrugged. "Some. Rivers are more common in Dracwood. They're nice too, but often the currents are too strong for swimming."

"Would be nice to see one of those, too."

Sometimes it was easy to forget that Mariun had spent her whole life in one place. "It must be quite a shock to leave your home for the first time."

"Shock? No." Mariun grinned, tipping her face to the sky as if soaking up every stray sunbeam that stole through the thick canopy. "It's wonderful."

The talk of water suddenly had another part of Violet's anatomy protesting. She pursed her lips and whistled. They'd agreed to whistle instead of shout, hoping the noise would draw less attention in a forest filled with birds—in case any masked men were nearby.

Nox and Ryon halted and turned back with quizzical expressions. Violet waved them backward, and they met in the middle.

"I need to take a break," she announced.

Ryon scanned their surroundings and pointed to a downed log. "We can rest here, I bet."

Violet grimaced, shifting from foot to foot. "Not that kind of break. In the woods."

"I could use one too." Nox cocked his head sideways. "Ryon and I will take this side." He pointed in the opposite direction. "You two stick together over there, and we'll meet back here."

With that settled, they split up in their respective directions. Violet huffed, working double time to tramp through the thick underbrush without the blade's aid. She cursed under her breath as a thorn clung to her pant leg and scraped her ankle.

"You all right?" Mariun asked.

"Fine." She bent down and carefully extracted her pants from the prickly thornbush. "Just not a fan of hiking. You'd think I'd be used to it. My father loved dragging me out hunting in the woods when I was young. I always hated it."

"Sounds nice to me."

Violet cringed. She must sound so ungrateful. Mariun didn't have anyone growing up, and here she was, complaining about her father sharing his love of the forest with her.

They burst into a tiny clearing. "Is this far enough?"

Mariun nodded. "I think so."

Violet spotted a large palm tree on the far side. "I'm going behind that tree."

"Sure." Mariun pointed to a gnarled fruit tree. "I'll take that one. Meet back here when we're done?"

"Yep." Violet hustled over to the palm and hid behind it. Relief rushed through her as she took care of her pressing business. As she stood, pulling up her sweaty pants, crunching leaves in the clearing signaled Mariun had finished as well. Violet circled the palm, a wide smile on her face. "I feel much better no—"

The word died in her throat as she spotted a hulking masked man facing her. He spoke a foreign tongue in a deep voice that set Violet's pulse racing. She froze, assessing the man and praying Mariun would be smart enough to escape.

He swaggered closer, a huge, muscled brute with a wickedly curved blade strapped to his side. He wore a black-and-white mask atop his all-black clothing like all Thalass soldiers, his shaped like a snarling fox.

What was she going to do? She didn't have a weapon, and Ryon and Nox were too far away to come to her aid. Maybe Mariun could slink away and find them before the fox harmed her?

She couldn't just stand there and do nothing. He wouldn't understand her, but maybe if she started talking—acting like he was her savior instead of her captor—then she could stall him while he considered what to do with her.

Violet thrust her arms out wide and smiled. "I am so glad to see you!" She infused her voice with all the thankfulness she could muster, speaking loudly enough that Mariun, and perhaps even the guys, would hear her. "Our boat was shipwrecked; can you believe it? I lost my friends out here in the woods. Please, you need to help me." She stared at his mask with what she hoped was a pleading expression, her hands clasped together at her chest.

The fox cocked his head, his hand on the hilt of his blade.

"Do you have a village here? Can you take me to it? Maybe my friends made it there. I need to find them. You'll help me, won't you?"

He stepped closer, ignoring her chattering.

Violet backed away slowly until her shoulders rammed into the palm tree. "How about food? I'm starving. Do you have something to eat?" She mimed eating, hoping the man would realize she was requesting aid.

Please, have a heart, fox.

The fox reached for his belt, and for one pulse-pounding instant she was certain he was about to undo the buckle.

Was he planning to tie her hands with the belt, or worse, drop his pants?

Violet buried the urge to scream as she tracked the man's gloved hand. When he bypassed the buckle and dug into his belt pouch, she nearly wept with relief. He plucked out a small piece of dried meat. Her mouth watered.

"Is that for me?" She flashed a grateful smile. "Oh, thank you so much. I'm so glad I found you."

She inched closer. Was her act working? Maybe the fox would be friendly after all. Her shaky fingers closed over the morsel. Before she could shove it into her mouth, the fox snatched her wrist in his fist.

She tugged, blinking rapidly. "Um, do you want to share? It's a little small for that, don't you think?" She tried pulling her arm again, but the fox's grip was unshakable.

Blazes. This was bad.

Words spilled out from behind the mask. He jerked her forward, ignoring the meat as it slipped out of her fingers and landed in the brush. Violet shuddered, her heart sinking. Fox settled one hand on his blade and lifted it far enough to flash the glint of steel. Then he tugged her arm and set off toward the forest—in the opposite direction of their meeting place.

Oh no. Where was he going? With his hand clamped around her wrist hard enough to make her gasp, she had no choice but to follow. Violet dug her heels into the dirt and shrieked. "Let me go, you brute!"

Fox merely gripped her tighter. He jerked her so forcefully the joints in her arm flared with a sharp pain and her wrist cracked. It was clear she had no chance of overpowering the hulking man. It didn't stop her from trying. She tugged against his hold and yelled obscenities at him. Not that it seemed to help.

But maybe she had one trick up her sleeve. One he definitely wouldn't be expecting. She could recreate that blast of wind she'd used to knock down the last man who'd tried to capture her.

The last time, air had flooded through her instinctively. Not now. Violet fought to recall the lessons her mother had drilled into her over the years. Even without her magic talent surfacing, her mother hadn't neglected to train her about the ways of the mages of old, always in the guise of stories. Now that the time had come to put the lessons into action, her stomach clenched.

Call on your source. Easy enough. She sucked in a deep breath.

Clear your mind. Concentrate. That was bound to be a problem. How was she meant to clear her mind while being forced to march against her will?

"Hey," a voice called out behind her in a voice heavy with command.

Fox spun around, jerking Violet in front of him. The breath spilled out of her lungs and all thought of summoning vanished as she spotted Mariun.

Blazes! What was she doing? With all the time that had passed, she'd been certain Mariun left to fetch Ryon and Nox. Apparently not.

Mariun stood in the center of the small clearing with her fists stacked on her hips. She launched into a conversation with the fox in Thalassian. The guttural tones echoed around Violet, and she gulped, praying Mariun could think of something to make the fox unhand her.

After a few volleyed words back and forth, where Fox appeared to grow increasingly agitated, he lifted her wrist high over her head. Violet gasped, forced to balance on her tiptoes.

Violet's gaze flitted between the fox and Mariun. The enormous man was unreadable beneath the menacing mask, his fingers biting into her skin. Mariun stood her ground with a fierce tilt to her brow and her lips pursed in a grim line. They were both silent and seemed to have come to an impasse.

Let me go. Just let me—

Fox dropped her hand. Blood rushed back into her tingly fingers. She hurried toward Mariun, but before she made it two steps, the fox shoved her down. With her body already in motion, she had no hope of righting her balance. Violet went flying, and her head thwacked the dirt hard.

She groaned, her eyes slamming closed and her hands rising to cradle her pounding skull. More voices sounded—ones she recognized—but with her head ringing, she couldn't concentrate on anything but the pain.

A strange buzz filled the air, momentarily overwhelming the agony. Violet cracked her eyelids open in time to spot the fox smack into the ground, convulsing. Mariun hovered over him, hand outstretched.

Violet's jaw dropped. "Mariun, what did you do?"

Not on His Watch

Nox's gaze flashed around the forest as he and Ryon watched the girls disappear into the trees. The island was entirely too quiet for his liking. There were no happy chittering monkeys in the canopy like back home. Not even the trickling of streams in the distance. Once they'd trekked inland, even the crashing waves faded, leaving them with only an occasional bird call or drone of a fly to break the eerie silence.

Worse than all that, he couldn't shake the dread coiling around him like a serpent. *"Something's about to go wrong. I can feel it."*

"Hey, I thought I was the pessimist between the two of us." Flint, always the voice of reason, jumped in to soothe him. *"It's all in your head, my friend. Chances are there's nothing to fear out there, and everything to gain."*

"What about the masked patrols? Then there are cliffs to fall from, wildlife to avoid, and oh yeah, an active volcano." Nox gritted his teeth as he selected a tree to duck behind. *"Besides, I don't want to* gain *anything."* He scanned the forest again as leaves crackled beside him.

His heart galloped, and he crouched into a fighting stance. When Ryon emerged back from his break, Nox's racing pulse only slowed marginally.

"Just me. You expecting trouble?" Ryon lifted a brow.

"Can never be too careful," Nox replied.

"*See, nothing to fear,*" Flint added soothingly.

"*Maybe you're right. I just can't stop—*" He cocked his head and grabbed Ryon's arm.

"What is it?"

"*What is it?*"

Ryon and Flint asked just out of sync, causing a strange echoing sensation that made Nox want to cram a finger in his ear.

They halted, and Nox raised a finger to his lips while answering Flint, "*Shh. I heard something.*"

Nox concentrated, waiting for the noise to repeat. Ryon stared with a perplexed frown, his normal hearing clearly picking up nothing out of the ordinary.

There it was again. Louder this time. A thud that was far too heavy to belong to any of the tiny woodland critters they'd spotted so far. Then a branch snapped.

Nox's stomach dropped. "*Someone or something is headed this way. I'm sure of it.*" It couldn't be the girls. They both knew not to sneak up on them without signaling with a whistle.

"*Good. You have the advantage. Hide and pounce,*" Flint urged.

Leave it to a jagoth to think about pouncing... but it was a good plan.

Nox pointed in the direction he'd heard the noise and handed the blade to Ryon. Heart pumping, he located a tree thick enough to hide his profile and ducked behind it.

Ryon caught the hint, even without a word spoken. He creeped behind a gnarled fruit tree trunk with the blade held at the ready. After they'd both hidden, the soft pounding of footsteps and the crackle of underbrush was loud enough that Ryon must've heard it too. They waited silently, ready to leap out and take down the masked man who was bound to appear from the forest.

Nox stared at his fists, willing the claws to emerge. He'd given the blade to Ryon, assuming he'd have his strange new boon to rely on. Since he'd wished on the bloodfeather, the jagoth claws had emerged more than once. Now, when he desperately needed them to defend himself, the telltale tingle in his fists was nowhere to be found.

"C'mon, claws."

"You don't need them," Flint said.

Nox sucked in a steadying breath as a stick cracked, clearer than ever. Maybe Flint was right. Whoever this guy was, he was clearly not taking appropriate steps to cover his footfalls. If he wasn't expecting to run into trouble, then they'd definitely surprise him.

Another snap. He peeked around the trunk. Still nothing to see, but the footsteps sounded much closer.

Nox caught Ryon's gaze. Nodded for him to take the lead. Ryon's hand tightened around the blade's hilt.

A bush across from them quivered. Ryon leaped out, blade lifted over his head, ready to strike.

Nox glimpsed a pair of wide gray eyes at the last instant. Rot and decay! He lunged and gripped Ryon's arm, blocking the blade from its target.

"Mariun," Nox hissed. "What are you thinking creeping up on us like that?"

Ryon blanched. "Guano. I nearly killed you."

Mariun rose from the crouch she'd fallen into when she'd spotted the blade flying at her. "Shh," she whispered frantically. "I need your help. It's Violet. He has her."

"What?" Nox lowered his voice when he was dying to scream. "Who?"

"A Thalass guard. Come on, we need to help her." Mariun didn't stick around to make sure they were following, but hurried back the way she'd come without another word.

Ryon barreled after her with even less thought to where he was stepping or how much of a ruckus he was making. Nox caught up to him and whispered as loudly as he dared, "Watch where you're walking. We have to be quiet."

Ryon met Nox's gaze and winced. He clenched one fist at his side, the other wrapped so tightly around the blade his knuckles were white. Nox had a sneaking suspicion Ryon was battling the urge to scream, too.

"*What's going on?*" Flint asked.

"*Violet. She's in trouble. Mariun came to warn us.*"

"*You'll find her.*"

Nox's pulse pounded as they rushed through the forest. Violet had to be all right. If something happened to his niece... he didn't even want to consider it.

Mariun led the way, darting a quick glance back now and then, but mostly rushing onward like a woman on a mission. After they covered a short distance, his keen ears caught the hint of voices. He was still too far to make out what they said, but the female voice was unmistakably Violet. He'd bet his life on it. Hearing her speaking soothed the panicked thud of his heart. Until a man's voice rose, the growling tones the same as he remembered from his imprisonment.

The tingle arrived, rippling across his fists at the same time a wash of rage spread through him. Pain sliced through his hands as the claws emerged. Nox gritted his teeth, ignoring the burn. He would withstand a thousand times the agony if it meant he had the means to protect his family from those killers.

The masked men would not take another person he loved away from him. Not on his watch.

He ducked and wove through the underbrush, doing his best to stay silent. Ryon and Mariun kept pace with him, each of them carefully treading closer. After another short distance, the voices grew loud enough that surely Ryon and Mariun could hear them. And they were loud enough for Nox to make out the words. He buried a smile as he clued into the act Violet was putting on. He hoped it worked. At least until they could reach her.

Mariun crouched low and slipped into a tiny space between two enormous fruit trees. Nox reached in and caught her ankle before she disappeared on the other side. "We can't fit through there," he whispered.

At that moment, Violet's voice rose in the distance, loud enough for all their ears. "Let me go, you brute!"

Mariun met his eyes. "Go around." Then she jerked her ankle free and rushed forward.

Nox pressed his fist into the dirt, swallowing the desire to yell after her. Now two of them would need saving. What was she thinking?

Ryon grabbed his elbow and yanked Nox up before jerking his head sideways and setting off around the trees. Nox followed, cursing inwardly with every step. It took them long moments to curve around the massive trunk, only to find their path blocked by a pair of gargantuan thorn bushes growing beside it.

Ryon gave up all pretense at being stealthy and hacked his way through. Nox cringed but kept silent, eager to follow Mariun. With the fight Violet was putting up, chances were the swish of their blade wouldn't be noticed.

They had to save Violet. Had to save them both.

"Hey." Mariun's voice joined the conversation ahead.

Nox's stomach somersaulted. Rot and decay. He and Ryon were still so far off. And with the thick tree cover, there was no hope of seeing what was happening. Then Mariun switched to Thalassian, and the male voice answered in kind, ensuring he had no clue what was said.

"*Why must they speak in that rotting tongue?*" He had half a mind to whisper at Ryon for a translation, but he thought better of it. All that mattered was getting there.

"*Hurry,*" Flint said, voice full of panic.

"*I am.*" Just a little further.

The conversation cut off abruptly. Nox held his breath, inching slowly closer. A group of palms were bunched together ahead, but he glimpsed a flash of white hair beyond them.

Violet. She'd been silent so long he'd worried... What was she doing, standing there so still? Nox's gut lurched, but then she began to move. He squinted, wishing he could see more than just a tiny sliver of the clearing beyond the palms.

Violet's hair jerked sideways, and then a sickening thump struck the ground.

"Violet!" Ryon flew into motion, racing for the clearing. He trampled everything in his path, whacking the underbrush mercilessly with the blade.

Guess the surprise was out.

Nox fell in on his heels. "Squirt! Mariun!" If they were screaming, they might as well go all out. Maybe it would distract the man enough that Mariun could make a break for it.

They reached the palms just as a familiar *buzz* rang through the air.

Oh no. If that man had one of those horrid poles, they'd have a vicious fight on their hands. Especially if that bastard was using it on one of the girls.

Rage ignited, coursing up and down Nox's spine. He was a dead man.

But when the view of the clearing was finally unimpeded, it wasn't the girls he found writhing on the forest floor.

Nox jolted to a stop, chest heaving. Ryon raced across the clearing for Violet, who lay in a heap on the ground. Violet lifted her head far enough to stare across the clearing. "Mariun. What did you do?"

She must have used their shouting to distract the masked man, who cowered, whimpering and clutching his body as it shuddered uncontrollably. Nox turned to Mariun, expecting to see a pole in her fist.

Mariun's hands were empty.

Shock sped through his veins, zinging through every limb. His claws retracted, vanishing as swiftly as they'd come.

"Explain," Nox barked. "Now."

Mariun flinched, tugging her arms against her chest. "I will. I promise I will. But we need to tie him up first. Quickly, before he comes to."

"Here." Ryon tugged his pack off his back and tossed a coil of skinny rigging rope at Nox. Nox caught it and bent to the task, wrenching the fox-masked man none too gently for all the trouble he'd caused.

"He's lucky I don't slit his throat for what he did to Violet."

"You have him?" Flint asked. *"The girls are all right?"*

"Yeah. No thanks to me. Mariun... did something to knock him out before we got here."

"Ah. She's scrappy. I like her more already."

He sighed inwardly. *"She didn't fight him off with her fists. I thought she had one of those poles. The ones they used on me. But she didn't."*

"What? I'm not following."

"Me either. Don't worry. I'll get some answers."

While he'd been tying the fox and chatting with Flint, Mariun had rushed over to help Ryon with Violet. As Nox tugged the last knot into place, he turned to them.

"Are you all right, Vi?"

Violet nodded slowly, wincing. "Yeah. I hit my head pretty hard, but I think I'll be fine."

"Good." He shifted his attention to Mariun. "He's tied. Spill it."

Ryon sneered. "Why did we tie him? Say the word and I'll cart him back to the cliff and toss him over."

"No." Mariun stood, arms crossed. "He's too valuable."

"What?" Nox barked.

"The eggs." Mariun stalked over and kicked the still-whimpering man in the ribs. "Where are they?"

Ryon cleared his throat. "You might want to say that in Thalassian..."

Mariun blinked, cheeks flushed. She repeated the question. The fox quivered, stinking and blubbering like a baby. She kneeled and yelled in his face. When she reached out a hand, palm splayed and aimed for his shoulder, the fox shrieked a pitiful yowl that spoke of ultimate pain. He broke into a string of chatter, shooting the words out rapid-fire. When he finally stopped jabbering at Mariun, Nox turned to Ryon. "Did you catch all that?"

Ryon nodded once. "What do we do with *him*?" He spat out the last word, his nostrils flaring.

Nox grabbed the blubbering mess and lifted him high off the ground. Then he smashed his head as hard as he could into the forest floor. With his hands and legs tied, the fox put up no defense, and the single blow knocked him out cold.

Violet sucked in a shaky breath.

Nox sent her a wobbly smile. "Relax, Squirt. He's still breathing. We can't have him escaping his bonds and chasing after us." He lifted the man's dead weight and tossed him into the underbrush. "Hopefully if another patrol happens by, they won't spot him until we've finished."

"More than he deserves, if you ask me." Ryon's gaze was glued on Violet. "A man who harms a woman doesn't deserve to draw breath."

Violet patted Ryon's arm. "I'm all right."

Nox swung around and found Mariun watching him while chewing on her lower lip and shifting on her feet. "Time to come clean, Mare."

She glared at him. "I told you not to call me that."

"I don't care. Why should I care about anything you want when you're keeping so many secrets? What was that?" He waved his hand at the brush. "How did you drop him? And what about the rotting storm last night?"

Mariun seemed to shrink in on herself while he stacked up question after question. But once he'd finished, she drew her shoulders back and met his gaze. "I told you I'd tell you and I will." She glanced at the others and her expression softened. "We don't have much time to find the eggs. Come on. I'll tell you everything while we walk." She sighed wearily and helped Ryon lift Violet to her feet. "Everything will make sense when I finish telling the story I started a few days ago."

A Daughter's Gift

Mariun gaped, staring in awe at the massive circular room. She'd never seen anything so big. She forced her open mouth to snap closed as she followed Seneca and the boys inside the drafty chamber. Rows of benches lined the walls, enough to seat thousands. All of them sat empty, staring down silently but giving proof to the stories she'd been told.

They lived in a massive city, Thalassia. Her instructors had explained the intricacies of city life. They'd detailed all the different jobs and shown them pictures, preparing them for the day when they would either return to their families and become a productive member of the city, or become the lucky one to help their father rule.

Until today, it had just been stories. They'd spent their entire lives together in the tiny suite of rooms, cut off from everything. She'd always wondered why. Why keep them as prisoners in everything but name? Why couldn't they spend their childhood with their mothers, their families, when the test only took a single afternoon of their lives?

It was the way it had always been done, her instructors said. Don't question the Supreme.

Now that she stood here, in a room big enough to house half the city or more, the thought sprung to her mind anew. It wasn't fair. She'd been forced to live a life of drudgery with only her classes to keep her occupied. History, arithmetic, writing.

During those long days of endless classes, she'd always remind herself that one day it would end. One day she'd be set free to return to her mother. To learn what it was like to live in a big, bustling city. Now she'd have to live with a single glimpse. This massive room would be her lone taste of freedom before her demise.

"It's almost over, Mare." The words cut her to the core. Whit squeezed her hand, sending her a tremulous smile, not grasping the finality in that statement. "Are you ready for the rest of our lives to begin?"

Mariun squeezed back and forced a smile. "I'm ready."

They stopped on a dirt floor in the center of the massive room.

"What is this place?" Whit craned his neck and stared up into the empty stands.

Seneca opened her mouth to reply, but before she spoke, a door swung open and a group of people filed in. A man wearing a fierce black-and-white spider mask, clothed head to toe in black, led them inside and directed them to stand against the walls of the huge circular chamber.

The rest of the people sported worn clothes, their faces painted with a mixture of emotions. All the instructors she'd met over the years were there, along with a handful of strangers. A few cried, holding tight to their companions as they spotted them standing silently in the center of the dirt ring. Others remained stoic, arms crossed, watching with curiosity. There were even a few children, clinging to their parents and staring with wide eyes.

Among the strangers was one face she recognized. Her mother watched with tears in her eyes, her hand tightly clutching a man who met Mariun's gaze and smiled sadly. A pair of children hovered beside them, talking quietly with each other and seeming oblivious to the world around them.

Her family. A jolt of pain pierced her chest. She'd always wondered if her mother had more children. What they'd look like. Now she knew. The knowledge didn't bring any comfort. She'd never get to know them. Never learn what it was like to be one of them, lost in their own little world, giggling together.

She stared back at the man who her mother claimed was the father, not just to her siblings but *her* true father as well. She'd never talk to him. Never learn his name. She could only stare across the cavernous room and meet his stare this once before he watched her die.

The door slammed again, drawing her attention. A man strolled onto the dirt floor with his head held high. Long black hair floated around his shoulders, and a deep-purple robe trailed behind him as he stalked toward them.

Seneca bowed deeply as he halted before her. "Your Grace, I present your progeny." She thrust out her arm, staring at them expectantly.

Heart hammering, Mariun shook off the shock of finally meeting the Supreme and stepped forward, bowing low. She sensed movement beside her as the others did the same. They'd been trained for this moment, but it still felt surreal. Like watching it happen from outside her body. As if she were a distant observer and not the one inside her flesh, demanding her head bow and her eyes stay trained down at the Supreme's shiny black boots.

"Rise," he demanded, voice like steel. "Let's get this over with."

Mariun shivered as she complied, but kept her eyes downcast. Maybe it was silly of her to expect a man who'd fathered hundreds—who'd never even bothered to meet her—to show a hint of affection upon their introduction. Even now, knowing he wasn't her true father, his cold dismissal stung.

"Joben, step forward," Seneca said.

Across the room, someone gasped. The woman waved, her face lit with joy. All the Supreme's children had dark hair and similar features. But if she looked close enough, she could see the resemblance between the two. That woman must be Joben's mother. How sad that she didn't even recognize him until Seneca uttered his name.

Joben hesitated long enough to suck in a single breath, and then he strode forward. He was the eldest of their quartet, and the biggest. If the test measured brute strength, he would be the one to pass.

Jurdan the Supreme closed the space between them. Joben was tall for twelve, but only came up to Jurdan's chin. Joben trembled, his head lowered, fists clenched.

"Eyes up," Jurdan demanded.

Joben tilted his head and met the Supreme's gaze. Jurdan clasped Joben's head in his hands.

This was it. Mariun's pulse pounded, skin tingling with anticipation. Everyone gathered watched the pair intently, the cavernous room so silent she heard immediately when the sound started.

A gentle *buzz* rent the air. Her gaze locked on Joben, his face held immobile between the Supreme's hands. At first, he stood there unmoving, his mouth ajar, staring back at their leader like he was mesmerized. But within only an instant, that changed.

The *buzz* amplified, and Joben began to shake. His fists unclenched and his fingers wobbled. Then his arms. The jerking increased, radiating across his body until he trembled from head to toe, and his eyes unlocked from Jurdan's and rolled back in his head.

Jurdan sighed and removed his hands. Joben crumpled to the dirt. He lay there twitching, writhing in agony.

Jurdan made no move to help him—his own son. He merely stepped sideways and barked, "Next."

Mariun's eyes widened, her chest flaring with every panicked breath she drew. Was no one going to help him? She almost stepped forward, but as she lifted her foot, Joben gasped and jolted up. He sat there looking stunned for half a heartbeat before he scrambled to his feet and returned to their line-up.

She glimpsed his face before he halted beside her. A tear slid down one flush cheek, and his jaw trembled. Mariun wrinkled her nose as his scent reached her, and she suddenly understood the need for the thick undergarments. But she only spared a quick moment of sympathy for Joben's embarrassment.

Seneca cleared her throat. "Malik. Step forward."

Malik took several mincing steps, already shaking. Mariun shook, too, fear and disbelief swimming in her veins. She had to watch this again. She had to *do* this soon.

Jurdan strode to him and barked out the same command. "Eyes up."

Malik complied. The Supreme gripped his face. The air buzzed.

Malik's reaction was swifter than Joben's. His whole body shook at once, even while the *buzz* was only a gentle hum. He held Jurdan's gaze for only a bare instant before his eyes rolled back.

The effect was much the same. Jurdan released Malik's head, and he collapsed, convulsing.

"Next." Jurdan wiped his hands on his fine robe as if cleansing himself of Malik's touch.

It took Malik longer to roll off the ground on shaky legs, but soon he returned to stand beside them. Mariun shuddered and shared a glance with Whit. He met her eyes and smiled gently.

Would she be next, or him?

Seneca's gaze trailed over them both. The glimmer of hope that'd been there that morning when she'd spoken of their passing had faded, replaced with a blank dullness. "Whit. Step forward."

Across the ring a woman wailed. She lurched toward them, her face red and blotchy from her tears. The spider barked out a low command and turned in her direction, but halted when the man beside her grabbed her around the waist and hauled her against his chest.

Mariun's heart ached as she watched her friend step forward. Maybe Whit would be the one? If he passed, then she wouldn't even need to be tested. He could become Jurdan's heir and she would be allowed to join her family. To live.

Whit was smaller than the other boys. Slimmer and shorter, despite being fed the same diet all their lives. But out of all of them, he was the calmest. He strode forward with his head held high and met Jurdan's eyes without having to be told.

A ghost of a smile tugged at the Supreme's cheeks. It looked like Whit's bravery in the face of almost guaranteed pain was finally something he approved of.

Mariun didn't have long to ponder the thought. Jurdan clamped down on Whit's cheeks, and another *buzz* interrupted the ghostly quiet. Even the wailing woman had stopped, her gaze locked onto Whit and Jurdan as the sound slowly increased.

A heartbeat passed. Then two. Three. Mariun's breath caught in her throat. Whit stood solidly, not a single tremor in any of his limbs. He stared at Jurdan, eyes blazing with triumph. But as three beats turned into four and five, Whit's expression shifted. His nose crinkled and the very tips of his fingers shook.

No. Mariun's stomach lurched. All the hope she'd held that she'd escape the test evaporated like vapor. It took Whit three times as long as Joben, but soon he crumpled to the floor. He popped up quicker, not even giving her the benefit of a longer wait before it was her turn.

Jurdan shook his head, his lips twisting as he watched Whit scramble back to his spot in line. Then his gaze narrowed on her. "Step forward and let's be done with this."

Seneca shifted, rubbing her elbow. "This is Mariun, Your Grace."

Jurdan waved a hand, beckoning her forward. She gulped, then stepped out of line. Four strides brought her abreast of him. She tried to channel Whit's strength. To meet the Supreme's gaze cooly, without flinching.

It was a hard task to accomplish. Her gaze kept straying to her family standing silently beyond him. Tears rolled down her mother's and father's cheeks. Even the children looked on with sympathy painted on their faces.

A sudden spear of anger jolted in her chest. Why had her parents brought them? Did they really want their children, her siblings, to watch her die? She had half a mind to race across the room and demand they leave.

But Jurdan's deep voice brought her back to the present. "Eyes on me."

Her gaze shot to his, and she sucked in a nervous breath. His eyes were a brown so dark they were almost black. His face was unreadable. Huge hands reached for her an instant before his clammy palms suctioned to her face.

Even before the sound started, she began to tremble. This was it. She was about to die. Her lashes fluttered closed like they had a mind of their own, worn down by the grief burdening her heart. She wasn't ready. She didn't want to die.

Jurdan's fingers clenched tighter. "Open," he barked.

Her eyes shot open, and she locked gazes with him once again. The buzzing started, and his grip increased at the same moment a gentle tingle thrummed across her skin. If it weren't for Jurdan's crushing hold of her face, she might have marveled at the sensation. But all she could focus on was his clenching fingers, his hands so large his fingertips reached back into her hairline.

Was this how the others had felt as it began? She could sense her body trembling all over, but was it from fear of her impending death or caused by the insistent *buzz*? It was so much louder with Jurdan's hands on her body, so demanding. The *buzz* sank into her skin and hummed deep in her skull. Her veins were alive with it, swimming with the startling sensation.

All the while, she stared into his mesmerizing eyes. Time seemed to slow as she lost herself in the dark depths of his gaze. This man would end her life without thought. He'd fathered hundreds, only to drop them to the dirt and abandon them forever when they couldn't meet his strange demand. What did this test prove? What was he searching for?

If she concentrated hard enough, maybe she would glimpse the truth before she succumbed to the test. If she just looked—

Suddenly, Jurdan released her. Mariun stumbled and staggered, but she did not fall. Why did he stop? Surely that wasn't the end of it...

Her gaze flicked back to her family and found them wide-eyed and gaping. She shook her head as the buzz's last lingering remnant departed, shivering across her skin and leaving her weak in the knees but still standing.

She was alive. Mariun sucked in a shaky breath and clutched her chest. Her mother was wrong. She almost laughed as relief washed over so intensely she practically fell to her knees from the force of it. But confusion rose to take its place.

That couldn't have been all of it. Jurdan would clamp his hands back on her skull and finish what he'd started. Mariun eyed him closely, ready for him to bark out another command. Instead, he turned to Seneca. "What was her name?"

"Mariun, Your Grace." Seneca's eyes shimmered, her smile so luminous Mariun flinched. What was happening?

Jurdan whipped around, facing the folk gathered along the walls. "Who is her mother?"

Mariun's mother tentatively raised her hand, sheltered in the circle of her husband's arms. "I am, sir."

"Your name?" Jurdan asked.

"Arrietty."

"Mariun. Arrietty. Follow me." Jurdan started out across the room, back toward the door he'd entered from. Mariun sent a quick glance back at Seneca, only for her to shoo her away with an insistent flick of her wrist, beaming.

Arrietty peeled herself out of her husband's arms and grabbed his hand, tugging him forward with her and waving at her children. "Come little ones, you heard the Sup—"

"No," Jurdan barked. "Just you."

Jurdan reached the spider-masked man's side and stood waiting. Mariun took one look at his hard face and scrambled across the dirt floor toward him. She arrived at his side at the same time her mother did.

The Supreme ran his gaze over both of them. A slow, deliberate perusal that made Mariun's stomach churn. Then he spun back to everyone gathered in the room and raised his voice. "You will remain here. No one leaves."

Jurdan nodded at the spider, who opened the door. Mariun swallowed the lump in her throat and followed. Arrietty kept step with her, her gaze flicking all over and her hands clenched in the skirt of her long brown dress. She tugged it up to her knees as they ascended a narrow staircase.

Where were they going? It was yet another piece of city Mariun had yet to see. Their boots echoed loudly as they climbed the deserted stairs. After a few flights, her legs began to tire, but Jurdan kept a steady pace while whispering to the spider a few steps above, so quietly she couldn't hear anything over the *clomp* of their footfalls.

She almost asked for the men to slow, but before her legs gave out, they arrived at the top. The spider held open another door. Jurdan strolled through calmly and paused, waiting for them to follow.

The Supreme's stare made it hard for Mariun to catch her breath. Arrietty seemed to be in a similar state. She huffed and puffed beside her, but after only a moment's hesitation, she stepped through the door.

Mariun spared a glance for the spider as she followed. He was even more muscular and frightening up close, with that fierce arachnid mask covering his features. A hood disguised his hair, and he wore long black gloves to hide his hands.

The masked were legendary in Thalassia. The strong right arm of the Supreme, tasked with keeping peace in the city and patrolling their borders. Mariun's instructors had shared countless stories about them over the years. But somehow, being in the spider's presence wasn't as comforting as she'd expected.

Mariun brushed off her reaction and set her attention on the space she entered. She suddenly understood the need for all those stairs.

They'd returned to the same circular room and floated inside an opulent box wedged between the rows of benches.

Two huge cushioned chairs dominated the space. Jurdan walked to them and thrust out an arm. "Sit."

No sooner had she and her mother sat than Jurdan stalked off, back through the doorway. The spider stayed behind with them, blocking the door.

Mariun's stomach buckled. What was happening? Where was he going?

She stared down at the ring. Everyone still waited there, shuffling their feet and chatting excitedly. Whit caught her eye and sent her a wide grin and a little wave. Mariun's brow furrowed. She waved back but couldn't find it in herself to smile.

"Do you know what's happening?" she whispered to Arrietty.

Her mother tore her gaze off her family below and faced Mariun. "I was wrong." She cut a glance back at the spider, then lowered her voice even more. "I don't know how, but you passed the test. You're going to be Jurdan's successor."

Mariun jerked back in the fine chair. "No. Surely not."

"It's true." Arrietty leaned closer. "Do you not realize how much time passed while he was testing you? I swear it must've been a quarter hour."

"It was?" Mariun's heart raced. It hadn't felt like that at all. She'd thought barely a moment passed before Jurdan removed his hands and released her.

"I don't know what you experienced, but I watched it all. That awful buzzing grew so loud every person down there covered their ears. But you just stood there." She squeezed her hand, a tentative smile on her lips. "Mariun. It's you."

Mariun closed her eyes, trying to wrap her mind around this new information. If her mother was right, and she *was* meant to be Jurdan's successor, then what happened next?

A door slamming below made her eyes shoot open. She leaned forward, watching movement in the ring.

Jurdan strode out, his arms stretched out wide. "All these years. Every test a failure. No longer." He looked up at the box and met her wide-eyed stare. Mariun's pulse drummed in her ears.

Halting in the center of the ring, Jurdan swung his gaze over everyone. "You were witnesses to my heir's test. You've all been connected in some way to her upbringing. I'm so very grateful to you all." For the first time since she'd met him, Jurdan's face broke out in a grin. The people below seemed to take comfort in it. Stiff shoulders relaxed, and nearly everyone wore an answering smile.

But not her. Mariun still couldn't stomach the conflicting emotions swelling within her. Jurdan might speak of gratitude, but she couldn't find it in herself to be thankful. She was too baffled. Too overwhelmed knowing she'd miraculously passed the test that should've been her end.

Jurdan waved the folks standing by the walls forward. "Come closer now. I have something very special to share with you all."

Seneca was the first to hop forward, glancing over her shoulder and clicking her tongue to ensure the boys followed. Soon everyone crowded around Jurdan, murmuring softly to each other, their faces lit with excitement.

"Gather around." Jurdan beckoned them closer still. If not for his height, she'd have lost track of him within the crowd. His voice boomed out among the throng. "Come forward and claim your reward."

As those words rang out, she did lose sight of him. Mariun inched forward in her chair, desperate to see what was happening below. Had he bent down to hand out something?

But then the most awful sound rose to her ears. That same maddening *buzz* that hummed through her limbs during the test split the air. Crumpling to the ground, writhing in agony, the crowd around Jurdan fell.

Mariun spotted him again, that horrible smile still spread across his face. He'd sunk his fingers into the ground up to the knuckles.

"No!" Arrietty screamed. She leaped to her feet, scrambling for the railing. Before she could take more than two steps, a gloved hand clamped on her shoulder. The spider hauled her back, clutching her to his chest while she wailed and tore at his arms.

Mariun sat dumbfounded, watching in horror. She stayed glued to her chair, unable to move, speak, or look away from the gory sight below. The people convulsed, only the whites of their eyes showing. A putrid stench wafted up, and she didn't have to guess what the dark stains on the folks' trousers were from. But worse was when little rivulets of blood dripped from their ears and eyes. Blood-red tears stained the cheeks of the only people she'd ever known.

He was killing them. Everyone she'd known. Every single soul she'd spent time with in her short life.

Mariun's gaze caught on Whit—the boy she loved like no other—and her soul shattered. Many of the others had already stilled, succumbing to the violence. But not him. He still writhed, hanging on so long that he was the only one moving, blood coating his entire face like a scarlet mask.

How could Jurdan do this? Why?

Finally, even Whit stilled. Jurdan rose from his crouch, picking out the few spots of dirt among the sprawled corpses and stepping gingerly around them.

Arrietty wailed. "No! My babies." The heartbreak in her voice tore Mariun apart.

The door below slammed on its hinges, momentarily drowning out her mother's cries. Mariun's pulse surged. Jurdan was on his way back up.

How could she face him after what he'd done? He'd just murdered a room full of innocent people. Mariun's palms sweated, her hands clenched so tightly to the arms of the fine plush throne she was probably leaving nail marks.

The door opened, and Mariun flinched. Jurdan strolled in. His face was perfectly stoic, giving no hint of the crazed killer who'd just sent so many to their graves.

"You monster!" Arrietty screamed, spittle flying out of her mouth. She jerked in the spider's arms, fighting to free herself.

Jurdan merely waved a hand. "I'm no monster. I'm protecting our daughter."

Mariun jolted like she'd been slapped.

"Now there are none who may claim my heir's affection. None who might seek to harm her before she comes into her power." Jurdan turned from Arrietty and stared straight at Mariun. "I've waited so long for you. I've seen what cruel desires live in the hearts of men. You must be protected from the common rabble."

Mariun's throat stung with bile. He'd killed them for her? *Because of her?* She was going to be sick.

"My children wouldn't have harmed Mariun. Nor my husband. They loved her. You're a liar and a murderer!" Arrietty screeched out the words, clawing desperately at the spider's arm. But when her speech ended with no reaction from Jurdan other than a single scoff, she wilted. "Kill me too. I can't live without them."

"Oh, I'm afraid I can't do that." Jurdan smiled condescendingly. "There's a reason I always bed women who are freshly flowered. Now that you've proven you can produce heirs worthy of me, I shall want another. Maybe a boy this time, hm?"

Mariun's chest burned. When she'd started her courses last year, Seneca had said that she'd flowered... Did that mean Jurdan had bedded her mother and forced her to bear a child—to have *her*—when she was the same age as Mariun was now? No wonder the poor woman couldn't bear to repeat the process when she'd failed the first time.

Arrietty appeared no more eager to appease Jurdan now. She lifted her red-flushed face and sneered. "Are you insane? You killed my family and you want me to lie with you?"

"Your wants are immaterial. You will do as your Supreme commands."

Her fight seemed to die with that calm demand. Arrietty whimpered, her limbs boneless within the spider's arms.

"Come. I'll show you to your new rooms." Jurdan spun on his heel and strode swiftly to the back of the box.

Mariun hesitated as a fleeting urge rushed to the forefront of her mind. They were so high up. If she dove off the railing headfirst, she could erase the clawing ache in her heart. She could join her friends in the calm embrace of death and steal the one thing that vile man wanted more than anything else.

With the spider occupied holding her mother, and Jurdan beside the door, surely she'd make it. But Arrietty's sniffles chased the morbid thought away.

Mariun couldn't leave her alone. She didn't know her mother well, but Arrietty had cared enough to seek her out and warn her before the test. Then she'd been forced to watch her children and husband murdered. If Mariun took her own life in front of her and left Arrietty alone with Jurdan's wrath and insistent demands, what kind of coward did that make her?

She detached her clenched fists and followed, keeping her head down. She still hadn't said a word since the killing had started. Her mind whirled, bombarding her with memories. Seneca nursing her when she was ill. Laughing and playing hide and find with the boys. Listening to the made-up stories Whit whispered in the dark.

That was over now. She'd known today would change her life. But never in a million years had she expected this.

She wasn't sure how long they walked or what direction they traveled, but before long, Jurdan tore open a set of doors and ushered them inside. By now the spider was practically dragging Arrietty, and her grief was so great that she didn't yelp when he knocked her head against the door, lugging her inside.

Mariun's head swam as she studied the room. It was far grander than any she'd ever seen. An enormous bed draped with lush pale-cream blankets took up nearly half of it, and a pair of couches occupied the other half. Bookshelves bursting with colorful tomes lined the walls, and a closet sat open in one corner, overflowing with fine gowns in rainbow shades.

The spider dumped Arrietty unceremoniously on the bed. She curled in a ball, shuddering.

Mariun sank down on the couch and watched Jurdan warily. He turned to her and smiled. "This is your mother's room." He pointed to the far corner. "That door leads to your room." His hand snaked out to point in the opposite direction at a second door. "That leads to my chambers. See that you knock before you seek to enter. And if you find it locked with no answer, leave me in peace. Understood?"

Mariun nodded dutifully, her hands balled in her lap. Jurdan stalked to the door he'd just pointed at, jerking his head at the spider to follow. As soon as the door slid closed, Mariun hopped up and joined her mother on the bed.

"Arrietty. M-mother." She traced her back gently, unsure of what to say. *What can be said to someone whose life was just upended in the worst way possible?*

Arrietty popped up and met her stare with bloodshot eyes. "I-I can't do it." She seemed to notice for the first time that they were alone. Then she shook off her sadness and rose with a determined stance. Her head flitted all around, searching the room, before she raced for the closet.

"What are you doing?" Mariun stood beside her while she crammed her body into the small space, flinging the gorgeous garments around carelessly. "I don't think making a mess is going to help matters."

Arrietty sighed and shoved out of the closet, then crossed to the bookshelves. She walked a circuit of the room, examining everything with her gaze. Then she ripped open the adjoining room's door and stuck her head inside, only to shut it again after a long look.

She drove her fingers into her long hair, tugging at the strands. "Oh, it's no use."

"What is?"

Arrietty spun to face her, wild-eyed. "You'll need to do it."

"Do what?"

Her mother sank to her knees and clutched Mariun's waist in a deathly grip. "I-I know it's selfish. I know I don't deserve your trust or your love. But please. Mariun, please, you have to help me end it."

Mariun shook her head. She couldn't be asking for what she thought she was asking... "End what?"

Arrietty leaned back on her heels and met her eyes. "My life."

She couldn't be serious… But as she stared down into those eyes that mirrored her own, she didn't see a single shred of hesitation.

"Please, Mariun. I-I can't. What he's asking of me… *I can't.*"

Mariun's legs buckled, and she wobbled on her feet. How could Arrietty ask that of her? She would be alone—truly alone—with that monster.

But as she gazed into her mother's eyes, her battered heart wrenched open. Could she condemn her for having the same thoughts she'd just entertained? And what was the alternative? Could she rest comfortably in her bed at night, listening while the man who had killed her family forced himself upon her mother?

No. Her mother had given her the gift of life. She would give her mother the gift of death.

"Close your eyes," Mariun whispered.

Arrietty nodded. A smile painted her lips as her lashes fluttered closed for the last time.

Mariun wrapped her hands around her mother's neck, and the silent room came alive with a familiar *buzz*.

Burden of Power

Leaves crunched beneath Ryon's boots as they followed the fox's directions through the forested island. They'd nearly reached the spot where the man claimed the eggs rested while a million questions flooded his mind.

That story... Could Mariun's awful tale actually be true?

Ryon was the first to break the silence. "You killed her? Your own mother?"

Mariun hung her head low. "I-I did. It's been more than a decade, but I still wonder if I made the right decision."

Violet squeezed Mariun's hand, her eyes swimming with unshed tears. "Blazes, Mariun. I'm so sorry they put you in that position. It was an impossible situation. An impossible decision for someone so young to make."

Ryon could certainly relate. He hasn't been much older when tragedy had prompted him to make a disastrous decision of his own.

Nox cleared his throat and spoke in the softest voice he'd used since Ryon had met him. "Sometimes a clean death is the kindest gift you can give."

Ryon lifted a brow. Maybe it was his imagination, but from the faraway look in Nox's eye, it sounded like he was speaking from experience.

Violet shuddered. "Jurdan... I knew that man was vile just from looking at him, but how could he kill so many? All those innocent people."

"I've noticed over the years how demanding and possessive Jurdan is. When people don't fall in line with his wishes, he becomes unhinged." Mariun sighed wearily. "He said he killed them to protect me. Maybe in his twisted mind, he convinced himself that was what he was doing. But I think he wanted to erase everyone I had known before him. To keep me beholden to him and him alone."

Ryon's stomach quivered. What a cruel, disgusting thing to do. And Mariun had been forced to live with him. To pretend to be his daughter. A man who would cut down so many just to keep her isolated. It was sickening. "What happened after? What did Jurdan do when he discovered what you'd done?"

Mariun wrapped her arms around her chest. "I was so scared. I thought..." She shook her head. "Spider saved me."

Nox's foot skidded in the thick underbrush. "The masked man who always shadowed you?"

Mariun nodded. "He found me crying hysterically over her body. I clammed up. Wouldn't say a word about what happened. I was sure Jurdan would kill me."

"Then what?" Violet asked.

"Jurdan burst in while Spider was questioning me. H-he convinced Jurdan it was a mistake. That the magic he'd awakened in me must have come out inadvertently."

Shock reverberated through Ryon's core. "And you'd just met the spider that day?"

Mariun nodded again. "I don't know why he stuck up for me." She shrugged. "Jurdan assigned him to watch over me. Said if anything like that ever happened again, it would be on his head."

"Did it ever happen again?" Nox asked.

"No. I used my powers, of course. I had to learn to control them to keep Jurdan happy. But Arrietty is the only person I've killed. By my own hand, at least." Mariun added the last in a voice barely above a whisper.

Ryon's blood ran cold. "What are you talking about?"

"I'm sure you wondered how the city can survive under the sea." Mariun pursed her lips. "It's powered by magic."

Nox rubbed his shoulder. "Those weapons"—he stared at Mariun's hands—"you powered them too, didn't you?"

"Yes. Jurdan had always handled it alone, but once he found me, he made me help him." Mariun shuddered. "I hated it. I hated knowing the magic I'd been given was being used to harm those poor animals. To hurt people. But obedience was all I knew. Once I learned about the games, I avoided them at all costs. Until one day, I had enough of hiding. Enough of pretending to be the dutiful daughter he wanted me to be. I convinced Spider to let me look after the prisoners." She smiled down at her feet. "That's when I met Iggy."

Nox cursed under his breath.

"Iggy told me stories about the land he came from. I decided then I'd do whatever it took to escape. That one day I'd find a way out of Thalassia." She shrugged. "When I saw my chance, I took it."

Violet ducked beneath a low branch the rest of them were forced to circle. "So, you dropped the fox with your magic?"

"I did. And I stopped the storm." Mariun frowned. "I've never done anything like that before. I can't really explain it. I just knew I needed to go out there last night. The storm called to me." She twisted her lips. "It felt right using my power as something other than a weapon for a change."

Silence fell again as they absorbed her words. Now that Mariun's story was finally out, Ryon couldn't help feeling sorry for her. What a strange, lonely life she'd lived. Even having such an incredible power had been a burden rather than the blessing it should have been.

It was a hard tale to wrap his head around, but he supposed it made sense. Only she had still left so much unsaid. Like her power. What was it and where did it come from? How did she get it if she wasn't Jurdan's daughter, but an imposter like she claimed?

Ryon opened his mouth to press for more, but then his lips slammed closed and his eyes widened. "Guano. I think we found them."

The forest parted ahead, revealing a massive clearing at the base of a dark mountain. Heat pooled in the air, seeping off the black rocks. The sun beat down, sinking into the ground and making the surface they creeped out on feel ten times as hot as the forested coast.

But it wasn't the heat that was the most shocking part of the landscape. Not even the enormous mountain bubbling with slow-moving streams of molten red leaking out of the top. It was the gargantuan boulders sheltered at the mountain's base. Four massive ovals rested in the clearing, arranged in a perfect semicircle. The dragon eggs.

Violet rushed forward and pressed her palms against the closest egg. It towered over her and was so wide it would take three of them with their arms outstretched to circle it completely. "These are the eggs? I mean, they don't look like any egg I've ever seen." She frowned as her fingers traced the hard shell. "It feels just like rock."

Mariun joined her, reaching out tentatively. "You're right. Maybe that's why the dragons need to be the ones to break out." She knocked on an egg and winced, rubbing her knuckles. "There's no way we're opening it from the outside." Mariun's gaze flicked from Violet to Nox. "Can either of you bond with them?"

Violet's brow furrowed. "I-I don't hear anything." She turned to her uncle. "That's how it works, isn't it? You communicate in your thoughts."

Nox tore his gaze off the egg on the semicircle's far end. "Yes. That's how it works." He met Violet's eyes and cocked his head at the eggs. "Do you feel drawn to any of them in particular?"

She backed away and scanned each boulder. "No. Should I?"

He rubbed the back of his neck and shrugged. "I'm not an expert, Vi. With only a few of us out there who can bond an animal, it's hard to say what's supposed to happen."

Violet's nose twitched, and she sneezed. "The ash in the air really tickles." She returned to her task, running her hands across a different egg this time.

Ryon stepped beside her, lips pursed. "Does this one feel any different?" He set his hand gently on the egg, silently agreeing with her earlier assessment. If he didn't know any better, he'd have guessed it was rock, too.

"I don't think so." Violet glanced at him and whispered, "What if it's not meant to be me who bonds with one of them?"

Ryon's heart ached at the quiet note of defeat in her voice. "Then it'll be your uncle, I guess." Nox hovered at the forest's edge, looking lost in thought. He was the only one who'd yet to touch the boulders. Ryon had to wonder if that was by design.

Nox paced closer, but instead of touching the eggs, he stopped in front of them. "Looks like we might be here for a while. I spotted some ploomfruit a ways back. I'll grab a few. We might as well have a bite while we wait."

Before any of them spoke in protest, he spun on his heel and back-tracked through the forest.

Should I follow him? The masked were still out there. It seemed foolish to split up.

A sob from Violet erased the thought from his mind.

"Hey, what's wrong?" he asked.

Violet clasped her mouth and buried her head in his chest. Ryon tugged her against him, wrapping her tightly in his arms.

"I'm sorry. I shouldn't be so emotional. I-I just wanted so badly for it to be me." She peeked at him and rubbed her teary eyes with her sleeve. "I can't help worrying that my parents were wrong. What if I *have* been skipped? Maybe I was never meant to have a bondmate..."

Ryon held her, wishing he knew what to say to comfort her. As his stomach churned, he had to admit he could use some comforting of his own. If they'd come all this way only to discover that nothing could be done to save the dragons, then what was next? Would fate be so cruel to give them a glimpse of what they were seeking and then snatch it out of their grasp?

Mariun patted Violet's shoulder. "We've only been here a few moments. Give it time."

Violet sucked in a shaky breath and straightened her spine. "You're right. I've barely started trying." She pushed out of his arms and walked back to the eggs. She rapped lightly on the hard surface. "We're getting you out of here. I promise."

Ryon grinned. "That's the spirit."

He only hoped it was a promise she wouldn't be forced to break.

Proximity and Danger

Nox plodded through the forest, fighting to reconcile the revelations falling into his lap. He'd spent the short trek back to the ploomfruit tree catching Flint up with Mariun's heartbreaking past. As if learning about her incredible power wasn't enough, now there were those stupid eggs he had to deal with.

"We always knew it was a possibility," Flint said.

"Rotting awful one." Nox buried the urge to slam the ripe orange fruit he'd plucked into the ground. *"I don't want another bondmate, Flint. What if I can't handle it?"* That familiar wash of dread swam in his stomach, so thick it felt like he'd been weighed down with sludge. And it wasn't just some story in a book. He'd lived it. Nearly died because of it.

"You managed with two before, and you can do it again." Flint was silent a moment, and then he asked, *"Are you sure it's even meant to be you? What about Violet?"*

"It's me all right. I couldn't stop staring at the one on the end. Couldn't stop picturing the wee dragon inside." A crooked grin lifted

the corner of his mouth before he swapped it out for a scowl. "*I had to hightail it out of there while I could still think straight.*" Nox shoved another fruit in his bag, certain he'd be washing sticky juice out of the fabric later.

"*What if she's destined to bond one of the others? Maybe you can put it off until you're... feeling more like yourself.*"

"*No. You know how it works.*" Nox shrugged. He'd told a little white lie to Violet back there. After five bondmates, he wasn't blind enough to miss the obvious. "*Proximity and danger. That's what you need for a bond to form. Violet was under plenty of danger when she was abducted by the fox. If she was meant to bond a dragon, they would've busted out to help her. Or warned her—something.*"

"*Look on the bright side. You couldn't have picked a better creature to bond with next.*" Flint's voice was laced with humor. "*I mean, it's no jagoth, but think of the lifespan. You'll never have a better chance of your bondmate outliving you.*"

Nox brightened slightly. Flint knew how much he loathed watching his bondmates die. It was like a little piece of his soul shriveled and decayed every single time. But a dragon... they lived for centuries.

A tiny smile curved his lips. "*You have a point.*"

"*And think of how cute the little critter will be,*" Flint added, a hint of a purr in his tone.

"*I don't know if* little *is the right word for a dragon.*" Nox sighed. "*I guess there's nothing for it but to break out my new bondmate and its siblings.*"

"*That's more like it!*" Flint sounded more excited than he had any right to be. "*So how do you bond with him? Or is it a her?*"

"*I'm not sure yet. About what it is, I mean.*" He cinched his bag closed and hitched it over his shoulder. "*As far as bonding goes, we have the proximity handled. The danger is another story.*" He frowned, stepping away from the tree and picking a trail through the underbrush toward the clearing.

"Danger, hm?" Flint mused.

"It's not wise to wait for the masked men to find us. If what Mariun said is true, they might even hold back and wait for us to hatch the eggs before they bother us. But I don't know what the alternative is."

"I might have an idea about how to arrange some danger a little sooner."

"Please tell me it doesn't involve me hiking that mountain and dangling above lava." Nox shuddered. *"I've had about all the heights I can handle."*

Flint chuckled. *"No. My plan doesn't involve any climbing... but I don't think you're gonna like it any better, my friend."*

He swatted away a fly buzzing close to his ear. If it got him off this rotting island faster, he was willing to chance it. After all, how bad could it be? *"Lay it on me, Flint."*

Nox drew a deep breath as he emerged from the woods. Even the second time, the massive fiery mountain and the gargantuan eggs were a sight to behold. His gaze shot unbidden to the egg on the end. An insistent pull tugged at his heart, but he did his best to ignore it. He returned to the group instead, where they hovered beside a different egg. Violet's hands pressed against it, her brow wrinkled, eyes closed to a slit.

"Any luck?" Nox asked.

"No." Violet sighed.

"Best take a break, then." He tugged his bag off his shoulder and opened it wide. The girls dug in without delay, but Ryon frowned at him and crossed his arms.

"Violet's been driving herself crazy trying to reach the dragons. I hope you had fun picking fruit."

"Ryon," Violet chided, her cheeks flushing.

"What?" Ryon glared at Nox, unapologetic. "The least he could have done was touch them once before he ran off to the woods."

"He's right." Nox planted the bag in Ryon's hands. "I'll do it now."

Nox halted in front of the first egg and set his hands on the rock-like shell. From up close, miniscule flecks of silver and copper glinted in the dim afternoon light. It was incredible when he stood back and thought about it. This enormous thing had housed a dragon for the last twenty years.

He paused at each egg until he reached the one on the end. A smile curved his lips as soon as his fingers made contact with it. Warmth spread through his veins, infusing his soul with a feeling he'd not allowed himself to grasp on to since he'd watched Flint fall. Hope.

He nearly brushed it aside, swarmed with guilt. But Flint spoke before he could tear his hands off the egg. "*No. It's all right. It's time, Nox.*"

Nox removed his hands slowly and turned back to the others.

"Well?" Violet stared at him, eyes bright.

He shook his head. "Nothing."

Violet's shoulders fell. "Oh."

Mariun patted Violet's arm. "Don't worry. We'll think of something."

Nox walked over to Ryon and grabbed his bag.

"Sorry." Ryon rubbed the back of his neck. "I thought—"

"It's fine." Nox forced a smile. "Matter of fact, I could use a favor, if you don't mind."

"Sure," Ryon agreed easily. "What is it?"

He pulled out an empty waterskin. "Would you mind heading back to the stream we spotted just inside the tree line? I forgot to fill this earlier, and my feet could use a rest."

Ryon nodded, flicking his long dreadlocks behind his ear.

"Would you mind going with him, Vi?" Nox tugged his tunic, drawing their attention to the sweat-stained fabric. "That way, you two can fill all the waterskins at once. We're bound to need more to drink if we're stuck here awhile, and it sounds like you need a break."

"Sure, Uncle Nox. I don't mind." Violet hurried to collect everyone's waterskins, and then they disappeared into the trees.

Nox sucked in a deep breath. "*Why did I let you talk me into this again, Flint?*"

"*Because it will work. Stop pussyfooting around and get it done.*"

Sitting cross-legged in the dirt, her long black dress tugged across her knees, Mariun chewed on a ploomfruit. She glanced up as he stalked over and stopped in front of her. He didn't sink down beside her, but stood directly above her, making her crane her neck.

"What?" She scrambled to her feet and backed up a pace. "Did you need something, Nox?"

"Yeah, I do." He cracked his neck and took a slow step closer. "I don't remember much from when I was attacked with one of those Thalass *poles*." He spat out the last like the taste of it sickened him. "Your good friend Iggy told me you were there with me."

Mariun swallowed. The half-eaten ploomfruit dropped into the dirt. She backed up another pace, her wide eyes locked onto his. "I-I was. I was there *healing* you."

She barked out the words with such accusation Nox almost cringed and called it all off. But Flint was right. It was the only way...

"It's funny, I vaguely remember the moment it happened. I guess pain that intense never truly goes away." He took another step closer. "Even if you're drugged out of your mind."

Mariun's shoulders collided with a dragon egg. She leaned back, looking for all the world like she wanted to dart away. Nox didn't give her the chance. He planted his fists on either side of her, boxing her in.

"You know what's strange, Mare?"

Fire burned in her gaze. "I told you not—"

He spoke loudly over her. "When I woke the next day, it wasn't just my shoulder that burned. My wrist did too."

Mariun's gaze darted sideways, landing on the exact spot.

"Funny how you're looking right at it, even when I didn't tell you which arm."

Her gaze shot back to his. "I-I..."

"Do it again."

"What?"

He grabbed her hands and planted them on his chest. Her eyes widened, mouth opening and closing silently.

He leaned even closer and wrapped his hands around her neck. "Do it or I'll finish what I started in that cage." A wave of disgust erupted from deep in his gut at the sight of his hands wrapped around her slender throat. He ignored it. He squeezed just enough to cut off her air for a heartbeat, then let up.

Mariun gulped in air. "Nox, no." She shoved at his chest. "I can't. I *won't*."

Nox stared into her stubborn, beautiful face. She knocked his hands off her neck, calling his bluff.

"*I told you*," he said to Flint.

"Good thing we aren't counting on her."

His keen ears picked up the crunch of leaves in the forest. The others were returning, but not fast enough. Mariun wouldn't stand there forever. Not unless he distracted her.

"I don't know what's gotten into you." Mariun inched sideways, clearly intending to sneak away.

Nox's arm shot out like it had a mind of its own, blocking her retreat. She turned to him, questions swimming in her big gray eyes. He silenced them all with a blistering kiss.

Mariun gasped against his mouth. He was sure she would push him away. That the shoving she'd done when his hands had been wrapped around her throat would pale in comparison. But after an instant where she seemed frozen in shock, her arms snaked up and wrapped around his neck. Her mouth opened, and he dove in, groaning when the bright tang of ploomfruit hit his tongue.

He'd never tasted anything sweeter. And she was kissing him back! It nearly killed him to pull away when he heard the clamor of footsteps and the echo of voices coming closer.

Nox pulled back far enough to meet her eyes. "I'm sorry," he whispered. He wrapped his hands around her throat again and squeezed hard enough to make her yelp. She let go of his neck and shoved at his chest again, harder than ever.

And from the forest, someone growled.

"Look out behind you!" a new voice shouted in his mind.

There it is.

Nox loosened his fingers from Mariun's neck and stepped back just as Ryon slammed into him. A fist flew at his face. Bones cracked. But Nox couldn't stop smiling.

"What is wrong with you? You're crazy if you think I'll let you hurt her!" Ryon screamed. He grabbed Nox's tunic and shook, his brows screwing up in confusion in the face of Nox's glee.

"*I'm coming!*" the voice yelled.

Behind them, one of the dragon eggs cracked. Nox couldn't help it then. He laughed.

Hatching

Violet raced out of the forest, dropping the waterskins in her haste to discover what had Ryon so riled. He'd approached the clearing a few paces ahead of her and bolted out like he was ready to commit murder.

Her stomach dropped to her feet as she emerged from the woods. She froze, gaping, trying to make sense of the peculiar scene. Mariun leaned against a dragon egg, clutching her neck and sucking in huge gasps. Nox was sprawled on the ground with Ryon atop him. Though his nose bled, Nox was smiling, the thin line of fluid leaking down his lips and painting his teeth a lurid red.

"What is wrong with you? You're crazy if you think I'll let you hurt her!" Ryon grabbed Nox's tunic and shook him.

Violet hurried forward just as the egg on the end cracked. Was it hatching? Her heart skipped a beat as a line appeared on the massive boulder's smooth surface. Nox's laughter spilled into the air, boisterous and more than a touch crazed.

"What in the blazes is going on?" Violet approached Mariun first. "Are you all right?"

Mariun blinked and dropped her hands to her sides. "I'm fine." She frowned at the egg as another line marred the surface. "I-Is that egg hatching?"

Violet crossed the dirt to where Ryon still hovered over Nox. His hands were clutched in Nox's tunic, but he'd stopped shaking him. Ryon's body appeared as frozen as hers had been, with only his eyes moving, flicking between the crackling egg and her cackling uncle.

Violet placed a hand on Ryon's shoulder. She nodded to Nox. "Perhaps you should let go until we get an explanation?"

Ryon detangled his fists from Nox's tunic and vaulted to his feet. "I-I don't understand." His brow creased.

Violet kneeled at Nox's side. "Nox is going to tell us. Aren't you, Uncle?" She held her breath, praying he'd still his manic laughter and explain. He just kept on cackling, great big belly laughs that seemed so out of place. His nose was likely broken after all, and his constant jerking with mirth wasn't helping stem the flow of blood.

Her stomach kinked up with knots. Her parents had warned her about the madness that sometimes overcame humans with bonding magic. Was Nox going mad?

She sighed and waved a hand behind her. "Mariun, could you find some bandages? And Ryon, would you grab the waterskins we dropped? I need to clean him up."

Violet's nerves slowly frayed the longer Nox's laughter went on. His gaze was locked on the egg, which continued to crackle and snap. Both sounds mingled together and echoed in the valley, making the place feel even more eerie than it had before.

She might not have confirmed it yet, but it seemed pretty obvious that Nox had bonded with a dragon. Her heart sank. She'd tried so hard to connect with one, all for nothing. Would she ever find a bondmate?

"Here." Mariun thrust a clean rag into her hands.

"Thanks." Violet pressed it to Nox's bloody nose.

Nox winced, and his laughter cut off abruptly. "Ow." His gaze snapped away from the egg and he sat up, snatching the rag out of Violet's grasp.

Violet rocked back on her heels and glared at him. "Good. Now that you're done laughing, you can tell us what the blazes is going on."

Ryon approached and tossed a waterskin into Nox's lap. "Yeah. Why were you choking Mariun?"

Violet gasped. She hadn't seen it, but it explained why Mariun had been clutching her neck. And why Ryon had been so quick to defend her.

But why had Nox done it?

She'd never known her uncle to be a violent person. Especially not with women. If the rumors floating around Flamesmoat could be believed, he was very popular with the ladies.

Mariun spoke up before Nox. "He wanted me to hurt him while you two were gone."

Violet's brow furrowed. "What?" Maybe he *was* going mad...

Nox cleared his throat. "Had to. I lied earlier, Vi. I know exactly how bonds work."

Hearing him speak again calmed a bit of the wild clawing in her gut. But she didn't like what he was saying. Not one bit.

"Why would you lie to me?" A pang of hurt lodged in her chest. Was he determined to keep the dragons for himself?

He turned to her with compassion in his eyes. "Once you're close enough, either you or your bondmate need to be in danger. If it were meant to be you, then you would've known when the fox grabbed you."

"Oh," Violet whispered.

"I had to put myself in danger." Nox spun to face Ryon. "I figured with the way you kept going on about throwing the fox off a cliff for shoving Violet, you'd want to hurt me when you got back."

Mariun crossed her arms. "And me?"

"Plan A and plan B. One had to work." Nox shrugged and pulled the rag away from his nose. The bleeding had stopped, but his nose was swollen and bruises were forming beneath his eyes.

"It was all an act?" Ryon rubbed the back of his neck.

"For the most part." Nox stood, tossing the bloody rag on the ground. "I did really choke her, though. Just long enough for you to see. I had to make sure you'd come at me so my new bondmate would sense the danger." Nox turned to Mariun. "I'm sorry. Did I hurt you?"

She shook her head. "I'm fine."

Violet glanced at the cracked egg. Tiny lines covered it from top to bottom, and one side was beginning to bulge. "And it worked. You bonded with one of them."

Nox grinned. "Yeah. Little chatterbox. Flint's keeping her entertained."

"It's a girl?" Violet clapped her hands together.

"You still hear Flint?" Ryon asked.

"They can talk to each other?" Mariun added.

Nox rubbed his temples. "Rot and decay. One at a time, *please*. I have enough going on in my head without you ganging up on me, too."

Violet frowned. No wonder Nox was having a hard time dealing with the new bond.

He sucked in a deep breath. "Yes, my new bondmate is female. Not sure about the rest yet. And I can hear them both"—he tapped his forehead—"in here. Flint never left. Adding another bondmate takes some getting used to, but I'll manage."

Another loud crack resounded, but something was different about this one. It took Violet a moment to realize why. "The other eggs are hatching!" She backed up and spotted a jagged line marring the egg farthest from Nox's. A heartbeat later, the boulder next to it cracked too.

"Can you speak to all of them?" Mariun asked.

"No." He nodded to the egg that held his bondmate. "But she can."

"You coax out the first and she gets the others to follow," Mariun said. "I can't believe that old story actually worked."

"Maybe not well enough." Ryon stopped in front of the last egg. While the other three crackled and snapped, it stayed silent and remained perfectly smooth and unblemished.

Violet's stomach dipped. She'd grown up on a farm. She knew it wasn't unusual for animals to lose some of their young. "Is it dead?"

"Hold on." Nox was silent for a moment, and then he chuckled. "No. Not dead. Just stubborn from the sounds of it."

The first egg splintered with a loud clamor, drawing everyone's attention. Shards of broken shell clattered into the dirt. Violet's heart hammered as the tip of a sharp claw tore through a tiny opening in the boulder.

This was it. She was about to meet a dragon! Even though she knew none of the hatchlings were meant to be her bondmate, chills spread up her arms and legs. It had been twenty years since anyone had seen one of the mythical beasts alive.

More and more rocky shell fragments spilled into the dirt. The hole widened enough that she caught glimpses of the dragon's leathery scales. Nox's bondmate was a gorgeous shade of green. As the tip of a wing emerged, the sun lit tiny flecks of bronze and copper shimmering in her scales.

"You're almost there." Nox smiled, looking more himself than he had since Flint fell in the ring.

Holes soon formed in the other two eggs that had begun to crack. Violet spotted more claws tearing through from the inside. But before the others got close to breaking free, the first dragon tumbled out. She hit the ground with a thump and rolled into a ball, sheltered beneath her large wings.

"It's all right," Nox said gently.

The little dragon peeked her head out of the protective shelter of her wings. Violet's breath caught. She was magnificent. A miniature version of the enormous beasts that featured on so many grand tapestries and paintings back home.

Even as a newborn, she looked fierce. Long, sharp teeth glinted in her mouth. And though she was nowhere near the size of a house like the adult dragons in the pictures she'd seen, she was already far larger than any of them. As she stood on shaky legs, and Violet got the first clear glimpse of the hatchling's size, she gulped. She was as large as a horse already, and who knew how quickly it would be before she grew even bigger?

"Um, are all the dragons this size?" Violet asked.

Nox shrugged. "Most likely." His new bondmate approached him and sniffed, then nudged Nox with her head. He patted her neck, smiling widely.

Violet couldn't still the grin that rose as she watched them silently communicate. But her stomach clenched at the same time. "Will they fit on our ship?"

Mariun frowned. "It will be a tight squeeze, but I think our boat can handle the added weight."

Ryon arched a brow. "Can't they fly?"

Nox shook his head. "They're babies. It'll take them time to learn, like any other flying creature."

Violet sighed. It certainly would've made things easier if they could just fly away from here. There were four of them and four dragons the size of horses. But it seemed dragon riding would not be happening anytime soon.

"Fetch those waterskins." Nox waved an arm, not taking his eyes off his bondmate. "Do you mind? She's thirsty."

Violet hopped to the task. A wave of dizziness washed over her as she bent down and lifted the first of the heavy containers.

"Hey." Ryon steadied her elbow. "You should have a bit as well. The heat will catch up with us if we don't drink while we're here."

Violet sucked down a few cool sips. Then she gathered another skin and returned with Ryon to the baby dragon.

"Thanks." Nox grabbed the first skin and lifted it to the dragon's mouth. She opened her jaws, and he poured water down her throat. Once she was finished, swallowing with a massive gulp, all the skins had been emptied.

"I guess we better get more for the others," Ryon said.

"We could lead them to the stream," Mariun suggested. "Might be simpler. If Jurdan's men are still keeping to the same schedule, there won't be another patrol planned until dark."

"No." Nox patted the green dragon's neck. "They need to conserve their strength." He turned to Violet. "You don't mind fetching more, do you? It's not far."

"You're right." She patted Ryon's arm and scooped up a few empty skins. "We'll get more." Violet's heart twinged. It meant she would likely miss the moment the other dragons first emerged from their shells. But keeping them healthy was more important than standing around and gawking.

She and Ryon cut through the forest quickly. The stream was only a short hike away. Violet kept her eyes peeled for any sign of the masked, but it appeared Mariun was right. They were alone for the moment. She drank her fill of the cool mountain stream before filling the skins and setting off back to the clearing.

A gasp spilled out of her lips upon her return. Another dragon had hatched, this one a brilliant shade of sky blue. The dying sunlight sparkled on its scales, highlighting flecks of white and silver.

"Wow." She approached slowly, not wanting to interrupt the heartwarming scene. The hatchlings were rubbing flanks, twining their long, sinuous tails together in an adorable manner that reminded her of kittens at play.

"A male this time," Nox announced.

The dragons drew apart, and the younger approached Nox, opening its massive jaw.

"Here." Ryon held out a skin with a chuckle. "Looks like he's thirsty too."

Violet dropped most of the skins at Nox's feet but carried one to Mariun. She stood by the eggs, watching intently as the third hole expanded.

"Drink up, Mariun. We can't have you fainting when it's time to leave." Violet thrust the skin at her.

Mariun grasped it and lifted it to her lips absentmindedly. She handed it back halfway drained. "Make sure Nox drinks some, too."

"I will." Violet returned to her uncle's side as he finished emptying the skins down the blue dragon's gullet. He reached out and twiddled his fingers, clearly intent on giving his portion to the baby. She shook her head. "This last bit is for you."

"Thanks, Vi." He drained it quickly, then wiped his arm over his sweat-soaked brow. "Do you mind going again?"

Violet's feet ached like crazy. She was all but certain her left foot would have a blister come morning. But she nodded and set off with Ryon once more.

By the time they returned, the sun had sunk so low it was a struggle to see in the darkened forest. She nearly tripped twice, but righted herself before she dropped the skins and sprawled in the dirt. The deeper dusk grew, the more Violet's anxiety rose. Mariun's words kept replaying in her mind, and she pictured the masked leaping out of each shadow she passed.

The clearing was still faintly lit by the day's last sunlight as they emerged. Violet smiled, finding not two but three babies cuddled up together beside the last egg. The new sibling was a brilliant white, its scales shimmering with tiny dots of silver and gold. "What's this one? Boy or girl?"

"Another male." Nox grabbed the skins, dumping their contents down the white dragon's throat. "We're going to need names for them soon. I've been calling them by their colors in my mind, but little green is not a fan of my system."

Violet's chest warmed. Who knew they'd be thinking up names for baby dragons? "We need to find good ones. Like their parents'."

"What were the parents' names?" Mariun tilted her head.

"Their father was my aunt Kayda's bondmate. Druturion the Black. She called him Dru," Violet answered. "Their mother was Belstasia the White. They called her Bela for short." She bounced on her toes. "We should think of names like that. Fancy and formal but easy to shorten."

"I like that idea." Nox was quiet a moment, and then a wide grin spread across his face. "Green likes it, too."

Ryon scratched his bearded chin. "Why are they all different colors?"

"The color of their scales signifies what magic they wield." Violet pursed her lips. "Bela was white. She could manipulate water. Dru, being black, was a fire dragon. Green must mean earth and blue air."

Mariun stared at the last egg, its surface still completely smooth and unmarred. "I bet that one is black." She rubbed her temples. "I once heard a story. A dragon of each element was needed for... something." She shook her head. "I can't remember it all."

"Doesn't matter," Nox said. "What matters is getting the last egg to hatch."

"Why hasn't it?" Ryon asked.

Nox shrugged. "Green's been talking with her, but she's not inclined to listen."

Violet hummed. "Oh. Another girl."

Mariun approached the last egg and placed her hand gently on the shell. "We might have to leave her here if she won't come out."

"Over my rotting dead corpse, we will," Nox growled. He puffed out his chest and practically snarled like a momma wolf protecting her pups. "All those babies are coming with us."

Mariun squared off in front of him. "What do you propose we do? Roll this massive boulder through the forest and toss it down the cliffside?"

"If we have to, yeah." He turned to his new bondmate. "But we won't need to."

"What do you mean?" Violet asked.

"Whatever you're planning, we better do it fast." Mariun shuffled away from the egg and peered into the dark forest. "It's been hours since we left the last patrol tied up in there. It won't be long before someone notices he's missing. Once they do, they'll send out more men to look for him. We can take out another patrol, but if they come in force..."

"Don't worry." Nox grinned slyly. "This won't take long at all."

Helping Hand

Nox smiled, doing his best to give off an air of surety. Mariun was already twitchy, eager to run off and leave the last egg behind. After hearing her story, he knew the last thing she wanted was to end up captured and return to Jurdan. But leaving one of the dragons when he'd been assured all it needed was a little more time... he wasn't about to sit by and let that happen. Not on his watch.

"*Don't worry,*" Green said soothingly. "*I've been talking with the others, and they think it will work, too.*"

"*It better,*" Nox replied. "*We can't stay here forever.*"

"*Give them a shot, Nox,*" Flint insisted. "*They can do it.*"

Nox rubbed his temples, still getting used to having not one but two voices in his mind. "*Yeah. I hear you both. Let's do it.*"

The dragons rose from where they rested, curled together in the clearing. They stalked toward the last egg.

"What's happening?" Violet asked.

"The hatchlings are about to give their sister a helping hand." Nox waved at the others. "Back up. They need some space."

"Will that work?" Ryon tilted his head as the blue dragon scratched at the last egg with a claw.

Nox nodded, infusing his voice with confidence. "It will. They'll take turns so they don't become too worn out." He toed at one of the deflated skins lying in the dirt. "We'll need more water to help them keep up their strength."

"That's gonna be a problem. We could barely see on our last trip." Violet lifted her face to the darkening sky. "It's bound to be even worse in there now."

"Won't be a problem for me." Nox scooped up an armful of skins.

"What are you talking about?" Ryon crossed his arms.

Violet nudged him with her elbow. "He can see in the dark. It's one of his boons."

"Boons?" he repeated, his brow furrowed.

Nox grabbed his pack and stuffed the skins inside. "When you bond with an animal, you share certain physical attributes. Great night vision is one I've been granted."

Ryon shrugged. "Works for me. Here." He detached the blade from his belt and handed it over. Nox took it and secured it to his belt.

Mariun kneeled beside Nox and snatched up a few skins, stuffing them inside another pack.

"What do you think you're doing?" Nox's voice cracked, echoing the clatter of dragon claws on the rocky shell.

"I'm coming with you." Mariun cinched the pack closed and slung it over her back.

"Don't be ridiculous. You can't see in there, can you? You'll only slow me down."

"Slower than making two trips?" She glared at him as she stood and planted her hands on her hips. "You can't carry all that water alone without overheating. Besides, what if something happens? We're safer staying in pairs."

"She has a point," Violet agreed.

"*Take her with you,*" Green chimed in.

"*Who?*" Flint asked.

"*The snappy girl looks like she wants to gather more water.*" Green turned her head away from the egg and met Nox's eyes. "*Distract her from trying to leave before we're through.*"

"*Good plan,*" Flint replied.

"*All right, all right. You don't have to gang up on me.*"

Nox cracked his back before tugging the sack onto his shoulders. "Fine. Stay close and do what I say." He held out a hand. "And don't let go. I don't want to be scraping you off the forest floor or hunting for you when you get lost."

Mariun grinned and clasped his hand. Nox set off, ignoring the tingle spreading up his wrist. She followed easily until they walked a few paces into the forest. A gasp escaped her lips before she clamped them shut.

"It's not too late to turn back." Nox inched forward, keeping his pace slower than he needed.

"Can you really see in here?" she whispered.

"Duck, now," he ordered.

She obeyed a little too slowly, and the top of her hair tangled in a dead branch. "What *is* that?" Her breathing sped up and her fingers shook. "What's in my hair?"

"Relax and hold still." He dropped her hand.

Mariun quivered. "Where did you go?" Panic flooded her voice.

"I'm right here. Let me untangle your hair from this branch."

"It's a branch?" She laughed nervously. "Why didn't you say so?"

"I just did," Nox bit out. "Did you want me to stitch you a tapestry?"

Mariun snorted. "No." Her laughter tapered off as he finished untangling her hair and grabbed her hand. She sighed, clenching his fingers tightly.

"Do you believe me now that I can see?" He gently tugged her forward.

She nodded. "I'll listen, I promise."

He knew what the others had said. She could benefit from the distraction. Even so, he couldn't help giving her another out. "I can handle gathering water on my own."

"I see that." Mariun took another mincing step in the dark. "But you shouldn't have to. Anyway, seems like you're the most important one out of all of us now."

What was that supposed to mean? "Duck."

Mariun obeyed immediately this time, shimmying low beneath a branch hanging heavy with inedible berries. "If something happens to you, we'll have no way to talk to the dragons."

Nox rolled his eyes. "So what? You came to protect me?"

"Is that so hard to believe?" Mariun rose and trailed carefully where he led her. "I have a few tricks up my sleeve in case we run into trouble."

That was certainly true. With her powers, she'd have no problem dropping another masked man if it came down to it. He'd always had Flint, and before that, his other bondmates, but as far as people went, he was used to being on his own. It felt strange having someone watching over him, protecting him. It sent a rush of tingles spreading through his chest.

"Almost there." He led her down a small hillside. "Careful, it's a little slippery—oof."

Mariun tumbled into his arms. He caught her easily despite her scrambling feet searching for purchase.

"Relax, I have you." Her cheek landed on his chest, and he tightened his arm around her back until she found her footing.

"Thanks," she whispered.

Her breathless reply made his blood pump faster. He flashed back to that kiss. With her pressed against him so intimately, it was all he could think about. Her soft lips moving against his own. Her tongue tangling feverishly with his. He could bend down and kiss her again so easily.

He loosened his hold on her instead. She was frightened. All alone with him, out in the dark. He wouldn't pounce on her again. It wasn't right of him to jump her like that the first time. He slipped his arm off her back, took a step backward, and tugged her gently forward.

Mariun's hand dropped off his chest. But only a heartbeat passed before she grabbed his neck and hauled him closer. "Wait," she whispered against his throat.

Nox closed his eyes, reveling in the wash of her warm breath on his skin. She pressed her curves against his chest, and his fingers itched, needing to touch her. He tilted his nose, breathing in the light floral scent clinging to her hair beneath the volcano's char. "What am I waiting for?"

Her fingers traced up his neck until her nails gently scraped through the stubble on his chin. Nox held himself immobile, letting her take the lead. Her other hand floated up his arm, leaving a tickling trail of sensation in its wake. She planted her palm firmly on his shoulder and lifted on her toes.

Mariun whispered against his lips, "For this." She placed a gentle kiss on the corner of his mouth.

The last time, it had all happened so fast. And he'd had half a mind on listening for the rustle of leaves and pounding footsteps approaching. This time was so much different.

Mariun's lips pressed sweetly against his. Her fingers trembled. If he didn't know better, he'd think this was her first kiss.

That thought hit him like a blow to the gut. His hands shot out, gripping her hips and dragging her closer. He deepened the kiss, swallowing her little breathy moan. Still, he held back, keeping his movements languid, while the thought of being the first man to kiss her had him feeling feral.

She kissed him back so eagerly. Her arms wound around his neck tightly, and she wedged even closer.

Nox's pulse pounded, blood rushing through every limb. He wanted so badly to take things further. Instead, he pulled back and rested his forehead against hers. "Mariun," he whispered, "they're waiting for us."

She nodded, breathing hard. He was certain if he could see color clearly enough in the pitch black, her cheeks would be flushed. But the smile that curved her lips he spotted all too well.

A stick snapped. Nox tensed. He grabbed Mariun's hand, squeezing hard at the same time he lowered his mouth to her ear. "Shh," he whispered, barely audible. "I heard something."

Nox closed his eyes and concentrated solely on his hearing. Rhythmic scratching flooded his ears, but he expected that. He tuned out the dragons' attempts to open the last egg and—

There it was again. A snap, coming from a different direction. His stomach lurched. It might be an animal. Some nocturnal hunter out on the prowl.

But then the unmistakable hum of voices—far too quiet for him to understand, but unmistakable nonetheless—whispered on the breeze.

Nox gulped and spoke again, keeping his voice so low only Mariun would hear. "People. Far away but coming closer. Get down."

Mariun dropped to her knees. The little hilltop she'd tumbled down would keep them hidden, he hoped. Nox sank beside her. He grabbed her ankle and pulled her lower, arranging her so she'd be invisible to anyone higher in the forest.

He bent to her ear once more. "I need to stop them. Stay here."

Mariun clutched his wrist tightly, her nails digging in. "No," she hissed. "You can't leave me. I can help."

His skin prickled. She'd barely made it here in one piece. Now someone was out there, hunting for them. "Not in the dark. Too dangerous. I'll lead them this way if I can't handle them on my own." He stroked the back of her hand. "I promise."

Her nails slowly detached from his skin. Nox stood, and with one last look at Mariun crouched and hidden, he climbed the hill.

He considered reaching out to Green for help, but the idea fled his mind as soon as it arrived. She had enough to worry about with the egg. If there were masked out here searching for them, then all the more reason for them to break their sibling free and escape.

He'd have to take care of the men on his own. He had Mariun to fall back on if it came to it.

Nox creeped through the forest, using every boon. His catlike balance and ability to navigate in the dark allowed him to move silently, his ears pricked for every little sound. The men out there were good, keeping their footsteps quiet and their whispers low. But they clearly weren't expecting to encounter someone with enhanced hearing.

Within moments, he spotted a dim glow ahead. That had to be them. He smiled to himself. Another advantage. With that light burning, they'd never see him coming.

He circled the light until he was close enough to see them clearly. Two masked carried a torch between them. He squinted, making out the animals on their masks. The first was clearly a bogbeast, the fearsome reptiles that lived so close to his home. The other made his breath catch. A dragon.

They headed on a meandering path through the brush, moving with familiarity. It was soon clear exactly where they were headed. For the volcano and the eggs. The frantic scratching pulled them forward like a beacon.

He scanned the brush ahead of their path, searching for the perfect spot to lie in wait. He channeled Flint as he settled behind a gigantic oak, the perfect ambush predator. His nerves came alive the closer they came. He waited, his heart pounding in his throat.

Just as Dragon walked by, he slashed out with the blade. Nox caught the back of his knee, sending him sprawling.

Dragon cried out a string of words Nox couldn't understand. No matter. Nox was already moving, slamming his foot into the bogbeast's gut before he could draw his sword.

Bogbeast fell back. The torch flew out of his grasp and skidded across the ground, but stayed lit.

Nox couldn't give them time to recover. He darted for the bogbeast and delivered a hard kick to his mask. Bogbeast's head slammed into the dirt, and he stopped moving.

That left Dragon. Nox turned, expecting to find him on the ground, cradling the deep gash in his leg.

"Duck!" yelled a voice from the woods.

Nox heeded Mariun's warning, dropping low. A blade whizzed over his head. Dragon hobbled backward, using the tree to support himself.

That was close! Nox lifted the hilt of his sword and whacked Dragon's temple. The blow landed just behind his mask with a resounding *crack*. He slumped sideways against the trunk and slowly slid into the dirt.

The men lay alive but unconscious at his feet. It would be easy to end them. To slit their throats or drive his blade through their hearts. But the thought made him queasy. These men were just acting on orders. Killing them while they were defenseless would be an act of evil he couldn't stomach.

He used his blade to sever a long length of vine. And another. By the time Mariun wandered over, drawn in by the torchlight, he'd gathered enough to tie them.

"Here." He handed half the vines to Mariun. "Hurry. We still need the water."

She kneeled beside the bogbeast and started tying his wrists. Nox worked on the dragon, swiftly looping the vine and knotting it firmly. "Thanks for the warning."

Mariun ducked her head. "I saw the torch and ran when I heard you fighting. It's lucky they walked past me."

He frowned at the forest as he went to work on the dragon's feet. He couldn't see the hilltop he'd left her hidden behind... "Hm. Sure you didn't come looking?"

She shrugged. "Maybe."

He should probably lecture her for not listening. She could've taken a tumble and broken a leg. Or drew the masked's attention to her. But he shrugged off the urge. She *did* just save him from a blade to the throat, after all.

He finished tying Dragon and rushed to Mariun's side. He held out a hand to help her up. She took it and rose, clenching his fingers tightly.

"I'm going to stomp out the torch, all right?" He kept his voice low. "There might be more of them out there."

"Can you hear them?" Mariun asked.

Nox shook his head. "Nothing for now. But I can only hear so far. We better hurry." His boot snuffed out the fire, washing them in darkness again. Mariun's grip tightened.

Green's voice made him jolt. "*Hey, what's taking so long?*"

Nox tugged Mariun forward, taking careful steps in the dark. "*Ran into a little trouble. We took care of it. Grabbing the water now.*"

"*What trouble?*" Flint asked. "*Are you all right?*"

"*Yes. Fine. Nothing to worry over. We tied two more masked up for a while.*" He grinned. "*How's the egg holding up?*"

"*Almost got it. Hurry back,*" Green said excitedly.

"*Working on it.*"

Flint and Green began to chatter back and forth. Nox rubbed his temple with his free hand. "*Listen, you two. I need to stay sharp out here. Can you save the discussion for later?*"

"*Fine,*" they grumbled in unison.

Nox sighed. He hadn't wanted another bondmate, but even with how crowded his mind felt, it warmed his heart all the same. Even as an infant, Green was a force of nature. A chatty, demanding little thing, smart as a whip and so damn happy to be alive. Her enthusiasm and glee bled into his mind, infusing him with a sense of wonder and a determination he couldn't remember ever feeling so strongly.

Maybe having a new bondmate wouldn't be so bad after all.

And Mariun. He hardly knew what to think about her. He kept flashing back to that awful story. The things she'd been made to do... the impossible choices she'd needed to make. The terrible people who'd wrapped themselves up in her life without ever showing her any love.

But the girl whom no one loved seemed to care about him. She'd put herself in danger for him. Kissed him.

He couldn't help feeling like he didn't deserve it. More than that, like he'd never be enough for her. She wielded so much power she could destroy them all if she wanted. Maybe he should fear her for that reason alone, but when he searched deep down to the very pits of his soul, he couldn't find a shred of alarm where she was concerned.

How had it changed so quickly? Just days ago, he *knew* he couldn't trust her. Had a single story and a few kisses really been enough to prove her point that she deserved a chance?

Nox brushed aside the thought as they arrived at the stream and bent to fill the waterskins. There would be time to examine his confusing feelings for Mariun later. He had dragons to save.

Unending Clamor

Ryon tugged his sweaty tunic away from his chest and threw another log on the fire. Violet had scolded him when he'd first left to gather sticks, not wanting to draw any attention to their impromptu campsite. Once the scratching began in earnest and the sun disappeared completely, she'd relented.

Black clouds blanketed the starless sky. Even the moon hid behind the mountain, providing them with no reprieve from the shadow the volcano threw across their little clearing. It would be the perfect place to get some shuteye, if not for the unending clamor of claws raking against stony shell.

It was a miracle the noise hadn't attracted any unwanted visitors already. His fingers tingled, clasping and unclasping around the spot on his belt where the blade had once hung.

"You all right?" Violet asked.

"Yeah. I just wish I didn't feel like a sitting gull out here."

Violet slipped her hand in his and squeezed, stopping his fingers from moving. "They needed it more than we did."

"Hm?" he replied absentmindedly, his gaze flicking across the forest.

"The blade. If anyone shows up here, we have a trio of dragons to defend us."

Ryon squeezed back and flashed a lopsided grin. "I suppose you're right."

Still, he couldn't stem the worry that weighed down his gut like a thousand rocky shell fragments. Who knew how much help the dragons would be in a fight? Would they even lift a claw to defend them without Nox here to protect? Would they have the strength after all the effort they'd expended attempting to break free their stubborn sibling?

He curved a hand through his sweaty dreads. Of course, he did have his small belt knife and his feathers to fall back on. If it came down to it, he could wish for claws like Nox. Or super strength. Maybe even perfect aim so he could send the sharp shell fragments sailing at his enemies' eyes like arrowheads.

The options were endless, after all. Still, he held off. They might run into more trouble in the future. He had to be strategic. Stingy, even. If he used all the feathers now, and a time came one day where it could be the difference between life and death, he'd feel like the ultimate fool.

Rustling in the forest made him grab his belt knife. His stomach dropped to his feet. He was a heartbeat away from ripping one of his locks to shreds when a voice called out quietly but clearly.

"We're back." Nox emerged, leading Mariun by the hand. They jogged to the fire, both of their sacks hanging heavy off their backs. Their hair was disheveled, and their boots and clothes covered in mud, but they were all in one piece.

"What took you so long?" Violet bent beside the sack her uncle had dropped into the dirt and dug out a waterskin. "Felt like you were gone forever."

Mariun kneeled beside Violet and lifted a waterskin in Ryon's direction. "Thanks." He snagged it, quickly gulping a few tepid mouthfuls that slid down his throat like the finest wine.

"There were masked out there, but we handled them." Nox grabbed Violet's skin before it slipped out of her shaky fingers.

Violet's voice trembled as much as her hands. "Masked? How many? Are there more coming?"

Nox sipped deeply before answering. "Just two. For now, at least. I doubt that will be the last of them, but they were the only ones we spotted. We left them knocked out and tied up a little ways away from the stream."

Mariun stood. "We need to leave."

"We will." Nox squared off in front of her. "As soon as we can. Green says they're almost finished."

Ryon tore his gaze off the darkened forest and glanced at the last egg. A hole decorated the side, but it was still far too small for a dragon to crawl out of. What's worse, it appeared there would be no crawling happening. While the other eggs had cracked from the force of the beast scratching from within, this one didn't. Whatever dragon lay inside still wasn't contributing to its release.

The realization made Ryon's stomach clench. Was something wrong with the little critter? Why wasn't she moving?

To make matters worse, the three scratching at the egg appeared to be flagging. When they'd started, they would take long moments between swapping. Each dragon had scratched a dozen times or more before resting. Now, they barely managed a handful of swipes.

"Help me give them some water?" Nox nodded at Ryon.

Ryon gulped, fighting to hide his own hands shaking. Was he brave enough to chance coming within arm's length of those massive teeth? How long would water sustain them when they were exerting so much energy?

Despite the questions swirling through his mind, he bent and grabbed Mariun's discarded sack. The dragons stilled as they approached, turning their shining eyes toward them.

Nox hefted his sack. "We'll split it between them this time. Two each. We'll save what's left for the rest of us."

Ryon peeked into his bag. Three waterskins stared back at him. The dragons opened their massive mouths in unison. Nox got to work immediately, dumping water down his bondmate's throat.

Ryon inched closer to the dragon nearest to him. The blue-scaled hatchling sat waiting, his big eyes tracking Ryon's movement as he dug out the first skin. Ryon held his breath as the water cascaded past countless jagged teeth. After he finished dumping the second, his racing heart slowed.

The dragon gulped loudly as he tucked the empty skin back into his pack. That just left the one to go. Ryon joined Nox in front of the white dragon. He poured the rest of his water into the hatchling's mouth and only flinched a little when the dragon snorted after gulping it down.

The dragons returned to their task. Scratching rang out. After the near silence that had fallen while they'd rested, the sound was so jarring he cringed.

Ryon circled back, fighting the exhaustion pouring over his body. With the storm last night, he'd barely slept. Not to mention a full day of trekking through the jungle. He was ready to collapse. But there was still so much to do.

As he shuffled back to the fire, all traces of weariness burned away. "Violet? Mariun?" Where were they?

"Over here," Violet answered.

Ryon exhaled in a great whoosh. The girls strode into the circle of firelight, their arms laden with sticks and dried leaves.

Nox raised a brow. "We're making enough noise to wake the dead already. Probably smart to keep the fire small."

"This isn't for the fire." Mariun dumped her burden on the ground and glanced at the trees. "We'll need torches if we want to reach the coast before dawn breaks. You can't hold all our hands."

Nox looked like he wanted to argue, but he clenched his jaw and nodded.

Ryon's feet ached from the thought of another long journey through that tangled forest. But they really had no other choice. They had to lead the dragons out of here. Now that not one but three masked were missing, it wouldn't be long before the others arrived in force. If they found them here, they'd be in trouble. Would they abduct them and force them to take part in those violent games? Or kill them on the spot and trap the dragons?

Ryon sank down beside Violet. "Can I help?"

"Sure." She shifted her legs and scooted the pile of wood closer to him. "Thanks."

Nox tilted his head, his gaze on the darkened trees. "Green will let me know when they're through. I'm going to keep watch."

Mariun rolled her eyes at his retreating back. "So much for sticking together."

"He's the best suited for watch." Violet shrugged.

"His boons didn't keep him out of Jurdan's dungeons last time," Mariun grumbled.

Ryon's stomach churned at the reminder. With the drugged darts the masked possessed, they could sneak up on them and knock them out. The thick tree cover would make the task easy.

"We had no idea anyone was stalking our boat last time." Violet snatched a stick off the ground so forcefully he was surprised it didn't snap. "They won't catch us unawares again."

Her words sounded like a promise. One he was determined to help her keep.

A deafening clamor made them all jerk. Ryon whipped his head toward the egg as Nox came racing back from the forest.

"The last egg." Nox motioned them up. "It's hatching."

Ryon hopped to his feet and hurried forward. After hiding all night, the moon burst through the cloud cover, illuminating the valley more fully than it had been since the sun set. It gave him a perfect view of the strange sight that greeted him.

Unlike the other three eggs, which merely had large holes in their sides, this one was shattered almost completely. His jaw dropped, confusion swirling through him as he spied the curious ball seated in the center of the remaining fragment.

A brown fleshy sack large enough to contain a hatchling pulsed and quivered before falling still.

"What is that?" Violet asked. "A birth sack? Shouldn't that have dissolved by now?"

They gazed at Nox expectantly, and he shrugged. "What, since I'm bonded to one of them, I'm an expert now? I honestly have no clue."

"Maybe that's why the little one didn't want to break out," Ryon mused.

"Could be." Mariun inched closer, then turned to Nox. "What are you waiting for? Slice her loose."

Nox tugged the blade off his belt, only to freeze a heartbeat later. "Green says to leave her in there."

"What do you mean? We can't stay here waiting any longer." Mariun's voice trembled. "Jurdan can't capture us. Please."

Nox slid the blade back on his belt and squeezed Mariun's shoulder. "Don't worry. The hatchlings have a plan." He flicked a glance at each of them. "Let's light those torches. Grab everything we're bringing. Let's get out of here."

Ryon paced back to the fire but couldn't resist asking, "What are they planning to do?"

"You'll see," Nox replied with a crooked grin.

Within moments, they'd gathered their things and lit the torches. Nox kicked dirt over the fire, dousing it.

The hatchlings hovered around their sack-wrapped sister, their heads bent together like they were deep in discussion, though not one made a sound. Then they circled the sack, taking spots on three sides. They wedged their wings beneath it and lifted their sister into the air.

Ryon gulped down a gasp when the sack slammed into the ground. His eyes widened. He expected the ball to rip open and the hatchling to spill out. But the fleshy bag remained intact, only rolling forward a bit before stopping a short distance closer to the forest.

"Will they carry her all the way to the coast?" Mariun asked.

"Carry. Roll. A bit of both, I think," Nox answered. "Green says those sacks are nearly as hard to break through as the shell, but much lighter."

"If it works, it works." Violet grinned, lifting her torch high and setting off for the trees.

Ryon hurried after her. "Hey, better let me go first."

Violet slowed and cocked a brow. "Why? Are you that desperate to protect me?" She chuckled sweetly.

"No. I just remembered how turned around you got back in Thalassia."

"Oh." She patted his arm. "Hm. Why don't you take the lead?"

Ryon grinned and ducked into the forest. Blackness soaked the trees. Little moonlight reached the forest floor. If not for the torches, they'd barely be able to see their own hands held in front of their faces.

He pivoted, heading directly for the cliffside where they'd left their boat anchored. They must have made a strange sight. Four weary travelers doing their best to hide their torches while a trio of dragon hatchlings followed in their wake, half rolling, half carrying the oddest ball he'd ever seen and making an awful racket. Luckily, no one burst out to stop them immediately.

Hopefully the masked would wait until morning to send more men after them. They certainly wouldn't have trouble locating them now. But if they wanted to bring all the dragons, they had little choice but to deal with the noise.

The trek took less than half the time it had earlier, now that they weren't searching all over. Still, his ankles and feet felt swollen when crashing waves finally joined the cacophony of smashing and rolling behind them.

Then, like a miracle, they arrived at the cliffside. He creeped over to the edge, his heart racing wildly as he scanned the dark waves.

"There." Nox pointed down the beach. "I can see the boat's sails. We aren't too far off."

Ryon breathed out a sigh. He'd feared for a moment they'd gotten lost and would need to spend half the night searching for their ship.

The moon hung high in the sky as they worked their way south, following the cliff's edge until they reached the spot where they'd climbed. The guide rope was still in place, the top wrapped around the boulder. Ryon dropped his torch and stomped it out. Where they were going, he wouldn't need it.

"Do we climb back down?" Mariun asked.

"How will the dragons handle that steep cliffside?" Violet crossed her arms. "And what about the last dragon?"

Nox leaned over the edge. "We won't need to climb. The water's risen. If the tide's in, then we can jump in and swim easily enough."

"How can you tell?" Ryon squinted over the cliffside, but even with the cloud cover thinned enough for the moonlight to wash over the dark waves, he couldn't be sure of the water's depths below. His stomach twisted. Those jagged rocks he'd spotted earlier littered the seafloor... If Nox was wrong, they'd be impaled.

"I can see in the dark, remember?" Nox clapped him on the shoulder. "The water is nearly at the spot where you tied the first guideline."

If that was true... "All right. Let's jump."

Violet squeaked, "You can't be serious."

Nox stood, brushing off his knees. "I am. Green and the hatchlings even volunteered to go first."

Mariun shrugged. "If they can make it, then surely we can." She frowned. "Can dragons swim?"

"Like fish, apparently." Nox chuckled.

Violet wrinkled her nose. "All right. I guess if you're all fine with jumping, then I am, too." She grabbed Nox's forearm. "Wait? What about her?"

They all stared at the unhatched dragon. The fleshy covering was battered and scraped in dozens of places, but there was still no sign of the baby forcing its way out.

"Green says they'll keep her afloat." Nox darted a glance at the forest. "I don't think we have much choice. In fact, we better hurry."

"Do you hear something?" Mariun tugged her hair over one shoulder, smoothing it restlessly.

Nox closed his eyes. "Noise coming closer. Still too far away to be sure, but we might have some company soon."

Ryon's pulse pounded. If the masked were on their way, then they definitely didn't have the time to climb.

The hatchlings wasted no time. Together they rolled their sister to the cliffside's edge. Then, with one on each side and another behind, they lifted her between them and leaped as one.

Splash!

The hatchlings kicked up a gargantuan spray as they hit the surf. Ryon raced to the cliff's edge and peered down. His heart beat in time with the angrily smashing waves. Where were they?

There! The dragons resurfaced, the dark blob of their sister balanced between them.

"Who's next?" Nox inched away from the edge, and his skin paled.

Ryon offered his hand to Violet. "Jump with me?" He turned to Mariun and cocked his head toward Nox. "Maybe you two should pair up as well. In case you're afraid."

Mariun shook her head but walked over to Nox. "We'll be right behind you."

Violet sucked in a deep breath. Her small fingers slid into Ryon's hand, and she squeezed. They stopped at the cliff's edge.

"We jump, then swim for the dinghy." He squinted directly below. "Looks like it's still attached to the end of the rope. We'll meet there if we're separated, all right?"

Violet nodded. "I'm ready."

"On the count of three?"

She nodded again and clutched his hand tightly.

"One, two, three."

Salty air rushed past him before he smacked into the warm water. Dread slammed into him at the same moment the water soaked him. Even after watching the dragons, he kept envisioning those black rocks waiting to impale him. But after sinking fast, he began to slow without hitting the bottom.

Ryon tugged on Violet's hand hard and swam for the surface. His lungs burned. He could suck in a mouthful of water and relieve the ache, but he ignored it instead. No sense wasting time spewing up a lungful of water when he resurfaced.

It seemed Violet had the same idea. She gasped and sputtered as soon as they bobbed to the top.

"You all right?" Ryon helped Violet flick her long hair off her face.

Her eyes glowed in the moonlight. "I'm good. Let's find the dinghy."

They swam together, covering the short distance quickly. Tied next to the cliffs all day, the dinghy had taken a battering, but it still floated. Ryon helped Violet climb inside, gripping her thighs and lifting her. She went for the oars as he clambered in after her.

He sprawled on the wet dinghy floor, breathing hard. "That was fun."

"Can you untie us?" Violet settled on the front bench and lifted the oars. "We won't get very far otherwise. I'll row out far enough to scoop up Nox and Mariun once they jump."

Ryon smiled sheepishly and crawled to the rope. He shook his head. Nox and his intricate knots. It would take him forever to untie this, unless... He grabbed his belt knife and cut just above the knot. "Got it."

They sliced quickly through the water. Ryon stared back at the coast. Once they'd pulled far enough away, he spotted two figures frozen on the clifftop.

"What's taking them so long?" He hoped Nox's fear of heights wasn't paralyzing him.

"Um, I think we have another problem," Violet announced.

Ryon whipped around. She wasn't staring at the cliff. Her gaze was locked on the water ahead of them. He frowned, seeing nothing.

All three dragons bobbed to the surface, and he gasped. "How many times have they slipped under?" The hatchlings were struggling to keep their sister afloat. They still had a long swim before they reached the boat. But maybe that was a one-off, and they just needed to adjust their grips?

Violet's face was grim when she replied, "That's three times now."

Before she finished speaking, the hatchlings' burden slipped again. "Guano."

There had to be some way to help them. The dinghy was far too small, and he and Violet wouldn't be much help to hold the heavy dragon. Or maybe not...

Ryon fingered a dread and lifted his knife just as a shout from the cliff sliced through the night. He spun to the sound and spotted Nox and Mariun careening down to the sea. Nox's body was stiff and straight as an arrow, but Mariun's limbs flopped wildly... Why would she—

His stomach dropped faster than they did. When a crowd of masked appeared on the clifftop and sent a rain of darts into the sea after them, the fear only spread.

Nox popped up on the waves and screamed, "Mariun!"

Oh no. Ryon's mind whirred, making connections at a sickening speed. If Mariun was shot before she fell, then she must still be sinking. Nox wouldn't be able to hold his breath long enough to reach her. Ryon could swim for her instead of the dragons, but he'd never find her in the dark. Nox, on the other hand...

Ryon cut off a dread and tossed it on Violet's lap before the echo of Nox's shout faded. Then he gritted his teeth and tore the blade across his palm, opening a deep gash. He tossed the knife at Violet's feet.

She gaped at him. "What are you—"

"Go back. Tell Nox to make the same wish we did. He's the only one who can see well enough to save her." He clasped his bloodied hand around one of his dreads, knowing the blood would take a moment to sink in. "I'll meet you on the ship. Stay safe, Violet."

As warmth spread up his hand, Ryon closed his eyes and made a wish. Then he turned and leaped into the ocean.

A Dragon's Boon

Nox stood atop the cliff, his palms sweating and his heart thumping out of control. Why did it have to be heights? He could handle pretty much anything, but knowing he had to leap from this rotting cliff made him want to curl up in a ball and hide.

"*You can do this,*" Flint urged. "*Just one little jump and you'll be safe in the water.*"

Nox drew in a deep breath, fighting to keep his hands steady. "*There's nothing little about that jump.*"

"*I did it. You can do it, too,*" Green chimed in. "*Come on. The water feels great!*"

Nox nearly laughed in the face of her unbridled enthusiasm. But then he peeked down again, and the world spun. He backed away, gulping hard.

"They climbed into the dinghy," Mariun announced. "Looks like they're rowing out so we don't smash into them." She turned from squinting at the water and glanced at him. "Are you all right?"

Nox shook his head. "I-I just need a moment."

Mariun marched over to him and grabbed his hand. "Come on. We'll go together."

Nox let her lead him to the cliff's edge, but his feet dragged like his boots were weighed down with stones. He knew the others had done it. Even the massive dragons had made the jump without injury. But fear gripped his heart and squeezed like a serpent. It was all he could think about. All he could see and hear, playing over and over in his mind until the leap into the dark water morphed into an endless, dizzying fall into a black pit.

"Do you trust me?" Mariun asked quietly.

"What?"

"Close your eyes." She squeezed his hand.

Nox frowned but lowered his lashes. Not being able to see the drop calmed him somewhat. But he still knew it was there. As soon as he opened his eyes again, the fear would rush right back in to freeze him.

"Keep your eyes closed. When I tell you to jump, jump. All right?" Mariun spoke soothingly and stroked the back of his wrist gently.

Maybe it would work... He could let her be his eyes. Take a blind leap and hope that nothing went wrong. Nox nodded and clenched her hand tightly.

"I'll be with you the whole way. Ready?"

Was he? No. But he couldn't stand there forever. Nox sucked in a final breath. "Ready."

"Jump," she yelled.

Something whizzed by his head as Nox leaped off the cliff. He dropped like a stone and slammed into the water. His eyes popped open. Panic tore through him as he continued to drop, sinking into the sea's black depths. It was like the pit from his worst fears was real, sucking him down, down—so far and so fast he'd never escape.

Nox swam like mad, slicing through the water and pushing to the surface. He burst into the night air, and with the first breath he drew, the all-consuming fear faded. Slicking his hair off his face, he treaded water while he fought to catch his bearings.

His hand. He stared at it. Mariun was supposed to be holding his hand. "Mariun!"

Where was she? He spun in place, praying he'd see her black hair bobbing to the surface. But all he spotted was the dinghy ahead and the cliff behind him.

What happened? Recalled sounds filled his ears. The crunch of grass. Whispered voices. Signs that made their mark on his mind but he'd ignored in the face of his own fear. Comprehension crushed him like a boulder.

That whizz by his head wasn't just some insect.

Rot and decay!

He dove under the water, scanning the seafloor. Darkness blanketed the ocean. Not just the water, but the rocks and the sand. How would he spot her, with her black hair and black clothes? He swam in a tight circle, gaze darting everywhere. Nothing. His lungs screamed for air, and he popped to the surface.

He nearly cracked his head on the dinghy.

"Nox!" Violet leaned over the edge. "Take this." She thrust out her hand. "Wish to breathe water as well as air."

Nox grabbed on instinct, his fingers working quicker than his mind. He stared at the small blade and thick lock of hair resting in his palm. The bloodfeathers!

Pain cut through the panic consuming him as he sliced his palm. He clenched the dread tightly in his fist and wished. *I wish to breathe water as well as air.* He tossed the blade back into the boat and spun around. Warmth spread up his arm as he dove again.

He sank lower this time, blowing out the air trapped in his lungs. If that wish worked as well as the last, then he wouldn't need to stick close to the surface. He swam on, scanning everywhere, and when the urge to breathe became too strong to ignore, he sucked in a lungful of water.

His chest burned. Rot and decay! It wasn't working. He'd made a terrible mistake.

But as fast as the burn came, it faded away. Water rushed in and out of his lungs, and the need for air disappeared with it.

That was when he spotted something. A bit of creamy white mixed in with all the darkness. He sank lower, darting through the water with the power and strength he'd been given as his very first boon.

Within a heartbeat, he was at her side. Mariun was slumped on the seafloor, her body curled around some dark rocks, one slim arm floating above all the rest, waving slightly with the current.

Thank the Mother! He grabbed her wrist and tugged. She didn't budge. He tugged harder. She jerked up, dislodging from the rocks. Strips of her dress tore off, but she was in his arms.

Nox swam for the surface, clenching her tight to his chest. Every stroke and kick compounded the fear strangling his heart. If she died because he had hesitated… Because his stupid fear had paralyzed him, he'd never forgive himself. The water rushed past, and he burst into the air.

He spun around in place. Where was the dinghy?

A gout of water spewed out of his lungs, and he nearly dropped Mariun. He clenched her tighter, turning his head aside as he floated on the surface, coughing and hacking like mad.

"Give her here," Violet called out.

Nox spun sideways, spotting the dinghy floating just behind him. He lurched toward it and thrust Mariun up the best he could while salty water continued to spill out of his lungs. Violet grabbed Mariun's shoulders and leaned back, fighting to lift her out of the water. Nox shoved from below, and together they maneuvered her onto the wooden boat bottom.

By the time she was in, he'd stopped coughing. Violet grabbed Mariun and beat on her back, tipping her sideways. Time seemed to slow as he treaded water, waiting for that same gout of water to spill out of Mariun's lungs.

If he'd found her too late...

Mariun jolted and coughed. As water poured out of her mouth and painted the boat bottom, the vise around his heart finally loosened.

Nox considered hopping in with the girls, but shrugged off the urge. He grabbed the rope they'd used to tether the dinghy and swam for the boat instead. With his boon aiding his strokes, it wasn't long before he reached the hull. He circled the boat, hunting for the rope ladder.

There. He climbed the ladder, a smile on his lips. He'd done it. They were back at the boat, safe and alive. But when he turned to help the girls up, the smile died.

"What's wrong?" His voice cracked, his throat aching from the saltwater retching he'd done. But that pain and the sting in his palm were the last thing on his mind.

Violet crouched beside Mariun. Her fingers wrapped around one of Mariun's legs so tightly her knuckles were white. Mariun's chest slowly rose and fell, but she was so rotting pale. Too pale. His gaze darted to the boat bottom, and he bit back a gasp. The thin layer of water on the floor stared up at him, far too dark to be only water.

"She's bleeding. Bad." Violet's eyes swam with panic. "Help me lift her."

Nox reached for Mariun in a daze. With Violet helping from below, he pulled her into the boat and set her gently on the deck. Violet joined them a moment later and dropped beside Mariun, applying pressure to her leg again.

"How bad is it?" Nox stood and paced, wringing his hands. "We can stitch her up, can't we? There's plenty of fishing line—"

Violet shook her head gravely. "I-I don't know. There's so much blood. I've never seen so much blood."

"*What's wrong?*" Flint asked. "*Green. Nox. You're too quiet.*"

"*Almost there,*" Green replied, her voice barely a whisper.

Nox jerked into motion, rushing to the side rail. How had he missed the dragons? How had they passed them? They should have made it to the boat first. And why did Green sound so damn exhausted?

He reached the side just as something slammed into the hull hard enough to rock the boat. Leaning over, he spotted them. The hatchlings floated in the water, ringed around their unhatched sister.

They all looked so spent. How would he help them up? With Mariun bleeding out, he couldn't spare the time even if he had the strength.

"*Get out of the way,*" Green yelled in his mind, her voice dripping with urgency.

Nox lurched aside just as the unhatched dragon flew out of the sea and landed on the deck. His jaw dropped. It rolled once, then settled.

"*How in the world?*" Nox inched forward, determined to help the others any way he could. Before he could take more than a step, the next dragon appeared. Then the next. Each weary hatchling bounced out of the water as if some force was propelling them from below.

"*Your friend helped us,*" Green explained as she landed and spotted the perplexed look on Nox's face.

Ryon. Nox hadn't even thought to look for him. He'd been so consumed with saving Mariun.

Sure enough, his dreadlocked head popped out of the water a heartbeat later. Nox scrambled into motion and grabbed his hand. Pain was his reward.

"Ryon, you're crushing me!" he screeched. Ryon dropped his hand like it were a hot coal, and Nox cradled it against his chest.

"Sorry. Guano, I'm sorry. I didn't mean—"

"Forget it." Nox jumped to his feet and hurried back to the girls. A small pool of blood shone beneath Mariun, sparkling in the moonlight. In the back of his mind, he could hear Green filling Flint in on what was happening, but he ignored it as best he could.

"Is she all right?" He winced as the words spilled out of his mouth. He could see she wasn't. "What can I do?"

"I'm not a healer." Violet's lower lip wobbled. "If only Lark were here." Violet lifted her palm and peeked underneath at Mariun's leg. Her face paled, and she shook her head before slamming her hand back down.

Mariun groaned and her eyes fluttered open. "I-I don't feel so good." Her voice was hoarse and thready. Her eyelids drooped like she could barely stand to keep them open.

Nox brightened. Violet wasn't a healer, but Mariun knew a thing or two. If he could keep her awake long enough with that rotting dart's sleeping tonic still poisoning her, then maybe she could help.

"Mariun." He sank beside them and worked his fingers under her shoulders, then lifted her carefully into a seated position. "You've been cut. By the stones on the seafloor, I'm guessing. I need you to take a look and tell us what to do."

Nox nodded to Violet, and she removed her hand. Blood gushed out of a deep gash in Mariun's leg, spilling onto the boat bottom.

Mariun glanced at the wound and lifted her trembling fingers to his cheek. "Nothing. Do nothing."

"No." Nox's brow furrowed. "No!"

Violet shook her head and pressed on the cut.

Mariun hissed. "You're only de-delaying the inevitable. T-that cut is far too deep and bleeding much t-too fast."

"No." Nox's eyes slammed closed. There had to be something they could do. The feathers! Nox's eyes jerked open. "Ryon, give her a feather," he shouted.

Ryon grabbed for his belt. "My blade? Where is it?"

"In the dinghy." Violet pointed frantically toward the rope ladder where they'd left the dinghy tethered. "Hurry."

Ryon bolted for the side rail.

Mariun squeezed Nox's cheek, drawing his attention. Rot and decay. She was so pale. His stomach clenched.

"It's all right," she whispered. Her lips curved into a tiny smile. "T-thank you."

"What? No."

"Shh, listen." Her voice firmed, some of the wispiness fading. "Thank you for taking me with you. F-for trusting me. All those years I was trapped down there, i-it's all I wanted." Her gaze flitted away from his, her gray eyes pointing toward the stars. "I-I never imagined it would be so beautiful." Mariun's smile widened, and then her lashes lowered and her hand dropped.

Ryon's boots pounded behind Nox, then halted. "She has to be awake to make a wish."

Nox shook her shoulders. "Mariun. Wake up. Rotting wake up!"

It was no use. Her head lolled on her shoulders, and she didn't so much as whimper.

It couldn't be the end. He refused to accept it. They had to save her. If he could just think of something... His hand shot out to Ryon. "Give me a feather. I'll wish for her to be healed instead."

Ryon backed away. "It doesn't work like that. You can't change someone else. Only yourself."

"Wait." Violet gasped. "I-I can try to summon." She pursed her lips. "Earth magic used to heal wounds like this. I just need to remember... Green! I need something fresh and green."

Nox scanned the boat. They'd just been on an island swimming in greenery, but now—wait. He gently set Mariun down and tore the pack off his back. The contents were waterlogged, but maybe... "Here!" He lifted a few scraggly ploomfruit leaves out of his pack.

Violet slid them under the wound and closed her eyes.

Nox waited, his patience wearing thin the longer they sat there with nothing happening. He'd been healed with magic once. He could recall so clearly the tremor that shook him to his very core and rocked the earth beneath him. But the boat was unchanged, only swaying gently with the surf.

Violet was obviously having trouble summoning. If only Lark were here to guide her. Or even—

"Kayda," he blurted on a gasp.

Violet's eyes popped open. "Hm?"

"Kayda told me once what boons dragons bring." Nox's gaze flashed to Green hovering with her siblings beside the unhatched egg. "She said she could access Dru's elemental power." His gaze shot back to Violet. "Move."

Violet frowned. "Wait. She told me that story, too. Didn't that happen at the battle in the Abandoned Lands? The same battle where she *died*? If you try this, you could die, Uncle Nox."

"I don't care." He kneeled beside her and stuck out his hands expectantly. "I said move."

Violet's shoulders trembled. "We *need* you. I-I'll keep trying."

"There's no time." Nox gritted his teeth. "This is my fault. If I hadn't frozen..." He shook his head gravely. "I need to try this. Please, Violet. Move your hands."

Violet relented, releasing her grip on Mariun's leg. Nox took her place, wedging the green leaves tightly against the jagged cut. Sticky, warm blood coated his fingers.

"*Green, I need you to summon.*" He looked up from the wound and met her eyes.

The little hatchling paced away from her siblings, walking toward him. "*Summon?*"

Nox bit back a scowl. "*Dragons can make magic. Your parents could do it. You can do it too. Open your mouth and spit it out.*"

Green cocked her head and seemed to consider his words. Then she cracked open her jaw and sucked in a deep breath through her nose. A tiny rumble rocked the boat as a stream of earth shot out of her mouth. Little specks of dirt rained over the deck, but the bulk of the blast flew over the side and splashed into the sea.

Green jolted, her jaws snapping closed. "*Ha! I did it!*"

"*Good.*" Nox glanced at Mariun's face. His heart pounded. "*Do it again, Green. Don't stop.*"

"*What are you doing?*" Flint asked.

"*Saving her.*" Nox bit his lip, fighting to concentrate as another gout of earth spewed out of Green's mouth and the boat shuddered. "*I'm using Green's boon. If I can just figure out how...*"

Boons were not all made the same. Some worked naturally, boosting skills he already possessed, like agility or hearing. But others he'd needed to learn, like Flint's blocking technique. Nox had a sneaking suspicion this wasn't one that would come easily.

He took a deep breath and closed his eyes. Flint and Green kept silent, instinctively knowing he needed the quiet. Maybe this would be like Flint's trick...

Nox visualized Mariun's wound in his mind's eye. He pictured it healing, the torn skin weaving back together and reforming. He set that image in his mind, and then he dug inside his heart. *Please work. Please let her be all right.*

His hands pressed into the wound, but no tremor came. No magic shook through his body. Just the gentle rocking from Green's blasts of earth. There had to be more... something he was missing.

Nox dug deep down to the very depths of his soul, where the love he felt for Flint and Green wrapped around him like a soothing balm. He grabbed hold of that feeling, tugging it into his mind. He drew on it while he pictured Mariun again.

His fingers trembled, and warmth pooled in his hands. Yes. Nox could sense it now. The magic swirled within him, sucked up through his bond and pouring through his skin like his body was one big sieve. He gave into the sensation. Let the magic roll through him and into Mariun. *Please, please let her live.*

The boat quaked. Violet gasped. And Nox crumpled to the deck.

Dying for Ages

"Nox!" Violet jerked into motion despite the terrible way the boat heaved. She fell to her knees beside her uncle, her heart in her throat.

Please be all right. If he died, she didn't know what she would do.

The stream of earth pouring out of the green dragon cut off abruptly, and the boat's awful lurching stopped. Green padded over to Nox's side and nudged his motionless body with her head.

Nox groaned and his eyes cracked open.

Violet rocked back on her heels, clutching her chest. "Blazes. You scared me!"

"I'm fine," Nox grumbled, shoving Green's head away and rubbing his temples. Then he jolted up. "Mariun!" He scrambled to his knees and heaved out a deep sigh. "It worked!" He laughed uproariously. "Her leg. It's good as new!"

Violet leaned over and took a peek. He was right. The deep gash was completely gone, replaced with smooth flesh without even the smallest scar. "You did it." She turned to her uncle as his laughter cut off and he wobbled sideways.

"Hey." Ryon caught him before he tumbled to the deck again. "You better get some rest."

Nox blinked repeatedly before shaking his head. "Can't. We need to sail away. Now."

Violet frowned, standing up beside him. "Ryon's right. Whatever you did healed Mariun, but it's clearly exhausted you. I can handle the sailing, with Ryon's help."

Nox stuttered, "I-I...Y-you."

"Don't argue," Violet demanded. Time to try another angle. "Besides, Mariun needs you to watch over her again. She's lost a lot of blood. She'll need to rest as well. Let the effects of those darts wear off."

"Fine," Nox grumbled.

Violet bent beside Nox and helped him stand. "Can you carry Mariun below and set her in a hammock?" she asked Ryon.

Ryon glanced at his hands, seeming hesitant, but he nodded finally. Then he leaned over and lifted Mariun in his arms so easily it was like he'd lifted an infant and not a fully grown woman. Violet cocked a brow but forced her questions aside. She was too busy fighting to help her unsteady uncle wobble his way into the cabin.

They made it there first, and Nox flopped into a hammock. She helped him fling his legs up into the swaying ropes and bent to untie his boots.

Nox spotted Ryon gently laying Mariun in the hammock beside his. "No," he whispered, holding out his arms. "Bring her here."

Ryon shot Violet a dubious glance. She shrugged.

"Please," Nox added. "I can't watch her from over here."

Ryon sighed and placed Mariun beside Nox. The hammock sank with the added weight. Nox wrapped an arm gently around her waist and closed his eyes.

Violet finished tugging off her uncle's boots and got to work on Mariun's.

"Are you sure we should leave them together like that?" Ryon hissed in her ear.

Violet wrinkled her nose. "It's how I found them the other morning. She didn't seem to mind it."

Violet pulled off Mariun's boot. Both of their gazes shot to Mariun's face as she stirred, humming gently in her sleep. She rolled, rubbing her face against Nox's chest and curling her arms around him, all without opening her eyes.

Ryon raked a hand through his hair. "I just—what if he hurts her again?"

"He won't." Violet jerked off Mariun's second boot and placed it on the floor. She turned for the door. "That was all a show, remember? He wanted you to hurt him."

Ryon followed her out. "I know. I just can't stand watching a woman being hurt." He sighed. "My ma used to stay with a man who hit her. Back when I was a lad, too small to do anything about it."

Violet's heart pounded. "Oh, Ryon. I'm so sorry." No wonder he was so adamant about protecting Mariun from Nox back in that clearing. "Do you want to talk about it?"

Ryon marched to the helm. "It's a long story, and we need to get going."

Violet swallowed her sympathy. "You're right. But once we're moving, I'm here to talk, if you want to."

Violet took the lead, calling out orders. Ryon helped without complaint, even though she sensed he was just as weary as she was.

By the time the island grew small behind them, dawn broke on the horizon. They'd spotted no sign of boats following them out to sea, but Violet's stomach fluttered anxiously. The dragons' added weight made their boat sink much further in the water than it had on their trip there.

Ryon stopped beside her, shading his eyes from the dawn sun. "I can't believe we actually did it. That was one wild journey, wasn't it?"

"Yeah, it sure was." Violet sighed. "But it's not over yet. What are we going to do now? I'm heading west for Dracwood, but it's so far away. I don't know if we'll make it there if any of those masked men give chase. Or if we'll have what we need to travel through the Still Sea with the few supplies onboard."

Ryon squinted behind them at the island. "Looks like we're alone so far. Maybe we'll get lucky."

Violet shrugged, but she couldn't help worrying that their luck wouldn't hold out for that long.

"I don't know about you, but I'm starving." Ryon wiggled his brows. "How about I catch us some breakfast?"

"You don't mind?"

Ryon shook his head. "I'll hop in the dinghy with the net. Think you can swing us close to some fish?"

"Sure." Violet scanned the sea, searching for a dark patch of water nearby. Nox had taught her that those patches often signaled where a school of fish swam close to the surface.

There. She turned the boat, angling it so that the fish would swim right past where the dinghy was tethered.

"Got it!" Ryon yelled.

Violet corrected their course and paced away from the helm. She arrived at the rope ladder just as Ryon appeared, a huge grin on his face and a net absolutely bursting with squirming fish the size of her thigh. There had to be more than a dozen, probably close to twenty.

He dumped them on the deck with a *thump*. The dragons perked up. The hatchlings had been sleeping next to their unhatched sister. Now they wandered over, sniffing and alert, staring at the fish hungrily.

Ryon backed away from the net, chuckling. "I figured I better grab some extra for them."

The white dragon snatched a fish first, biting down on the poor creature with a wet crunch. The other hatchlings dove in, tearing through the pile of fish.

A single fish flopped over to Violet's feet. She bent and lifted it, groaning at the weight. Her belly clenched. It was a struggle for her to lift one. "How did you carry all these fish, Ryon? They're so heavy." She grunted, nearly slipping as she fought to hold the squirming creature.

"Here." Ryon took the fish, lifting it in one hand easily. Then he grabbed its head with his other hand and squeezed. A deafening crack rang out, and the fish fell still.

Violet backed away, cocking a brow.

"Before I jumped into the water to help the dragons, I wished for increased strength." He flashed a halfhearted smile. "I can't seem to turn it off. I don't think I'll be much help handling anything with a delicate touch from now on." His smile fell.

Violet's pulse pounded. Is that why he'd looked so reluctant to lift Mariun? But he'd done that without hurting her, hadn't he? She placed a hand on his shoulder.

"That's incredible, Ryon." She smiled at him. "You'll get used to it. I know you will."

He set the dead fish on top of a barrel and stared at his hands. "It's so strange, all these consequences piling up. I've always rolled with them before, but this one feels different."

"Why is that?" she asked.

"This strength could so easily be a curse." His hands trembled. "When Nox helped me on the boat, I crushed his hand." He lifted his tired eyes to hers. "What if I hurt someone else?"

Violet grabbed his hands. He started to tug them away, but she gripped them tightly.

"Violet, please. I don't want to hurt you."

"You won't." She searched his wild eyes before stepping closer and wrapping his arms around her waist. "I know you won't."

"What are you doing?" Ryon's voice shook as badly as his hands.

"Proving it to you." She laid her head on his chest and wrapped her arms around his torso, hugging him tightly. "See? I'm holding you tighter than you're holding me." She peeked at him, and her breath caught. He stared at her and licked his lips.

She tried to pull away. "I-I didn't—"

Ryon's arms tightened around her waist, making her gasp. His face fell, and he instantly released her. "Did I hurt you? I knew I—"

Violet grabbed his forearms, tugging him back. "No, you didn't hurt me. I just..." She settled his arms back around her, frowning. "I wasn't trying to..." She gulped. "The consequences," she blurted.

"What?" His arms relaxed around her, but his eyes flitted across her face, brows drawn.

"You're only drawn to me because of the bloodfeather's consequences. I wasn't trying to make it worse." She stared at his chest, unable to meet his eyes. "I just knew you wouldn't hurt me. That's all."

Ryon slid a finger under her chin and tipped her face up. Then, with an achingly soft touch, he trailed a finger over her cheek. "You didn't."

"Huh?" What were they talking about again? With him staring at her and caressing her so sweetly, she was having trouble following.

"You didn't make it worse. I've been dying to kiss you again for ages."

Violet gulped. Her gaze moved to Ryon's lips. He tugged her closer, bent down, and kissed her softly. She closed her eyes, reveling in the sensation. Maybe it was wrong of her to let him kiss her when it was only magic that made him want to, but with his strong arms wrapped around her, she couldn't bear to push him away. It felt too perfect. Too blazing good.

Was it so bad to want to feel good for a change? All the exhaustion in her limbs faded away. All the aches and pains from dragging herself up a cliffside and trekking for endless hours disappeared. It was just the two of them, kissing on a boat in the middle of the sea.

Violet slid her hands behind Ryon's long locks. But with him bent to reach her, she couldn't get as close as she'd like. He slipped his hands down her back, and then with one swift tug, he lifted her into his arms. Her eyes popped open to find him shoving the fish to the back of the barrel so she could perch on the edge.

"Is this all right?" he asked, staring at her eye to eye.

She nodded and spread her legs, tugging him close. His lips landed on hers again, and she wrapped him tightly in an embrace. Mm, that was better. She smiled against his lips before he deepened the kiss. Her toes curled inside her boots.

A jerking motion against her back made her gasp. They both glared at the blue hatchling as it backed away, their fish clenched in his jaws.

"Hey." Ryon turned, aghast. "I saved that one for us, you greedy little—"

Violet slapped his chest, her eyes popping wide. "Blazes, Ryon. Look!"

He curved a hand through his dreads. "What?" He trailed his gaze over the deck and across each dragon. "Wow, I can't believe they demolished all those fish already."

"Not the fish." Violet hopped off the barrel and hurried to the nearest dragon. "The hatchlings. They're bigger." What had seemed too strange to be believed was perfectly clear once she stood beside the happily chewing blue hatchling. "He used to be a head taller than me. Look at him now."

She gulped as the dragon swallowed and lifted his head. It dangled a good deal higher over her own now. At least two heads over, perhaps even three.

"Guano. You think eating made them grow?" Ryon frowned.

"I don't know. But if they grow this much after every meal, then there's no way we're making it through the Still Sea on this boat." She walked to the side rail and peered over. The boat sat low on the waves, with the salt spray threatening to splash the deck already.

Ryon joined her at the railing. "I think you're right." He stared into the water flatly, and then his expression brightened. "We can go to my island. The dragons too. We can hide out there while they learn to fly."

Violet pursed her lips. "Maybe." She was already planning to go with Ryon to meet Mother Orea. Surely Nox wanted to bring the dragons back to Dracwood as soon as possible, but a detour made more sense, with them growing so quickly. "We'll bring it up to Nox and Mariun when they're awake."

Violet tore her gaze off the water and scanned the horizon. She sighed deeply, exhaustion creeping up on her again. But she couldn't rest yet. "I better get back to the helm. The wind is trying to blow us off course."

Ryon sighed, too, and spun back to the deck. "And I better catch a new fish for breakfast." He leaned closer. "I'll use a pole this time. Maybe those greedy hatchlings won't be so eager to steal it if there's only one."

Violet giggled nervously. "Yeah. I think we've fed them enough already."

She paced back to the helm, forcing her desires aside. All she wanted was sleep. Well, if she were being perfectly honest, she wouldn't mind a few more kisses, too. But she had to see this through. The boat needed someone to sail it. The hatchlings needed protecting. Nox and Mariun needed a chance to heal.

She might not be the perfect person for the task, but for now, she was all they had. Honestly, when she thought back on her failures, it made her want to cry. She couldn't use her magic to save herself from being abducted or to heal Mariun. And the dragons... she'd wanted to bond one so badly.

Truth was, she might never find a bondmate. She might spend her whole life without figuring out how to access the elemental power trapped inside her. But she could do this. She could sail them to safety. That was enough for today. It had to be.

Dusk washed over the ocean. Violet stood at the helm, sheer force of will the only thing keeping her awake. Nox and Mariun still hadn't emerged from the cabin, and she wasn't planning to wake them.

She'd peeked in a few times throughout the day to check on them. Each time, she'd been greeted with quiet snores, and spotted their eyelids flickering as they dreamed. She might have a thousand minor aches and pains plaguing her, but she hadn't escaped the brink of death like they had. She hoped a good rest would be enough to heal them fully.

Ryon stopped beside her. "Still no sign of sails behind us." He nodded to the helm. "Want me to take a turn?"

"Sure." Violet backed away, rubbing her shoulders and sighing.

"Do you want to head below for an hour or two?" Ryon quirked a brow. "I can handle keeping us steady."

"No. I'm fine. Besides, you're just as tired as I am. Who's to say you won't fall asleep on your feet?" She nudged his side with her elbow. "We'll keep each other on our toes until we drop."

Ryon chuckled, but the sound cut off abruptly, shifting into a deep yawn. "Drop sounds about right. I'm ready to sleep on the deck at this point."

Violet giggled. "Me too." She pointed at the hatchlings asleep on the floorboards. "It's comfy enough for them."

The hatchlings dozed the day away after gobbling all those fish. Surely they needed the rest after working so hard to save their sister so soon after their birth. The egg sack lay in the sun, kept extra warm from the hatchlings curled around it.

A sudden thought made Violet's heart skip a beat. "The hatchlings need heat to hatch, don't they?"

Ryon nodded. "Wasn't that why they were hidden beside the volcano?"

Violet rubbed her neck. "What happens when the sun sets?" Cool evening air was already curling through the breeze. The sun lingered on the horizon, but once it set fully, there would only be the hatchlings keeping their sister warm. What if it wasn't enough?

Ryon lifted a hand off the helm and squeezed her forearm. "She'll be all right. I can feel it."

Violet met his eyes, fighting to ignore the tingles racing up her arm. "I hope you're right."

"Have you been thinking about their names?" Ryon put his hand back on the helm. "I have a few ideas."

"You do?" She leaned back on her heels, flicking a glance at the snoozing dragons. "Let's hear them."

"Nox seems so fond of calling his bondmate Green. I thought maybe they'd like Greta. She could be Gretillia the Green." He cocked a brow. "Or Gretishia, maybe?"

"Hmm. The second one sounds better to me." Truth be told, she wasn't crazy about either of them, but she wasn't about to tell him that. Not when she wanted to hear the rest of the names he'd thought up. She tapped her chin. "We'll have Nox ask for her opinion, of course."

"Of course." He grinned.

"Did you think of any others?"

"The white one's scales remind me of the decorative crystals Ma likes to use when she's braiding hair."

His mother was fond of braiding hair? Perhaps she was the one responsible for Ryon's unusual look. She tucked that little nugget away to examine later.

"I was thinking Crystalus the White, or Crys for short," he continued. "And the blue hatchling's scales look like the ocean and the air. So, maybe Ocearius the Blue. We could call him Ari for short."

"Those are great." Violet paced over, examining the hatchlings more closely in the dusk light. "I think they suit them perfectly."

Ryon shot her a crooked grin. "Really?"

"I do. The males, for sure. I think Green's might need some tweaking."

Ryon's face fell.

Violet rushed to assure him. "Who knows, she might love it."

"Yeah. We'll see." He shrugged.

"Have you thought of anything for this little one?" Violet strode to the final hatchling, stepping carefully between the slumbering dragons. Green cracked an eye and gazed at her lazily, but went right back to sleep.

"No. I haven't," Ryon said. "Feels a little premature when she hasn't hatched yet."

"I don't know about that." Violet rested her hand on the rubbery egg sack. "What if she just needs someone to believe in her? If we give her a name like all the rest, then she's bound to fully hatch."

Ryon chuckled. "It's worth a shot, I suppose." His gaze lifted to the sky, and his expression turned pensive. But before he could supply any names, an idea struck her.

"I think I have one for her."

"Yeah?" He tilted his head. "What is it?"

"If Mariun's guess is right, then this will be a fire dragon. A black. Her father, Druturion, was a black too. It might be nice to give a little nod to him with her name."

"Hmm. I like that. Bet they will, too." He smiled. "What's the name?"

"Menadru the Black, Mena for short." She patted the sack gently. "What do you think in there? Do you like it?" She'd not been expecting a response. She nearly stumbled over Green when the sack rippled beneath her fingers.

"Wow." Violet giggled. "I think she approves." She faced Ryon with a wide grin. The egg sack rippled again, making her gasp. She backed up, staring at the fleshy sack as it quivered.

"Your instincts were right, Violet. She needed a name. Mena's finally hatching." He left the helm and joined her on the deck.

The dragons must've noticed their sister stirring. They yawned and stretched as they woke, and each of them watched the sack tremble from the force of the hatchling working her way out.

Violet grabbed Ryon's hand and squeezed. "Blazes." She glanced at the cabin door. "What about Nox? Do you think we ought to wake—"

Her words cut off as the door slammed open. Nox shuffled out. His hair was tousled and faint rope lines were etched on his cheek, but his eyes were as alert as ever. "What's happening? Green wouldn't shut up until I—" His brows shot up, and he halted beside them. "She's hatching?"

"Uncle Nox." Violet threw herself into his arms. "I'm so glad you're all right."

"Hey, Squirt. Sorry if I scared you back there." He hugged her tightly and then pulled back, his gaze on the horizon. "Have I slept all day?"

"You needed it. But now that you're looking so well rested, I hope you don't mind if Ryon and I take a turn sleeping next. We're exhausted."

"I bet you are." Nox nodded to Ryon. "Go on, then. I can take over."

"And miss this?" Ryon stared at the egg sack as it quivered violently. "I've stayed up for nearly two full days. Another few moments won't kill me."

Violet silently agreed with him, refusing to move. She was dying to see the new dragon, too. And she knew just what to occupy herself with while she waited for the hatchling to break free.

"Ryon and I thought of some names. Do you want to run them by Green? See what she thinks?"

Nox relayed the names to Green. "Ari and Crys will do for the males. Mena is good too. Green's not fond of Greta."

Ryon twisted his lips. "Violet wasn't either."

Nox fell silent for a moment. "She likes how you gave Mena part of their father's name. What was their mother's name again?"

"Belstasia," Violet answered.

Nox rubbed his temple, and then his face split with a wide grin. "Gwenstasia the Green. Gwen for short."

Violet's heart warmed. "Gwen, huh? I love it."

"Me too." Nox beamed. "It was Flint's suggestion."

"So that's settled. Crys, Ari, Mena, and Gwen," Ryon said.

The sack tore, and out of the hole ripped in the side, Mena burst free.

Violet pursed her lips. "Oh. We might need to rethink the name. She's not black after all."

Mena's scales shimmered in the dying sunlight; a brilliant white shot through with tiny flecks of purple and pink. Violet quirked a brow as she inched closer. Her scales were different from Crys'. Something tickled the edges of her mind as she examined them closer.

Mena opened her jaw and yawned. Violet gasped as she spied a burning ember glowing deep inside the hatchling's throat.

"Wait... she *is* a fire dragon!"

"I don't understand..." Ryon frowned. "Why isn't she black?"

Violet bounced on her toes. "She's albino. She's albino like me!"

Nox slapped a hand on his knee. "Rot and decay. I think you're right, Vi."

Violet couldn't stop smiling. But then Mena opened her eyes. Gorgeous reddish-blue orbs stared back at her. The colors swirled together, looking violet in the dusk.

Violet's knees buckled. "Ryon." She grabbed his arm. "Your riddle. What was it again?"

"Hm?" He cocked a brow.

"Riddle?" Nox chimed in. "What riddle?"

"When Ryon first came looking for me, they sent him searching for the answer to a riddle." She shook his arm. "Tell me again. Please."

Ryon took a deep breath. "Look for one with a gull's egg gaze."

"Her eyes," she interrupted. "They're just like mine—"

"Hatched in the moonlight..." Ryon continued.

"You thought it meant my hair, but remember how the moon shone down right when her shell cracked?" Violet spat, her words spilling out frantically.

Ryon's gaze flicked over the horizon. "...baptized in dusk."

Violet spread out her arms. "It fits. She fits the riddle." Her arms fell to her sides and her stomach sank. "It was never me."

"No." Ryon shook his head, his brows scrunched. "No, it's you. I know it's you."

Violet forced a smile, burying the disappointment raging in her soul. "I guess now we know we're making the right call. We have to stop at your island. Mena needs to meet Mother Orea."

Failure or Fated

Ryon collapsed into his hammock. Moonlight lit the small cabin faintly, but his eyelids sank like they'd been weighed down with rocks. He toed off his boots, letting them clunk haphazardly on the floor.

He and Violet checked on Mariun when they first entered the cabin. She swayed peacefully in her hammock, and the worrying pallor covering her that morning appeared to have faded a good deal. Ryon sighed and pushed his concern for her aside. Mariun was tough. She'd pull through. He bet in the morning she'd be out on deck, giving Nox a hard time.

His hammock swung, and the hypnotic motion nearly lulled him to sleep. Until a quiet sniffle tickled his ears. His eyes popped open in the dark cabin. "Violet? Is that you?"

"Go back to sleep," she replied, her voice thick.

Like he could, now that he knew she was crying. "What's wrong?" His heart pounded, and though his body wanted no part of it, he forced his limbs to move, shifting to sit on the wobbly hammock.

"I'm fine," Violet insisted.

Ryon barely resisted rolling his eyes. "Do you always cry when you're fine?" He threw his legs out of the hammock and nearly tripped over one of his boots.

"What are you doing?" Violet hissed.

After grabbing his hammock to steady himself, he kicked his boots into the corner. "I'm coming over there."

"Don't." The word shook, choked out of a throat fighting back tears. "I'm a mess."

"Scoot over," he ordered. Violet obeyed silently, and he climbed into her hammock with her. She held herself stiffly at first. His hands trembled before he forced himself to relax. He shoved aside the ever-present fear that his newfound strength would harm someone and reached for Violet. Once he gently tugged her to his chest and wrapped his arms around her, she melted against him and sniffled again.

Ryon rubbed her back. He was dying to know what was bothering her. Honestly, it wasn't a surprise she needed a good cry. She'd been forced to watch Flint die in the ring. Nox and Mariun had both nearly died. And with them constantly on the go, they'd had no time to linger over their emotions. Yet, he didn't press her. If she wanted to pretend to be fine, then he'd pretend too. But he drew the line at letting her cry all alone in the dark.

Violet hid her face in his chest. She barely made a sound, but his tunic grew progressively wetter. He held her while she cried, rubbing gentle circles across her shoulders.

Eventually, her tears stopped falling. Ryon stilled, waiting for her to speak. After a long moment of silence, his eyelids fluttered closed. She must have fallen asleep. He sighed, too exhausted to even consider returning to his hammock.

"I'm sorry." Violet's fingers curled into his tunic. "I wrecked your shirt."

Ryon twisted sideways, sliding Violet's cheek off the wet fabric and onto his biceps. "It's just a shirt."

Violet toyed with his collar. "Aren't you going to ask why I was crying?"

"Nope. You're fine, remember?"

She shoved his shoulder gently, and he spotted the faint gleam of her teeth. But her smile faded fast. "Have you ever felt like a failure?"

"Yes," he answered honestly. "Every full moon night for decades."

"Full moon?"

"Mm-hm, when I tried to earn a golden bloodfeather." He tucked the arm Violet wasn't lying on behind his head. "To gain an audience with Mother Orea, petitioners bring silver on every full moon. Every time I entered the Aviary, so hopeful that night would be *the night*. And each time I left, failure sinking into my bones and seeping through my marrow."

"You did that for decades?" Violet smoothed his tunic, sending tingles across his chest. "You must have been so young when you started."

He nodded. "I was eleven."

"Eleven?" Violet's fingers curled around one of his dreadlocks. "Why did you seek an audience at that age? What wish is worth decades of failures?"

"My brother, Rovan. I need the wish for him." Ryon sighed. "It's a long story. I promise I'll tell you, but after you tell me why you feel like a failure."

Violet let go of his lock and dragged her hand down her face before tucking her fist beneath her chin. "I'm supposed to have all this magic, but when I try to use it, I can't. I couldn't save Mariun. I couldn't even save myself from the fox."

Ryon frowned. "You and Mariun are safe. That doesn't sound like a failure to me."

"No thanks to me."

"No thanks to me, either." Ryon shrugged. "Nox and Mariun might have done the saving, but we all followed the map together. We found the dragons, just like we set out to. That's not a failure. That's a win."

"Maybe... but I can't help feeling like everyone was wrong about me."

Ryon pulled his arm from behind his head and gently rubbed Violet's shoulder. "Who was wrong?"

"My parents." Her shoulder stiffened beneath his palm. "You."

His stomach clenched. "Oh? And how were we wrong?"

"My parents told me I was special. That I'd need the magic I was born with for some important quest." She clicked her tongue. "My mother had a vision, apparently."

Violet might not see it, but the more she told him, the more certain it made him that she *was* important. That fate made sure she embarked on this journey any way it could.

"What vision?"

"It was as vague and confusing as your riddle. But now we've saved the dragons. We'll be returning to Dracwood soon. And all I used my magic for is knocking one man away from me. Seems her vision was wrong, just like the riddle." Violet exhaled a shaky breath. "Sure, the quest was important, but I didn't need to be here at all. Nox won the map and helped the dragons hatch, not me."

His jaw dropped. She didn't really believe that, did she? "But if you hadn't gotten Muse into that dinghy, then you'd have never found me.

We would have never found Aren or Thalassia. Lark and Nox would still be stuck there."

"I suppose"—Violet yawned—"that's true."

"You're not a failure, Violet. And yeah, saving the dragons didn't require your magic, but the quest isn't over yet."

"You're not a failure either." Violet yawned again. "We'll bring Mena with us." A third yawn made her words garbled. "Get you your golden feather."

His heart twinged. He hated that she didn't believe she was the answer to the riddle anymore. But he wasn't about to argue about it while she was clearly exhausted. "Shh. We will. How about we get some sleep first?"

Violet cuddled closer and blinked a few times before closing her eyes. "Goodnight, Ryon."

"Goodnight." With her warm weight curled around him, and her confession playing through his mind, Ryon drifted to sleep.

"Fish!" a voice yelled. "Fish! Fish!"

Ryon groaned, rubbing his ears. "Damn gulls." He cracked open his eyes, expecting to find Violet still sleeping beside him, but he was alone. He stretched and flung his legs onto the floor. A smile curved his lips when he spotted Mariun's hammock empty as well.

After snagging his boots out of the corner and stuffing his sore feet inside, he made his way above deck. Bright sunlight shone down, making him squint.

"Good morning," Violet greeted, all signs of her sadness from last night washed away. She beamed at him from where she sat cross-legged on the mid-deck and waved him over. "Are you hungry? We just cooked some fish."

Ryon took the wooden plate she offered and settled beside her. "I'm starving. Thanks." He shoved a bite of meat into his mouth and chewed thoughtfully. Something was different this morning. It wasn't just Violet's sunny attitude. He peered around, fighting to pinpoint exactly what he sensed that was so odd.

Nox and Mariun chatted quietly at the helm, sharing a plate of fish. The dragons stood in pairs, two on each end of the boat with their backs turned toward him. What were they doing? Watching the fish swim as they floated by?

The wind whipped the sails, drawing his gaze upward. It reminded him of the night of the storm before Nox demanded they tie down the sails. He glanced off the boat's side as another gull flew past strangely slowly.

He gulped and grabbed the waterskin Violet had placed between them. "Are we moving faster?"

Violet nodded. "Isn't it incredible?"

Ryon slugged a mouthful of water. "But how? I thought we would be slower than ever with the dragons gaining weight after every meal?"

He swung his gaze back to the pair at the bow. It was Ari and Mena. Even from afar, he could tell they'd grown. Especially Mena. She'd been a good deal smaller than her siblings when she'd hatched last night, but now she was only a head or so smaller than her blue-scaled brother.

Shouldn't the boat be even slower now? He glanced at Violet, his brows scrunched.

She smiled. "Can't you feel it?" She rubbed her arms and tipped her gaze to the sky. "It's magic. They're summoning."

Ryon concentrated on the sensations around him and nearly laughed. A gentle tingle hummed on the breeze. Moisture swirled around the deck, making the air feel more like it would on a foggy day, despite the bright sun beaming on them. No wonder he'd been so sure something was different.

He stood and walked to the side rail. At this angle, he could see the stream of water spilling out of Ari's open jaw. Mena sat beside him, her mouth and eyes closed, their tails coiled together. He shifted to stare at the stern and spotted Crys and Gwen in the same position. Crys' jaw gaped open and air swirled around him. Gwen rested peacefully beside him.

Violet joined him at the side rail. "Nox talked them into trying last night. This was how they traveled through the shallow waters around the southern continent back home before the battle in the Abandoned Lands. Human mages did the summoning then, but the hatchlings were able to replicate it. Ari is manipulating the water beneath us to boost the boat higher in the water, and Crys is creating more wind to speed us along."

"Wow." He tilted his head. "What about Mena and Gwen? Why do they look like they're sleeping?"

"They're joined, sharing their talent," Violet explained. "It helps them summon longer without tiring."

"How do you know all this?" he asked.

"My mother was a mage. My father, too. Well, kind of." She scrunched her nose. "They both told me hundreds of stories about how elemental magic used to work." She chuckled and shook her head. "I guess I should say *works* now."

"Yeah, it's definitely working." He grinned, but then a heartbeat later, his smile fell. "Hey, why are they stopping?"

Streams of magic cut off from the dragon's mouths, and their jaws snapped shut. The tingle and moisture in the air faded. The hatchlings shuffled back toward the mid-deck as the boat slowly sank deeper into the waves and slowed.

Violet sighed. "Even with joining, they can't keep it up forever. The boat I was telling you about had shifts of mages working around the clock and giving each other plenty of breaks."

Ryon scanned the horizon, wondering if he might glimpse his island off in the distance. "Even with breaks, it's pretty amazing. I bet we'll reach my island in no time."

"Speaking of," Nox cut in, "we need to talk about that plan."

Ryon stopped hunting for his island and spun toward the helm, his stomach sinking.

Violet turned to her uncle with a frown. "What do you mean?"

Nox crossed his arms. "When you told me about your idea to stop there, I agreed because I didn't want to end up stuck in the Still Sea while the dragons outgrew the boat." He waved a hand at the hatchlings. "I don't think we'll have that problem now."

"Are you sure about that?" Mariun asked. "They seem pretty ravenous after they summon."

Violet nodded. "It's true. They've demolished two breakfasts already. Even if they're speeding us along, they're growing just as swiftly. Do you really want to chance it?"

Ryon held his tongue even though he was dying to argue. But he'd given Violet his word that he'd never force her to return with him. He wasn't planning to force her uncle or the dragons, either.

Nox rubbed his forehead. Then he huffed out a deep sigh. "Fine. I know when I've been outvoted." He threw his hands up. "But we're getting those hatchlings flying fast. We need to return to Dracwood."

Mariun stiffened, and her face paled. Ryon stepped toward her, but Nox got there faster. He slid an arm around her shoulders.

"Hey, you all right?" Nox bent to look into her eyes. "Maybe you ought to lie back down."

Mariun's gaze flitted across his face. "No, I'm fine. It's just—"

Violet cut off whatever Mariun was about to say. "Um, problem. Big problem."

Ryon whipped around. Violet pointed at the sea, gesturing frantically.

"What is it?" he asked.

Violet grabbed his face and angled it forcefully. "There. Are those sails behind us?"

Ryon squinted, and his stomach dropped. "I think they are." From so far away, it was hard to be certain, but without the hatchlings' aid, it wouldn't be long before whoever was out there caught up to them.

"How did they gain on us?" Violet asked. "There's no way they should've been able to with the dragons' summoning."

Mariun joined them at the railing and stared at the ocean. "Look at the direction they're sailing. I don't think they followed us from the volcanic island. That's one of Jurdan's patrols."

"Guess that clinches it. Let's hope your island is close." Nox sent Ryon a nod, then hurried back to the helm.

Stalked In the Water

V iolet inhaled a nervous breath, her gaze flicking between the boats chasing them and the island looming ahead. It had taken most of the day, but eventually they'd spotted Ryon's island on the horizon. The sight of the grassy plains topped with a massive rust-hued mountain only brought her momentary relief. It was hard to feel anything but fear with the masked men drawing ever closer.

The dragons had done their best to keep ahead of their pursuers. Still, it wasn't long before they realized it was not one but two boats stalking them. Even with the short blasts of magic boosting their speed, the ships had closed much of the distance. A few times they'd drawn so near Violet could spot men dressed in black staring with their eerie animal masks in place.

Thankfully, the hatchlings always recovered in time to put more distance between them. But with each hour that passed, the boats closed in a little more. She could only hope that once they landed, they'd think of some way to outrun the masked.

Ryon dumped a net full of fish onto the deck. The dragons tore into the squirming pile, their appetites unquenchable.

Violet's belly heaved as she watched the hatchlings make a mess out of the silver fish wriggling on the wooden boards. Blood coated everything, darkening the deck and making it slippery. By now, the boat sat so low in the water the waves sloshed onboard every time the hatchlings took a break to eat.

The dragons had been so much smaller when they'd hatched. How they had grown from the size of a horse to this in such a short time was mind-boggling. They'd all nearly doubled in size in barely more than a day.

"Almost there." Ryon stopped next to her. "One more push from the dragons and we should be close enough to drop anchor."

Mariun burst out of the cabin, her arms loaded with stuffed sacks. "I packed everything I could find that might be useful." She thrust a pack into Violet's and Ryon's hands.

"Thanks." Violet shouldered the pack. "Why didn't you tell me what you were up to? I would've helped."

Mariun frowned at the boats behind them. "It's all right. I needed something to occupy my mind." Suddenly her eyes widened, and she dropped the two packs she'd been holding.

Violet followed her gaze, biting back a gasp. The boats were so close she could pick out individual masks. A shark and a hawk were stationed on the bow. And at the helm—a spider.

"Nox," Violet yelled. "We need to hurry!"

"I see them," Nox yelled back. He raced out onto the deck, shooing the dragons toward their ends of the boat. The hatchlings' slumped posture and slow movements betrayed their exhaustion.

Violet's heart jerked. With the hatchlings being so young, they'd agreed it was too risky to ask them to use their magic to fight the masked. Not to mention they were outnumbered and practically weaponless. That left running as the obvious solution. But what would they do if the hatchlings couldn't summon? They'd be captured again as soon as the masked came close enough to shoot their toxic darts.

Thankfully, the hum of static and the cool touch of moisture flooded the air. Their boat lifted and shot forward. Violet exhaled, wiping sweat off her brow.

"Ryon thinks we'll make it with this push. Do you think so, too?" she asked Nox.

"I wager they have enough left in them to get us close to shore." He sighed. "They're just so thirsty. Gwen can't stop complaining about it."

Violet's stomach clenched. They'd fed the hatchlings plenty of fish, but they'd run out of fresh water hours ago.

Ryon shaded his eyes, staring at the coast. "I know where we are. There's a freshwater spring a short hike from where we're about to land. Tell them water is close."

Nox brightened. "That is good news."

Violet's gaze fell to the ruined deck. Their stolen ship had served them well, but the thought of being back on dry land bolstered her spirits. In fact...

"Uncle Nox, I have an idea." She grinned at him. "What if we can bring the hatchlings to that water even faster?"

He lifted a shoulder. "I think they'd be pretty pleased with that. What are you thinking?"

"Let's beach the ship." She flicked a glance at the dragons. "Assuming they have the strength to summon for that long."

Nox pursed his lips.

"The plan is to teach the dragons to fly, right?" she continued. "We won't need the ship again if we're going to fly out of here."

Mariun nodded. "You're right. And it will give us a head start. They'll drop anchor and ferry inland on smaller crafts."

"Gwen agrees." Nox clutched the helm tightly. "This might be a bumpy landing. Everyone better grab something."

Violet hurried to the side rail. Ryon rushed beside her. "Mariun, get over here too." Mariun joined them, and Ryon nudged her until she settled at the rail. "You two huddle together and let me stand behind you."

Mariun plastered herself against Violet's side. Violet gulped as Ryon leaned against them both and spread his arms wide, gripping the rail tightly. Her pulse raced, and her gaze locked on the shore as the boat sped ever closer.

"Almost there. Hang on!" Nox ordered.

The boat slammed into the sand. The awful clamor of wood splintering crashed in her ears. Violet's chest jerked painfully against the rail, and Ryon's hard muscles smacked into her back, wedging her pack so tightly something inside jabbed her ribs. She closed her eyes, certain the boat was about to break into a thousand pieces. But when she pried them open a heartbeat later, they'd skidded to a stop in the sand above the breakers.

"Let's go," Nox shouted.

Ryon peeled himself off of her and Mariun, and the three of them hurried to the ship's bow. The dragons hopped down first, kicking loose sand everywhere.

Violet's boots sank into the sand, and she nearly tumbled sideways. Ryon was there to catch her. He gripped her elbow tightly, and she winced, an involuntary gasp spilling out of her lips.

Ryon tugged his hand back like he'd been stung. "Guano. Are you all right?"

Violet nodded vehemently, resisting the urge to rub her elbow. "I'm fine. Come on. You better lead the way."

They trudged through the sand to the tall grass beyond it. Ryon hurried to the front of their group, a frown etched on his face. Violet's heart twisted, and she wished she could take back her stupid reaction. He wouldn't want to touch her now. She buried the thought, and the overwhelming wave of disappointment that came with it.

Ryon hadn't been lying about the spring being close. Soon the trickle of running water played on the breeze, overpowering the surf's rolling as they trekked further inland.

Ryon brushed a clump of tall grass aside. "Here it is. We need to hurry. The masked won't be far behind."

The dragons didn't even wait for the words to fully leave his mouth before they barreled forward and dipped their heads to slurp up the gurgling spring. Violet halted at Ryon's side, giggling.

"They sure weren't kidding about being thirsty." She smiled, watching them fight for turns to lap up the bubbling water. It burst out of a small rock formation and created a tiny pool and even smaller stream that cut through the grassy landscape on a course for the ocean.

Mariun tapped Nox's shoulder, her gaze glued behind them. "Can you see if they've landed?"

Nox frowned and squinted behind them. "No. Let me ask Gwen." Gwen extracted herself from the pile of hatchlings and lifted her long neck toward the beach. Nox shook his head. "She can't see the ocean either. We've hiked too far inland."

"We should assume they're still following us," Violet said. "There's no way they would turn around now when they've chased us this far."

"You're right." Mariun shuddered. "If Spider is there, he won't stop until he captures me."

"Hey." Nox tugged her against his side and wrapped his arm over her shoulder. "We won't let that happen. I promise."

Ryon cut in. "As long as we arrive at the mountain before them, we'll be safe."

Mariun bit her lip. "You keep saying that, but I don't know if it's true. You don't know Spider like I do. He always follows Jurdan's orders. If Jurdan told him to find me, he won't give up. Masked are worse than hounds, obedient to the end."

"The mountains will keep them out." Ryon's voice rang with confidence. "Trust me."

"We just need to make sure we get there faster." Nox squeezed Mariun's shoulder, then pulled away. He shucked the sack off his back and dug inside. "Everyone, fill your waterskins."

Violet pulled her pack off and fished her waterskin out.

Ryon held out a hand. "Here, I'll fill it for you."

"Thanks." Violet smiled shyly and handed it to him. Ryon met her eyes for a heartbeat and paced away without returning her smile.

Her heart sank. Was he planning to beat himself up about gripping her too tightly forever?

Violet turned away and wandered over to Mariun's side. She'd given her waterskin to Nox to fill. The girls stood and watched as Ryon and Nox closed in on the spring. They both seemed reluctant to inch too close while the massive dragons crowded around it, jostling each other as they fought for a turn to gobble the water.

Mariun lifted her fingers to her throat and wobbled. Violet shot out a hand, helping her steady her stance.

"Are you all right?" She quirked a brow at Mariun. "Maybe we should sit down."

Mariun nodded, and they settled on the tall grass. This island was far different from the last. No thick forests surrounded them, just rolling hills stretching out until they butted up against the string of red mountains. Insects chirped and birds sang. The dying sunlight warmed Violet's face. If not for the impending threat of the masked catching up with them, it would be peaceful enough to lie down for a nap.

"How are you feeling after everything yesterday?" she asked. "We haven't had many chances to talk."

Mariun shrugged. "I'm fine. A little wobbly here and there. I guess that's to be expected when you lose so much blood."

"I suppose you're right."

"I'm grateful, too." Mariun's gaze glided to the spring and landed on her uncle. "Nox told me how Gwen healed me. If he hadn't thought to ask her to use magic... I know he just felt guilty about hesitating before we jumped, but I'm glad for it, anyway." She looked away and curled her hands idly through the long grass. "I'm sure he'd be happy to be rid of me."

"I don't think that's true at all." Violet grabbed Mariun's hand and squeezed. "We all started out distrusting you, but can you really blame us? By now, I think you've shown us how wrong we were in the beginning. I don't want to be rid of you. And I doubt Nox does either."

Mariun flushed, her gaze darting back to Nox. "You think so?" Her gray eyes were softer than Violet could ever remember seeing. Her face lit with a soft smile as she stared at Nox fighting his way in between the dragons to fill the waterskins.

"I do." She paused, unsure if she should say anything when Nox seemed eager to downplay his role. "It wasn't just Gwen who saved you. Nox used her boon. He could have died trying it."

Mariun's eyes bulged. "He didn't tell me that."

Violet's insides warmed. Mariun was clearly infatuated with Nox. And if the way Nox insisted on holding her while they slept was anything to judge by, he felt the same way about her. It was strange that neither of them realized it when she could spot the signs so easily. Or maybe they did, but they weren't willing to admit it.

Nox and Ryon hurried back, and Violet stood, holding a hand out to help pull Mariun to her feet.

"Everything all right?" Nox's brow furrowed and his gaze slid over Mariun.

"Yep," Violet answered. "Just resting while we can." She turned to Ryon. "How far of a walk is it to the mountains?" Her feet ached at the thought of another long hike across another huge island.

Ryon handed her waterskin over, then shaded his eyes and stared at the mountain. "If I'm remembering right, it will take about a full day. That's if we don't stop to sleep. If we camp for the night, it will be even longer."

Nox kneeled and lifted his pack off the ground, then stuffed his waterskin inside it. "It won't take nearly that long."

"If you expect us to run, you might have to carry me instead of that pack," Violet replied, hands on her hips.

"We won't be running." Nox rose from his crouch and shouldered his pack. "We're riding."

"Riding?" Mariun pursed her lips. "Riding what?"

Nox flicked out his arm toward the hatchlings. "There are four of us and four dragons. It's kind of perfect, wouldn't you say?"

Excitement welled in Violet's chest. It wasn't quite as exciting as flying on a dragon, but riding one was still probably the most thrilling thing she would ever do. "Are you sure they have the strength? After all the magic they used to bring us here, they must be exhausted."

Nox grinned. "Gwen says they can handle it." He shrugged. "If they get too tired, we can always hop down and walk. What do we have to lose?"

"You don't have to convince me." Ryon beamed. "I'll gladly take a ride on a dragon over another long hike."

"Who's riding who?" Mariun asked.

Nox glanced back at the dragons. Gwen cocked her head in his direction and backed away from the spring. After a few moments, Nox said, "Vi, you're the smallest, so you should ride Mena. Gwen wants me with her." He split a look between Mariun and Ryon. "You two, take your pick."

Once the hatchlings drank their fill, they sauntered over and crouched low in the grass. Mariun clambered atop Crys' back, and Ryon hopped on Ari.

Violet waited for Mena to approach. She'd grown a great deal since hatching, but she still hadn't caught up to her siblings yet. Violet held her breath as Mena bent low beside her. Her white scales sparkled like the fine gems her aunt Kayda wore on special occasions. Even as the smallest, she was still massive. She folded her huge leathery wings against her sides and curved her sinuous neck sideways to glare at Violet, seeming impatient.

Violet gulped and climbed atop Mena's back. She clenched the dragon's neck and wrapped her legs tightly around her torso. Noise echoed behind them, and a pit formed in Violet's stomach. Were the masked landing on the beach? No wonder Mena looked so eager to leave.

The hatchlings took off, with Ryon and Nox in the lead, hollering at each other over the dragons' pounding footsteps. Though they were surely graceful when they flew, on land the hatchlings were awkward mounts. Violet held on tightly, certain she would tumble off and into the tall grass. Eventually, she grew used to Mena's gait and relaxed enough to look around.

The island was as lovely as she remembered. She'd stuck close to the coast before. This time, they raced across countless rolling hills, drawing ever closer to the enormous mountain.

As the dragons fell into a steady rhythm, Violet's mind began to wander. With each long stride, they put more distance between themselves and their masked pursuers. Still, she couldn't allow herself to accept the feeling of safety that arose at the thought.

Would they ever be safe again? If the masked would follow them here, couldn't they just as easily follow them anywhere? Even Dracwood?

They might hide on the mountain long enough to fly away, but would it matter if what Mariun said was true? The spider would keep hunting for her. Jurdan would never allow her to escape. Were they asking for trouble by allowing her to come with them?

But how could they possibly send Mariun away after everything they'd been through? Maybe once they arrived home, she could slip away. She could hide in the snowy mountains of Doln or the vast jungles of Raimire.

The idea made a riot of bubbles explode in her belly. It wasn't fair to make Mariun hide. She should be free to live her life as she chose.

Jurdan had already ruined Mariun's youth. Now, even after she'd escaped, he held her future in a stranglehold. If only there was something they could do...

A Sure Bet

Ryon grinned from his perch on Ari's back. Dragon riding sure beat walking, although it was murder on the thighs. If he had known he'd spend the evening with hard scales chafing his skin, he would have exchanged his skirt for a pair of the stolen masked men's trousers.

He chuckled to himself. Who knew there'd come a day when he'd long for those confining garments? But he could certainly see the benefits with his knee-length skirt bunched high on his thighs, threatening to give everyone a peek at his undergarments.

Luckily, the sun setting behind the mountain washed the grassy hills they traversed in shadow, and Ari's wings flicked beside him, helping hide his bottom half from view.

They'd elected him and Ari to lead the way. At first, he'd struggled to keep the lumbering hatchling on track. Finally, Nox assured him a swift kick to Ari's side wouldn't hurt him at all. Now, whenever he needed to adjust their course, he had a way to, even if it made him wince each time his boots smashed against the hatchling's scales.

All the same, it was good to be back. He'd never imagined leaving his island before. It made sense that he'd be homesick. It would be good to see Ma again. And Rovan.

Excitement welled in his chest. His years of hard work were finally about to come to fruition. With Violet by his side, he'd be granted his audience with Mother Orea. The orecolns might be greedy for silver, but they always kept their word. He couldn't wait to feel the golden feather in his hands. To finally set right the awful mistake he'd made so long ago.

Ryon glanced back at Violet. He'd promised to tell her about his brother last night, but with both of them so exhausted, he'd forgotten. To be honest, the thought of telling her made acid churn in the pit of his stomach. What would she think when she learned what he'd done? Would she still look at him the same? Or would the longing he'd glimpsed in her eyes when they'd kissed disappear for good?

That kiss... His heart fluttered at the memory of her soft lips. If he hadn't been on a boat with her uncle within earshot and those mischievous hatchlings ready to butt in, those few stolen kisses might have turned into much more.

Was he ready for that? In the past, he'd never allowed himself to grow close to anyone, mainly out of guilt. If Rovan couldn't be happy, then why did he deserve happiness?

Violet made him want more. More of her sweet smiles and bubbly laughter. More of her gorgeous eyes staring at him with desire.

How did he end up so smitten?

Was there any truth to Violet's assumption? Did his wish on the bloodfeather when they'd first met make him drawn to her? He searched his feelings, but he couldn't say for sure whether he'd have liked her any less without his wish. In the end, what did it even matter? His feelings were real regardless of where they originated. He just hoped he could convince her to see it that way, instead of using it as an excuse to push him away.

Wings fluttered beside him, drawing Ryon from his reverie. Silver feathers shone on the bird, even in the shaded light of dusk. He tilted his head, carefully scanning the orecoln circling him. He whistled, "Quill? Is that you?"

"Ryon!" Quill whistled back, filtering instantly to words in Ryon's mind. "Hmph. I should be insulted. You meet a few dragons, and you don't even recognize your old friends."

Ryon chuckled. "Come now. I'm just not used to seeing you from this angle."

Quill continued to fly, swooping around Ari's head in slow circles as he marched toward the mountain. But it seemed the hatchling wasn't fond of his new follower. When Quill circled Ari's face again, he opened his mouth wide and blasted a spray of ice chunks at him.

The bird squawked, barely dodging. "How rude!" He flapped his wings angrily and lifted higher into the air.

"Hold on," he whistled before Quill flew out of earshot. Ryon bit back a smile and turned to Nox, who rode close by on Gwen. "Hey, that bird is a friend. Tell Ari to leave him alone."

Nox frowned but nodded. A few heartbeats later, the dragons slowed, then halted. Nox hopped off Gwen and motioned for them all to follow suit. Ari bent low, and Ryon slid down. The ground thumped as the girls jumped off their dragons.

"We didn't need to stop." Ryon shook out his legs and stretched.

Nox tugged his pack off his back. "The hatchlings are thirsty." He raised his voice. "Share some of the water in your skins." Nox turned to Ryon. "You can call your bird back. They'll leave him alone."

Ryon whistled loudly, "You're safe to come back." He grabbed his waterskin and sucked down a few mouthfuls before pouring the rest into Ari's wide-open jaw.

"Look at the size of those teeth," Quill said as he landed on a hill beside them.

Ryon grinned. The fear that had filled him the first few times he'd fed the hatchlings was completely absent now. It was strange to realize he'd grown used to the mythical beasts so quickly. "They're not even fully grown yet," he told Quill.

Violet wandered over. "Who's this?"

Ryon smiled as she scanned Quill closely with narrowed eyes. The orecolns likely appeared a little odd to someone who hadn't grown up around the gull-sized birds with spindly legs. "Quill. He's one of the silver orecolns I told you about."

Her face lit with a jaw-dropping smile. "I thought those feathers looked familiar."

"Odd friends you've made," Quill chirped, bouncing on his long legs and cocking his head at Violet. "Why's this one so... colorless?"

His stomach wrenched, and Ryon fought the urge to make the tactless little bird take back his words. He whistled sharply, "She's albino. The dragon she's riding is, too."

"Albino... Ah, I see." Quill hopped on the hillside, his silver head tilting this way and that as he surveyed them. "I've been out looking for you every day."

Ryon's heart warmed, cooling the ice spreading through his veins. "You have, have you?"

"The priests offered extra silver to whoever brought back word of your return."

Figures it had more to do with silver than him. "Still greedy as ever, I see."

"Hey. Can't make a bird change their feathers." Quill stopped scanning the party and gazed at him directly. "Besides, I knew you'd be back. It was a sure bet."

That statement had warmth spreading again. It was certainly nice to know Quill had faith in his return.

"What's he saying?" Violet's brows scrunched and her head bobbed as she followed their whistling.

"He's out looking for me. The priests want word of my return," Ryon explained.

She scratched her head. "Is that good or bad?"

"Good, I hope. It means we might have help waiting for us when we arrive at the mountain." Ryon beamed. He'd been certain he'd need to climb, but now... He turned back to Quill. "What are you waiting for? Go tell them I'm back."

Quill shook out his feathers. "Maybe I shouldn't bother, if that's the welcome you have for me. Gone for ages, and you can't wait to get rid of me."

Ryon barely resisted rolling his eyes. "Quill, you know I'd love to chat, but I'm hoping to have the priests' help when we arrive." He scanned the darkening sky and then pointed to the mountain. "At the rate we're going, the village will be asleep when we get there. But if the priests are forewarned..."

Quill lifted his beak. "Fine. But you owe me. When all this is said and done, you better dig up that last batch and let me at it."

"Done. Fly safe, buddy," Ryon said.

Quill rose with a few graceful beats of his wings and tore off into the darkening sky. Ryon smiled as he watched him fly away.

"That was interesting." Mariun cocked a brow. "I didn't realize you could talk to birds."

Ryon shrugged. "There's a bunch of us who can in my village. You'll get used to it after a while."

"Hopefully we won't be there long enough to get used to it." Nox waved a hand. "With any luck, the hatchlings will learn to fly sooner than later. Come on. Let's move."

They climbed back onto their dragons. Hillside after hillside slid beneath them, bleeding into a monotonous blur. Until they spotted a herd of tritusks in their path.

"What's that?" Nox yelled. The herd was still far ahead, but the dark shapes of their massive dark-furred bodies were spread out before them, blanketing the landscape like ants swarming a mound.

"Tritusks," Ryon yelled back, his heart thudding faster. The three tusked beasts didn't look so scary from afar, but he recalled the fear of being squashed when they were on the run all too well.

"Should we be worried?" Nox frowned.

Ryon's lips thinned. "They feed on grass, so no need to worry about them trying to attack. Although, if we spook them, they might start running." His gut clenched. "Stampedes aren't pretty."

"I can imagine," Nox replied dryly. "So, we circle around, then?"

Ryon nodded. "I think that's wise."

Ari marched forward, and Ryon waited for the hatchling to speak to Gwen and turn aside. It would likely cost them an hour or so, dodging a herd so large. Still, it was better safe than squashed. After a few moments without turning, Ryon nudged Ari with his heel. The blue hatchling continued forward, even with another harder tap to his side.

"What's going on?" he shouted to Nox. "I thought we decided to go around."

Nox patted Gwen's flank, and a moment later she sped up, closing the distance between her and Ari. "The hatchlings want to go through.

They said they won't spook them." He shrugged and lowered his voice. "I think they're getting tired."

Ryon gulped. If the hatchlings ran out of energy in the middle of that herd, it would be disastrous. But if he pushed to circle them and they grew so tired they needed to rest before reaching the mountain, would that be any better? One way or the other, they had to take a chance. They were being hunted. Any advantage they might have to put more distance between them and the masked, they ought to take. "All right. If they think they can do it, then let's do it."

The dragons tucked their wings close to their sides and strode forward slowly. Ryon's pulse raced, his veins pumping with adrenaline. It seemed foolish to imagine that the tritusks would just sit idly and allow a group of predators to wander through their herd unchecked. But who knew? They were used to being the biggest beasts around, with only wild mountain cats and his people hunting them.

Even then, their fast pace and thunderous strides were enough to save them most times. Whenever hunters took down a tritusk, it was always one that couldn't keep up. If the beast was sickly, that meant the meat was too poor to be eaten, and they'd have to settle for harvesting their bones and hide. But when they picked off a young bull, or one that had been recently injured, then the whole village would feast.

Ryon's stomach rumbled, but he shoved the memory of their delectable meat aside before his mouth watered uncontrollably. He needed to stay alert. One wrong move and they might find themselves in the midst of a stampede.

The dragons slowed their movements as they carefully closed in on the herd. Crys inched into the lead, overtaking Ari's position at the front. Mariun sent him a befuddled look as she passed, clinging tightly to Crys' neck.

Ryon glanced back at Nox and cocked a brow.

"They want Crys to go first through the herd," he explained quietly with a shrug.

A crackling buzz filled the air, making the hair on Ryon's arms stand on end. He turned forward and spotted Crys' mouth open. The wind kicked up, blowing the tall grass on either side of their path. A strange familiarity tickled the back of his mind, but he shook off the perplexing feeling before it fully formed.

When the air reached the first of the great lumbering beasts in their path, it lifted its head out of the grass and shuffled sideways. Nearby tritusks reacted the same, raising their heads and chasing the breeze.

The hatchlings wasted no time marching down the small pathway Crys' magic cleared through the herd's center. The tritusks ignored them, content with shaking their furry hides in the cool air and munching on grass.

How had they known that would work? Ryon was dying to ask, but he was too afraid of drawing unwanted attention to speak up. They were good and truly surrounded now, with massive beasts on every side. The herd even shuffled around to block the path behind them, making retreat unlikely. If anything went wrong—

"Ah-choo!" Violet sneezed, and Ryon's heart plummeted to his knees. He nearly broke his neck, spinning around to watch the mayhem that would undoubtedly follow.

A tritusk just behind Mena jolted and reared. Its enormous hairy front legs rocked the ground a heartbeat later. It spun and bolted, racing away from them. Nearly a dozen tritusks joined the skittish animal on its flight.

Eyes widening, he held his breath, waiting for more beasts to join in. He'd seen it dozens of times. One moment, the herd would be calm and content, and then they morphed into a racing wave of death, trampling everything in their path.

But this time, luck was on their side. The few tritusks who ran were all behind them, and the larger bulk of the herd remained where they were.

Ryon's speeding pulse finally slowed. Violet and Mena, being in the rear of their little group, were likely the only thing that saved them from inciting a full stampede. He spared a glance back at Violet and frowned. She clasped a hand over her nose and her head hung low, but not low enough to disguise her flushed skin.

She was already feeling like a failure. Now this. If only he could hold her again, like last night...

Ryon shoved the thought aside as he spotted Violet's arm. Her sleeve had ridden up, exposing a dark-purple stain around her elbow. Disgust raced up his throat, burning like bile.

He shouldn't be going anywhere near her. Violet had tried to play it off like nothing, but he *knew* he'd hurt her when he'd grabbed her elbow. So far, when he concentrated enough, he'd been able to keep his touch gentle. But today showed him that when emotions were high, he still couldn't trust his own strength.

How long would it be before he hurt her again? If he couldn't find some way to control his strength all the time, then he didn't belong with any woman. He couldn't be that man, harming his lover one moment and begging for her forgiveness the next. Ryon had watched his mother live with that nightmare for half his youth. He refused to become the same monster.

He whipped around and set his gaze on the path ahead. The herd's musky stench tickled his nose. With every step the hatchlings took, the closer they drew to his mountain. While the thought should fill him with glee like it had earlier, he couldn't shake the image of that bruise from his mind. The sky darkened further, mirroring his black thoughts.

By the time they worked their way through the herd, night had fully fallen. Thankfully, the cloudless sky sparkled with countless stars, illuminating the grass. Still, he was glad the dragons had excellent night vision and that they were so close to the mountain already he couldn't get lost.

Soon they arrived at the mountain's base. Ryon squinted, scanning the rocky outcroppings in the near dark. It was no use. He needed light. He opened his mouth, ready to insist they light a torch, when he finally spotted something familiar.

He kicked Ari's side, nudging him to follow the curve of the mountain.

"Where are we going?" Nox craned his neck and eyed the steep rocky cliffside dubiously. "Is there some secret way to climb this? Because I have to tell you, it looks impossible from where I'm sitting."

"It's only impossible if you don't know where to start." He waved an arm, urging the others to follow. "Come on. We're almost there." They rounded the base of the mountain for so long he counted four separate yawns from his companions. But finally, he called for a stop.

Nox patted Gwen's neck, and a moment later, the dragons sank to the ground, allowing their riders to slide off. Ryon gulped as Ari practically collapsed beneath him. His boots thumped onto the rocky grass. He rounded Ari's side and spared the exhausted beast a sympathetic glance in time to see his massive eyelids snap closed and his head fall on his forelegs.

Good thing they'd made it when they had.

"Are you sure we're in the right spot?" Mariun asked. Violet halted beside her and joined her staring up at the mountain.

It was an imposing sight. The cliff was so steep it was perfectly vertical in dozens of spots all the way up. From below, it was impossible to see anything of the village hidden in the clouds above. Even on a clear night like tonight, a few fluffy layers clung to the mountaintop, perpetually ringing the mount like the halo of seeds on a dandelion.

"Yeah. This is it." Ryon frowned. He'd been sure Quill would come through. That the priests would come to their aid. But it looked like he might be climbing after all.

Ryon began stretching his sore muscles. He was normally well rested when he made this climb—during the day. His skin prickled with gooseflesh as he considered climbing by feel in the dark. But surely if anyone could do it, it was him. They didn't have any time to lose.

"What are you doing?" Violet dropped her gaze from the mountain and faced him.

"Stretching." Ryon couldn't see her roll her eyes in the dim moonlight, but he was nearly certain she had.

She tapped her foot repeatedly. "Why?"

"There's a lift at the top. We use it when hunting parties take down a tritusk. I'm going to climb up and let it down so we can haul the dragons up."

"Now?" Mariun gasped. "Are you crazy? Wait until the morning, at least."

"No time. Not if we want to be up there and out of sight before our masked friends catch up to us." Ryon sighed. "It takes nearly an hour to send the lift up and back down. And it's not very big. We'll need to take four trips, one for each dragon."

Nox paced to the cliffside and touched the dark red-orange stone dappled with sporadic spots of off-white stains. He pulled his hand away quickly and stared at it. "How are you even supposed to climb with this gunk covering everything?"

"What is it?" Violet asked curiously.

"Guano," Ryon replied.

"Huh?" Mariun whipped her head around behind them. "Is there trouble?"

Ryon shook his head and chuckled. "We have a habit in my village of using that word like a curse. This is what it really is—bat droppings."

Violet lurched back a few paces and smoothed her hair while Nox frantically wiped his hand on his trouser leg. Ryon bit back a laugh.

Only Mariun remained confused. "Bat? What's a bat?"

"Nasty little flying vermin," Violet said. "A few made a home in our barn one year. They made such a mess."

"They're not so bad. I wouldn't be able to make this climb without them." Ryon dropped one elbow and grabbed the other, his upper arm aching as the muscles stretched.

"Why not?" Nox asked. "Their guano makes your hands stick better or something?"

"Not quite. There are caves all along this section of the mountain. Over the centuries, the bats have made countless holes in and out. There are a few spots above where they're the only available handholds."

Violet grabbed his shoulder as Ryon finished stretching his arms. "I don't like this. Mariun's right. You shouldn't be climbing in the dark."

Ryon turned to her, and careful to not apply too much pressure, he pulled her into a gentle hug. He ought to leave her alone, but the tremble in her voice had him reaching for her before he could talk himself out of it.

"I'll be fine." He pulled back so he could gaze at her beautiful face in the moonlight. "I always used to joke with Ma that I've made this climb so much I could do it blindfolded. Remember what I told you about the silver? It was here. I climbed down to hunt for it before every full moon."

Violet's nose crinkled. "I don't want you to get hurt." She stared at the mountain. "What happens if you fall?"

Ryon's heart pounded, but he refused to show a single shred of the fear trickling through his veins. "I won't."

He retracted his arms and stepped aside, then marched over to his first handhold. "Don't worry." He raised his voice. "And don't be alarmed when an empty lift comes down after me. It should be able to fit one of you and one dragon inside at a time. I'll have to stay there to work the ropes at the top. Tug on the rope five times when you're loaded."

"Good luck," Nox called.

"Be safe," Mariun added.

Ryon turned back to Violet, who stood silently with her arms crossed. "Don't worry. I don't need luck."

With that, he began the climb. His body quickly fell into a rhythm born of repetition. The fear chilling his veins evaporated, and even though his tired muscles complained, with every step upward, his soul rejoiced.

Home. He was finally going home.

Ryon's hands and feet moved almost without conscious thought. His entire world narrowed down to the climb. The darkness did little to slow him. He reached for each new grip automatically, knowing by heart where it would be. And here, at least, he found a reason to be thankful for his wish. The strength he'd been granted allowed him to climb faster than ever.

Suddenly, a shout from below broke his trance-like state. Holding tightly to the cliff wall, Ryon paused and listened carefully.

Nox's voice pierced his ears, drenched in panic. "Ryon! Look out!"

Downright Disrespectful

"Ryon!" Nox's stomach lurched as he watched the huge contraption slide down the mountain. With his advanced night vision, he was likely the only one at the mountain's base who spotted it. The massive lift was just moments away from whacking Ryon down the steep slope.

Violet clutched Nox's arm, confirming his guess a heartbeat later. "What's happening?" she demanded.

"The lift. It's headed right for him." He fought to keep the panic out of his tone as Ryon continued upward, oblivious. He hadn't exaggerated his climbing skills in the least. He was already high enough that a fall would likely cripple him, if not kill him outright. "Ryon! Look out!" He swallowed and yelled again. "Look out for the lift!"

He heard, finally. Ryon clung to the cliffside, his head whipping all around.

"What's he doing?" Violet's voice squeaked. "Is he climbing back down? Will he make it?"

"I-I..." Nox stalled for time, not sure how to tell her Ryon wasn't climbing down. He'd stopped moving except for his head, which bobbed slightly, tracking the massive lift as it descended.

He wasn't the only one who had spotted Ryon's predicament after all. Gwen chattered at Flint, their voices echoing in the back of his mind. Nox fought to ignore them, along with Violet's increasingly intense questioning.

Rot and decay! If Ryon didn't start climbing, he'd be squashed. Why wasn't he moving?

Nox's gut plummeted, and he lurched toward the mountain, even though he didn't have any chance of reaching Ryon in time. But he couldn't just stand there and do nothing.

Before he reached the cliff wall, Ryon finally moved. He leaped for the lift just before it smashed into his head.

Nox gasped as the lift swung violently. Ryon grabbed something beneath it and hung on while the platform rocked. After a moment, the swaying settled, and the contraption continued to descend with Ryon dangling from the bottom.

"He's all right." Nox backed away, relief rushing through him. "He caught a ride."

"What?" Violet asked.

"You'll see." Nox's speeding pulse slowed by the time the lift approached the bottom. Ryon jumped off and rolled out of the way before the lift smashed into the ground.

"Looks like Quill found the priests after—oof." Ryon's delighted statement cut off when Violet launched herself at his chest. "Hey." He tentatively patted her back as she clung to him. "I'm fine."

"*You humans sure are affectionate.*" Gwen giggled. "*Shouldn't we be moving?*"

Nox cleared his throat loudly and moved closer to the lift. "Who's first?"

Violet jerked out of Ryon's arms. "We better send up Mena first. We have to make sure she gets to Mother Orea."

Ryon frowned. "You should go with her, too."

"Me?" Violet shook her head. "I can't talk to your priests. You need to be the first one up."

Nox could practically see the argument on the tip of Ryon's tongue. But they couldn't afford to stand there squabbling. "Vi's right. I'll make sure she's on the next lift." He hooked Ryon's elbow and pushed him toward the lift. "You were already headed up first. Time to finish what you started."

"Tell Mena to hop in there. She's going up first."

Gwen nodded and turned to her sister. Mena stepped closer to the lift, only to halt a few steps away.

"What's the holdup?" Nox asked.

"She's scared," Gwen replied quietly. *"Are you sure that thing's safe?"*

Ryon circled Mena and approached the lift. "Let me show you how to open the basket. You planning to head up last, then?"

Of course he was. He refused to leave Violet or Mariun by themselves. "Yeah. Gwen and I will go last."

Nox peered around Ryon's shoulder. Ryon leaned over the tall side and unlatched three locks holding the enormous box's wide railing in place. With a grunt, he tugged the railing away from the box. The opening was large enough that the hatchlings would have little trouble squeezing through, though there was clearly only room to lift one at a time.

Nox shuffled closer to Ryon and whispered, "You're positive this will hold them?"

"I've seen it lift three stacked tritusk carcasses at once." Ryon rubbed the railing. "It'll hold."

"Tell Mena she's safe. This thing lifts those beasts on the plains. Surely they're as heavy as you."

"Excuse me?" Gwen's voice took on an offended lilt. *"You think we're as heavy as those scruffy land beasts? I hope not or we'll never learn to fly."*

"Then it ought to be even more of a non-issue." Nox buried the urge to chuckle. *"Come on. The longer it takes to get started, the longer the rest of us are stuck here like sitting sparlings."*

Gwen went silent, and then Mena finally strode forward. Ryon followed her inside, dragging the gate with him and re-latching it. "Make sure you secure the railing." Then he hopped onto Mena's back and tugged the rope dangling inside the caged lift. "Five pulls signal whoever is at the top to haul the lift up. Don't give the signal until you're ready."

A few moments after his last tug vibrated the rope, the lift hoisted into the air. Violet waved, her voice full of false cheer. "See you soon, Ryon. Mena. Stay safe."

The basket creaked something awful, but it ascended swiftly. Soon Violet and Mariun resorted to squinting while trying to track the basket's upward movement in the dark. Nox watched easily until the lift disappeared within the lowest clouds.

Nox swallowed, forcing down a lump in his throat. He had no reason to distrust Ryon. At every turn, he'd been there to help them, though he was little more than a stranger. Still, they knew next to nothing about his people. Only what Ryon had told them...

"Don't look so worried. Your hairy friend will send the lift back for us," Gwen insisted.

Nox shrugged. "*You're likely right. But I've been fooled before. Better to be prepared for anything.*"

"*Gwen's right,*" Flint chimed in. "*He's clearly smitten with Violet.*"

"*Not Squirt. She's too young for him.*" Nox blinked furiously, staring at his niece and remembering her distress when Ryon had been in danger. And he'd have to be an idiot to miss how protective Ryon was of her. Sure, he'd spotted the stolen glances... but he'd dismissed it as a passing infatuation brought on from proximity.

Gwen snorted and shook her head. "*Is she? Then you might want to tell her to stop kissing him.*"

"*What?*" Nox tugged on the back of his neck. "*When did they even have the time?*"

"*Back on the boat,*" Gwen answered.

"*Pretty sure you were busy cuddling Mariun.*" Flint snickered.

Nox wasn't sure how to feel about that revelation. Shocked, certainly. Insulted, even. He and Mariun were recuperating from nearly dying, and Ryon was moving in on his niece while his back was turned. It was downright disrespectful.

Gwen cocked her head toward Mariun. "*Are all humans so fond of coupling up? Or is this unusual?*"

"*Not all...*" Flint began explaining. Nox rubbed his temple, tuning out the rest of their conversation. He stalked over to Violet instead.

"Can I talk to you, Vi?"

Violet turned to him, abandoning her attempt to squint at the mountain's peak. "Sure. What is it?"

Nox tugged her away from Mariun and lowered his voice. "What's going on with you and Ryon?"

Violet bristled. "I-I'm not sure what you're asking."

"Gwen said she saw you two kissing."

Violet crossed her arms and glared at the hatchlings before spinning back to him. "So?"

"So?" Nox gritted his teeth. "You just met."

"You mean like how *you* just met *Mariun*?" Violet hissed. "Don't act like it isn't exactly the same."

"He's too old for you."

Violet cocked a brow and raised her voice. "Hey, Mariun, how old are you?"

Nox's stomach dropped. He'd never asked her for the exact number, but he had a feeling Mariun was a good deal younger than him.

"I'm twenty-seven," Mariun called back. Nox winced. That was a six-year age gap. He imagined it was larger with Violet and Ryon, but not by much.

"Thanks!" Violet replied loudly over her shoulder before lowering her voice again. "Well, isn't that interesting?" She jabbed a finger at his chest. "I'm on this journey, just like you. I've met someone I like, just like you. And guess what, he's older than me... just... like... you." She punctuated her last words with another set of jabs.

Nox backed away, rubbing his chest. "I guess you have a point."

Violet smiled triumphantly.

"Look, I—You're my kid niece. I don't want to see you get hurt."

Her expression softened. "I appreciate that. I really do. But I'm not a kid anymore. And you don't need to worry about me and Ryon. He won't hurt me." She sighed. "I swear I must be doomed to repeat this conversation."

"What are you talking about?"

Violet scrunched her nose. "He wished for increased strength to save Mena from drowning. Remember?"

Nox stared at his hand. "Yeah. That's why he nearly crushed me when I was helping him back into the boat."

With everything that had happened immediately after, he hadn't given the strange event much thought. In hindsight, it made perfect sense. If the hatchlings were struggling to hold their sibling, there's no way an average man would make a difference. Once again, Ryon had proved with his actions he could be trusted.

And here he was, immediately thinking the worst of him. Nox felt like something had crawled into his gut and died.

"Now he's afraid he'll hurt me." Violet shook her head and sniffled. "You saw what happened when he was almost crushed. He would barely hug me back afterward. Ryon won't let himself get close to me again. You have nothing to worry about."

Nox's heart twinged at the hint of sadness in her voice. Clearly he'd misjudged the situation—badly. "Vi, I'm sorry. I didn't—"

"The lift's coming back," Mariun yelled.

"Forget it." Violet squeezed his forearm. "It's fine. I'm next." She started walking away. "C'mon. You need to help me into the lift."

Nox followed her slowly. Tension curled through the air like smoke, making his lungs ache. He'd just made everything worse.

"*Who's next?*" Gwen asked, drawing him from his thoughts. "*Should we send Ari or Crys with the little one?*"

Nox rolled his eyes. For someone who was so adamant about not being called by a color, she sure didn't mind calling all of them something strange. "*Violet can head up with Ari.*"

Gwen turned to her blue-scaled brother. He perked up and slowly lumbered up from where he'd been dozing. "*He's ready,*" she announced. She tilted her head. "*Mena says it's lovely up there.*"

"*You can still hear her? Even from so far away?*" Nox gazed at the cloud-shrouded mountaintop.

"*Yes.*"

Hm. He filed that fact away. It might come in handy in the future.

Ari had time to stretch before the lift finally settled. Nox jumped forward, unlatching the side and dragging the heavy railing out.

"Wait." Violet lifted a hand, stopping Ari from barreling inside. She grabbed something off the floor. "Here." She tossed a full waterskin at Nox's chest.

He caught it and drank gratefully. He sucked down a few more gulps when Violet bent again and sent a second skin sailing toward Mariun, then lifted a third for herself.

"*You planning to share?*" Gwen asked.

Nox dumped the rest of his skin into Gwen's mouth. The others followed suit, Violet sharing with Ari, and Mariun with Crys.

Nox collected the empty skins and stuffed them in his pack. "You ready, Vi?"

Violet stepped aside, ushering Ari into the lift. "Yes. See you up there."

Nox shoved the side closed and latched it. Violet grabbed the rope and tugged the way Ryon had shown them. The lift took off, ascending with an ear-splitting *creak* that made his stomach tense. He stood for a long while, watching as the lift disappeared into the night's dark clouds.

A soft touch on his arm made him flinch.

"Hey. You all right?" Mariun asked.

"Fine." Nox stared at her hand on his sleeve until her fingers lifted and tangled nervously in her long black hair.

"What about Violet? She seemed a bit subdued after your little chat."

Nox sighed wearily. "I should've kept my mouth shut."

"That's usually wise where you're concerned." She chuckled lightly and shifted closer. "Nothing serious, I hope?"

"No." He frowned. "Did you know about Vi and Ryon?"

"You mean that they like each other?" Mariun lifted one shoulder and sent him a crooked smile. "It was pretty obvious."

Nox's frown deepened. "I tried to warn her away from him. Said he was too old for her."

Mariun's laughter tinkled through the air. "Let me guess. That's when she asked my age."

"Yep." He spun to face her and spotted her flashing a knowing grin. Guess Violet wasn't the only one whose feelings were obvious.

"For what it's worth, I don't think you need to worry about Ryon. He's always so sweet and gentle. He won't hurt her." Mariun stared back at him, her big gray eyes and delicate features bathed in moonlight.

Nox's heart pounded. Why did she have to be so rotting beautiful? He wanted nothing more than to taste her lips again. But did he deserve to when he couldn't promise her the same thing?

"I won't be gentle and sweet." And like the hypocrite he'd proven himself to be, he reached out, brushing a silky strand of hair behind Mariun's ear so softly she shivered. "I'll hurt you." He trailed his fingers down her neck. Across the delicate column that once bore bruises from his hands. That same soft skin he was dying to mark with his mouth. "I won't be able to stop myself."

Back away. He begged her with his gaze. But the stubborn little fool stepped closer and cupped his cheek.

She cocked a brow. "Is this your way of warning me away from you?" she whispered. "Stop trying to scare me. I could drop you right now if I wanted to."

Nox gulped, the ghostly memory of that awful shock reverberating through his veins. Mariun traced his face softly, her touch so soothing he leaned into it subconsciously.

"I'm only speaking the truth." A voice in the back of his mind demanded he pull away, but he didn't listen. His hand kept moving, dragging down her neck and skimming the tempting valley between her breasts. His nails caught on her tunic, and his fingers itched to rip the fabric away. He looked straight into her eyes. "I'm more animal than man."

She scoffed and planted her palms on his shoulders. "You don't feel like an animal to me." She slowly traced his chest. Tingles sprouted everywhere her teasing touch lingered. The air crackled between them, and blood sped through his veins like molten fire.

"Stop."

"Why should I?" she asked breathlessly.

Nox clenched his teeth, fighting to keep his voice steady. "Because I won't." He gripped her waist and hauled her closer. "I won't stop until you're screaming." He bent beside her ear as her hands stilled their exploration. "Is that what you want?"

He leaned back, waiting for her answer. His gaze locked on her lips as heartbeats ticked past.

"I-I..." She licked her lips.

"*Um... sorry—*"

"*Not now,*" he barked.

"*But the lift is here,*" Gwen finished.

"*Already?*" He stepped away from Mariun just as the lift slammed down beside them. "*I thought Ryon said it would take longer.*"

"*Mena and Ari are up there helping.*"

"Nox, wait," Mariun said.

"Your turn," Nox insisted as he hurried to the lift. "We can talk about this later."

Or never. His stomach churned as he admitted the truth. Mariun didn't want him. Not really. She wouldn't have hesitated so long if she did. He'd tried to scare her away, and he'd succeeded.

Probably for the best. He would only disappoint her in the end. Or end up going mad one day and leave her like everyone else who'd disappeared from her life. She deserved someone like Ryon, who would be gentle with her battered heart.

It's better this way. Maybe if he told himself enough times, he'd start to believe it.

Cloistered

Violet held tight to Ari's neck as they ascended into the clouds. The lift shuddered, jerking upward swiftly but not smoothly enough to keep her stomach from lurching. After a wave of vertigo had slammed into her, she'd stopped looking down. Violet craned her neck up instead. While standing at the mountain's base, the rust-red peak appeared to go on forever. Now, if she squinted, she could almost see the top. What would they find up there? Who would be there to greet them?

Her belly wobbled more furiously the longer she lingered over the question. Sure, Ryon was amazing, but would the rest of his people be so welcoming? It was clear they led a sheltered existence on this mountaintop. They might not be happy to admit strangers into their midst.

More than that, they were practically fugitives. How would his people react when they learned they'd been driven there out of desperation? That the men hunting them were certain to follow them inland?

Ryon had been so insistent that they'd be safe... but would they really? Her gaze trailed across the steep rock wall. It seemed nearly impossible to scale this mountainside. The longer they ascended, the more it baffled her that Ryon had managed it. But if he *could* climb it, then what was to say the masked couldn't as well?

Violet saw the summit clearly now. Bobbing lights flickered along the edge, enough that she suspected the help Ryon asked for had arrived in force. As the lift jerked up the remaining length, she drew in a deep breath and shoved her apprehension aside.

A group of men rushed forward as the lift cleared the cliffside. A few not holding torches grabbed the contraption, tugging it forward. The heavy box settled on the clifftop with a mighty *thump*. Violet scanned the strangers, her heart twinging when she didn't spot Ryon among them.

"Violet." Ryon's voice made her twist so quickly she nearly tumbled off Ari's back. Ryon left the trio of robed men he'd been chatting with, half-hidden behind Mena's big body. He jogged toward the lift, reaching it as the men tugged the gate open and Ari barreled out onto the mountaintop.

Ari tore off directly for his sister and didn't stop until he was close enough to rub hides with her. Ryon flashed a bemused grin, and after a few soft words for the men hovering around the lift, he turned and hurried to her side again.

Violet struggled to slide off Ari's back. The hatchling seemed to have forgotten to crouch down to let her off in his eagerness to reunite with his sister.

"Here." Ryon held out his arms. "Let me help you."

"Thanks." Violet reached for him, and with a gulp, she leaped. Ryon caught her easily, and their gazes collided as he slowly lowered her. Tingles lit her skin where his fingers gently gripped her waist.

"You all right?" he asked quietly, making no move to release her even after her boots were firmly on the ground.

She nodded, unable to tear her eyes away from his. She'd been so sure he wouldn't touch her again. Now that he was, she didn't want him to let go. "I-I'm fine." Somewhere behind them, a throat cleared loudly, breaking the spell. Violet unlocked her arms from Ryon's neck and backed up a pace, her cheeks warming.

The trio of men approached, their faces lit by delicate oil lamps the two in the back carried. The one in the lead began speaking. Of course, she had no idea what he was saying. But while he chattered on, Violet took a moment to study them.

All three wore long black robes trimmed with silver and gold stitching. Their long black hair shone in the lamplight, the strands brushed silky smooth and decorated with feathers and shimmering gems. The two in the back were young, likely around her age. They stood silently behind the leader as he chattered, darting quick glances at the dragons and then back at her.

The leader appeared to be a few decades older. A smattering of gray dotted the hair above his temples, and faint wrinkles lined his face. He finally fell silent and turned from Ryon to her. He met her eyes with a kindly smile, then crossed his arms with closed fists pressed against his shoulders and bowed his head slowly.

Ryon nudged her with his elbow. "That's a greeting of respect here. You should do it, too."

Violet mimicked the man, crossing her arms and bowing. When she looked up from dipping her head, the man beamed at her like she'd hung the moon.

"Who is this?" she asked Ryon.

"These are priests from the Aviary. Violet"—he held out a hand to the man grinning like a loon—"meet Brother Tham." He pointed to the first young man, this one slightly shorter and stouter than the other two—"Brother Lennam"—and the final man, who was the lankiest of the trio, with a long, hooked nose—"and Brother Pip."

"Hello. It's lovely to meet you all." Violet brushed off the urge to stick out her hand and bowed again to each of the younger men. When she finished, all three wore matching smiles. She smiled back, feeling slightly uncomfortable with the attention, but reassured by it at the same time. At least she didn't need to worry Ryon's people would throw them out of their village immediately now.

She tore her gaze off the grinning priests and glanced around. She'd been so caught up in the introductions that she hadn't inspected her surroundings yet. But now... nerves pulsed beneath her skin.

"I thought you said there was a village up here?" The clifftop was as barren and unwelcoming as she'd expect a clifftop to be. Rock stacked on more rock, with no sign of anything approaching a dwelling.

Ryon chuckled. "Don't worry. There is. It's just not near the lift."

"Oh." Violet's nose wrinkled. She spun around just as the dragons moved, heading for the men operating a complicated-looking system of cranks and levers. The basket was already gone, the creaking rattle of it descending once again loud in her ears but slowly dimming.

Brother Tham began chattering again, gesturing wildly to the dragons as they hovered beside the lift operators.

What could the hatchlings want? Were they as curious as she was about how the strange contraption worked? No. She watched them eyeing the men working and instinctively sensed what they were after.

Violet tugged on Ryon's sleeve. "I think they want to help."

Ryon spoke up, first to the priests, and then he darted closer to the lift and shared a few words with the men there. One of them nodded and kneeled, digging a long length of rope out of a sack and attaching it to the controls. He handed the other end to Ryon.

"Thanks." Ryon grinned and walked the other end over to Mena. She opened her jaw, light spilling out of her throat from the fire in her belly, and snapped down on the rope after Ryon dropped it.

With the dragon lending her strength to the men, the noisy cranking increased. From the smiles painting the men's faces, she assumed that whatever they'd done was helping.

"Smart thinking." Ryon returned to her side. "Mena wandered over there earlier, but I didn't think anything of it. With them helping, we ought to save some time."

Warmth pooled in Violet's chest. Finally, she'd contributed something. Even though it was only a small thing, not the lifesaving magic she'd hoped for, it felt nice to have helped. "It was nothing. I'm sure you'd have thought of it without the priests distracting you."

Even before her statement left her lips, the trio of robed men approached again. Ryon smiled wanly and turned back to listen to Brother Tham.

Violet took the opportunity to observe the men working the lift. They were dark-haired like the priests but dressed differently. Instead of robes, they sported plain tunics and knee-length skirts, much like the one Ryon preferred. She edged behind Ryon as she spotted one fellow leering at her legs.

Suddenly, the conversation heated. She might not understand what they said, but tension curled through the air, so thick it was tangible. The men volleyed back and forth, Brother Tham's posture and tone apologetic and Ryon's unmistakably irritated. Finally, Ryon dragged a hand through his dreads and stalked off in a huff.

Violet hurried after him and grabbed his arm. "Hey, what's wrong? What did he say?" Panic bled through her veins. What if he demanded Ryon send them back?

Ryon's gaze collided with hers, and his eyes widened. "Nothing dire, I swear." He leaned closer. "It's about Mother Orea. I wanted to take you and Mena there tonight, but the priests won't let me."

"Oh." Violet blew out a breath. "That's—I was sure they told us to leave."

Ryon's brow crinkled. "No, nothing like that. Couldn't you tell they were delighted to meet you?"

Violet speared him with a shrewd glare. "Why exactly would that be, hm?"

"We don't get a lot of visitors?" Ryon's answer sounded more like a question.

"You're a terrible liar." She punched his shoulder weakly. "What did you tell them about me?" She hadn't missed how he'd included her *and* Mena in his request to see his strange bird deity.

"I just said I wasn't sure who the *one* was Mother Orea needed to meet." He shrugged. "Although I still think it's you."

Her heart pounded. She refused to linger over that possibility. After all, Mena fit the riddle perfectly. "Why can't we see her now?"

Ryon's gaze darted to the priests. "They said Mother Orea demanded the Aviary be cloistered just before we arrived. No one in or out until the next full moon. The orecolns are holed up inside. They even made Quill go in once he'd reported our location to the priests."

Violet cocked a brow and scanned the moon. It was nearly half full tonight, so they'd be waiting for days. "Does that happen a lot?"

"A cloister? No. Practically never." Ryon shifted from foot to foot. "The last time they did, a new Mother Orea had just hatched."

"Do you think that's what happened now?" Violet's mind swam, recalling Ryon's explanation about how the orecolns' magical head bird was chosen. Once in every generation, a new Mother Orea hatched. "What if the new Mother Orea doesn't care about the riddle at all?"

Ryon grabbed her hand, giving it a gentle squeeze. "I honestly can't say. I don't even know if that's why they're cloistered. I tried to get Brother Tham to tell me more, but he wouldn't. I'm sorry."

"I guess we can always ask the old Mother Orea. She'll still be there, won't she?"

Ryon's face turned grave. "No. She won't. When a new Mother Orea hatches, the old one always dies within a few days." He exhaled a shaky breath. "If a new one hatched earlier tonight…"

His voice trailed off, and Violet's stomach churned. "We need to get in there. Can't they make an exception?"

"I'll ask again, but I don't think it will be any use. The priests are as stubborn as they come when it involves a direct command from Mother Orea. I doubt we'll convince them to budge."

Violet stared at her feet as Ryon wandered back to chat with Brother Tham. A sinking sensation spread through her chest. If they traveled all the way here, just in time for the enigmatic creature who'd summoned them to die, then she might go mad. It hadn't seemed so dire before—with all the chaos of finding her aunt and then recovering the eggs—but now, the question of what exactly Mother Orea wanted with them burned in her mind like the hottest of coals.

She stood there, lost in thought, until the lift returned. Mariun slid off Crys' back as soon as the hatchling allowed it and wandered over to her side, looking a little green.

"Are you all right?" Violet asked.

Mariun clutched her stomach. "Yeah. Just didn't expect that lift to be so jerky."

Ryon excused himself from his conversation and strode over to join them, but detoured before reaching them. His gaze slid over the rocky soil, and he ambled around in a loose circle. Violet opened her mouth to ask him what he was searching for, then closed it when he bent and plucked a small green-and-white weed out of a patch of soil.

He jogged over and offered it to Mariun. "This is beeweed. If you chew the leaves, it will settle your stomach."

Mariun took it with a soft, "Thank you."

That was incredibly thoughtful. Warmth spread through Violet's chest as she turned to Ryon. "Any luck?" She nodded at Brother Tham.

Ryon sighed. "No. I'm afraid not."

"What's going on?" Mariun stuffed a few leaves into her mouth and grimaced, chewing carefully.

Violet filled Mariun in on the situation. By the time she'd finished, Mariun's skin appeared normal again, and she'd released her tight grip around her belly. Then the brothers popped over, and Ryon made introductions. Once they'd finished, the rattle of chains was already increasing, signaling Nox and Gwen's arrival.

Violet hurried to the lift as it settled on the mountaintop. "Uncle Nox." She grinned. "No trouble down below?"

He shook his head. "No sign of anyone."

Ryon arrived at her side. "If the masked are traveling on foot, they won't make it to the mountain until morning at the earliest. Maybe even longer. I bet they'll have trouble tracking us since we went through that herd instead of around it."

Violet's spirits lifted. "I hadn't even considered that." As much as she didn't want to wait, it appeared they had little choice but to spend a few days here. It would certainly be nice not to spend it all worried the masked would scale the mountain and confront them.

The priests approached with Mariun in tow. Nox gave the brothers a cool appraisal from his perch on Gwen's back. "Who are they?"

Ryon made another round of introductions. Then Brother Tham motioned for them to follow. Nox hopped off of Gwen's back to round up the hatchlings, and they all followed the priests away from the cliff's edge.

"Where are they leading us?" Violet asked. "Back to your village?"

Ryon shook his head. "The dragons would cause an uproar if we brought them to Avion. They can stay at the Aviary. Well, not inside, but on the grounds. Word will likely reach the village about them eventually, but no one would dare to intrude while Mother Orea's called for a cloister."

Nox scratched his head. "Cloister?" Violet quickly filled him in. Once she had, he nodded and said, "The hatchlings will work on learning to fly while we wait to meet with your Mother Orea." He frowned at Ryon. "But what of the masked? We can't just forget about them."

"I already told Brother Tham about our *company*," Ryon explained. "He's arranging a watch, both to ensure no one ventures down below and to keep an eye out for the masked's arrival. He promised to tell me immediately if anything changes."

"I suppose that ought to do, for now." Nox's shoulders sank.

Exhaustion tinged his words, and the same weariness weighed down Violet's bones. It had to be halfway until morning by now. The priests must have somewhere for them to sleep. Perhaps even a proper bed. A tiny smile curved her lips as she allowed her mind to linger on the notion. She could almost feel the soft sheets caressing her skin.

Rocks crunched under her boots, and her breaths came hard and fast. The longer they trekked, the more it wore on her until her head pounded with every step she took. She glanced at her companions and spotted Nox and Mariun flagging, but not Ryon. "Is it just me, or is it harder to breathe?"

"It's the elevation," Ryon said. "You'll get used to it."

"It doesn't seem to be bothering you." Mariun rubbed her temples.

Ryon lifted a shoulder. "I can definitely feel the difference, but I guess my body's adjusted to it from living up here."

Nox shared a look with Gwen, and then Crys drew closer. "Stop for a moment."

"Why?" Mariun asked warily.

"So I can feed you to Crys," Nox said dryly. He grabbed Mariun's arm, tugged her against his side, and slung his other arm around Violet's shoulders. "Just breathe."

Crys stopped in front of them and snapped open his jaw. Tingles spread across Violet's skin as a cool gust of air wrapped around her face. She inhaled deeply, and the tightness in her lungs instantly lessened. After several deep breaths, even the ache in her head dimmed.

"Thanks, Crys." She grinned at her uncle. "You too, Uncle Nox. I feel much better."

Brother Tham and the other priests chattered excitedly, halting to watch. But before long, Brother Tham began waving his arms again, clearly wanting them to follow.

"We better go." Nox squeezed Violet's shoulder. "I'll have Crys conjure us more air when we arrive where we're going."

"It's not far now." Ryon pointed to a large mound ahead. "Once we circle those rocks, we'll be able to see the Aviary."

Violet hurried after the priests, feeling reinvigorated. She wasn't sure whether it was the burst of air or the promise of an end to the trek, but either way, her feet practically flew around the mound.

She bit back a gasp as she spotted the Aviary. Even lit solely by moonlight, it was an impressive sight. The circular structure rose high into the sky, towering over the one-story brick building beside it. As she gazed upon it, goosebumps erupted across her arms. She couldn't quite put her finger on why, but the sight of the building lit a fuse of energy within her soul.

Violet forced her gaze away from the Aviary to examine the surrounding grounds. Beyond the rocky crags they'd traversed rested a hill-covered plateau rich with grass and dotted with tiny flowers. It was such a strange sight to find atop a mountain; she had the urge to rub her eyes to make sure it wasn't a figment of her imagination.

Beyond the two buildings, lights winked in the sky, but though Violet squinted, she couldn't make out their source. Was that Avion? She shoved the question aside. She'd worry about visiting the village after she got some sleep.

If not for the Aviary dwarfing it, Violet would've been impressed with the size of the building perched beside it. She guessed it covered as much ground as Kayda's castle, Kings Keep. She expected the priests to lead them there, but they set off toward a dilapidated old barn on the plateau's far corner.

When Brother Tham threw open the doors, Violet wrinkled her nose. "Is this where the dragons will stay?" She paced inside and slid a disdainful glance over the dusty interior. Her nose itched. "It could definitely use a thorough cleaning." She sneezed.

Ryon sighed. "Actually, we'll all need to stay here. For tonight, at least."

Mariun crossed her arms. "Why can't we stay in that big castle out there?"

"That's where the priests live. Outsiders aren't allowed inside." Ryon shrugged. "Unless you want to dedicate your life to serving Mother Orea as a priest…"

"Yeah, no thanks." Nox waved the hatchlings inside. "I'd rather stay with the dragons."

Bowing, Ryon grabbed the oil lamp Brother Lennam handed to him. "Tomorrow we can walk into the village. We'll arrange some better accommodations. But for now, this is the best we're going to get."

Violet sneezed again. "We'll make it work." Exhaustion creeped up on her, so much that even the old piles of hay shoved inside the rows of stalls looked welcoming. It might not be the bed she'd been hoping for, but it would do.

As the priests said their goodbyes and swung the door closed, Violet sighed. They were safe—for the moment, at least—and everything would look brighter in the morning. But though the thought should've comforted her, something in her mind wouldn't quiet. A strange sense of urgency spooled in her chest, bothering her even more than the tickle in her throat or the tightness in her lungs.

"You all right?" Ryon asked.

Violet shook off the feeling and sent him a weary grin. "Yeah. I just need to rest."

Nox threw open the big barn doors. "Here, this ought to help." The hatchlings had gathered at the back of the barn. Crys stood at the front of the pack, and each hatchling touched him. Gwen tangled her tail with his. Ari rested the tip of a wing on his shoulder. And Mena leaned against his flank, her eyes closed.

Crys opened his jaw again. Violet's skin prickled all over as he aimed a blast of air at the floor. Dust and little bits of debris shot into the air, making her shut her eyes and cover her face. The rush of air sped through the barn and out the doors. After a few heartbeats, the harsh stream subsided. Violet cracked open an eye as Nox shut the door again. Crys kept summoning, but the air swirling around the barn was much gentler now. Her head and lungs rejoiced as the cool air filled her lungs.

"There," Nox announced. The dragons broke apart and Crys' jaw snapped shut. "Better?"

Violet sniffed, smiling when she didn't feel the urge to sneeze. "Much better."

Mariun moved closer to where Nox stood, parting her lips.

"Goodnight." Nox stalked off to the back of the barn, slamming a stall door.

"What's gotten into him?" Ryon asked.

Mariun stiffened. "I'm going to lie down, too. Goodnight."

Violet watched her walk into another stall before she turned to Ryon with a shrug. "I guess we should sleep." She met his eyes briefly before looking away shyly. "Goodnight, Ryon."

"Violet." Ryon's voice cracked around her name. She glanced up, quirking a brow. He looked like he wanted to say more, but his gaze darted to the back of the barn and he sighed. "Goodnight."

Violet wandered into a stall and sank into a pile of dry hay. A million worries bombarded her as she lay down, so many she was sure it would take her ages to fall asleep. But as the lamplight slowly faded away to nothing, sleep chased her racing thoughts away.

The Tour

Ryon stretched, a loud *creak* waking him just before light spilled across his eyelids. Hay crunched as he stood and gazed around the old barn.

"Good morning." Brother Tham shuffled inside. His arms were laden, a huge bundle of clothes stacked nearly to his chin.

Brothers Lennam and Pip followed closely behind him. Each was likewise burdened, but instead of clothes, they carried food and drink.

Brother Pip huffed, and Ryon nearly laughed, wondering why the scrawniest youngster was chosen to cart the heaviest load. He dropped a massive pitcher of what was likely wine on a wooden bench beside the door, setting a stack of cups beside it. Brother Lennam plunked a covered basket next to it.

Though Ryon couldn't yet see what lay inside, a delectable aroma wafted toward him. Stomach rumbling, he shoved open the stall door and wandered over to meet the priests. "Good morning. Is that"—Ryon sniffed, closing his eyes briefly—"tritusk sausage I smell?"

"Indeed," Brother Tham answered with a grin. He plopped the pile of clothes beside it. "We've brought food, drink, and fresh clothes for you and your companions. I'm sure your friends will be grateful to rid themselves of their traveling attire before they venture into the village."

Violet emerged, covering a yawn. Ryon didn't miss the quick glances the brothers shot at her trouser-clad legs.

"Thank you, Brother Tham," Ryon replied. "I'm sure you're right."

"Good morning." Violet stopped in front of Brother Tham, bowing to him and the brothers, making all three beam, and a blush spread across her cheeks. "Is that breakfast for us? I'm starving."

Ryon chuckled, walking over to the basket. "Me too. Let me grab you something."

"Thanks." Violet ducked her head, then shot a glance backward as another stall door jerked open.

"Morning already?" Nox grumbled.

Mariun wasn't far behind him. She excused herself to the outhouse while Nox strode over to check on the dragons.

"I suppose I better save some sausage for the hatchlings," Ryon mused as he dug through the basket. He set four cloth napkins on the bench, then began doling out a portion of food atop each, leaving most of the meat in the basket for the hatchlings. "Luckily, Brother Tham brought enough to feed a small army."

"Or a quartet of dragons," Violet quipped, appearing at his elbow. Brother Pip busied himself pouring the jug, which Ryon was pleased to discover did hold wine.

Apparently, Violet wasn't so pleased. She wrinkled her nose after grabbing the cup Pip handed to her. "Wine? For breakfast?"

Ryon shrugged. "Why not?" They drank wine at practically every meal in his village. "It's a mild variety. Sweet and crisp. Give it a try. I think you'll like it."

Violet stared into the burgundy liquid dubiously, but after giving it a cautious sniff, she lifted it to her lips and sipped. "Oh. That's delightful."

"What's delightful?" Mariun strolled inside, hitching her skirts and eyeing the pile of clothes.

"The wine," Violet replied, taking another sip.

"Wine? What's that?" Mariun leaned close to the pitcher, her face lit with curiosity.

"You've never had wine before?" Violet asked.

"No. But if it's so delightful, then I'd like to try it." Mariun held her hand out to Brother Pip, who handed her a cup.

Ryon's heart twisted. The more he learned about Mariun, the more he cursed that villain who had kept her caged away from the world. It was so odd to learn such simple pleasures had been denied to her.

Nox returned, cocking a brow as he spotted what the girls were drinking. He shot a look at the brothers, then leaned close to Ryon. "Getting us drunk before breakfast? I thought these brothers of yours were pious?" Despite his reprimand, Nox accepted the cup Brother Pip offered and drank deep.

Ryon chuckled. "That they are. You'll have a hard time getting drunk on that blend. It's barely strong enough to be called wine." He finished doling out the food and grabbed the basket, handing it to Nox. "For the hatchlings."

With a crooked grin, Nox took it and strode to the back of the barn.

"He seems to be in much better spirits this morning." Violet watched her uncle as he set the basket on the floor and the hatchlings circled him.

"We'll see how he feels after I tell him the brothers brought him a clean skirt to wear." Ryon gestured to the clothes still folded neatly on the bench.

Violet waved a hand. "I doubt that will faze him. You should see what they wear in his village."

Mariun's gaze darted between the clothes and Nox. "What do they wear?"

Violet's smile turned mischievous. "Barely anything at all."

"You're kidding." Mariun's eyes bulged.

"'Fraid not. The jungles of Raimire are so hot and muggy it's torture wearing anything other than the luct fabric crafted in their villages. But the weave is so sheer, you can see right through it." Violet leaned over the bench and grabbed a small cube of cheese. "I've been to visit a time or two. It's quite comfortable, actually."

An image of Violet clad in see-through clothes rose to plague Ryon, and he choked on his wine.

"You all right?" Nox reappeared in time to slap him on the back.

"Yes. Fine," Ryon bit out as soon as he'd finished hacking. "Swallowed wrong."

Brother Tham cleared his throat. "I see you're settled for the moment. We shall take our leave. Please knock at the rectory if you need anything."

"Of course, brother. Thank you." Ryon collected himself enough to hand back the empty basket and bow before the brothers shuffled out of the barn doors.

They gathered around the benches and began to eat. Ryon bit into a sausage and smiled as the savory flavor hit his tongue. It was good to be home.

"So, what's the plan for today?" Violet asked.

Ryon swallowed. "I'm heading into the village to find somewhere more comfortable for us to stay tonight. Would you like to tag along? I can take you on a tour."

"That sounds lovely." Violet trailed her gaze over to Nox and Mariun. "Should we all go?"

Nox shook his head. "I'll pass. I need to stay with the hatchlings. Help them practice flying."

Mariun polished off her cup of wine, her cheeks rosy. "I think I'll hang back as well. I could use a day to rest."

That was understandable. Nox was the obvious choice to remain with the hatchlings. And Mariun must still be weary from their travels—not to mention practically dying.

Ryon's stomach fluttered. Now that he'd have a moment alone with Violet, he could tell her the whole story about Rovan. And maybe, if she didn't hate him afterward, he would take her home to meet Rovan and Ma.

He selected a hunk of brown bread, pairing it with a flaky cheese. "That's not a problem. Violet and I will come back later once we've made new arrangements for tonight." Ryon popped the morsel into his mouth and chewed.

Violet eyed the pile of clothing. "That was nice of the brothers to bring us fresh clothes. Do you want to choose first, Mariun?"

Mariun set down her cup and ambled over to the pile. She selected a dark-blue knee-length skirt from the top and lifted it to her waist. "What do you think?"

Oh no. The brothers would be scandalized the moment she stepped foot out of the barn... Ryon coughed. "Better pick one of the longer ones."

"Oh?" She smiled coyly and held it out to Nox. "I guess this one's for you."

Nox scowled at the fabric but snagged it anyway. "At least it's clean." He folded the skirt, tossed it over his shoulder, and continued eating.

Mariun dug through the pile, pulling out a floor-length burgundy skirt and a pale-pink tunic. "I think this will do."

Violet popped her last bite of bread into her mouth and joined Mariun hovering over the clothes. Ryon bent over his food, shoveling in another bite of sausage and a chunk of bread. Violet disappeared into a stall before he got a look at her selection.

"Did the brothers say anything about the masked while they were delivering breakfast?" Nox asked quietly as Violet's stall door slammed closed.

"No, but the watch will let us know as soon as they arrive."

Nox tilted his head toward Violet's stall. "I trust you'll keep her safe today."

Ryon met his eyes and buried the urge to shy away from his intense stare. "Of course."

Nox nodded curtly and wiped his hands on his trousers. Then he rose from the bench and snagged a few more clothes from the dwindling pile. Ryon gathered the discarded napkins and cups, tidying them before grabbing what was left and retiring to his stall to change.

He pulled on a light-brown tunic embroidered with golden feathers on the sleeves. The dark-brown-and-tan pinstriped skirt matched it nicely, though it was a little fancier than the plain skirts he favored. Still, the fresh cloth was smooth and free from tears and stains, which was more than he could say for the worn skirt he discarded.

Stall doors banged open and closed while he relaced his boots. The brothers had provided them with new socks and undergarments, but he was glad they'd not tried to pass along the leather moccasins the brothers preferred. With all the walking he'd be doing today, his well-worn boots would serve him well.

Ryon was the last to emerge from his stall. Nox hovered next to the dragons, seeming perfectly at ease in the new clothes. Mariun's skirt swished as she halted beside the wine jug and poured herself another glass. Violet's stall stood open, but she wasn't anywhere in sight.

Mariun must've noticed him staring at the empty stall. "She went out already."

"Thanks." Ryon strode through the barn doors. His breath hitched as he spotted Violet standing a few paces away. With a hand shading her brow from the dawn sun, she spun slowly, taking in the scenery. "You ready?"

Violet turned to him, a stunning smile lighting her face. The hem of her purple skirt dragged in the grass, and she tugged the lilac tunic's sleeves over her palms. "Definitely. Your village is so lovely. I can't wait to see it up close."

Ryon had to agree. From their vantage, with the sun shining on the brightly colored cabins, the village looked picturesque. Soon the market would come alive with hawkers, and folk would flock to the streets. But in the early morning calm, only a few people were about. They were still too far to pick out any individuals, but he spotted the occasional figure striding swiftly from one house to the next.

"Let's go, then." Ryon set off at a brisk pace toward the Aviary.

Violet cocked her head as they drew closer, her gaze flicking between the village and the orecolns' home. "Are the village and the Aviary on the same peak?"

"Good eye. No, they're not. But don't worry. A bridge joins the two mountaintops so we won't need to do any climbing."

"How did your people find this place?" Violet raised her hand again, scanning the Aviary closely as they strolled alongside it. "We couldn't see anything from down below."

"I'm not sure if anyone remembers clearly. But we've been here for generations. There are a few tales, all revolving around the orecolns seeking us out, though the details differ depending on who tells it."

"I'd love to hear a few—" Violet's eyes widened, and her steps halted at the same time as her request. "What is that?"

Ryon followed her outstretched finger with his gaze, and his stomach clenched. "Oh. That's one of the orecoln grooms." As they watched, a small boy of perhaps ten scaled the Aviary, a heavy belt dotted with leather pouches swaying across his waist. "They clean the orecolns' nests. It's a great honor to be chosen."

"But he's so high. Isn't that dangerous?"

"Yes." Ryon's mouth went dry. "I've been—"

"Ho, Ryon," Brother Tham called. Ryon whipped around and spotted the same trio of brothers approaching. "Are you two headed into the village?"

"Yes. We are," Ryon replied. "I'm giving Violet a tour and finding us somewhere with proper beds to rest tonight." He gulped, his words flying out in a rush. "Not that we don't appreciate the accommodations."

"It's all right, son." Brother Tham chuckled and waved a hand. "We're headed to the village as well. Would you mind if we joined you?"

"Not at all." Ryon smiled politely, cursing his luck. He turned to Violet. "The brothers are headed into town, too. They asked to join us."

"Oh. Sure." Violet's head bobbed as she bowed to each brother.

Ryon bit back a scowl. He'd been looking forward to having Violet all to himself. But perhaps they could still talk. The brothers didn't understand her language, after all.

"Shall we?" Brother Tham led the way, the younger brothers falling in on either side of him. Ryon sent Violet a lopsided smile and followed, keeping his pace slow enough that they ended up trailing a few paces behind.

"Anyway, like I was saying," he began, only to snap his mouth closed. Footsteps pounded from ahead, punctuated by the labored breathing of someone who'd run far and fast.

"Brother Tham," a voice squeaked, "I need your help!" A teenager jolted to a stop in front of the brothers, her wiry limbs shaking with exertion and her sweaty black hair plastered to the sides of her face.

Ryon shouldered past the brothers as recognition struck him. "Deanna? Is that you?" His stomach knotted, and he sensed he knew exactly what had driven his neighbor here.

"Ryon?" She bent at the waist, sucking in big gulps of air. "Good. You should come, too. Your Ma sent me for Brother Tham. Rovan is having one of his—episodes."

Violet caught up, peeking around Brother Lennam's shoulder. "Ryon? What's wrong?" Brother Tham thanked Deanna and set off immediately. Ryon's feet itched, demanding he follow. But he couldn't abandon Violet without an explanation.

He grabbed Violet's shoulder. "It's my family. Brother Tham and I need to help them."

Violet hitched up her skirts. "Okay. I'll come with you."

"No," he barked more forcefully than he'd intended. But the thought of Violet wandering in to meet Rovan blindly made his heart clench. "I can't take you on a tour now, but I promise I will after." He gestured to the barn. "Head back and wait for me? Please?"

"Are you telling her to return to the barn?" Brother Lennam spoke up. "Brother Pip and I are still walking through the village. We can accompany Violet in your stead."

It wasn't what he wanted. He'd been looking forward to showing Violet his home. Seeing the wonder in her eyes as she saw the market vendors for the first time. Pointing out the fish and waterfowl in the river they'd pass. But he hadn't been expecting this either.

Ryon turned to Violet. "Brothers Lennam and Pip said you can go into the village with them instead. I'm sorry, Violet. I'll be back as soon as I can."

He didn't wait for her reply. His feet began speeding away before the words had even left his lips. Then he faced forward and ran.

His family was in trouble, and he had to help them.

Flying Practice

Nox led the hatchlings behind the Aviary. The dragons loped along, playfully jostling each other as they traversed the grassy fields.

After talking with Gwen, they'd decided to head back to the mountainous terrain they'd hiked through last night, rather than practice within eyesight of the Aviary and the village beyond it. There'd be plenty of smaller rock formations for the hatchlings to climb and jump off of while attempting to fly, and less chance of some curious villagers arriving to gawk.

He only hoped that they'd manage the task quickly. Who knew how long it would be before the masked tracked them here? Sure, the mountain was daunting, but given enough time, they'd discover some way to scale it. He didn't want to be here when that happened. Much less to lead such violent men to the peaceful brothers who had taken them in.

If they flew away on the dragons, the masked would leave, too, wouldn't they?

"*Why do you look so glum?*" Gwen asked. "*It's a beautiful day and we're safe. You should try to enjoy it for once.*"

Nox bit back a scowl and tipped his head up to the sky. The sun shone on his cheeks, and a cool breeze drifted through his hair. The tightness in his lungs had vanished. Still, it was hard for him to live in the moment when so much uncertainty lay ahead. He sighed.

"*Something else bothering you? Or someone?*" Flint asked slyly.

Leave it to Flint to bring up the one person he was eager to ignore.

"*Oh, she definitely is,*" Gwen replied. "*You should have seen how much glowering he did last night after she got in that lift. I don't understand why you humans need to make things so complicated.*"

Nox rolled his eyes. "*She's the daughter of the man hunting us. Of course it's complicated.*"

Gwen snorted. "*But—*"

"*Just drop it. The only thing you ought to be worried about right now is learning to fly.*"

Gwen stared at him closely but let the subject rest. Nox rolled his shoulders back and pressed on. Soon the crunch of grass beneath his boots gave way to hard rock. Once they reached a small plateau littered with a handful of enormous stones, he halted.

"*There.*" He pointed to a rectangular outcropping that loomed just over Gwen's head. "*I bet that's high enough for starters.*"

Tilting her sinuous neck sideways, Gwen said, "*Looks easy enough to climb. I think it'll do.*"

"*Who's first?*" Nox leaned against a smaller rock and eyed the hatchlings curiously.

Hatchlings might not be an appropriate way to think of the dragons any longer. All four towered over him, well on their way to being the size of his hut in Raimire. Who knew they'd grow so quickly?

After a moment's pause, Ari scrambled atop the rock, sending a rain of small pebbles skittering down. He reached the top and sat there staring at all of them, hesitant.

"*Tell him to spread his wings and jump,*" Nox instructed. "*To glide.*"

Gwen cocked her head at her brother and shook out her wings. Ari blinked at her, then did the same. The other dragons backed away, all eyes lifted to their blue-scaled brother.

Finally, Ari leaped. Nox's breath caught. He wanted so badly to watch him gracefully glide on the breeze and land lightly on his feet. Instead, he choked down a laugh as Ari dropped like a stone and smacked into the ground so hard the earth trembled beneath his boots.

Of course it couldn't be that easy. Nothing in life ever was. Nox turned to Gwen with a grin. "*Who's next?*"

They practiced for hours. The dragons took turns climbing the stone and jumping. And every time they slammed down gracelessly, without a single glide in the mix. When the sun hung overhead at midday, Nox called it quits.

"*C'mon. Let's take a break and grab some lunch. You've all done well,*" he told Gwen.

"*That's what you call well?*" She snorted. "*At this rate, we'll be stuck here forever.*"

Flint spoke up. "*Don't doubt yourself. You will fly. I know it.*"

Nox nodded. "*Flint's right. This was your first try. You just need more practice.*"

Gwen hung her head. *"I'm sure you're right."*

His heart squeezed. He only hoped he and Flint weren't wrong. It was hard to watch the hatchlings fail over and over. And it was even harder to wonder if he was doing the right thing. After all, what did he know about teaching a dragon to fly? He was in unprecedented territory, winging it and hoping for the best.

What if it wasn't enough?

The dragons trudged ahead, their heavy steps and downtrodden attitudes far different from their playfulness this morning. Hopefully after a meal and some rest, they'd be ready to try again.

The barn door hung open when they returned. Gwen bolted inside, heading for the big pile of old hay in the back where she'd curled up with her siblings last night. Nox hovered in the doorway, watching the hatchlings settle down to rest and trying not to be alarmed that the drafty old building was completely empty.

Violet and Ryon had planned to head into the village, but Mariun was supposed to be resting. Where was she? He'd expected her head to pop up out of one of the stalls when the dragons lumbered inside, but it hadn't. Unless she was dead asleep...

Nox paced the barn, peeking over the stall doors.

Gwen laughed. *"You should see how creepy you look right now."*

The glare he sent the silly hatchling only made her laughter increase.

"What's he up to now?" Flint asked.

"Peeping in the stalls." Gwen's chuckles finally subsided. *"You can give it a rest. She's not here. I would've heard her breathing if she were asleep."*

"I'm going to knock for the brothers. See if I can't find us something to eat. You guys hang here and wait, all right?"

Gwen lifted her head. *"Go. We're just gonna rest."*

Nox nodded absently, his stomach churning. He'd completed his circuit only to prove what he'd immediately suspected. Mariun wasn't inside. His gaze snagged on the bench where they'd gathered to eat breakfast. The pile of discarded napkins and cups was gone as well.

He left the barn and walked toward the brothers' brick building to beg for lunch. Perhaps Mariun had awakened with the same idea. As he rounded the barn and spotted black hair peeking out of the long grass ahead, the tension in his shoulders eased.

She sat on the ground, her gaze glued to the strange cylindrical monument Ryon had dubbed the Aviary. Nox spared the crumbling tower a glance. It was certainly unexpected to find a building so tall on the top of a mountain. Much less one that stood out so oddly from all the surrounding structures.

Unlike the village cottages and the squat, sprawling rectory the brothers lived in—which appeared to be built of the same orange-red stone that made the mountain—the Aviary was a shiny gray. Countless holes peppered the sides. Though he couldn't see it clearly from where he stood, he suspected from the way light shone out of the openings that the structure didn't have a roof.

Where did the stone come from to build that thing? And how long had it been there? He guessed from the decaying exterior it was much older than the buildings surrounding it.

"How was practice?" Mariun turned and looked up at him, and he shoved those questions to the back of his mind.

"Fine." He shifted, then nodded to the rectory. "They needed a break. I'm going to grab some food."

"Nox, wait." Mariun pushed to her feet. "Can we talk?"

Nox frowned. "The brothers—"

Mariun waved a hand. "Don't bother. I woke ages ago and brought the dishes here. Some brother grabbed everything from me and slammed the door in my face."

"Sorry." He winced.

"It's all right." Mariun sent him a wry smile before staring at her boots. "I'm used to being ignored."

Nox's chest ached. Here he was, prepared to do the same. Just like he had last night before they'd gone to bed. "What do you want to talk about?"

Mariun glanced at him, her cheeks turning pink. "I-I..." She sucked in a deep breath and squared her shoulders. "What you said last night..."

"What about it?"

"I don't believe you."

"I told you I'd never lie to you, Mariun." Nox inched closer. He stopped once he was close enough to touch her, but he kept his hands plastered to his sides. "Are you calling me a liar?"

Mariun rolled her eyes. "No. I just... I don't know what I mean." She shook her head. "Forget I said anything."

Nox grabbed her wrist as she turned to leave. Her pulse galloped wildly beneath his fingers, sending tingles up his forearm. "And if I don't want to forget it?"

Mariun stared at his thumb tracing idle circles on her wrist. "I've spent my whole life in one place. The Supreme's progeny. Everyone there, they never looked at me and saw *me*. They saw me as an extension of him. A dangerous bird in a gilded cage." She met his eyes. "No one's ever looked at me the way you do." Her gaze flicked to her wrist again. "No one would dare touch me when they knew what he'd do."

Nox dropped her hand like he'd been scalded. Was that all there was behind her actions? Her tempting kisses in the dark? A yearning to be treated like her own person?

"You're free of him now. I'm sure you'll find plenty of men willing to touch you," he spit out, the words burning his throat like acid.

Her big gray eyes flashed at him. "You—"

The rectory door flew open with a loud *bang*. A pair of brothers hurried out in matching robes, carting a basket and a new jug and cups. Their faces lit with smiles when they spotted them standing beyond the door, seeming to take no note of the tension curling in the air.

Nox frowned, not recognizing either from the night before. Mariun sent him one last glare and spun to the beaming brothers with a bow. The fellow with the basket began chattering at her, and Mariun replied smoothly. Nox ground his teeth, wishing for the hundredth time that he could understand.

His gaze landed on Mariun as she smiled back politely. Then it flew back to the brothers. The one holding the jug hadn't said a word, but that didn't stop his gaze from roving appreciatively over the full length of Mariun's body. Nox scowled, his fists clenched at his sides. It appeared she wasn't being ignored any longer.

She turned to him after the long back-and-forth conversation wrapped up. "They're insisting on carrying that back to the barn for us," she explained.

The brothers left the doorway and ambled across the field. Nox fell in behind them, burying the urge to groan when the talkative brother with the basket started chatting again, demanding Mariun's attention.

Something the brother said made her laugh. The glorious sound filled his ears and made his stomach clench.

She deserved more laughter in her days. After all the hardships Mariun had been through, she deserved a chance at a normal life. She wouldn't find that with him. Especially not now that he'd bonded a dragon.

Gwen perked up from her spot on the floor as they entered the barn. Both brothers' eyes widened comically, and the chatty one with the basket finally fell silent.

Nox took the opportunity to snatch the food out of his hands. "Thanks for this." He bowed, hiding his smirk with his downturned chin, though neither brother bothered looking at him. They were too busy staring at the hatchlings as they stretched, sniffing the air.

Mariun reached for the pitcher and spoke a few quiet words. The brothers bowed, then retreated the way they'd come.

"He had a lot to say. Anything I ought to know?" Nox asked.

"The village is planning a feast in our honor tonight."

"Are they really?" He dug through the basket, divvying up a small portion for him and Mariun and leaving the rest for the dragons. "Think I'll pass. Stay with the hatchlings."

"I'm going." A wistful smile curved her lips as she poured wine into two cups. "Sounds like fun."

Did he really want her out there with countless men, looking for *fun*? Nox's gut churned. He plopped a loaded napkin in front of Mariun on the bench.

"You sure you don't want to go?" She stared at him, her eyes wide and pleading. "After all, they're being so nice to us. Surely we should accept an invitation to a gathering held in our honor."

She had a point. And he was curious to see the village. "Fine. I'll go." He yanked the basket off the bench.

Mariun clapped her hands. "Oh good. You'll see. It'll be great."

Nox shook his head as he wandered back to the hatchlings. A night spent celebrating while he should be securing their escape didn't sound that *great* to him. Guess he'd find out soon enough.

"*Here's lunch,*" he announced. "*Eat up, and then we better practice some more. They're planning a gathering in the village this evening.*"

"*Do we get to come?*" Gwen asked.

He shrugged. "*I'm not sure, but I'll find out.*"

Gwen bent over her meal. The dragons gobbled their meat quickly, pushing and shoving each other to snatch up the choicest bits.

Nox returned to the bench. "Did they say whether the dragons were invited to this feast?"

Mariun swallowed. "No. But I can find out, if you'd like."

"Thanks." He folded his lunch in the napkin and waved an arm for the dragons to follow.

"Wait, Nox. We didn't finish talking earlier. I—"

He headed to the door. "Can it wait? If we're meant to spend the night celebrating, then we really ought to practice first."

"Fine." Mariun's voice rang with command. "Find me before the feast. I mean it, Nox."

He nodded and left the barn. Maybe he was a coward for avoiding her. Scratch that—he definitely was a coward. But knowing that didn't stop his feet from moving.

He could sense from the look in her eyes that whatever she'd been about to say would be big. He sighed. Was it too much to ask for one rotting day without his world being rocked by one revelation or another?

For now, he was fine slinking away with his cowardice. But he wouldn't put her off forever. Tonight, he'd hear her out. He just hoped whatever she had to say didn't hurt as much as her silence had.

Home

The kitchen door to his family's cottage slammed behind Ryon. He'd raced home, ignoring everyone who shouted greetings as he'd passed. Even so, he'd barely caught up to Brother Tham before they arrived.

Sunlight shone in the windows, highlighting the simple table and chairs. Dishes lay haphazardly on the counter, their scattered nature telling him at a glance that all was not well in his home.

"Brother Tham, thank you for coming." His mother grabbed Tham's hands, her gaze flicking to Ryon briefly as she ushered the priest further into the house. "I'm so sorry to ask again, but would you mind singing for Rovan? You know it's the only thing that calms him down when—"

"My dear, say no more. I'm happy to help." Brother Tham disappeared down the hall, heading toward the back bedroom where a rhythmic thumping rattled the walls.

Ryon jerked into motion, only for his mother to halt him before he'd taken two steps.

"Stop. Brother Tham will handle it." She trailed her hands across Ryon's stiff shoulders, then tugged him into an embrace. "Son. I'm so happy you're back."

"What happened?" Ryon asked. The first verse of a merry tune began, Brother Tham's melodic tenor muffled by the closed door. "I came as soon as I heard."

Ma pulled out of his arms. "Oh, you know how Rovan is about his routine. He wasn't pleased when Deanna banged on the door to tell me the news this morning." She tsked gently. "The silly girl was a little too eager to be the first to tell me you were back, and the racket upset him." She waved a hand. "But it'll be fine now that Brother Tham is here."

Ryon peered into his mother's smiling face. Faint shadows hung below her eyes. Being here in her presence warmed him in a way nothing else could. But a frigid chill creeped up his spine, chasing away the warmth. It was news of *his* return that had set Rovan off. His fault, once again, why Ma's smile was a touch too pinched.

"I'm sorry, Ma."

She patted his chest. "Don't be. I'm delighted you're back." Ma frowned, her gaze trailing across his hair. She lifted a lank dread off his shoulder. "What have you done to my marvelous work? Sit. Please. I can't have my boy walking around the village like this."

Ryon allowed Ma to direct him to a chair. Truthfully, he had no desire to have his hair pulled and prodded, but he wouldn't fight her on this. He knew Ma well enough to realize that styling hair was soothing for her. She didn't just do it for a living. She enjoyed making people shine, and he wasn't about to deny her an activity that would calm her after what was most likely a difficult morning.

"So, tell me. Is what they're saying true?"

Ryon grimaced. "What would that be?" He wasn't surprised news of his return had already spread. In a village as small as his, it was hard to keep anything secret.

Ma chuckled. "That you returned with a trio of traveling companions and a herd of dragons."

"A herd?" Ryon rolled his eyes. "Only if you consider four a herd."

A gasp spilled out of Ma's lips, and Ryon cocked a brow. Sure, flesh-and-blood dragons were hard to believe, but she was being awfully dramatic...

Ma squeezed his shoulder, and her voice held a hard edge. "Ryon. How much of your hair did you cut?"

Oh... *that* reaction made a bit more sense. He grinned crookedly and shrugged. "A bit?"

Ma threw her hands up and muttered, "Guano. What am I to do with you, Ryon?" But only a heartbeat later, her fingers were back in his hair. "Don't worry. I can fix this. Why don't you tell me about your voyage? Did you find the answer to the riddle? Was it a bird? Oh! I bet it was a dragon."

"I did." He settled back in the chair and told Ma about his journey. By the time he'd finished, Brother Tham had sung three more songs and his mother had moved on from transforming his hair to attacking his beard with the trimmers.

"Oh, Ryon. It sounds like such an exciting journey." Ma sent him a shrewd glare. "Your friends. When can I meet them? There's talk of a feast tonight, but I'd love to be introduced before." She brightened. "I could braid their hair. Why don't you bring them by later this afternoon?"

Ryon smiled. "Sure, Ma, I'll invite them."

Brother Tham appeared, closing Rovan's door with a gentle *snick*. "Rovan's calmed down. He's sitting at his desk, working on his trinkets."

Ma set down the trimmers and clapped her hands. "Bless you, Brother Tham."

"And you, as well." Tham smiled and paced toward the exit. "I'll leave you to it. You're looking wonderful, Ryon. Beautiful work as always, Vera."

"Thank you, brother." Ma beamed at the priest's praise. "And thank you for singing to Rovan." She followed him to the door and closed it behind him.

Ryon rubbed a hand across his chin, feeling lighter with his thick beard shorn close to his face. "Are you done?"

Ma hurried back to the table and picked up the trimmers. "Not quite. Relax."

He sighed and settled back, steeling himself for more poking and prodding. "Do you know where I can find lodgings for my companions? I promised to look for somewhere better than the brothers' old barn."

"Hm." Ma's eyes narrowed. "I just might. Give me a little while to ask around. You can stay here and keep Rovan company while I go see."

Ryon's stomach twisted. More than anything, he wanted to give his mother a break. She'd likely been cooped up in their cottage much more than usual with him gone and Rovan to look after. But still... "Are you sure that's wise? I don't want to disrupt his routine even more."

"No better time than now," she answered breezily. "Brother Tham's singing always leaves him in a good mood for the rest of the day. Besides, he's missed you. I can tell."

If only that were true... Ryon sighed. "I've missed him, too." He buried the sick wash of regret that always overcame him when he thought of his brother. "It won't have to be like this for much longer. On the next full moon, I'll finally get a golden feather. I know it."

He expected his mother's smile to match his own, but the grin she sent him barely tugged at her cheeks. "Are you sure about this?"

Brow furrowing, Ryon met her gaze. "Of course I am. This is what I've been working toward for decades, Ma. I need to fix him. I—"

"But the sacrifice," Ma cut in, tears pooling in her eyes. "What if it's more than you can bear to give? What if by saving him, you curse yourself?"

"That's a chance I have to take."

Ryon's heart sped up. He'd long ago decided that any cost was worth saving Rovan. Even if it hadn't been his fault, he'd have still wanted to save his brother. They'd been so close they'd finished each other's sentences. He wanted that back. He *needed* his brother back. Whole and fully aware, not the shell that was left after that awful day when everything changed.

"Ryon, please. Think about the future. Your future." She set down the trimmers and grabbed his hands. "Your story... I couldn't help noticing how you spoke about Violet. You care for her, don't you?"

Ryon sighed and nodded.

"What if the sacrifice you make to save your brother stops you from helping her?" Ma kneeled and stared straight into his eyes. "I just want you to consider it from every angle. I know what happened to Rovan wasn't fair, but we're fine. We've managed this long, and that won't change."

"Don't you see, Ma? You shouldn't have to just *manage*." He shook his head. "I'm making the wish. And whatever sacrifice it requires, it will be worth it to give Rovan his life back." He squeezed Ma's hands.

"To give *you* your life back. I love you both too much to keep watching you suffer when I can fix everything."

Ma released his hands and stood. "I see you've made up your mind." She carefully removed the apron she'd settled on his clothes to catch his hair trimmings. "Come along. Let's go see what Rovan is up to."

Ryon pushed out of the chair and brushed his hands across his shoulders, flicking off a few black strands that his mother missed. "Do you need to sweep up first? I can help."

"No." Ma waved a hand. "Don't worry about that. I'll take care of it once I get you boys settled."

Ryon resisted the urge to roll his eyes. They were nearly thirty years old. Guess to Ma, he and Rovan would always be her *boys*.

He sucked in a deep breath and followed Ma down the hall. Who knew what mood Rovan would be in when he spotted him? Despite her assurances that Brother Tham's singing calmed him, Ryon mentally prepared himself for the opposite. There'd been countless times over the years where his brother took one glance at his face, only to start screaming—or worse—crying. And just as many days when he'd regarded him with cool indifference.

What would happen today? Only one way to find out.

Ryon halted at his mother's elbow as she eased open Rovan's door. His brother's room was brightly lit, the sun streaming in through the wide-open window. Shining gems and feathers hung on every surface. So many more than he remembered.

"Rovan's been busy," he muttered just as his mother stiffened. "What?"

Ma spun around and lifted her trembling fingertips to cover her mouth. "Rovan... he's gone."

Ryon circled his mother and entered the room. She was right. Rovan's room was empty. He stalked to the open window and stuck his head out, praying his brother would be standing within eyesight.

No luck. Guano.

Ryon whipped around and met his mother's teary eyes. "Don't worry, Ma. We'll find him."

A Familiar Face

V iolet watched Ryon race ahead, her stomach knotting. Why wouldn't he let her help? It had to be serious if he was speeding into town so quickly.

She bit her bottom lip as the last glimpse of Ryon faded into the distance. Then she sighed and did her best to concentrate on the scenery. It wouldn't do to spend the whole day obsessing over what may or may not be happening with his family. She had a village to explore, after all.

Violet smiled at Brother Lennam and Brother Pip. They'd been kind to offer to accompany her in Ryon's stead. Sure, she could return to the barn and wait for Ryon to take her later. She'd been tempted to do just that but had quickly decided against it. For one, who knew how long he'd be? In the end, the curiosity welling in her chest demanded she continue onward, rather than spend the afternoon bored in that dusty barn.

They strolled at a leisurely pace. The brothers chatted quietly for a time but soon lapsed into silence. Brother Pip repeatedly tugged on her sleeve, pointing out colorful birds along their route and once at a rock formation that, though clearly natural, resembled a couple dancing. A massive black bird with an elongated beak perched on the head of the "man," making her giggle. A bird certainly made a ridiculous hat.

The wind whipped at her clothes. Violet shivered and tucked her fingers inside the long sleeves of her purple tunic. The borrowed clothes were thicker than what she'd brought with her, and she was certainly grateful for it when the cold breeze kicked up.

Soon, rushing water tickled her ears, overpowering the whistling wind. Violet gulped as she spotted the source. A massive river lay between the mountain that held the Aviary and the one where the village rested. It rushed through a canyon well below their elevation. Far enough that she was certain a fall from where she stood would be a death sentence.

Brother Pip tugged her sleeve again and pointed. Violet sent him a wobbly grin as she spotted a massive bridge ahead spanning the two peaks. Her stomach clenched, and she nearly begged off the rest of the journey and returned to the barn.

Something about bridges always made fear claw at her chest. It was an irrational reaction—one she'd been working hard to overcome.

It's perfectly safe. You can do this. Eyes ahead and one foot in front of the other.

With her inner pep talk playing on a loop through her mind, she took her first step onto the wide stone bridge. Thankfully, the bridge was large enough for several men and a few carts to cross at the same time. A stone railing spanned each side, guaranteeing nothing would spill into the gurgling river. Still, the hair on Violet's neck lifted, and she gritted her teeth until she stepped safely on the other side.

As her nerves settled from the crossing, pure excitement rushed in. It wasn't a long walk from the bridge to the village's edge. The brightly painted houses stood there cheerily, and people dressed in long skirts wandered the streets.

Violet followed the brothers onto a cobblestone road. A young woman leading a little boy by the hand stopped to greet them. When the woman spoke to her in a cheery tone, Violet gulped. She settled for bowing like she had to the brothers, which earned her a smile and a bow in return.

The brothers spoke to the woman for a short while, then started walking again. Violet trailed along, pausing every time someone approached to speak to the brothers and bowing politely. Nearly everyone they passed had something to say, and though she enjoyed greeting the villagers, she began to grow weary of the interruptions.

Just when she thought she couldn't stand to bow again, the brothers turned onto a bustling road packed full of people. Carts bursting with goods lined the road. To the left, she spotted a cart stacked with folded cloth. To the right, an old woman stirred a massive pot. A teen stood beside her, handing a steamy bowl of fragrant stew to a man who barely hesitated to dig in.

"A market. How wonderful!" Violet exclaimed.

Brother Lennam faced her with a quizzical expression. She pointed around the road and clapped her hands, hoping the clap and her wide grin would be enough to communicate her delight.

Brother Lennam returned her smile with one of his own and led her further into the market. They passed carts and wagons with all manner of goods. She stopped to smell a few soaps that caught her eye, her smile widening when she picked out some familiar scents hidden among the foreign floral notes. But the hawkish woman running the cart barked at her after she lifted the third bar of soap to her nose.

She cringed and set it down. Had she offended her somehow? "I'm sorry. Am I not allowed to smell them?"

Brother Pip cut his conversation with a portly villager short and hurried to her side. After a few quick words with the woman, her frown disappeared. She lifted the soap Violet had just set down and handed it to her with a nod and a smile.

Violet lifted it to her nose, closed her eyes, and inhaled the fresh aroma. She picked out a hint of mint and something floral she couldn't pinpoint. Opening her eyes, she smiled and extended her arms to hand it back. The old woman shook her head and clasped a wrinkled hand over her fingers.

"Oh, you want me to keep it?" she asked.

The old woman nodded vehemently. Violet wrinkled her nose and shucked off her pack. She suspected the woman meant it to be a gift, but she couldn't stomach the thought of taking it without paying. It smelled quite lovely, after all.

She dug into her coin purse and pulled out a coin. When Violet tried to hand it over, the woman stared at the little circle of metal with a furrowed brow. She shook her head and closed Violet's hand around the coin.

How odd. Did these people not use money? Or was she simply refusing payment?

Violet returned the coin to her purse and spotted the small journal she'd brought with her from home in her pack. She'd barely had time to even consider writing, but she'd smashed a few blooms into the pages during her travels. She grinned. What better gift for a soap maker than new flowers?

She selected a few bright-pink blossoms she'd harvested on the island where she'd found Uncle Aren. The woman's eyes lit up when

Violet handed them to her. She sniffed them cautiously, then flashed a radiant smile.

Violet cinched her pack closed when the woman attempted to hand them back. "Please, keep them. A trade."

The woman bowed, and Violet returned the gesture, a rush of warmth flooding her veins. Then she left the cart and ambled down the road, examining the carts she passed.

She kept the brothers within eyesight, but with their distinctive robes, she wasn't worried about losing them in the crowd. Both of them remained busy, greeting people, talking about who knew what. Violet was grateful for the break from bowing at everyone who approached. It was much more fun studying the wares.

Her eyes widened. She'd spotted a cart selling the loveliest trinkets—bright flowers and feathers painted in every shade of the rainbow decorated with shimmering gems. A woman and her daughter browsed the delicate creations, the little girl giggling as her mother lifted a pair of white feathers to her hair. The mother set the feathers back, then ushered her daughter to a different stall.

Violet strolled closer, her gaze locked on a silver feather adorned with golden beads that reminded her of the bloodfeather Ryon had gifted her. She traced her finger along the edge, noting the subtle differences. This feather was slightly larger, and the color a touch more iridescent. Despite that, it was lovely. She smiled and pulled her pack off her back, motioning for the slim man guarding the stall to come forward.

"Hello." She smiled and pointed to the silver feather. "Can I buy this from you?"

She selected a coin and offered it to the man. He frowned and shook his head. Violet pulled two more coins from her purse, adding them to the first. Still, the man shook his head. She sighed and dropped the coins back into her pack. Perhaps once she learned what these people accepted as payment, she could return.

Violet tugged her pack onto her back and wandered away. She breathed deep, reveling in the delicious scents from the food vendors. She chuckled under her breath as a trio of laughing children rushed by. This little slice of normalcy warmed her heart more than she cared to admit. After the danger they'd faced, it was nice to spend time among people who had no worries other than finding the perfect trinket or what to eat for lunch.

A cry pierced the air. Violet stilled, cocking her head. People bustled around her, none of them seeming to note the sorrowful noise.

There it was again. A sob rang out, followed by a man humming a merry tune that sounded particularly peculiar when the voice responsible for it was clearly not merry at all.

Frowning, Violet scurried toward the sound. Her feet led her away from the market, down a side street. In the back of her mind, she knew she was being foolish. She shouldn't be wandering off on her own. At the least, she ought to find the brothers. But that voice... Even though she couldn't make out any words, it struck her as oddly familiar.

She ignored the warning in her head and followed her ears—and her heart. She rounded a corner and wiggled in between a clump of trees. Her pulse pounded as she burst into a small clearing surrounded by greenery. She gasped, her gaze darting over the gorgeous park. Flowers burst from the ground in a myriad of colors. And in the center of it all sat a lone man perched on the edge of a bubbling fountain.

Violet inched closer. The man's head hung low, staring at the running water as he hummed, but as she drew closer, he lifted his face.

Shock washed over her like a flash flood. "Ryon?" As soon as the word left her mouth, she wanted to snatch it back. This melancholy fellow wasn't Ryon. The hair was all wrong, for one—the right shade, but much shorter. She frowned, noticing a dark bruise on his forehead that his bangs did little to hide. And his eyes, though the exact shade of brown, even down to the little flecks of amber swimming within them, showed no sign of recognition when he met her gaze. Quite the opposite. They swam with confusion.

All the same, she instantly recognized him as Ryon's kin. The resemblance was so uncanny she suspected they were twins.

"Hello." She smiled gently and edged closer. "I'm Violet. I'm a friend of your brother's."

He didn't attempt to reply. By the time she'd finished speaking, he'd turned back to the fountain and begun humming again.

Blazes. Of course he couldn't understand her. She racked her brain. What had Ryon called his brother...

"Rovan. That's your name, right?" Rovan's gaze flashed to her, and his humming cut off. She smiled and sat beside him on the fountain's edge. "Rovan. I'm Violet."

His brow wrinkled. Rovan stared at her, not saying anything.

Violet gazed into his eyes and sensed he wouldn't reply. And not just because of the language barrier. The confusion she'd first noted still shadowed his eyes.

Rovan held her gaze for another moment, then glanced at his hands. Violet bit back a gasp when she spotted what he had.

"Do you make those lovely trinkets in the market?" She gestured to the gorgeous feather and string of beads in Rovan's hands. It was similar to the one she'd tried to purchase, only the feather was black and the string of red beads was only partially strung.

Rovan dug into his pocket and pulled out a tiny crimson bead. He lifted a thin string and meticulously knotted it before sliding the bead into position. As he worked, he hummed, the tune sounding so forlorn Violet's chest ached.

What was he doing here? He was clearly upset. About what, she had no clue, and even less of a chance of figuring it out. She needed to help him. She could go back for the brothers... but what if when she returned, Rovan was gone? A smile crossed her face at the same time a new idea popped into her head. If those trinkets were meant to be woven into hair, then Rovan must want to help his mother. What would be better than bringing her a new customer?

She cleared her throat, capturing his attention, then began running her hands through her hair. "My hair, it's such a mess." She sighed deeply and started braiding her long locks haphazardly. She hoped that making an absolute mess of the braid would be enough to set him in motion.

Rovan barely watched her for a moment before he shook his head. He stood and beckoned her to follow.

Violet's heart raced as she followed Rovan. He led her away from the market and through a winding route that ensured she lost her bearings completely. Rovan kept a few paces ahead and hummed all the while, sneaking peeks at her every now and then.

Maybe she should be frightened. She was following a man she'd just met through an unfamiliar village. He'd yet to say a single word. Were it any other man, she'd likely be shaking in her boots. But Rovan set her at ease. Even without words, she felt calm in his presence. She *knew* he wasn't leading her anywhere dangerous. In fact, she hoped he was leading her exactly where they both needed to go.

Rovan stopped in front of a small cottage. He silently pushed open the door and nodded inside. Violet peered around him, spotting a warmly lit kitchen. A woman sat at the table, her face cradled in her hands.

"Hello?" Violet stepped inside.

The woman flinched and glanced up. Her gaze slid over Violet quickly and snagged on Rovan behind her. She lurched out of her chair and rushed over, a stream of words spilling out rapid-fire.

Violet dodged the woman's grasping hands, smiling warmly when she used them to pull Rovan into a tight embrace. Footsteps echoed down the hall. Another familiar voice rang out, speaking in the language she still didn't understand.

"Violet?" Ryon halted as he entered the kitchen, his gaze flying from her to Rovan and back again. His eyes bulged so comically Violet choked down a laugh. "What are you doing here?"

Shameful Confessions

R yon whipped his head around the kitchen, his gaze darting between Violet, Ma, and Rovan. When he and Ma returned home after so much fruitless searching, the last thing he'd expected was for Rovan to arrive in the company of one of his friends.

"Oh, my dear boy," Ma clucked at Rovan, smoothing her hands down his clothes. "Where did you wander off to? You gave me such a fright."

Heart thumping, Ryon ducked his head as Rovan's focus shifted away from Ma and across the kitchen.

Oh no. The last thing he needed was to set Rovan off again...

But Rovan ignored him completely. He tugged a hand through his short black hair and then nodded to Violet.

"Did you bring me a customer?" Ma smiled shrewdly. "Wonderful! You've done well, Rovan. Come, let's get you back to your room." She glanced at the half-finished feather ornament dangling in his hands. "Is that one nearly done? How lovely..."

Ryon tuned out Ma as she continued chattering away while leading Rovan toward the hall. He shifted, turning his face away from Rovan. *Maybe if he doesn't see me—*

Guano. Rovan halted directly beside Ryon.

Ryon held his breath and faced his twin. A war of conflicting emotions bombarded him. His brother... it had been so long since he'd seen him. The urge to hug him was nearly overpowering, but Ryon ignored it, allowing his gaze to only flicker across the face that was both impossibly familiar and utterly foreign.

Rovan... What will it be this time?

His brother scanned Ryon's face, his eyes swimming with confusion. Then Rovan's gaze flitted behind him and landed on Violet. A heartbeat later, arms wrapped around Ryon's chest. Ryon sighed and carefully hugged his brother back.

Ma watched from the doorway with tears spilling down her cheeks. Then she scrubbed her face with her sleeve and cleared her throat. "Come, Rovan. Your brother will visit with you shortly. Can't keep our customer waiting long."

Without a sound, Rovan retracted his arms and followed Ma out of the kitchen.

Violet stepped beside him and peered down the hall as Rovan's door closed. "I found him while I was exploring the market with the brothers." She splayed a hand across her chest. "Blazes. I forgot about them..." She lifted her skirts. "They're probably worried about—"

"Don't go. Just give me a moment." Ryon gestured to the table. "Have a seat. I'll be right back." He rushed out the door and knocked on his neighbor's cottage. After a brief conversation, he returned. "I sent Deanna to the market to tell the brothers you're here with me."

"Deanna?" Violet's nose scrunched. "The girl from this morning?"

"Yes. She lives next door. Helps Ma out from time to time."

"Oh." Violet's fingers bunched in her skirt.

Ryon sat across from her. "I suppose I owe you an explanation."

"I don't want to pry—"

"You're not. I've been meaning to tell you for a while now." He sighed. "Rovan... I'm sure you noticed he's not well."

Violet tilted her head. "He's mute, right?"

"He is." Ryon stared at his boots. "But he wasn't always. In fact, he used to sing so beautifully. Brother Tham said he had perfect pitch. If it weren't for me, Rovan would probably be a priest by now."

Violet grabbed his hand and pulled it atop her lap. "What happened?"

Ryon lowered his voice, his gaze flicking down the hall. "Remember what I told you about my ma?"

"You mean, about the man who hurt her?"

He nodded. "Our father died on a hunt when Rovan and I were still in swaddling clothes. The bastard who hit her, he was one of Da's friends who swooped in to help her after his death."

Violet's fingers squeezed around his palm. "Oh, Ryon. I'm so sorry."

Ryon forced a small smile. "He wasn't always so bad. He tried to be a good da at first. I have some fond memories of him tussling with Rovan and me when we were little lads. But somewhere along the way, he changed. He started picking fights with Ma. Hurting her." Ryon's fist clenched by his side, but he forced the hand in Violet's lap to remain perfectly still.

"Your poor ma. And you were just boys?"

He nodded sadly. "She put up with his abuse for years. Then one day, I couldn't stand it anymore. I jumped in between them when he was about to hit her." Ryon's fingers unclenched, and he rubbed his temple, the ghostly memory of that strike replaying in his mind, clear as the day it happened. "He tossed me into the wall. Knocked me out cold."

Violet gasped. "Blazes."

"I was all right. Just a little banged up. But I'd do it a thousand times over because that day, Ma tossed him out. She didn't do it quietly, either. She ranted and raved all through the village. Showed every woman who'd look the bruises she'd always been so careful to keep hidden."

"That must have taken a tremendous amount of courage."

"It did. I was so proud of her for standing up for herself. For protecting us even when she knew it would be disastrous for her standing."

"Her standing?" Violet's nose wrinkled. "I don't understand..."

Ryon pursed his lips. Violet and her uncle had told him about their coin. It wasn't surprising she didn't know what he was talking about.

"Social standing is very important to my people. We rely on it while trading and to make sure that goods shared among all are distributed to those who have done the most to deserve them."

"Your mother lost standing when she kicked out the man hurting her?" Violet's eyes flashed. "That doesn't make any sense. She should've gained it for doing what's right. She didn't just protect you—she protected all the women in your village by outing that monster."

Ryon grinned at her fierceness, but his smile fell fast. "I agree. But he was a hunter, like my da. With him gone, Ma was just a mother to two boys with no skill to speak of." He shrugged. "It made trading extremely difficult."

Violet's brow furrowed. "That explains so much. When I was at the market earlier, a woman didn't want me touching her soaps until

Brother Pip spoke with her. Then she turned around and gifted me one."

"The priests have excellent standing. Almost as much as hunters. She likely owed them a favor or two." He shrugged, realizing they were getting off topic. "Anyhow, back then, I knew it was up to me to help my mother. And I was already one of the best climbers in the village."

Violet squeezed his hand. "Let me guess... You volunteered to be one of the boys cleaning the Aviary."

"I did." He sighed heavily. "It was enough to give us a small boost. We still weren't trading as successfully as we used to, though. Ma found an older woman who offered to teach her to braid, but it was a long apprenticeship. I thought if Rovan joined me, then maybe Ma wouldn't need to worry about rushing through her training." Ryon closed his eyes. "Rovan was afraid of heights. But I wouldn't give up until he at least tried..."

He couldn't bear to look at Violet. With all he'd said already, she was bound to have pieced it together. She'd pull away for sure, her voice thick with revulsion. What kind of man goaded their own flesh and blood into making the worst mistake of their life?

But Violet's hands closed more firmly around his own, and when she spoke, her words were full of compassion he didn't deserve. "Blazes, Ryon. What happened?"

"Rovan fell. His safety line broke." He shook his head and opened his eyes. Violet stared back at him, not a smidge of disgust painting her face. Somehow, that only made the awful churning in Ryon's gut increase.

"And that's when Rovan became mute?" she asked gently.

"Yes. The healers said he damaged his brain from the fall. He hasn't spoken since. And half the time, he wanders around so confused. I never know what to expect when I see him. Sometimes he recognizes me, but not always. Some days, he'll just stare at the wall for hours. Or worse, bang his head against it."

Violet rubbed her forehead. "I noticed his bruise. Is that what happened today?"

Ryon nodded. "When Rovan gets like that, Brother Tham comes to sing to him. It's the only thing that calms him down."

"So, you need the golden bloodfeather to heal Rovan?"

"Yes. Once the healers told us there was nothing they could do, I started searching the rivers for silver to begin my petition. I had to. If I hadn't repeatedly badgered him, Rovan would've never..." His lip wobbled, and Ryon leaned over the table, covering his burning eyes with his free hand. "I should've *never* forced him to climb."

Violet let go of his hand, and Ryon's heart sank. He'd been expecting her to pull away, but that didn't make it hurt any less when—

His chair jerked back. He lifted his head just as a warm weight settled on his lap. Violet wrapped her arms around him and tugged his face into the crook of her neck. "It's all right."

Ryon's chest caved as he drew her closer. He had just enough presence of mind to ensure he wasn't cradling her too tightly before he gave into the heavy weight of sorrow pulling him down and sobbed. "He's missed so much. It's all my fault."

"No, it's not," Violet said fiercely.

Ryon shook his head. "Yes, it is."

"It was an accident." Violet pulled back far enough to stare into his face. "You said it yourself. His rope snapped."

That day... he could recall it so clearly, his brother's scream. The sickening thud that followed. And then the deafening silence that only lasted until a new scream rang out—his own. Ryon shuddered, his gaze falling to the floor. "But—"

Violet grabbed his cheeks and forced him to meet her eyes. "You were just boys. Two brave boys taking care of their mother. Fate was cruel that day, but you, Ryon..." Violet caressed his face, her soft touch at odds with the deadly seriousness of her tone. "You did the only thing you could think of to take care of your family. And when Rovan was hurt, you didn't give up. You dedicated your life to finding a cure." Her voice softened, but she never once looked away. Her beautiful eyes shone with a light that radiated into the depths of his soul. "You're not the villain of this story. You're the hero."

Her surety bled through his veins. He'd been so afraid Violet would look at him differently after he told her what he'd done. He never expected her to take the most shameful moment of his past and force him to look at it through her eyes. Or that she'd be the balm that soothed his aching heart.

"Violet." He closed the space between them and captured her lips in a searing kiss. Her hands tightened on his cheeks, then slid down his neck as she kissed him back.

All too soon, the sound of a door opening forced them apart. Pink bloomed on her cheeks as Violet scrambled off his lap. She slipped back into the chair across from him just before Ma reentered the kitchen.

Ma took one look at the scene—both of them breathing heavily, straightening their clothes—and smiled, glee practically bursting out of her eyeballs. She refrained from jumping up and down with delight, although Ryon was certain her head was full of visions of future grandbabies. "Ryon, aren't you going to introduce me to your friend?"

Ryon stood, and Violet followed suit. "Ma, this is Violet." He switched languages. "Violet, this is my ma, Vera."

"It's lovely to meet you." Violet smiled shyly, balling her fists and raising them to her shoulders. Before she could complete the bow, Ma tugged her into a hug. Violet giggled nervously.

"Dear girl, you don't need to stand on ceremony with me. Not when you've already captured both my boys' hearts."

Ryon shifted on his feet, thankful for once for the language barrier.

"What's she saying?" Violet whispered, still clutched tightly in his mother's arms.

Ryon cleared his throat. "She's pleased to meet you as well." He gently tugged on Ma's elbow and switched languages. "All right, Ma. Let her breathe."

Ma pulled back, only to thread her fingers through Violet's long, silvery tresses. "Violet, your hair is absolutely gorgeous." She turned to him, grinning radiantly. "You're right, Son. Just like a moonbeam."

Violet stared at him expectantly.

"She likes your hair," he explained. "The shade reminds her of a moonbeam."

Violet flushed. "Oh." She smiled at Ma. "Thank you."

"You must allow me to braid it for you," Ma insisted. "It's the least I can do to thank you for bringing Rovan home." Ma nudged him with her elbow. "Tell her I'll give her the loveliest style for the feast. The other girls will burn with jealousy when they see it."

"Ma's thankful you brought Rovan home. She'd like to braid your hair for the feast."

"Feast?" Violet quirked a brow. "What feast?" She let Ma lead her back to the chair.

"We heard about it when we were out searching for Rovan." Ryon sat across from Violet. "The village is planning a feast tonight to celebrate our arrival."

"How exciting." Violet smiled wistfully. "I always loved attending feast days back home." She frowned. "Should we go back and tell Nox and Mariun? I bet Mariun would love to have her hair braided. Do you think your mother would mind?"

"No. She asked to meet all of you this morning while she was fixing my hair."

Violet's gaze trailed across his head and beard appreciatively. "Ah. I was wondering why you didn't look as scruffy as usual."

"Scruffy?" Ryon scoffed dramatically, earning a giggle.

Ma sighed, a warm smile painting her face as she followed their exchange.

Ryon rolled his eyes. "Don't give me that look, Ma."

"What?" Ma lifted a brush and started detangling the tips of Violet's hair. "I'm not looking any way at all."

"Sure." He stood. "Do you mind if I fetch the others at the Aviary?"

"Go. I'll keep Violet company." Ma grinned sweetly.

Ryon turned to Violet. "I'll fetch them now while Ma's busy with your hair."

"All right." Violet smiled just as sweetly. He took a step back, admiring the sight of Violet and Ma bonding. With both of their gazes locked on him—both of their breathtaking smiles directed at him—Ryon's heart melted. He hurried out of the door before he did or said something idiotic.

He shook his head as the afternoon sun warmed his face. How did he get so lucky? Even without speaking the same language, Violet had charmed his family so easily. She fit in perfectly. He could picture her fitting into his life for good.

When the orecolns had sent him looking for their one, he'd never known she would end up meaning so much to him. Now that he'd gotten to know her, he had to admit the truth. Violet wasn't just Mother Orea's one. She was his one, too.

His mother's warning returned to plague him. Could he still go through with his wish, knowing about the sacrifice it required? What if... No. Ryon steeled his spine and lengthened his stride. No matter what, he *would* save his brother.

But once Rovan was well, if he was still able, he would tell Violet how he felt. Ryon's gaze lifted as the crescent moon made an early appearance behind a cloud in the afternoon sky.

The full moon couldn't come fast enough... One way or another, it would be the most momentous night of his life.

The Feast

Nox threw open the barn door and frowned. "*Where is everyone?*"

Gwen's head perked as she trod through the door, her siblings trailing in her wake. "*Bet that feast already started. I hear music coming from the village.*"

Nox lifted a brow. "*I don't hear anything.*" Normally, his hearing was far superior to everyone around him. But with a dragon as a bondmate, it seemed he'd need to get used to being bested.

"*You sure you don't hear—Wait... do you* smell *that?*" Gwen bolted further inside and joined the other dragons around an enormous pile of food. Someone had dragged a worn wooden trough into the center of the room, and it overflowed with smoked meat.

Shaking his head, Nox scanned the barn. He'd been positive Mariun would be here waiting after her demand earlier. How was he supposed to find her before the feast when she'd left without him?

"*I'm going to see if the others are with the brothers.*" He turned to the door and halted. Parchment fluttered in the breeze, tacked just above the inner handle. Nox's gaze trailed across the page. *"Never mind. Looks like they've gone into the village already. Do you mind staying here? Apparently the brothers advised against you attending."* He clenched the parchment in his fist, trying not to let the fact that they'd excluded his bondmate bother him. *"You know what? Let me keep you company. I don't want to go to a silly feast any—"*

"Nox. Go," Gwen insisted. *"We're exhausted after all the falling—ahem—training you've put us through today."* Her voice, though weary, was thick with mischief. *"Besides, we ate all the meat. You won't get any dinner if you don't go."*

"Already?" Nox shot a glance at the back of the barn, only to confirm the hatchlings had devoured the huge pile of meat.

"If I'd known you planned to hang around and mope, I would've saved you some," Gwen replied.

"I'm not moping," he grumbled.

Flint cut in. *"I have to agree. A little fun might do you some good."*

"Fine." Nox stomped out of the barn. *"I'll take my bad attitude elsewhere."*

Flint's and Gwen's chuckles reverberated in his mind. They certainly liked to gang up on him lately. Always ribbing him. Dragging him out of his comfort zone. A tiny smile curved his lips as he approached the rectory's back door. He might grumble, and yeah, mope, but he was grateful for their teasing. He'd always had a hard time making friends that weren't animals. Sometimes he needed a push where people were concerned. Because there was one person he needed to talk to tonight.

He rapped on the door. After a brief wait, it swung open.

Great. The same chatty fellow from this afternoon stood in the doorway, a blank look on his face.

"Mariun left me a note. Said one of you brothers would take me into the village." He hated to bother them, especially this guy, who'd seemed happy enough to help Mariun earlier, but was decidedly less smiley now. But he had no clue where to go. Sure, he could trust his intuition and follow his ears, but that might not be the smartest idea on an unfamiliar mountain with dusk rapidly falling. Nox waved the parchment in his hand, then pointed at the village.

The brother closed the door, motioning for Nox to follow. They set off at a fast pace across the mountaintop toward the village. Thankfully, the fellow didn't bother to strike up a conversation. Even if they could understand each other, he wasn't feeling particularly friendly at the moment.

When a familiar dreadlocked head appeared on the path ahead of them, Nox's jaw unclenched. "Ryon." He waved, cocking a brow when he spotted the lit torch in Ryon's hands. The sky was overcast, but sunlight still lit the sky, making the torchlight a tad premature.

"Nox. I was coming to find you." Ryon jogged to them and exchanged a few words with the brother, who promptly turned and began retracing his steps. "Come on. I have something to show you before we head to the feast."

Nox frowned. "Where are Violet and Mariun?"

"They're at the feast already." Ryon took a sharp turn, veering away from the bright village lights.

"Where are we going?"

"A little detour. Don't worry. It won't take long." Ryon scrambled up an incline.

Nox followed, using all his concentration to avoid falling.

When he caught up, Ryon ducked inside a hollow cutout in the stone wall. "Come on. It's through here."

Heart thudding, Nox trailed after him into darkness. Ryon's torch sent shadows racing across the cavern walls. The chamber was dank and gloomy, about the size of an outhouse.

"What is this place?" Nox ducked beneath a massive triangular rock that grew out of the ceiling.

"Remember I told you about the bat caves? This is one of them. Follow me." Ryon bent at the waist and shimmied into a small opening.

Nox followed, moving easily through the dark cavern. He had once been bonded to a creature adept at traveling by feel in pitch-black tunnels like these.

The second chamber was much vaster than the last. Rushing water tickled his ears. The torchlight barely dented the gloom, and even with his boon, Nox couldn't see how far the back wall went.

Ryon stopped next to a lift similar to the one they'd ascended the mountain on, but much smaller. He held out the torch and nodded to a hollow carved into the wall. "You mind hanging this so I can untether the lift?"

Taking it, Nox made quick work of the task. Then he leaned over the precipice that the lift dangled over. Blackness stared back at him, just like the awful pit that lived in his worst nightmares. His stomach roiled, and he backed away uneasily. "What do we need to go down there for?"

"I need you to see something below the cloud cover. Don't worry. I've been on this lift dozens of times. It's perfectly safe. If we were to fall—which *won't* happen—we'd land in the deep pool at the bottom." Ryon slid open the contraption's door and hopped in. "Come on."

Don't look down. You'll be fine. Nox gulped and followed, his curiosity outweighing his fear.

The lift jolted into motion, sinking them into darkness. Ryon worked the rope expertly as Nox stood there, trying not to betray his feelings with how badly his fingers trembled on the railing. After countless heartbeats pounded through his ears, Ryon halted the lift. Nox squinted at the sudden brightness seeping into the cavern from beneath them.

"Almost there. Don't make any sudden moves or loud noises while we're exposed, all right? I'm going to drop us a little more," Ryon said.

Slowly, they inched further down. An opening about the size of a window rested on the cavern wall. Nox blinked quickly as his eyes adjusted to the light.

"Do you see?" Ryon asked.

Nox's brow furrowed. "See what?"

"Look down," Ryon added.

Rot and decay... exactly what he *didn't* want to do. Nox swallowed. Then he forced his gaze down. A few sparse fires crowded the mountain's base. They were far too high to make out any individuals, but men in black wandered around, erecting tents and looking well at ease.

Nox's blood ran cold. "Jurdan's men. They've found us."

"They've found the mountain." Ryon clapped his shoulder. "That doesn't mean they'll find us."

"Do the girls know?" Nox asked.

"Not yet. Brother Tham found me while I was on the way to fetch you and told me the lookouts just brought him word of their arrival. I figured you'd want to see for yourself." He gestured at the ropes. "You ready to go back up?"

Nox nodded. "I've seen enough. Let's keep this to ourselves—for tonight, at least. Let Violet and Mariun enjoy the feast."

"Good idea. Anyway, Brother Tham assured me he set watches to keep a constant eye on their camp. We're still safe."

All the same, a sickening sensation rolled through Nox's stomach. One that had nothing to do with the cavern's dark heights swallowing them once again, and everything to do with the threat at their door. No matter Ryon's assurances, Nox wouldn't feel safe until he'd put an ocean between the masked and his friends. He needed to get the dragons flying—fast.

Still, he didn't have the heart to worry the girls. Clearly, climbing that mountain was no small feat. Not one that the masked could hope to accomplish in a single night. Dusk was falling, and Ryon was likely the only man foolish enough to attempt climbing such a steep mountain in the dark. Surely the watch Brother Tham had set would be enough to alert them before anyone came close to scaling the mountainside.

They could tell Violet and Mariun in the morning once the feast was over. They deserved a night to relax and forget their worries.

After emerging from the cavern, they trekked across the mountaintop and over a wide stone bridge. Lights twinkled in cottage windows, making the small houses lining the straight village streets appear picturesque. Nox's boots rang out as he followed Ryon into the village.

"I've one more thing to show you before we head to the feast." Ryon pointed at two humble cottages. "Here's where we're staying tonight."

Nox scanned the buildings, noting nothing to set them apart from the homes beside them. "Are these what passes for inns in your village?"

"There are no inns." Ryon chuckled. "We don't get many visitors. We'll be staying with some friends of my ma's." He pointed at the house on the left. "This one belongs to an old widower. That's where you and I will sleep." His finger trailed over the one beside it, which looked identical except for the frilly flower-patterned curtains in the windows. "And his sisters who live next door have a pair of beds to spare for the girls. If you'd like to retire early, just head here and go right in. They're expecting us. They left the doors to the guest rooms open. Feel free to take your pick if the owners aren't back from the feast yet."

"All right." As they continued onward, Nox was careful to keep track of the route so he'd remember his way back.

He normally didn't reach out to his bondmates when he knew they were resting, and they were kind enough to do the same. But he might as well let Gwen know… *"Hey, you still awake, Gwen?"*

"Hm?" Her voice was groggy. *"Something wrong?"*

"No. Sorry I woke you. Just wanted to let you know Ryon found us beds in the village. Think you and the others will be fine on your own tonight?"

"Yes. Now enjoy your night and let me sleep."

Nox smirked at her surly tone. Maybe he was rubbing off on Gwen a little too much.

"Did I miss something funny?" Ryon asked.

"Just Gwen." Music and revelry filled the air. Nox's stomach churned as his gaze fell to Ryon's hands wrapped around the torch. His fingertips tingled as an old conversation with his niece replayed in his ears. "I've been meaning to ask you about those bloodfeathers of yours. Violet mentioned something about consequences."

Ryon winced. "I guess I didn't explain much when you were in your cell."

"I can barely remember what happened while I was drugged." Nox shrugged. "The consequences—is that why the claws that appeared when I made the wish in the ring keep coming back?"

"Yeah." Ryon glanced at Nox's fists. "I'm actually surprised they didn't stay like that for good."

"That could happen?" He shuddered.

"Maybe. It's all in how you word the wish." Ryon rubbed the back of his neck. "What did you wish for?"

Nox racked his brain, but he couldn't quite recall. He nearly reached out to Flint to ask if he remembered. No. He'd ask in the morning. Gwen needed her rest if the hatchlings had any hope of learning to fly tomorrow.

Ryon examined his expression. "Want me to ask Mother Orea when I'm granted my audience? I bet she'll have answers for you."

"Sure. Thanks." Just another example of Ryon being so *sweet*. Nox forced his fists to unclench. He had half a mind to ask Ryon about his own consequences. His hand ached with the memory of the uncontrolled strength Ryon had unleashed on him when he'd pulled him into their stolen boat.

Before the words formed on his tongue, they turned a corner. The feast spread out across a large square. A riot of smells, music, and laughter bombarded him all at once. Children ran amok, chasing each other and squealing. Gray-haired elders perched on stools on the crowd's edges, chatting animatedly with one another. Long-skirted women and short-skirted men wandered the streets, sipping from cups and wearing pleased grins.

Despite all the chaotic merriment, Nox scanned the crowd and almost instantly picked out a head of silvery-white hair among the dark-haired villagers.

"Violet," Ryon called, making her spin to face them.

Nox split a look between them. A slow smile curved his lips as he watched them dodge the crowd to meet in the road, their gazes locked on each other. Like two waves racing around jagged rocks, only to crash into each other on the shore.

Good thing he'd kept his mouth shut—this time. Obviously, the doubts Violet had shared before climbing into the lift were unwarranted. They both blatantly ignored him, though he kept pace with Ryon and stopped beside him.

Ryon trailed his fingers across a golden feather woven into Violet's hair—all the while staring at his hand with a dumbstruck expression, like he couldn't quite help himself from touching her. The man was clearly smitten, just like Flint had insisted. How had he missed it before?

Nox cleared his throat.

Violet flushed, finally noticing him standing at Ryon's elbow. "Uncle Nox." Her gaze only lingered on him for a heartbeat before it returned to Ryon. "You found him. Did you need to drag him back with you?"

"Not quite." Ryon dropped his hand. "Have you been enjoying the feast so far?"

She spun a half-full cup of wine in her hands. "Yes. The music is lovely." A tiny frown creased her brow. "I haven't tried much food yet, but it smells wonderful."

"You haven't?" Ryon tilted his head, examining the square behind them. "Let's fix that." His eyes lit up. "Have you eaten cloud bread before?"

Violet shook her head. "What's that?"

"It's an Avion specialty. You have to try it. Wait here. I'll grab you some." Ryon hurried off, crossing the street and lining up behind a stall handing out some puffy concoctions.

"Having fun?" Nox tugged a lock of Violet's hair, admiring the intricate weave. Half of the silvery strands were coiled atop her head in a pattern that reminded him of roses. The rest hung around her shoulders, layered with silver and gold feathers. "I like the new look."

Violet patted her head. "Ryon's mother styled it for me."

"So, he's already introducing you to his family." He quirked a brow. "That's good. Just what you wanted, right?"

She smiled shyly, her gaze landing on Ryon across the road. "I like it here. What do you think of Avion?"

A man strolled past them, carrying a tray filled with cups of wine. Nox snagged one as he passed, and shrugged. "Seems pleasant enough, I suppose. Definitely beats Thalassia." The mention of Mariun's home made curiosity crawl up his neck. "Where is Mariun?"

"She's around here somewhere. A few locals taught us a dance when we first arrived. I couldn't quite get the swing of it, but Mariun took to it like a fish to water. Last I saw, she was dancing near the bonfire." Violet tore her gaze away from Ryon long enough to point down the road.

Nox frowned. He scanned the crowd, but with what looked like the entire village crammed into the square, he couldn't see her. He swigged a sip out of his cup and winced. "Wow. That's stronger than I remember."

Ryon reappeared, his hands laden with fluffy white bread shimmering with seasoning. "That's feast wine. Different blend than the stuff we drank this morning."

Violet wrinkled her nose, staring at her half-filled cup. "Hm. I thought it tasted different. I should've warned Mariun to take it easy on the stuff. She kept going on about how much she liked the brothers' wine."

Ryon passed a piece of bread to Violet and held another out to Nox. "Here, I brought you some, too."

"Thanks." Nox crammed a bite of the sweet bread into his mouth and chewed, barely hearing Violet's comments about how delicious it tasted. He swallowed. "You two mind if I look around?"

Violet shook her head. "No. Go ahead. There's lots to see. If you spot Mariun, tell her about the wine."

"I will." Nox stalked off, heading straight for the central bonfire.

Where was she? Mariun might be older, but in some ways, she was even more naïve than his twenty-year-old niece. If he found her passed out in a corner somewhere, or worse—

The black thoughts fled his mind as he spotted her. She spun around the fire, skirts twirling, laughter bubbling out of her lips. A trio of teen girls danced with her. Mariun flicked the occasional glance at their feet and mimicked them when they changed the pattern of their steps, but mostly she swayed to her own beat.

Nox's breath caught as he watched the hypnotic swing of her hips. He lingered on the crowd's edge, nibbling on his bread and sipping his wine. One song turned into two, and his bread disappeared, along with the wine. Still, he stood there, mesmerized. She looked so happy. So free.

He would have likely stood there all night, basking in her joy, if not for the fellow who cut in. Some pretty boy in a checkered skirt tapped on her shoulder and bowed.

Nox tensed, clutching his empty cup so tightly the wood buckled. He studied Mariun's face. If she appeared even the least bit uncomfortable, he'd barrel through the crowd in a heartbeat.

But Mariun grinned and took the man's hand. Pretty boy tugged her away from the girls, spinning her through the dancers with practiced ease. He held tight to her hand and settled the other lightly on her waist.

Nox clenched his jaw until his molars ached. His gaze darted between Mariun's smile and that idiot's hands. His fingers twitched with the undeniable urge to rip them off her.

Rot and decay. He forced a deep breath into his chest. It was just a dance. Fun. Mariun deserved a little fun—hadn't he told himself that on the walk over?

But when the song ended, pretty boy didn't let go. He led Mariun away from the dancers and snatched two cups of wine off a passing tray. As Mariun lifted the cup to her lips and drained it, Nox jerked into motion.

He tore through the crowd with a few strides and plucked the empty cup out of her hand. "How many of these did you drink?"

He expected her gaze to shoot straight to him. For her brow to furrow and for her to bark some insult. But her glassy eyes slid across him leisurely, and a relaxed grin curved her lips. "Nox. You're here! Good. I thought for sure you'd decided to hide out with the dragons."

Nox frowned, not inclined to tell her how close he came to doing that. "How many, Mariun?" He jiggled the cup in front of her face.

"Dunno. Three? Four, maybe?" She tugged at her tunic and wafted a bit of air down the top. "Been dancing. I got thirsty."

Rotting wine... At least she seemed like a happy drunk. Nox had learned not to overindulge in spirits if he didn't want to end up crying into his cup by the end of the night.

Pretty boy, his gaze glued to Mariun's chest, spoke a few words and held out his hand.

Nox growled low in his throat and wedged himself between them before Mariun reacted. "That's feast wine. It's not the same as the brothers' blend."

"So? It's just as tasty." Mariun giggled. "I want to dance. Dance with me, Nox."

"No." She wanted to dance? She ought to be headed straight to bed to sleep off that wine.

She pouted. Nox stared at her, stone-faced.

Mariun sighed. "It's all right. You don't have to." She turned to pretty boy with a lopsided smile.

Before she could open her mouth and chatter in that maddening tongue, Nox bit out, "Fine." He shoved his and Mariun's empty cups into pretty boy's hands and flashed a grin. "You don't mind taking these, do you?" From the way the man's face drained of color, Nox imagined his grin was downright feral. Nox snagged Mariun's hand, dragging her back into the crowd of dancers.

She stumbled before smoothing out her stride. Then she spun in his arms, facing him with a coy smile. "Do you plan to scare off all my dance partners?"

He tugged her closer, wrapping an arm around her waist and resting his hand on the small of her back. "You're drunk, Mariun. I'm just looking out for you."

"Keeping me safe, are you?" She giggled again, peeling her hand out of his and wrapping her arms around his neck.

He let her set the pace of their dance, and though the drums thumped and the woodwinds sang a jaunty tune, she swayed slowly. With each step, she inched closer until their bodies were nearly flush.

He should pull back. None of the other dancers had been so close. For all he knew, the villagers were staring at them, aghast, wondering why they were pressed together so indecently.

But he swayed closer instead. With his free hand, he gently lifted her chin and lost himself in the shadowy depths of her gray eyes. The rest of the world faded away until all he could see was her staring at him so sweetly.

He leaned closer. Close enough they might as well be sharing the same breath. Until Mariun opened her mouth and licked her lips. The strong aroma of wine wafted around him.

Rot and decay. Nox pulled back. She was drunk. And here he was, a heartbeat away from mauling her in front of a feast full of people.

Her brow furrowed. "What's wrong?"

Nox tugged her hand, leading her away from the bonfire. Mariun stumbled into him, making him even more grateful he had the presence of mind to cut their dance short. He guided her across the crowd and down the street leading to their guest houses.

"Nox, wait." Mariun jerked his hand—hard. "Where are we going?"

He whipped around to face her. "You need to sleep off the wine."

She scoffed and ripped her hand out of his. "No thanks." She turned back to the feast, but Nox grabbed her shoulders and spun her around before she'd taken a single step.

"I'm not letting you go back there so some other pretty boy can put his hands all over you."

"Why not? You don't want to kiss me again." Her shrill voice rose until she was practically screaming. "Why shouldn't I find someone else who will?"

Nox dragged her farther away from the feast before someone wandered over to investigate. He pulled her to the side of the road and stopped once they were wedged between two skinny trees.

"It's not that I don't want to kiss you, Mariun," he explained softly.

"No? Could've fooled me. Seems like you've been going out of your way to ignore me." She crossed her arms. "You can't send me to bed like some misbehaving youth. I've put up with people bossing me around my whole life. Not anymore."

He tugged a slim braid between his fingers. Mariun's hair was plaited as well, and though the style was much simpler than Violet's, it was just as lovely. "You're drunk."

"That's a convenient excuse. What about last night?" Her eyes flashed. "That's right. You'd rather hurt me than kiss me." She jabbed his chest. "You don't think I've known pain? I'll scream all you want if you just stop being so confusing and kiss me."

"What are you—" Comprehension hit him square in the chest. Was she truly that sheltered? Did she freeze last night because she thought he'd wanted to make her scream in pain? A wicked smile crossed his lips. "Mariun, I want to make you scream with pleasure."

Mariun's eyes widened. "Oh." She burst into a round of giggles. "I'm such an idiot."

He was the idiot for assuming she'd understood his innuendo when she knew so little beyond Thalassia. Nox shook his head as she doubled over laughing—her reaction confirming once again that he needed to get her to bed.

"You're not an idiot." Nox grabbed her hands and gentled his voice as her laughter tapered off, determined to speak plainly this time. "I don't want to hurt you, but I can't promise that I never will. And I want to kiss you. But I want more than that, Mariun. So much more."

She wobbled closer, her lashes lowering. "I want that, too." She angled her face upward, lips pursed invitingly.

It would be so easy to kiss her. To take her back to one of those empty houses... No.

"Not tonight." Nox's firm statement made Mariun's eyes snap open.

"Why not?" There was that adorable pout again. It took everything in him not to lean down and wipe it off her lips.

"I'm guessing you've never been drunk before?" This morning, she'd admitted she had no idea what wine was, but he refused to keep making assumptions about her.

"No." Her nose wrinkled. "I don't see why that matters."

Nox slung an arm over her shoulder and started walking again, angling them away from the feast. "I've overindulged once or twice. Tomorrow you'll wake with a hazy memory and a pounding head. If you still want to kiss me, come find me when you're feeling better."

"I feel fine now," she insisted.

He chuckled. "I'm sure you do." It was odd explaining this, but he'd be damned if she went on thinking drunken trysts weren't typically riddled with regrets. "It's just that sometimes decisions that seem like a marvelous idea when you've had a bit to drink turn out to be disastrous in the morning."

He cringed inwardly as she wobbled beneath his arm, forcing him to steady her. Was it even worth it to explain this now? Who knew how much of this conversation she'd even recall... Clearly, that third—or fourth—cup of wine had not settled well.

"You know"—Mariun rolled her neck and glared at him, but the effect was less potent when it caused her to stumble—"for a guy who claims to be an animal, you spend an awful lot of time acting civilized."

Sure, because what kind of man would bring a woman to his bed when she could barely walk a straight line? "I said I was an animal, not a monster."

Mariun's expression softened. "Trust me, I know. I've been around enough monsters to tell the difference." She fell silent for a long while, only the gentle tapping of their boots on the cobblestones ringing out between them. As they turned down the road where they'd find their beds, she quietly said, "I think you're wrong about one thing."

"What?" Nox grinned, trying not to laugh at the way her words came out slightly slurred.

"I won't change my mind. Kissing you will still sound like a marvelous idea in the morning."

He leaned over and placed a chaste kiss on her forehead. "We'll see. Come on. Let's get you some water and find your bed."

Nox led her inside, all the while wondering if her drunken claim would prove true. Would she still feel the same in the bright light of day, or would Mariun wish she could snatch those words back? No matter what, at least she'd be making the decision with a clear mind.

His stomach twinged as he watched her collapse into her waiting bed. He helped her out of her boots and drew the blanket over her.

"G'night, Nox," Mariun whispered with a sigh. Her dark hair fanned out on the pillow, and her eyes fluttered closed. The sight of her lying there, so trusting and relaxed, made his chest ache.

"Goodnight."

He hovered in the doorway, as mesmerized by the sight of Mariun sleeping as he'd been watching her dance. Just days ago, he'd been suspicious of her every move. Sure, she still made his blood boil more often than not, but somewhere along the way, she'd wormed her way into his thoughts. She'd lodged there like a catchy tune, impossible to ignore.

It was insane. She was irrevocably tangled with Jurdan. Even though they weren't blood kin, she shared his power. A power so strong, if she chose to use it for evil, they'd be hard-pressed to stop her.

But as Nox watched her sleep, he couldn't shake the feeling that he'd been wrong. Wrong to suspect her of helping Jurdan. Wrong to push her away when he could've been leaning on her.

Mariun wasn't anything like that *thing* that called himself her father.

She'd put herself in danger to save Violet. Then when the masked closed in on them back at that volcano, she could have easily left him quaking with fear and saved herself before being shot. But she hadn't.

She'd stayed with the fool who couldn't stop punishing her for a death Jurdan orchestrated. She'd saved him even though he didn't deserve it.

Even after a lifetime of abandonment and seclusion, her heart remained pure. Watching the delight on her face as she discovered something new never failed to send a rush of tingles across his skin. She was honest, helpful—and though he hadn't admitted it to anyone—funny, too. He'd even begun to secretly look forward to her sarcastic comebacks when they argued.

And he'd have to be blind to deny how beautiful she was. Now that he knew her, he could see that her beauty wasn't just on the surface.

His heart clenched as he turned to leave, and in that moment, he admitted the truth. He wanted her more than he wanted his next breath.

And if Mariun changed her mind, it would wreck him.

Fate Conspired

Violet sighed. Her belly was full, music and laughter filled her ears, and Ryon hadn't left her side since he'd returned with Nox. She was having an incredible time at the feast. Still, as the night wore on, the tiny sliver of discomfort that had plagued her since she'd arrived in Avion became more insistent. Her skin prickled, and every movement in her periphery made her flinch.

"Something wrong?" Of course, it didn't take long for Ryon to notice.

She plastered a smile on her face. "No." She shook her head and stared at her boots. "Nothing I can put my finger on, at least."

Ryon cocked a brow, dodging a pair of little girls waving colored streamers. "Do you want to talk about it?"

"It's just this strange feeling." Violet's brow furrowed. "I don't know—"

An older woman approached, all smiles and full of chatter, seeming to either not notice or not care that she was interrupting their conversation.

"Hold that thought," Ryon told her, then turned to the woman with a smile.

Violet backed up a few paces, wishing once again she could speak their tongue. Maybe Ryon could start giving her lessons.

Now that she'd met his family, she was even more ready to learn. When he'd finally shared the full story of his past, she'd felt like her chest had cracked open. She couldn't even imagine how hard that must have been, growing up with a monster in their home.

It was obvious Vera was a kind, caring woman. Violet had known it when she'd watched how sweetly she'd handled Rovan. And then when Vera had insisted on braiding her and Mariun's hair, she'd effortlessly made them both feel at home.

To think her lover spent years abusing her, and Ryon and Rovan had had no choice but to watch it happen... Violet shivered.

She wasn't at all surprised that Ryon had jumped in to save her. That even as a child, he'd done what he'd needed to do to protect the people he loved.

Then poor Rovan... her heart twisted. It was clear Ryon blamed himself for his brother's accident. And once again, he went above and beyond to help him. She only hoped that once he received his golden feather, he'd finally forgive himself.

"Forgiveness is a lofty ambition when one's heart is weighed down with guilt," a feminine voice whispered, barely audible.

Violet blinked, her gaze darting around the feast. Where had that come from? Was that... Her eyes widened, and she replied in her thoughts. *"Hello? Are you there?"*

"Yes, child," the voice answered, even quieter than before. *"You must f-find me."*

Her hand flew to her chest, and Violet whipped around. *"How? Where are you?"*

But this time, no reply came.

Violet closed her eyes and focused on the connection blossoming in her soul. A gentle tug pulled her forward. Her eyes popped open as her feet began moving. She wove through the crowd of revelers with only one thought on her mind.

She had to find her bondmate. Proximity and danger. That's what Nox had said was needed for a bond to form. But she was safe, an honored guest surrounded by merry villagers. That only meant one thing. Her bondmate was in danger.

Violet wandered in a daze, relying on instinct to lead her through the empty streets. Shadows darkened every corner, making her regret her swift departure. She should have waited for Ryon. What if she got lost? She could wander off a cliff edge, and where would that leave her bondmate?

Noise clattered on a side street. Violet jolted and hastened her steps. Her heart thundered in her throat. She was a stranger in this community. A place where at least one man lived who delighted in harming women. What if someone was out there, just waiting to snatch her and pull her into the gloom?

Maybe the danger wasn't as one-sided as she'd assumed...

"Hey!"

Violet yelped and whirled around, her tense shoulders falling when she spotted Ryon racing to catch her. "Blazes. You startled me."

"Where are you rushing off to?" Ryon jogged beside her, carrying a lit torch.

Violet had already turned back to her task, following the nagging warning reverberating in her bones. "It's my bondmate. I finally heard her."

Ryon slowed to match her pace. "I knew you would. That's incredible news."

"Yeah, it would be if I wasn't certain she's in danger." Violet sucked in a deep breath. "I need to find her."

"All right. I'll help you. Did she say where she is?"

"No. She sounded so weak. I think she must have run out of strength to contact me before she could finish telling me where to go." Violet's hands shook. "What if I don't find her in time?"

"Don't worry. We will." Ryon grabbed her hand and squeezed gently. "How can I help?"

Violet smiled weakly. "Follow me. I-I think I can sense where to find her. At least, I hope I can."

"If you think you can, then you will." Ryon squeezed again. "I believe in you, Violet."

Ryon's faith warmed her chest. And with him by her side, the shadows didn't seem half as scary. Together, they hurried through the village until they reached the wide stone bridge leading back to the Aviary.

"She's over there?" Ryon quirked a brow. "Are you sure?"

Violet nodded. "She is. I can feel it."

Ryon started across the bridge. Violet ignored the fear pulsing up her neck and followed.

"What if it's Mena? Though I hope the hatchlings are all right," Ryon mused.

Violet nibbled on her lower lip. It was possible, but something about his guess felt wrong. Not so long ago, she'd wished to bond with a dragon more than anything. Somehow, the thought that she'd never bond with a dragon didn't sting the way it once had. "I don't think it's Mena."

"Well, whoever it is, we'll find them."

They hurried across the bridge and past dozens of rocky outcroppings. It wasn't long before Violet realized exactly where her intuition was leading her.

"Violet... are you heading to the Aviary?" Ryon's voice wavered, sending a wash of prickles down her back.

"Yes. She's in there."

Ryon halted, and the torchlight wobbled. "But the priests. They said we can't enter until the next full moon..."

Violet faced him, her pulse hammering. "I can't wait." The devastation painting Ryon's face nearly made her gasp. "You don't need to come with me. If you're afraid of what will happen with your audience, then I'll under—"

"No." Ryon's gaze flicked back to the village, but then he squared his shoulders and stepped forward. "I'm not leaving you. Come on."

They rushed across the grassy hillside in front of the Aviary. The slim, rocky tower loomed there like some ancient relic of a bygone era. It sent a shiver up her spine that seeped into her blood and chased its way to her heart.

What was happening to her bondmate in there? Had they made it in time to save her? The questions darted around her mind, and she covered the final distance at a jog, desperate to uncover answers.

The closer they drew, the more the building struck her as eerie. She'd felt nothing of the sort when she'd gazed upon it on their way to the village. At first, she couldn't grasp what was so strange.

But then Ryon shuddered, and she heard an audible swallow work its way down his throat. "Something's wrong. It's never this silent."

That was it. She'd soaked up the sweet melodies pouring out of the pockmarked structure earlier. Tonight, it was deathly still. Only the crunch of their footsteps in the grass and the light whistle of wind marked their journey.

Ryon led her toward a doorway. A brother lingered inside it. He tugged the sides of his cloak tightly across his chest as they approached and greeted Ryon with a weary voice. Ryon struck up a conversation. He halted beside the man and angled his body so that she was hidden. Then, with a subtle jerk of his head, he motioned her to continue.

Violet darted inside, passing the brother and not stopping when he shouted in alarm. Ryon dropped the torch, and the unmistakable sound of the men grappling rang out behind her.

She paid them no mind. The tingle in her blood had grown urgent. It pulled her forward into the dark recesses of the Aviary.

She'd only taken a few steps before fear choked her. It was no use. She couldn't see in the dark like Nox. Without Ryon and the torch, she'd have no way to find her bondmate. She might as well be wandering in a—

The moon stole out from behind a dark patch of clouds. The shining crescent shone directly upon the Aviary, lighting the structure dimly. Violet's breath caught, and she had the distinct sensation that this was exactly where she was supposed to be. That fate had conspired to bring her here at this very moment. That even the heavens were aiding her quest to find the creature she was destined to bond with.

As her gaze rose to admire the felicitous moon, a flash of gold at the very top of the Aviary caught her eye. She squinted, but before she could narrow in on the curious sight, the golden figure toppled over the edge and plummeted.

Violet's stomach dropped with it. Sudden instinct made her lurch forward. She raced for the tumbling creature and threw out her arms just in time to catch it.

"Oof." She landed on her behind with a squirming bird cradled in her arms. As soon as her gaze connected with the gold-ringed black eyes of the most beautiful golden-feathered bird she'd ever seen, Violet knew. This was what she'd been pulled here to do. She'd just saved her bondmate from smashing into the ground. *"Are you all right?"*

The reply came slowly and labored. *"For now. Thank you."* Her bondmate's voice was so melodic it was one step away from a song.

Violet frowned, scanning the bird all over for the source of her apparent exhaustion. She wasn't trained to heal animals, but she had grown up on a farm. After a quick once-over, she'd spotted nothing obvious that might be bothering her bondmate. Perhaps she just needed rest...

Ryon hurried into the room, his torch held aloft, lighting the moonlit chamber even further. Violet lifted her head, her eyes bulging as she spotted hundreds of beady eyes staring at her. Birds perched on every wall, shrouded in a riot of silver and duller gray feathers.

"Violet." Ryon halted beside her and gasped. "Why are you holding Mother Orea?"

"She's my bondmate." Violet smiled up at him from her seat on the floor. She turned back to study the golden bird. *"Are you Mother Orea?"* Shock reverberated through her, chilling her to the bone.

"I was. No longer." The golden bird stared upward.

Violet followed her gaze and spotted another flash of gold at the top of the Aviary. Ryon's explanation replayed in her ears, and Violet's stomach lurched. *"A new Mother Orea has hatched? But Ryon said when that happens..."*

"He's right. I'm dying, child."

"No!" Violet cradled her bondmate in her arms. She'd heard tales of the instant bond that formed between bondmates. Now she could say for certain it was all true. Even though they'd never set eyes on each other before this moment, a soul-deep connection drew them together. And the thought of her dying... Tears stung her eyes. *"Please, there must be something we can do."*

It couldn't be the end... The fate she'd just rejoiced in had turned on her, granting her one of her greatest wishes, only to snatch it away in the same breath.

Violet clutched her bondmate to her chest and burst into tears.

Introductions

Ryon kneeled beside Violet, his heart breaking. "Don't cry. Whatever it is, we'll figure it out."

"She's dying." Violet lifted her tearstained face. "I saved her from the fall, but she's still dying."

Ryon's stomach sank. It didn't make sense. Why have Violet save Mother Orea only for her to die? Could fate truly be that cruel?

A clatter erupted behind them. Brother Albus lurched into the doorway, a dark-purple bruise blooming under his eye. Ryon buried the urge to cringe. The portly brother wasn't one of his favorite priests in the Aviary, but he'd never imagined he'd get into a fistfight with him. He just prayed the actions he'd taken to help Violet wouldn't come back to haunt him when he was granted his audience.

"What are you two doing in here? I thought I told you—" Brother Albus gasped, his jaw dropping. "Mother Orea."

The bird in Violet's arms opened its mouth and sang. "Direct us to my funeral chamber. Thank you, brother."

Brother Albus startled, then whistled back. "B-but you're not..."

"I'm dead to *them*. That's enough for now."

Ryon's gaze darted around the Aviary. The orecolns that had been so keen to watch him during his petitions had turned their attention away. They stared upward, gazing upon the golden hatchling seated on the highest perch. Ryon blinked at the tiny chick, trying to fathom what would make the orecolns turn aside from the leader they'd followed for years, in favor of this infant.

"Follow me," Brother Albus said.

"Violet." Ryon cleared his throat. "Mother Orea ordered Brother Albus to take us... away from here." He couldn't quite bring himself to repeat the order verbatim when Violet was clearly struggling.

"That whistling... he can talk to birds, too?" Violet scrubbed her face with her sleeves and stood, carrying Mother Orea carefully in her arms.

Ryon nodded. "All the priests can."

Brother Albus led them out of the Aviary and toward the squat rectory perched beside it. Ryon's pulse pounded as they approached the door.

"We can't go in there," Ryon blurted. It was forbidden for any but priests to enter the rectory. Everyone knew that.

"Mother Orea's orders supersede our customs," Brother Albus chimed in. "Please, follow me."

A darkened hall spread out before them. The faint scent of candle wax permeated the air. Brother Albus snagged an unlit taper off the wall and gestured to Ryon's torch. "May I?"

He helped Brother Albus light the taper, then stomped out his torch at the brother's insistence. They followed his swishing robes down the hall, passing a handful of detailed tapestries of orecolns adorning the walls.

Brother Albus swung open a door emblazoned with an intricate carving of a golden orecoln in flight. He ushered them inside, using his taper to light several more tacked to the walls. The small windowless room was sparsely furnished, with only a single low table in the center and a pair of benches perched along the far wall.

"Thank you, brother. Leave us," Mother Orea sang from within Violet's arms.

"Brother Albus," Ryon cut in quickly. "I'm sorry about your eye."

Moccasins tapping, Brother Albus slid the door shut with a gentle *click*, not bothering to reply.

"Please, set me on the table, child." Mother Orea fluffed out her wings and perched on her spindly legs as soon as Violet deposited her atop the wooden tabletop.

Ryon frowned. "You don't understand her whistles, do you?"

Violet shook her head. "No. She speaks to me in my mind."

"I can both sing for you, Ryon, and relay my thoughts at the same time. I think you can handle speaking and communicating with me at once as well, Violet," Mother Orea insisted. "Now, I believe we shall need proper introductions."

Introductions? She clearly knew their names already. What was there left to introduce?

Violet's lip wobbled. "B-but what about you? Shouldn't we be looking for a healer?"

Mother Orea cocked her head. "No. I will explain why that's unnecessary. But first, I can't have you calling me Mother Orea. That phase of my life has passed."

"What would you like us to call you?" Ryon whistled. He quickly repeated the question in words, for Violet's sake.

"You may call me Orry."

"Orry," Violet repeated. "I'd really feel better if we sent for a healer."

"No need. Your boon shall heal me well enough."

Ryon's brow furrowed. "What boon?"

Violet gasped. "That's right! Humans always give their bondmates the same boon; they lengthen their lifespan." She clapped her hands and bounced on her feet. "Shadow, my father's bonded wolf, has already lived far longer than a normal wolf, and he's still going strong."

"Yes, since our bond began, I've already begun to feel invigorated. But I'm afraid it will not be quite the same," Orry replied sadly.

"What?" Violet's face fell. "Why not?"

"I may not look it to your eyes, but I'm very old. For an orecoln, at least. Since our bond was completed when I was already close to my end, your boon will not be so effective."

Ryon eyed Orry closely. With every moment that passed, her voice grew steadier, and she appeared less frail. It was a shame to realize that wouldn't last. His stomach clenched. "How long will you have?"

"A few weeks. Maybe a few months, if we're lucky." Orry inched closer to Violet as she wrung her hands. "Do not weep for me, child. You've given me an unimaginable gift. None other in my position will ever survive as long as I shall. And we have much to accomplish together."

Violet's lips thinned. "What do you mean?"

"There's a reason I sent Ryon to find you. You're not just my bondmate, Violet. You're the one."

Violet shook her head. "But Mena—"

"It was never her. I knew it, Violet. I knew it was you." Ryon beamed.

"I don't understand... I'm the one—for what?" She rubbed her temples. "Can you tell me that, at least?"

"You are the one who will save us all. There is a great evil plaguing our world. One that will not be easily destroyed. But you can stop it,

Violet, with the power that you alone possess. That and the boon you now have access to."

"My boon?"

"Yes, child. I shall tell you more in time. I promise." She cocked her head, eyeing Ryon. His heart jolted. Was this it? Was he finally about to learn if he'd done enough to earn a golden bloodfeather? "First—"

"Wait," Violet cut in. "Sorry." She winced. "Just one more question. How do you know all this about me being the one? How could you possibly know what the future holds?"

Orry spun back to face Violet. "There is a fish to thank for that."

"You can't mean... the dream elixir." Violet's brow furrowed. "But siltreak fish live in the Northern Depths."

Ryon pursed his lips, his head bobbing between them. What in the world did a fish have to do with dreams or telling the future?

"The siltreak do spend most of their lives in the icy north. But they travel to the Still Sea every spring to spawn their young."

"Hold on, I'm not following this at all," Ryon admitted. He cursed himself the moment the words popped out. He really ought to let them finish whatever this odd conversation was so he could learn what Orry had been about to say. Still, he couldn't deny his curiosity.

Violet turned to him. "Do you remember the vision I told you about? The one my mother had about me?"

Ryon nodded.

"My mother traveled to the Northern Depths to find a woman called the Winter Witch of the North. The witch harvested the dream elixir—the liquid that caused her vision—from within the siltreak fish." Violet pressed her palm against her chest and leaned over slightly. "It's all connected, isn't it?"

"Certainly seems that way," Ryon said.

"Now that I've answered your question." Orry spun back to him. "I'm so proud of you, son."

Ryon's eyes stung, and he blinked furiously.

"You've earned this, Ryon." Orry strode forward and plucked a shining golden feather off her chest with her sharp beak. "Hold out your hand."

With trembling fingers, he reached out. He sighed as Orry dropped it and the achingly soft feather floated down and landed on his palm.

This was it. All those years of toil digging up silver. The treacherous climbs up and down the mountain. Even the dangerous adventure he'd faced since meeting Violet.

All of it was worth it.

Now he could save him. He could finally save Rovan.

Ryon closed his eyes and exhaled shakily, clasping the feather tightly in his hand. "Thank you."

"I must warn you—"

His eyes snapped open. "I know about the consequences." His gaze flitted to Violet for a heartbeat. He swallowed. "Whatever is required, I'm prepared to give. I'd sacrifice anything for Rovan. I've made my peace with that."

Orry shook her head rapidly. "Son, you misunderstand. You've already sacrificed everything that's required."

Ryon jolted, nearly dropping the feather. "What?"

"Why do you think we make petitioners gather so much silver? There's a reason we force them to toil for years on end."

Violet gasped. "You're making them sacrifice in advance."

Orry nodded sagely. "It is a delicate balance. When the suffering occurs first, then a wish on a golden feather may be made freely. If not, there's no telling what you might be required to sacrifice."

Rubbing his brow, Ryon sighed. If he'd known that earlier, would it have made his years of toil a little easier? Probably, but it was too late to know for sure. "Well, that's good news." He reached for his blade.

"Wait. There is one more thing I must tell you. Golden bloodfeathers are not the same as silver. No matter how much pain and suffering you withstand after this, you will never be granted another. You must be certain that this wish is worthy of your sacrifice."

Ryon didn't even need to consider it. "It is. Rovan deserves his life back."

Violet smiled at him gently as he unsheathed his knife. Ryon sucked in a deep breath and nicked his palm. He pressed the golden feather against the tiny droplet and closed his eyes. *I wish for the damage to Rovan's brain to be healed so he can live a normal life.*

Heat rushed up his arm, much more than the gentle warmth that bloomed when he wished upon a silver bloodfeather. The molten rush shocked his eyes open, and he groaned.

"Ryon. Are you all right?" Violet rushed to his side, but before her fingers closed around his forearm, the sensation subsided.

"Yeah. Yeah, I'm fine." He turned to Orry, his heart beating with all the force of a tritusk stampede. "Is that it? H-he's healed?"

"Go, son. Find him and see for yourself."

Ryon spun toward the door. He halted with his boot in the air. "Wait. What about you two?"

"I must rest," Orry announced firmly. "Violet's boon shall keep me alive, but I'm still so weary."

"I'll stay with her," Violet said. "Go to Rovan. We'll walk into the village and find you in the morning."

Ryon spared Violet a grateful nod, and then he raced through the door. Maybe he should've offered to stay with them. After all, who knew how the brothers would react when they returned from the feast and discovered what had happened in their absence? But he couldn't bear to spend a single instant without knowing if his wish worked.

He'd spent his entire life after Rovan's fall dedicated to this moment. There'd been countless nights lying awake, wondering what it would be like when he finally had his brother back. Would Rovan blame him for the accident? Would he even remember that day at all? And what about the years he spent in a confused haze, trapped within his own head? Questions buzzed through his mind, each one louder than the last.

In the past, all those questions did was make his chest ache. But not tonight. One way or another, he would get his answers. Even if he had to wake Rovan from a sound sleep, he would finally hear his twin's voice again.

A smile lit his face in the moonlight. It had been so, so long.

Ryon sprinted over the bridge and jogged through the mostly empty village streets. Here and there people tottered home from the feast, their laughter stilted from too much wine. Ryon didn't slow for any of them, even the few who called out to him by name.

He passed close enough to the feast to hear that the merriment was still in full swing. But he detoured around it, even though going straight through the square was the most direct route to his cottage. He wasn't taking the chance of being waylaid by the demanding questions of one of the elders.

Finally, he arrived. His hands trembled as he pushed open the door.

He halted in the threshold. Was that...?

Ryon fell to his knees just inside the doorway. The most glorious sound wrapped around his soul, mending the shredded tears ripped into his heart the moment he watched his brother fall.

He wouldn't have to wake his twin after all. Rovan was singing.

Strange but Good

Sunlight streamed inside, waking Nox at daybreak. He groaned and rolled beneath his borrowed sheets before shoving the blankets off. Blinking, he rubbed a hand across his stubbly chin and scowled at the window.

Last night, before he'd turned in, he'd met the jolly widower who owned the house. The man seemed pleasant enough, and his body was truly grateful for a night spent in an actual bed. But really, would it kill the guy to hang a few curtains?

"Hey. You up yet?"

"If you mean still, then yes," Flint replied instantly.

Nox chuckled. *"How about you, Gwen?"*

"Nope," Gwen answered groggily. *"I'm still dreaming. And in my dream, you let me sleep."*

He rolled his eyes and stuffed his feet into his boots. *"You can sleep till I get back to the barn. I'm leaving the village now. See you soon."*

"How was your night?" Flint inquired quietly. It appeared he was so desperate to know that he was willing to chance waking Gwen.

Nox sometimes forgot that this must be strange for Flint, too. They'd spent nearly twenty years with just the two of them bonded. It was a bit of a transition, adding into the mix a third creature whose sleep schedule they had to be mindful of.

"Strange but good, I suppose." Nox sighed.

"Good," Gwen grumbled. *"He can tell us later, then."*

Flint fell silent. Nox finished lacing his boots and strode to the door, careful to keep his footfalls light. It wouldn't do to repay the hospitality he'd been shown by stomping all over the house at the crack of dawn.

He paused outside the wide-open door of the second guest room. The bed was still made, the blankets folded crisply. Did Ryon not return last night?

A jolt of adrenaline shot through his veins. Was something wrong? He'd assumed that Ryon would keep Violet entertained after they'd left the feast. Surely they would've called for him if something dire had occurred while he was sleeping, wouldn't they?

Then again, Ryon's family lived in this village. He probably headed home instead of sleeping with the old widower. Maybe his mother even knew that windows were meant to have curtains. Nox continued past the room, willing his speeding pulse to slow. Before he jumped to conclusions, he ought to look around.

Wind whistled in his ears as he stepped onto the empty street. A few birds sang, and somewhere far away the gentle creak of wood and rhythmic smack of wheels rolling on stone played on the breeze. Still, it appeared most of the village still slept, no doubt worn out from all the revelry the night before.

He glanced at the house beside his. Was Mariun still curled in bed, sleeping so sweetly? Or already awake, nursing a headache and a whole heap of regrets?

Nox had half a mind to knock. It was already clear he'd spend the rest of the day worrying over what she would say. He could tear the bandage off now... He shook off the urge. She was probably still asleep. He wouldn't cut short her rest just to calm the raging tempest in his gut.

Pacing toward the bridge separating the village from the Aviary, he frowned at the sky as a dark cloud hid the rising sun. More clouds gathered on the horizon, slowly moving toward Avion. Big black clouds.

Great. Another storm. That meant he needed to get the hatchlings moving if he wanted any chance of flight practice today. At least the impending weather would likely slow any attempts the masked made to climb the mountainside.

Breaking into a light jog, Nox swiftly crossed the bridge. But a curious sight made him stop before he passed the Aviary.

"Violet?" He spotted his niece's silvery-white locks emerging from within the rectory. Even more strangely, a golden bird hopped by her feet. "What are you doing out here so early?"

"Uncle Nox." Violet strolled over, a huge grin painting her face. "You'll never guess what happened last night!"

"I'm guessing something big, since you're not still asleep in that house with Mariun."

She nodded quickly. "It was huge!" She threw out a hand. "Meet my bondmate, Orry."

"Really?" Nox eyed the bird more closely. Birds flocked all over Avion, most of them species he didn't recognize. This one wasn't any more familiar to him. He scratched his chest. "Sorry, what kind of bird is Orry?"

"She's an orecoln."

"You're kidding." Nox did a double take. Come to think of it, she did look oddly similar to the spindly-legged silver bird who'd ticked off Ari the other day.

She beamed. "Nope. In fact"—she leaned in conspiratorially—"she's the one we came here to see, Mother Orea. Well, she was." Violet grimaced. "It's kind of a long story."

An idea took root as Nox studied Orry. "Hey, do you think she'd be any help teaching the dragons to fly?"

Violet quirked a brow. "Hm. I don't know. Let me ask."

It was as good a thought as any. Perhaps a flying creature might have better luck teaching a dragon to fly. It's not like he'd been very successful so far...

After a moment's silence where Violet silently stared at her bondmate, Orry opened her jaws and let out a swift melodic trill. Answering song echoed from the Aviary.

Violet turned to him with a grin. "She's asked some silvers to help. They'll meet you at the barn."

A crack of thunder boomed off in the distance, making them jolt.

"Blazes. Another storm? What awful luck." Violet frowned. "Do you mind if I fill you in later on how I found Orry? I promised Ryon I'd meet him at his ma's cottage this morning, and I'd rather not get soaked."

The storm clouds weren't *that* close yet. Still, her story could wait. Violet was practically humming with excitement, her gaze locked on the village. She was no doubt bursting with longing for her sweetheart.

"Sure, Vi." He shook his head, chuckling. "Well, at least you don't need to worry about Ryon ignoring you anymore."

Violet's brow pinched. "What? Why?"

"You bonded with his people's deity." He waggled his brows. "Hope you like being revered." He smirked and bowed, sweeping extra low.

"Very funny." Violet shoved his shoulder while he was still bent over. If he wasn't so nimble, he'd have landed flat on his ass. "I'll see you later."

Nox straightened and waved, though he needn't have bothered. She didn't spare him a backward glance.

He buried a chuckle as he passed the Aviary. A flock of silver birds erupted from the top, forming a loose V formation before swinging low overhead.

"Rot and decay." Nox ducked, one step away from cowering on the ground while the stupid flock tried to take his head off on their flight to the barn.

He exhaled shakily. "It's gonna be a long day."

Before long, he shoved the barn door open. A tingle creeped over his skin, and moisture filled the air. His eyes widened at the chaos that greeted him. The dragons stared at the ceiling, their mouths ajar, lobbing magic into the rafters. The orecolns perched on the wooden beams, dodging blasts of air and chunks of ice and earth.

"Are you rotting mad?" he shouted, bursting in just as a chill raced up his spine. He whipped around, spotting a fireball coalescing in Mena's throat. "*Gwen. Stop! They're here to help.*"

The magic cut off abruptly.

"*We were only having a little fun.*"

"*Fun?*" Nox threw his arms out, incredulous. "*Mena was about to lob a fireball at the ceiling!*"

Gwen shook her head. "*She was just trying to scare them down. She wouldn't have really—*"

"Yeah, sure." Nox dragged a hand through his hair. It was easy to forget he was essentially babysitting a bunch of kids. He'd asked so much from them during their short lives. Once they got out of here, he really needed to grant them some time to be young and dumb. Just not inside a flammable building with fireballs.

Gwen's long neck swung side to side while she chatted with her siblings. Crys snorted and stamped a foot.

"What's his problem?"

Gwen flicked a quick glance at the rafters. *"He was really looking forward to tasting them."*

"No. Absolutely no tasting. Those birds are the closest thing these people have to gods." Nox wagged a finger, doing his best to look stern. *"Relax. I'll grab you ravenous hatchlings some breakfast."*

He left the barn, frowning at the darkening sky, before stopping short. The rectory door hung open, and the same smiling brother stood beside it, chatting with Mariun. Neither of them glanced his way, and Mariun appeared to be listening raptly to whatever nonsense the brother spouted.

Nox resumed walking. "Good morning."

"Nox." Mariun bowed to the brother, then faced him. "He was filling me in on what happened at the Aviary last night. Have you heard?"

"That Violet bonded with their goddess? Yeah. I saw her on my way here. They even arranged for a few silvers to help teach the dragons to fly."

Mariun's brow furrowed. "I passed her, too, while we were crossing the bridge. Violet told me where to find you, but she was in a hurry. The golden bird with her, she's the one?"

Nox nodded.

"Wow." Mariun grinned.

"So, you were looking for me?" His heart pounded as their eyes met.

The brother chose that moment to speak. Mariun turned her attention to him. Nox gritted his teeth.

"The dragons' breakfast is ready," Mariun announced.

"Good." Nox forced his jaw to unclench. "That's what I came out here for. If we want to get any flying practice in, it'll have to be soon." He waved at the storm clouds.

She frowned. "But we need to talk."

He winced. "I know, but—"

Crossing her arms, Mariun whipped around, speaking so rapidly and with such force it wiped the cheesy grin off the brother's face. Nox choked down a laugh.

Three youths appeared, swimming in their long black priest robes and carting buckets full of meat. The head brother nodded curtly at Mariun and wheeled about, directing the young brothers toward the barn. They fell in behind them, and Nox didn't miss the smug smile painting Mariun's lips.

"What did you say to him?"

"I told him we'd need a brother to tag along with the hatchlings today. Someone to watch over their progress with the orecolns' training. That will free you and me to hang back and chat."

He hid a smile with a cough. "Really? And he agreed?"

She shrugged. "Who wouldn't want to watch dragons learn to fly?"

Nox spared the brother a glance. The fellow's grin was back, shining so brightly it was practically blinding. Seemed Mariun was right. This would likely be the most exciting day in the priest's life.

They arrived back at the barn, and he sighed when the door opened to reveal a much calmer scene than the one he'd left. Silver flashed in the rafters. A bird sang a greeting, and the priest answered with a series of whistles.

The hatchlings crowded around the trough, eagerly awaiting their breakfast. As soon as the lads dumped the buckets inside, they bent to their feast.

"*Hey, Gwen,*" Nox said.

"*What?*" Her head popped up, a sausage link dangling from her lip that she snapped up before dipping back down to her breakfast.

"*Would you mind if one of the brothers went with you and the silvers? Mariun has something she needs to talk to me about.*"

"*Talk, eh?*" Flint chuckled.

Nox rolled his eyes. Mariun chatted with the brother again, and the silver birds fell silent.

"*Sure. We can manage,*" Gwen replied.

Mariun crossed the room and halted beside him. "The silvers know of a spot to practice beside a cavern. They'll take shelter from the storm there until it passes."

"Great." Nox's pulse sped as he met her gaze. "Sounds like they've thought of everything."

He thought he spied a twinkle in her eyes before the cacophony of dragons' thundering footfalls and birds' fluttering wings filled the room. The brothers hurried out after them, leaving the pair alone.

Mariun wedged a board inside the doorway. Nox crossed his arms and cocked a brow.

"What?" She shrugged. "I'm sick of being interrupted."

Speaking of... "*I think I need a little privacy for this conversation.*"

"*Don't worry, we'll be fine,*" Gwen insisted.

"*Yes, we'll be here once you've... talked.*" Flint snickered.

Nox scowled at the floor, concentrating long enough to build a block in his mind. Then he lifted his gaze and gave Mariun his full attention. "How are you feeling?"

"Good." She squared her shoulders. "Great, actually."

"Really?" He stepped closer, unable to avoid being sucked into her orbit. "I could've sworn you'd wake with an aching head."

She flushed. "I did. My hostesses were kind enough to brew me some tea to ease the pain..." She waved a hand. "But that's not what I want to talk about."

Nox seated himself on the bench by the door. He patted the seat beside him. Mariun ignored the gesture, pacing instead.

Despite all her demands about talking, she didn't utter a word. He watched her skirt swish across the dirt floor, his heart pounding in time with the smack of her boots.

Finally, she stilled and speared him with a direct stare. "I have a lot to say. I need you to sit and listen. Can you do that for me?"

He bristled, tempted to argue just so the familiar response might help calm her nerves.

But then her eyes softened, and she added, "Please?"

He nodded.

Mariun drew a deep breath and smiled softly. "I spent so long feeling alone. I lived my whole life surrounded by people, but none of them ever truly saw me. The first time our eyes met in that cell, it was like a shock straight to my soul. You didn't see Jurdan's progeny or his successor. You saw me."

Nox's chest burned. He'd felt it then, too. The first time he'd stared into her gray eyes, it had cut him to the core.

"I suspected then what I've grown to know. You're a good man, Nox."

He said nothing, but something in his expression must have betrayed his feelings.

"You *are*. I've seen the way you treat animals. How you fight to protect your friends. The way you risked your life to save me."

A muscle in his jaw ticked. How did she know—Violet.

Mariun stepped closer and laid her hands on his shoulders. "You're a good man, Nox. But one thing has to stop."

Nox gulped, the heat from her palms soaking through his tunic and branding his skin.

"I know it looked like I had power when you were the one in the cage, but I didn't. My whole world—my whole life—was my prison. Fear made me fall in line. It made me docile and complacent. When I escaped Thalassia, I told myself that was the end of it. For better or worse, the choices I make are mine now. And no one, not even a good man like you, will sway me."

During her speech, Nox's gaze had drifted to her plump lips. She stood so close his fingers itched at his sides.

Mariun curled one hand up, grabbed a fistful of hair at his nape, and jerked. His gaze flew to hers on a gasp. Molten pools of silver stared back at him. "I need you to stop telling me what I should and shouldn't want."

Rot and decay. She was stunning. As he gazed at her fierce expression, she squeezed his heart just as strongly as she gripped his hair.

"What do you want?" His voice was all gravel, forced out of his heaving chest.

He waited for her to say it. One little word and he'd give into the burning desire racing through his veins.

You. Say I want you.

But the next words out of her mouth quenched the inferno.

"I should be dead."

Nox started to shake his head, but Mariun tightened her grip on his nape.

"I saw that wound. If you weren't there..." She loosened her fingers. "I almost died without ever really living. That's what I want. I want to live. I want to feel the sun and the rain. Joy and sorrow. Pleasure and pain. I want it all."

Her fingers trailed across his neck. He snagged her wrist, holding her in place. It was beyond time she knew. They weren't so different. In so many ways, they were kindred.

"Can you feel this?" He traced her fingers across the faint scar ringing his neck.

Mariun's eyes widened. "Yes."

"I should be dead, too."

She bent down to examine it and frowned. Then she settled on his thigh and tilted his chin up. Nox sucked in a deep breath, fighting to ignore the press of her weight on his lap and her tickling fingers on his skin.

"What happened?"

"My bondmate turned on me. He was under the thrall of an evil being using dark magic. If my sister hadn't been there to heal me, I would've bled out."

"You were healed with magic, too?"

He nodded. "Afterward, I was distraught. I'd never expected my bondmate to attack me like that. It shouldn't have been possible."

Mariun blinked quickly, her fingertips tracing the scar so gently it made his pulse pound.

"Eventually, I started to feel lucky. I'd come so close to death and escaped unscathed. Why should I deny myself any scrap of pleasure I could grab? I vowed to live my life like any day might be my last."

"Yes. That's how I feel exactly."

"It's not quite the same. Well, I hope not."

"What—"

He pressed a finger to her lips, stilling her voice. "You haven't grown jaded like I have. I watched a creature I loved like a brother try to destroy me. Since then, trust has been... illusive."

Her gaze dropped until Nox cupped her cheek. She met his eyes.

"You make me want more than the fleeting moments of connection I allow myself with others. I want more than that with you, Mariun."

"But you trust me now. Don't you?" Her voice cracked, her eyes shining with earnestness.

Not so long ago, his answer would've been an emphatic no. But now...

A crooked smile tipped up his lips. "I do."

Mariun's face lit up. As he watched all traces of uncertainty disappear from her expression, his heart clenched.

That smile. He'd put that smile on her face. If he could bottle up the pure contentment radiating around them, he'd do it in a heartbeat.

"Do you know what I want right now?" she asked.

"Whatever you want, it's yours."

"Kiss me."

Nox scooped her up in his arms and stood.

She squealed. "Hey, what happened to whatever I want is mine?"

He strode across the barn and kicked open a stall door. The door swung closed, hiding them from the outer chamber. He set her on her feet and planted a chaste peck on her lips. Despite his attempt to keep the mood light, the air between them heated the instant their lips met. "Happy?"

Mariun shook her head slowly. "No." She stepped closer and lifted her hands to his collar. "I told you already." Her nimble fingers popped his top button. "I want it all." Another button down. His skin prickled. "And I want it with you, Nox."

Her confession unleashed the animal inside. But instead of the feral howl he expected to reverberate through his bones, the beast growled a single word.

Mine.

He jerked his tunic off and crushed her against his heated flesh. He swallowed her gasp with a blistering kiss. She melted in his arms, and his heart felt full enough to burst.

The *pitter-patter* of rain fell on the barn roof. A heartbeat later, thunder cracked around them. Mariun jolted.

He looked to the heavens and smiled. "Thank the Mother."

She quirked a brow.

"What?" He grabbed her hand and tugged her down on the soft pile of hay and blankets. "You don't want to be interrupted, right?"

"Oh." She smiled, stretching out beside him. "You're right. I bet no one will dare to brave the storm."

Nox chuckled. "I wasn't thanking the Mother for the storm. I was thanking her for the thunder."

Mariun's brow furrowed, but her hands didn't stop tracing the divots in his bare chest and abs, making his blood blaze with every exploratory caress.

He slowly hitched her thick skirt up her leg.

"I told you I'd never lie to you, Mariun. Are you ready to scream for me?"

Nox and Mariun lay together, sated and curled in each other's arms.

"Wow," she breathed. "That was…"

"Loud?" He smirked. "I warned you it would be."

She giggled and playfully slapped his bare chest.

"Do you think the storm will last much longer?" he asked.

She snuggled closer. "I wouldn't mind if it lasted forever."

He slicked a damp tendril of hair off her forehead. "Once we return to Dracwood, then it can rain forever for all I care."

Mariun propped her head on her elbow. "Nox, there's something I've been meaning to tell you."

"All right. So tell me."

She bit her lip. "Promise you won't get mad?"

Nox frowned, his stomach sinking. He sat up, feeling like the world was about to be pulled out from under him. "What is it?"

"I'm sorry. I know I should have said something right away. But you all kept talking about sending me back to Dracwood with Lark and Aren, and I knew you'd need my help with the dragons." She cringed. "It's about your sister. Jurdan is planning something. I think she's in danger."

"Lark?" He clenched his fist. "Stealing her from her husband and son to perform for his sick amusement wasn't enough?"

"No. Not her. Kayda. Jurdan is going to disrupt her wedding."

"What?" Nox's hands burned, and he took a deep breath, fighting back the anger threatening to envelop him. "Why would he do that? What's he planning?"

Mariun shook her head. "I only know what I overheard, which isn't much. I think he's hoping to create a wedge between your country and Doln. Maybe even start a war."

Rot and decay.

Nox leaped up and started tugging on his clothes. His mind whirled as he tried to figure out how much time they had left. It certainly wasn't much. How many rotting moons had passed since he'd sailed away from Dracwood?

"Where are you going?" She stood, wrapping a blanket around her shoulders.

"The outhouse." He needed space. Time to swallow the urge to scream.

"I'm sorry, Nox. But there's still time to warn her. We can stop him."

He stalked out of the barn without replying.

Mariun... how could she have kept that from them for so long? Now Kayda was in danger and he was half the world away.

Nox sucked in several deep breaths on the way to the outhouse. He tilted his face, allowing the rain to cool his flushed skin. Soon, his panic faded with it.

She was right. They still had time. As long as the dragons learned to fly and they left soon.

Should Mariun have told them immediately? Probably. But he understood why she'd kept the news to herself. She'd assumed correctly that he'd have pushed for her to go to Dracwood with Aren and Lark. And where would they be now if that had happened? Would they have ever found the eggs without Mariun's help?

Maybe. Or they might be back in one of those cells under the sea.

Nox shuddered, and it wasn't the rain that caused a chill to creep up his spine.

After all, how could he be mad at Mariun when he was doing the same thing? He was still sitting on the secret Lark had shared with him just before they'd said their farewells. A secret about someone Mariun knew well.

Nox sighed. Trust was a tricky thing indeed. If he wanted a relationship with Mariun, he needed to share the truth with her. Surely she'd see he had his reasons for keeping the spider's true identity to himself, wouldn't she?

A prick on the back of Nox's neck interrupted his thoughts. He jerked and reached back. Rotting bugs. You'd think the rain would chase them away.

But his fingers swatted away something thin and pointy. What the...?

Nox collapsed, and the world went black.

Bridges

Violet sighed as her boots touched down on firm rock. She spared a glance behind her and shuddered. Stupid bridge. Mariun probably thought she was crazy with how fast she raced away from her. But she could hardly concentrate on their conversation when she was desperate to reach solid ground.

"Are you faring well, child? You appear a tad flustered." Orry cocked her head, golden feathers shining in what little sun remained with the dark clouds gathering overhead.

"It's the bridge. I can handle other heights, but something about crossing bridges always gives me the creeps." She sucked in a shaky breath. *"I'll be fine now that we've crossed. Come on. Ryon's house is this way."*

"I'm pleased to see your fear didn't stop you." Orry hopped along beside her, seeming much livelier after a night's sleep.

Violet shrugged nonchalantly. *"I'm working on it."*

"Bravery in the face of primal fear is quite rare and exceedingly commendable."

Violet shook her head. Orry and her sayings... Would she ever get used to having such a wise bondmate? Her heart wrenched, nearly making her stumble. She wouldn't have the chance to, would she? If only Orry wasn't right about how long she had left to live... Maybe there was something they could do? Some way to extend her years with magic.

Orry interrupted her musing. *"Well then, are you ready to learn more about your boon?"*

Her pulse kicked up. *"Yes. More than ready. What is it?"*

"I believe it will be a skill you'll master quickly."

"Sure." She snorted. *"How could you possibly know that?"*

"I told you about the fish last night, yes?"

"The dream elixir." Violet's nose scrunched. *"What about it?"*

"I know you more closely than you realize, child. In the dream, I've seen glimpses of your past—and your future."

"Blazes." Violet's eyes widened. *"M-my future. What—"*

"Now, now." Orry laughed an airy, melodic trill that sang through Violet's ears. *"Let's not get ahead of ourselves. You want to know what your boon is, yes?"*

"I do. Go on."

"I've seen the way you interact with others. You know things, too. Sense things deep down in your bones about people you've just met."

Violet flinched. *"H-how..."* She'd never explained it out loud. Not to her parents or any of her friends. But Orry was right. There'd been countless times in her life when she'd gazed into a stranger's eyes and knew whether they could be trusted. She'd always assumed it came with the territory of looking different. *"So, you're telling me my intuition is connected to your boon?"*

"It is. I suppose you could say you've been given the boon of enhanced intuition. The feeling that has always whispered in your blood will soon

start singing. When you look into the eyes of the worthy, you'll hear the song in their hearts."

Violet's stomach dropped. "*The song in their hearts...*" she repeated slowly. "*Heartsong.*" She halted, a hand on her chest. "*My mother. That's what her father said in her vision. Follow your heartsong.*"

Orry nodded sagely. "*Yes. Once you have mastered your boon, you'll be able to hear the song in your own heart as well.*"

Violet's mind raced. This was it! She'd been so worried her grand adventure had been a dud. But now, she had proof that there was far more to come. Once she knew how to listen to her heartsong, then who knew where it would lead her?

She tipped her face to the sky, her steps lighter than they'd been in ages. Not only had she found her bondmate, but she was one step closer to discovering the answer to that maddening riddle from her mother's vision. Could the day get any better than this?

But as she replayed Orry's words in her mind, a bit of that lightness receded. "*Wait. You said something about the worthy. What do you mean by that? Worthy of what?*"

"*A time will soon come when I'm not here to guide you. In the flesh, at least. With your boon, you'll still be able to determine who is worthy of our divine gifts.*"

"*Divine gifts?*" Violet shook her head. "*What gifts?*"

"*Wishes. You will know who deserves a feather, and on whom it would be wasted.*"

"*Y-you want me to give out feathers? But why? Won't you be with me?*"

"*Don't fret. I won't leave you until I must. Still, there will come a time when you and I must part.*" Orry puffed out her chest and stared straight into Violet's eyes. "*The journey you'll embark on will be fraught with danger. Young Ryon has done a commendable job of sharing his feathers so far. But the ones I shall entrust to you are much dearer."*

Violet rubbed her brow. *"You're going to give golden feathers to me?"*

"Yes, child. You are the one. The one who will welcome the bridge be-tween—" Orry cut herself off, shaking her head sharply. *"Never mind that. Now I'm getting ahead of myself. We'll talk more about this later. If I'm not mistaken, we've arrived."*

Violet wanted to demand an explanation. What was all that talk about bridges? But Orry was right. Ryon's cottage stood before them. One thing at a time.

She marched to the door and knocked. The door swung open, held in place by Vera. The brightest smile lit her face until her gaze trailed down and she spotted Orry hovering in the doorway. Vera's eyes fluttered closed and her body went limp.

Blazes. Violet lurched into motion, catching her before she smacked into the floor. She wobbled, unsteady with the weight of a fully grown woman clutched in her arms. Thankfully, Vera recovered from her faint quickly. As soon as she had full control of her limbs, she jerked out of Violet's hold and sank into a deep bow.

Violet arched a brow at Orry. They'd traveled into town so early the streets were deserted. This was the first villager she'd seen interacting with Orry. *"Do I need to get used to catching fainting women?"*

"I hope not." Orry cocked her head, her gaze darting around the kitchen. *"Where is Ryon? It appears he hasn't explained the details of our situation to his family just yet."*

Violet tapped on Vera's shoulder. "Is Ryon home?"

Vera appeared reluctant to rise from her bow, but after Violet re-peated the question and Orry hopped further inside, Vera stood and ushered them down the hall. She flung open a door in the back of the cottage.

Violet swallowed a gasp. Even the lone window's faint light couldn't dim the magnificence tacked to the walls. Gorgeous feathered trinkets in every color and pattern imaginable hung on nearly every available space.

A smile tugged at her lips. Ryon sat on the bed beside his brother, both of them atop the covers and fully clothed, their heads leaning against each other. Neither was completely reclined, their shoulders propped against pillows on the headboard. She had a sneaking suspicion they'd fallen asleep without intending to.

They looked so peaceful. So close. Violet didn't have the heart to wake them.

Luckily, Vera had no such problem. She perched on the bed beside Ryon and lightly brushed a lock off his head, speaking quietly.

Ryon's eyes popped open. "Good morning." He blinked repeatedly, shaking the dazed remnants of sleep from his eyes.

"Good morning." Violet giggled.

Rovan jolted awake—and spoke.

Violet's chest bloomed with a gentle heat that spread outward to warm all her limbs. "It worked?" She clasped her hands to her heart. "Oh, I'm so glad it worked!"

"Yes, it—" Ryon frowned, then switched languages. Violet patiently waited while Vera and Rovan listened to Ryon, only interjecting a word or two here and there. When Ryon finished speaking, Vera's eyes swam with tears. Next, he whistled to Orry.

Violet shook her head. It would certainly be challenging communicating with three languages in the mix.

"*Yes, of course.*" Orry's voice echoed in her mind while she whistled back to Ryon. "*But truly, their thanks should be directed to you.*"

"Did you explain that Orry isn't Mother Orea any longer?" Violet asked.

"Just now, yes." Ryon chuckled. "Ma said she fainted when she first saw her."

"She did."

Vera crossed the room, wiping her eyes with her sleeve. She spoke again, patted Violet's shoulder, and looked at Ryon expectantly.

"Ma's invited us to stay for breakfast," Ryon explained.

Violet smiled and nodded at Vera. "That would be lovely."

Vera clapped her hands and disappeared into the hall.

Violet turned her attention back to the men on the bed. They both perched on the edge now, slipping on their boots. Their looks and mannerisms were so similar, Violet's skin prickled.

"I suppose a proper introduction is in order." Ryon smiled widely, stopping between her and his brother. "Violet, meet my twin, Rovan." He switched languages to complete the introductions.

Violet thrust out her hand, grasping Rovan's automatically before remembering his people's greeting of choice. Rovan rolled with the shake, a slight widening of his eyes the only sign of his surprise before he squeezed back and shook eagerly. When he met her gaze, she was pleased to note the strange cloud of confusion was nowhere to be seen.

Rovan spoke again, his voice oddly similar to Ryon's yet different. His words were softer spoken, and the tone a touch more melodic.

"He says he remembers you." Ryon's voice wavered with a hint of disbelief. "And thank you for bringing him home. For bringing both of us home."

Now Violet was the one with tears in her eyes. She blinked them back. "It was no trouble."

Rovan let go of her hand and spoke softly to Ryon before exiting the room.

Violet smiled brightly. "What happened? I want to know everything!"

Ryon chuckled and pointed at the bed. "Have a seat and I'll tell you. Ma ought to be cooking for a while." She plopped down on the edge, and he seated himself beside her. Orry hopped onto the windowsill and stared outside.

"After I made my wish, I raced home, where I heard the most glorious sound."

"Rovan talking?"

"No. He was singing." Ryon sighed, his face lit with so much delight it made Violet's belly erupt with tingles.

She grabbed his hand and squeezed. "That's wonderful."

"We stayed up half the night talking." Ryon's smile fell. "There's so much he doesn't remember. I'm honestly surprised he remembers you." The corners of his lips quirked up. "Though maybe I shouldn't be. You know, since you're *the one*."

"Uh-huh." Violet rolled her eyes. "I bet it's just that I'm the only albino girl he's met."

"I don't know about that..." Ryon inched closer and slung an arm around her shoulders. "What about you two? Did anything else happen with the priests during the night?"

"No, not at all. A few brothers were crowded in the hall when we left this morning, but whatever Orry said made them clear out pretty quick." She grinned.

Ryon shot a look at Orry. "No surprise there."

"Oh, and on the way here, she told me about my boon." Violet couldn't disguise the excitement brimming in her chest.

"What is it?"

"It's increased intuition."

"Huh." Ryon drew back, pursing his lips. "What does that do?"

"She said I'd need it to know who was worthy. That one day, I'd go on a journey fraught with danger." She leaned in close. "She's going to give me golden feathers, and the intuition will let me know who deserves them."

"A journey fraught with danger... that's what they told me when they gave me these." He sifted a hand through his dreadlocks.

"Don't you see what it means?" Violet bounced her legs, making the mattress vibrate. "My journey doesn't end with the dragons like I thought it did. There *is* more to come. Orry even said the same thing that my mother heard in her vision all those years ago. I have to follow my heartsong."

Ryon grinned. "I knew it. What did I tell you? You've been the one all along."

Violet's cheeks warmed. "Yeah. I guess I am." It was odd to admit it. She'd spent so long wondering whether any of it was true. And just as long lamenting that the prophecies were an exaggeration. Or meant to point to Mena instead of her. But now, she couldn't deny it any longer.

The truth that she'd always sensed deep in her soul had finally been confirmed. She was far from ordinary. Somehow, someway, the actions that she took would change the course of the world. That fact should have felt daunting. But the only emotion she could muster was a bone-deep sense of rightness.

"What a day. Everything is looking up for us." Ryon squeezed her shoulder.

Just then, a peel of thunder reverberated outside. The gentle *ping* of raindrops hitting glass and wood registered in Violet's ears. She peeked out the window and realized the rain must have started some time ago, though she was too caught up in her conversation to notice.

"Everything except the weather. That looks like a nasty storm."

"Good thing we have shelter and a warm meal to keep us occupied while it passes." Ryon stared into her eyes, and a wash of prickles spread across Violet's skin.

"Should we see if your ma needs any help?" she offered.

"Sure." He stood and held out a hand to help her up.

They arrived in the kitchen just as Vera settled a platter of flat fried bread on the table. The delectable scent of cinnamon sugar perfumed the air, making Violet's stomach rumble.

Vera shooed them away when they offered to help, insisting everything was well in hand. Everyone settled at the table, even Orry, after Rovan pulled over a tall stool for her to perch on. Her golden head bobbed up and down as she nibbled on the ripe berries Vera placed in front of her.

At first, Violet was certain the meal would prove exceedingly awkward, with the language barriers in play. Soon they fell into an easy pattern of conversation that somehow felt comfortable, even with all the translating required. The morning passed in a blur of wonderful food, laughter, and so much smiling Violet's cheeks ached.

"Rovan." She faced him with a smile. Breakfast was long gone, and the boom of thunder had faded outside. "You make such wonderful art. Do you plan to keep crafting?"

He shook his head shyly. Despite their similar looks, the morning spent together had revealed a few differences. Rovan was a good deal more reserved than Ryon, and she needed to prod him to talk about himself. "No. I'd like to become a priest. If you think you can manage without me, Ma."

Vera clasped his hand in hers when he peeked at her. "Son, I want you to do whatever will bring you joy. Don't you worry one wit about your old ma." She nodded back to the hall. "Besides, it will take me a lifetime to weave the beauties on your walls into lucky customers' hairstyles. I'm all set."

Violet smiled at Ryon as he finished translating. With the full morning practicing, it had started to come by route now. So much that when Vera started talking, he immediately began to translate.

"What about you, Ryon? Now that you've healed Rovan, what will you do?" Vera asked.

Violet's heart jolted. She'd been wondering the same but was too scared to ask. Ryon had every right to stay. This was his home. He'd completed the task he'd spent most of his life striving for. But she had an adventure calling her name. One fraught with danger. And as much as she wanted to beg him to come with her, she wouldn't. Still, she couldn't help but hope he would offer to tag along.

Ryon's face fell as the last word of translation left his lips. He spun to face Violet. "W-well…" He stared into her eyes and leaned forward, inhaling deeply.

Please come with me. Violet released the thought she refused to voice. Ryon wouldn't kiss her if he'd planned all along to say goodbye, would he?

Pounding blasted the door, shaking the walls with its ferocity. Vera jumped to her feet and rushed to open it.

Brother Tham spilled inside, a blur of wet robes and wringing hands. He chattered rapid-fire, so fast that Ryon struggled to translate.

"It's the dragons. They returned from training with the silvers and won't settle down. Mostly the green one."

"Gwen?" Violet frowned. "What did Nox say?"

Her pulse pounded while she waited for Ryon to translate and Brother Tham to reply. "He didn't say anything. He wasn't there. Is he here with you?"

"What do you mean, he wasn't there?" Violet stood and paced. "What about Mariun? I saw her when I crossed the bridge this morning. She was headed to the barn to find Nox."

Tham answered, "Yes, one of our brothers saw her there, too. He left them together and went with the silvers to train the dragons. But when they returned, the barn was empty."

"And Gwen can't find him?" Violet's stomach dropped. "But they're bondmates. She ought to be able to find Nox." Where could they be? Her mind raced. She gasped. "The masked. What if the masked have them?"

Ryon shook his head. "No. The climb, remember? Even I wouldn't scale the mountain in that storm."

Tham explained, "I just checked on their camp. They're all still camped at the base of the mountain."

"Still camped?" Violet halted her pacing. "What do you mean, *still*?"

Ryon rubbed the back of his neck. "They arrived late yesterday afternoon. Nox and I thought it would be best to let you enjoy the feast before we told you."

Violet's heart stalled. Was she cursed to be forever kept in the dark by well-meaning people around her?

She had been conscious enough to communicate the conversation in her thoughts to Orry while they spoke, so it didn't surprise her when Orry started whistling, *"Brother, order the silvers to fan out. We won't find what we don't search for."*

Brother Tham disappeared out of the door at a jog.

Violet watched him go while she fought off a wave of dizziness so strong she wobbled on her feet. This couldn't be happening. Her uncle was missing—again. Without him, the dragons might never make it back to Dracwood.

Maybe she was overreacting. He and Mariun might be holed up somewhere, wrapped up in each other's arms and dead to the outside world. But as she glanced at Orry, those instincts she'd honed over a lifetime struck an ominous tune. It sang through her blood and reverberated deep within her bones.

Something was wrong. She *knew* it. Nox was in trouble, and they had to find him before it was too late.

Black

N ox's mind spun. A sharp pain in his skull bloomed, pulling him out of blackness. Voices echoed in his ears. Gruff, masculine voices. More of that tongue he couldn't understand.

And then, just when he'd been ready to give up and sink into the black, a new voice rose. One he couldn't understand but that was as familiar to him as his own.

Mariun.

He fought to open his eyes and quickly realized it was no use. The lids might as well have been sewn shut.

Where was he? What was happening? Confusion reigned, weighing down his mind with syrupy sludge he had to wade through to make sense of the world. Was he back in that dank cell under the sea, surrounded by broken men? Was this just a dream? The back of his skull smacked against a hard surface, and another blast of pain chased away that notion.

"Careful! You'll hurt him," Mariun cried. Soft hands landed on his face. Trembling fingers traced his neck and pressed against his pulse.

The maddening rumble of voices answered her. How many were there? And what were they doing to her? If they were hurting him, what was stopping them from harming her, too?

Mariun. He had to wake. Had to help her.

After a struggle that might have lasted an age but was likely only a few heartbeats, he pried his lids open a tiny sliver. Shadows danced across his vision. He glimpsed wood hovering above. Rafters. The barn.

Then came a flash of black hair wreathed around a face lined with worry. She was there. Right there looking down at him. The tiny peek brought him comfort that spread across his limbs like a healing salve. His eyes crashed closed.

Mariun would keep him safe. He could trust her. Yes.

But only a heartbeat later, her voice cut through the relief. A voice drenched in terror and panic. "No. Please. Anything but that."

More rumbling spread ice through his veins. Mariun and a man arguing in that awful tongue.

"I-I-I'll go with you. Just leave them in peace and I'll go." Mariun's voice was thick with defeat. But he sensed the steel in it all the same.

She meant it! Rot and decay, she couldn't mean it!

He could hear her weeping. Fat tears splattered across his face that spoke of the worst pain. His heart tore apart.

Nox fought inside his mind. He swore at himself. Finally, he forced his tired body to move the insignificant amount needed to tear open his eyes again. His lashes fluttered open in time to watch a figure rip Mariun off the ground. He begged his hands to move. To grab her dress and drag her back into his arms. But all he could manage was a bare flick of his littlest finger.

He was so weak. Why was he so rotting weak?

"Relax, you oaf," Mariun grumbled. "I said I'd come."

A masked man barked at her.

A masked man! They were here. With his eyes cracked, he could see the barn, though his vision was far too blurry for his liking. Comprehension lashed at him like a fire blast. This wasn't a dream. They were here, in Avion. The masked weren't still camped down below. They were among them—and they were *taking* her.

Rot and decay! What could he do? It had taken a gargantuan effort to open his eyes. His muscles were so weak he could scarcely lift a finger. And his mind so bleary he couldn't think straight.

If only someone... his bondmates! He reached for them and rammed right into the rotting block. The stupid block in his mind he'd erected to share a private moment with Mariun was now impeding him from reaching Gwen and Flint.

Mariun... His gaze rolled back to her, slow as molasses. She was making a show of gathering her things. Stuffing the few meager belongings she owned into her pack.

What was he going to do? He couldn't help her. Not like this.

Nox turned inward. If he broke down the block, then Gwen would come. He tore at the wall he'd erected in his mind. But it was as useless as when he'd tried lifting his fingers. It was like clawing at a brick wall with his bare hands. Utterly useless.

Despair filled him, overpowering the anger marinating in his gut. He couldn't just let her leave. He wouldn't...

Mariun clutched him tightly. "I'm sorry," she whispered into his ear. "I have to go. I—" She jerked away, and his head slammed into the ground yet again.

"No," Mariun shrieked. "Let me go!"

Nox's eyes cracked open another sliver. His throat worked, his mouth inching open. But the scream in his lungs escaped as a gurgle.

All the tiny sound earned him was more pain. A kick landed on his ribs. Another slammed into his shoulders. Agony exploded in his body, and he couldn't even curl into a ball to protect himself.

"Stop!" Mariun screamed. She switched to Thalassian, and though he didn't understand what she said, the intent was impossible to ignore. Her voice crackled with barely leashed fury, and a shiver of static snapped in the air.

The kicking stopped. But then something worse came. The sound of their footfalls receding and the door slamming closed.

No! This couldn't be it. They couldn't just waltz in and take her from him. He wouldn't allow it.

But what could he do? Pain screamed through his limbs. And the fuzziness in his mind wasn't abating.

Help. He needed help. He had to break down that block.

Again, Nox turned inward. He closed his eyes, focusing on the wall he'd built in his mind. He tore at it. Burned it. Tried to force it apart with the weight of his grief. But no matter which way he approached it, the barrier held.

Ugh. It was no use. He might as well just lie here and wait for the dragons' return...

But then Mariun would be gone. No. If he couldn't call on his bondmates, then he'd have to save her himself.

Get up. Get up, you rotting idiot!

Nox wrenched open his eyes. He breathed through the pain. Used it to funnel into his rage. Rage was all that he had left. The only force driving his drugged body to move.

He clawed his way out of the barn on his hands and knees, one slow lurch at a time. His battered ribs protested every motion, but he ignored the agony piercing his chest.

A blast of frigid air greeted him as he fought his way outside. The cold was a welcome relief. Another slice of pain he could use to fuel his mad scramble after the masked. After her.

He spotted a flash of black on the horizon. He crawled for it, and miraculously, from somewhere deep within, he found the strength to shove up to one knee. Then two. Then his feet were under him.

A manic grin painted his face as Nox staggered across the grass. He was doing it! He'd find her. He just had to keep pushing. Keep stumbling forward.

Rain pelted his face. His muscles screamed. And his vision blurred each time his feet slammed into the ground. Still, he pushed forward. One lurching step at a time.

Rock met his boots. The grin spread, curving into a snarl. Boulders rose on either side of his path, and Nox used them to his advantage, leaning his battered body on stone when he could scarcely summon the urge to stand. He rolled across the jagged formations in great lumbering jerks. Even when cloth tore and pebbles stabbed his flesh.

Through it all, he tried again and again to tear down the block. Yet even though he'd summoned a measure of strength to move his limbs, he couldn't say the same for his thoughts. After a dozen tries, he gave up, using his full concentration to pick out the subtle sound of men chattering ahead on the stony terrain.

Sweat beaded on his forehead despite the cold seeping into his bones. Wind whipped him forward, great billowing gusts laced with needles of ice. The rain shifted to sleet, slicking the rock and biting his cheeks. Still, Nox pressed on, desperate to stop them.

To find her.

He had to find her.

He almost couldn't believe it when he spotted them ahead. Through blurry eyes, his vision made even worse with the icy wind blowing tears into the corners, she appeared. His heart jolted, slamming against his chest with tremendous force, like it might leap out of his throat and dive straight into her hands.

Mariun shivered, clutching her arms around her middle. Black-clothed men hovered around her. Too many to count in his present state. A few shoved at a rock in the path, knees locked, teeth gritted, hands and shoulders heaving with exertion.

What were they doing? Nox brushed the question aside. It didn't matter. All that mattered was her.

He lumbered forward, rage propelling him. If it weren't for the thick ooze clogging his mind, perhaps he'd have thought to be stealthy.

Of course, they heard him. A group of masked raced forward to greet him, with one in the lead. He didn't even bother looking at him long enough to note what fierce predator graced the fool's mask. All he could think, all he could see, was her.

Beautiful, horrified gray eyes met his. "Nox. No!" Mariun screamed.

Hot blood splattered his face. His arm ached from the dead weight pressing upon it. From somewhere far away, his mind connected the dots. The claws that had failed him so many times had come to his rescue.

But it was too little, too late. Pain assailed him as blow after blow landed—on his head, his ribs, his gut. A blow to the knee followed, and he collapsed. There were so many. Too many for his weak, addled body to fight off.

A fist crashed on his temple, the blast ringing through his ears and making his eyes slam closed. Light speared the backs of his eyelids and the air sizzled. Men screamed, and bodies thudded into the rock beside him.

"I said leave hi—" Mariun's screeching command cut off sharply.

Nox forced his eyes open. She stood gaping, hand outstretched. But all too soon, she crumbled, caught in the arms of one of the masked. Another stood beside him, holding a wooden tube.

"Mare—" Nox lifted a hand, only to feel a dart sink into his palm. In the heartbeat that passed after, a thousand thoughts flooded his mind.

She was gone. He couldn't fight them off now. If it had been impossible with the contents of one dart weighing down his body, then what chance did he have with two?

None.

Where were they taking her? Would he ever see her again? His stomach revolted at the thought. This couldn't be it. It couldn't be the end.

But what could he do? He'd tried. He'd tried his rotting hardest, and it hadn't been enough.

Would he even survive long enough to go after her again? He'd followed her out in the middle of nowhere in a tempest. Would anyone find him before he succumbed to his injuries and the elements? Or had he sealed his fate by chasing Mariun—and losing her?

That last thought rang in his aching head as it slammed into the rock and the black returned to claim him.

Intuition

They burst into the barn. Ryon's chest burned from the race over, his breath catching in his throat. The dragons crowded the back of the space, but none of them were at rest. Gwen paced nervously, and her siblings stood watch, their heads bobbing as they followed their sister's steps across the dirt floor.

Violet rushed over to Gwen, who finally halted. "Where is he, Gwen? Why can't you find him?" she whispered, rubbing her hands down the skittish dragon's quivering flank.

Ryon eyed the pair warily. "Are you sure you should be so close when she's clearly upset?"

"Please." Violet pinned him with a withering glare. "She won't hurt me. Someone has to comfort her."

But did it have to be *her*? Ryon bit back another complaint. She was probably right. It didn't stop him from worrying, though. He turned his attention to the barn, hunting for any signs that might reveal where Nox and Mariun had gone.

Ryon approached the portly brother wringing his hands by the door. "You went with them to practice, right? Has Gwen been acting like that since you returned?"

The man nodded vehemently and tugged his black robe tightly around him. "Yes. She's been pacing for ages. But before that, she wouldn't stop sniffing the ground over there." His finger reached out, indicating a spot in the stall beside the door.

Ryon walked over and kneeled to examine the dirt. He spotted faint markings inlaid on the floor. Unmistakable ones. He might not be a fully trained hunter like many men in the village, but he knew enough to spot these. "Someone was here. Quite a few people."

"What did you find?" Violet left Gwen's side and crouched beside him.

"Bootprints." He traced a large print with his forefinger. "Too big to be from you and Mariun. And far too many to be just from Nox and me."

Violet gasped. But then her brow furrowed. "Wait, what about the brothers?"

Ryon pointed to the brother's feet. "They don't wear boots at all. See the moccasins?" He frowned at the ground in front of the doorway. He would expect to see a trail of them leading out of the barn, but it certainly wasn't the case. "I can't make heads or tails of the tracks over there."

"Looks like the dragons disturbed what was there when they came inside. But these..." Violet's eyes narrowed on the bootprints scattered in the stall. "I think you're right."

He caught a flicker of gold in the corner of his eye and spun to face Orry, whistling, "Can we convince more silvers to join the search? I'm almost positive someone was here."

Orry sang, "I will." With a few elegant flicks of her wings, she lifted into the rafters and disappeared out of a high window.

Violet shivered, curling her arms around her belly. Ryon glanced out the door. It was midafternoon, and though the storm had passed, the weather had turned frigid. He certainly didn't want to traipse around outside, but he couldn't see any way around it. Someone needed to join the search on the ground. The silvers could see only so much from above.

Perhaps he could at least convince Violet to stay behind, where she'd be warm and safe. It was bound to be slippery after the storm. And off the main paths, the climbing could be dangerous even in the driest conditions. The last thing he wanted was to lose her, too.

"I'm going to join the search for Nox and Mariun. I need you to stay here."

"What? No. I can help."

"I know. It's just... like you said. Someone needs to comfort Gwen and the other hatchlings."

Violet crossed her arms and cocked a brow.

He tried a new angle. "And what if they come back? Someone should be waiting here, too."

She sighed. "Fine. But I want to be the first to know when they're found." Her lip wobbled. "No matter what."

Ryon's stomach twinged, and he nodded swiftly. He already regretted keeping the masked's arrival from her. He wouldn't make the same mistake again. Violet deserved to be apprised of everything—good news and bad.

He just hoped the news today wouldn't be bad.

The flutter of wings flicked in the rafters, golden feathers flanked by silver. "Ho, Ryon." Quill stared down at him from above. "I hear you need some help. How did I know you'd be back begging for favors even after you got your wish?"

Ryon sent him a halfhearted smile, though he couldn't dredge up a playful retort. It didn't feel right cracking jokes when Nox and Mariun were lost. "Hey, buddy. You with me? I'm leaving."

"Sure." Quill seemed to catch wind of his dour mood. "I'll take the high route; you take the low?"

"Got it." With a curt nod, Ryon turned to the door.

"Wait," Violet cried. She grabbed his face with both hands and lifted on her toes, and heedless of the brother, Orry, and all the other eyes on them, she planted a firm kiss on his lips. "Please, be careful."

"I will. Promise." Ryon pressed his forehead to hers and breathed deep, soaking in Violet's sweet scent. Then he tore himself away and strode through the door.

Twilight was not far off. His breath clouded the air in front of his face. Ryon trailed his gaze across the landscape, wondering which direction to go. Rocks spread out in all directions beyond the brothers' plateau. And though he knew Avion like the back of his hand, he had no clue where to search. If only he had an inkling. Even a guess would be better than what he had. Some intuition.

A smile crossed his lips, and he turned back to the door.

"Where ya going?" Quill whistled. "Need to kiss your sweetheart some more?"

"Not exactly. Just wait." Ryon popped his head back into the barn. "Violet? Can you come out here for a moment?"

Violet lifted her skirt and followed him out of the barn. She shivered instantly but didn't let her chattering teeth stop her from halting at his side. "What is it?"

"You said your boon was increased intuition, right?"

"Yeah." Her brow furrowed.

Ryon grabbed her shoulders and spun her slowly to face away from him. "Close your eyes and tell me where to go."

Violet chuckled nervously. "I don't think that's how it works."

"We won't know if we don't try." Ryon kneaded her neck gently. "I'm taking a chance either way. I'd rather place my faith in you, Violet. I believe in you."

"All right." Her stiff muscles softened beneath his ministrations, and her eyes fluttered closed. "I'll try."

Her chest rose and fell in a steady rhythm. Her eyelids flickered. A muscle twitched in her cheek. Then, slow and steady, one delicate finger rose and pointed. "There," she declared firmly. "You should start your search there."

He followed her finger, burying the frown that fought to spread. She'd pointed toward the village, only slightly to the left. It wouldn't be long before the river impeded their path if they headed in that direction. Still, it was as good a place to start as any.

"Thank you. Now go back inside before you freeze." He gently pushed her toward the barn.

"Good luck. Don't forget, I want to know right—"

"Right away," he finished for her. "I got it. I'll even send Quill so word reaches you faster. If you see him return without me, then follow him to find me."

"All right. I'll bring Gwen, too. I'm sure she'll feel much better once she sees Nox again."

"Perfect." Ryon sent her one more smile and began his trek.

"Wait, son." The door to the rectory slammed open, and Brother Tham raced toward him, his robes whipping in the icy wind. "I've gathered more brothers for the search."

Ryon bowed. "Thank you, brother. Direct them to fan out. We need to search everywhere. Nightfall isn't far off." As he raised his head, he spotted at least a dozen men tugging their black robes closed and rushing to catch up with them.

"Yes, of course." Brother Tham cleared his throat and whistled, including Quill in the conversation. "Perhaps now that so many of us have joined the hunt, the orecolns can return to the safety of the Aviary."

"And disobey a directive from on high?" Quill laughed, an airy chuckle that seemed at odds with the wary optimism painting Tham's face. "I think not."

"Very well," Tham replied in a defeated tone. But when Ryon moved to leave, he blurted, "Please, at least take a few brothers with you. No one should travel alone."

That was a fair request, and prudent. The last thing he needed was to get in trouble and add another number to their search. "All right."

Brother Tham whistled sharply. Two brothers broke off from the pack and approached.

"Brother Pip. Brother Lennam." Ryon nodded to each of them. "Thank you for your help."

"Of course." Lennam stared ahead and frowned. "Are we heading back to the village to search?"

Ryon shook his head, pointing. "No. This way. I've a hunch that no one's thought to search the cliffs overlooking the riverbank yet."

Pip flinched. "Because no one goes there. Nothing but rocks that ought to be treacherously slippery after that storm."

"That's where I'm headed. Join the others if you'd like." Ryon's voice was firm, brooking no argument.

"We'll just watch our step extra carefully, won't we, Brother Pip?" Brother Lennam cut in, his tone far too jolly for a man facing a perilous journey. Still, Ryon appreciated his cheerfulness far more than Pip's negative remarks.

"Did you spot anything useful in the barn?" Pip asked.

"Just some bootprints." Ryon quickly filled them in. Quill took to the air, flying low and circling ahead. Ryon and the brothers slowed their pace as they approached the rocky terrain bordering the Aviary's plateau. They ventured off the well-worn path, searching carefully around each rock large enough to hide a body behind.

By the time they reached the river, Ryon's hands were cold as ice and his teeth wouldn't stop chattering. A thin film of sleet covered everything. Pip was right. Moving forward would be risky. One wrong step could send them careening down the cliffside and into the river far below.

What was worse, bright slashes of oranges and pinks painted the few clouds that weren't gray. If he was caught out here after dark, then the trek back would be even more dangerous.

Ryon turned back, squinting at the tip of the Aviary. Their meandering search had led them slightly off the path where Violet had pointed. If he wanted to speak the truth when he'd told her he'd searched where she'd pointed, then there was no choice but to hasten forward.

Still, he didn't need to subject the brothers to his decision. It was clear they weren't used to climbing like he was. "I'm going to head up a ways." He pointed in the opposite direction, down a much safer path. "Can you two search between here and the bridge? We'll meet back here before nightfall."

Brother Pip nodded forcefully, his relief evident.

"Are you sure?" Brother Lennam asked. "I thought we were meant to stick together?"

Ryon smiled gently. "Normally, I'd agree, but we're running out of daylight. If we want to cover more ground, then we need to split up." He lifted his gaze to the sky. "Don't worry. Quill will watch over me."

That explanation seemed to satisfy him. The brothers turned and began searching in the direction he'd sent them.

Ryon didn't waste much time watching them. He shimmied around a huge rock blocking the narrow path he needed to follow.

"Where are you going?" Quill whistled from above. "There's nothing over there. I just checked."

"This is where Violet pointed. I need to be sure they're not over here."

Quill tilted in the air, swooping back around. "If you say so."

Gritting his teeth, Ryon carefully balanced on the icy rocks. The sleet had stopped falling, but with the chilly wind blasting, he wagered the rocks wouldn't dry completely until daybreak. At this height, snow and ice could come any time of year. Although, late-summer storms like this tended to pass swiftly, and warm weather returned soon after.

But it appeared the cold was here to stay, for tonight at least. As his breath fogged the air, he admitted the hard truth. If Nox and Mariun were somewhere out here, lost and without shelter, the chances of them making it through the night without frostbite were pretty slim.

Before long, the curving path dead-ended in a small clearing. Beyond that, a steep rock wall rose at such an incline even he'd struggle to climb it. But he wasn't planning to bother. He knew for a fact nothing was up there. And with Quill there to confirm, there wasn't much point in checking.

He stood for a long moment, catching his breath and working up the nerve to turn around and begin the treacherous return journey.

"See?" Quill landed beside him. "What did I tell ya? Nothing here."

"Yeah. Guess I should've listened." Ryon sighed, fighting to bury his frustration. He'd been so sure Violet would know where to look.

Now he had to return and tell her Nox and Mariun were still missing. He frowned, then kicked a loose rock sitting next to his boot.

As he glanced at the ground, something curious stared up at him. His kick had dislodged the layer of ice. Instead of the dull orangey-red of the rest of the mountain, the spot under his boot was a dark crimson. It almost looked like—

"Blood." He swept his boot across the icy rock, knocking more frost loose. "Look, it's all over."

He followed the trail to the mountain's edge. His heart hammered as he gazed down the slope. Sharp rocks littered the descent, ending in the river valley far, far below. Anyone who fell there would be done for. Even if they avoided the rocks on the way down, the river was shallow enough to wade, not deep enough to cushion a fall by any means. And if by some miracle the fall didn't kill them, the river led back into the mountain. Anyone carried in its wake would eventually find themselves dragged into dark caverns and would drown from lack of air.

Quill descended, scanning the rock wall below. When he lifted back up and landed beside Ryon, his voice was strangled. "I spotted more blood. It doesn't look good."

Ryon's stomach dropped. It certainly didn't. Did they both fall to their deaths? But that didn't explain the blood in the clearing.

He backed away from the cliffside, following the trail of blood again. He made it back to where he'd first spotted it, then swept outward with his foot again. Maybe if he cleared all the ice, he would find another clue.

There! Another bloodstain and another trail. This one led in the opposite direction. Ryon followed it until it stopped at the cliff wall. His brow furrowed. Another dead end.

He kneeled, examining the stain, when his gaze caught on a narrow hole at the bottom of the cliff wall he'd missed before. Maybe because the hole wasn't empty at all. Crammed inside, covered in a thin layer of ice like everything else, lay a body.

Ryon's shivering fingers reached in, and he rolled the still figure toward him. "Nox!" Ryon shook him, but when he didn't wake, his heart fell. "I found him," he whistled to Quill while checking Nox over. Nox's chest rose and fell slowly. Though he was covered in blood, and his skin was much too cold for comfort, he appeared to be alive.

"What about the girl?" Quill asked.

"She's not here." The hole was too narrow to fit anyone else inside it. His gut lurched. Someone had fallen down that cliffside. They had the bloodstains to prove it. If it wasn't Nox...

But he had too much to do to grieve her loss now. "Fly back to the barn. Fetch Gwen. I'll carry him back to the brothers, but we need to bring him to the village healer as fast as possible."

"You sure you can manage that on your own?" Quill cocked his head at the slippery path back.

Ryon nodded. "I have to. What are you waiting for? Go!"

Quill took off, his silver wings flapping in the day's last sunlight.

If Gwen arrived to carry Nox, then maybe they had a chance to save him. But first, he needed to lug Nox's dead weight down that icy path. Ryon slapped his face, praying he could wake him. If only he had a little help...

It was no use. Nox was out cold. And the longer he sat here waiting, the colder it was growing. He had no choice but to push forward.

He grabbed Nox's shoulders, tugging him into the clearing's center. Out of the two of them, Ryon was bigger, and after years of rock climbing, he considered himself exceptionally strong. Still, carting another fully grown man was going to be a challenge. Luckily, he had his wish to help him.

Grunting, Ryon lifted Nox and slung him over his shoulder. His wish made handling the weight simple, but the position was awkward, threatening to throw off his center of gravity. He stayed far back from the cliff's edge as he grew used to the burden and took slow, careful steps on the icy rocks.

Soon, he'd completed the harrowing task. As he circled the last rock, he blew out a deep breath.

"Ryon!" Brother Pip raced forward. "You found him! What about Mariun?"

Ryon shook his head sadly. "There was no sign of her. Just a trail of blood leading to the cliff's edge."

"Oh no." Brother Pip's brow furrowed. "Why would they be over there? There's nothing." His gaze hardened as he stared at Nox's wounds. "He must have led Mariun there, and she fought him off."

Ryon's stomach dropped. "Don't go jumping to conclusions."

"He's right." Brother Lennam cleared his throat. "That doesn't explain the bootprints Ryon found in the barn."

"I don't see anyone else out here, do you?" Pip grumbled.

Whatever the answer, they wouldn't discover it by standing around debating. "He's in bad shape. Help me carry him to the bridge." Ryon shifted Nox's weight, allowing the brothers to each grab a leg. With them working together and the footing much more stable, they covered the distance swiftly.

They arrived at the bridge just as thunderous booms pounded the rocks behind them. Ryon turned, spotting Gwen racing for the bridge, Violet perched on her back. Quill flew ahead of them, leading the way.

Gwen slowed to a stop. Violet jumped down. "Nox! Is he all right?"

"He's alive, but he's not awake. Help me get him on top of Gwen so she can take him to the healer."

Violet's hands trembled, but she nodded. "How can I help?"

"My pack." Ryon shrugged it off his shoulder as he and the brothers maneuvered Nox's unconscious body atop Gwen's back. "There's rope inside. Grab it for me? We don't need him falling off."

"Where's Mariun?" She handed the rope to him.

"I'm sorry. I think she's gone." Ryon pressed his lips together.

She gasped. "What do you mean, gone?"

"We found blood. A lot of it. The trail led to the cliff's edge."

Violet blinked back tears and leaped into action, helping him with the rope. Soon, they'd strapped Nox to Gwen's back. Violet insisted on riding with him, and Ryon didn't protest. If she wanted to keep watch over her uncle on the trek to the healer, then he wouldn't stop her.

As they crossed the bridge, he and the brothers jogging to keep up with Gwen's hurried pace, Ryon finally allowed his mind to linger on the scene he'd found. Had Mariun really fallen, or had something more sinister happened? He'd been moving on instinct, saving Nox because it was the right thing to do. That and he knew Violet would want her uncle back no matter what. But now, he had to consider the possibility that he'd just saved the life of a murderer.

He recoiled at the thought. Surely there must be another explanation. Yeah, they could be a little prickly to each other. But with the way they'd been looking at each other lately, he'd been expecting them to work things out... maybe even do more than just work things out.

Nox wouldn't hurt Mariun, would he?

They traversed the streets quickly, not pausing to address any curious folks who came out to gawk. Finally, they arrived at a small cottage on the central square's edge.

Brother Pip banged on the door. "Open up!" he yelled.

Ryon hurried to detach the rope, breathing heavily from the jog. At least the exertion had warmed him. Sweat gathered on his brow despite the chilly breeze.

As he reached up to grab Nox, he frowned. Tears streamed down Violet's cheeks. "It's all right. The healer will know what to do."

Violet nodded sadly, her hands clenched around a handful of green leaves. "I hope so." She lifted tearstained eyes to Ryon's. "I tried again. I couldn't heal him."

Nox's weight shifted to his shoulders, and Ryon grunted. He wanted nothing more than to drop him and pull Violet into his arms.

The healer's door inched open, and the hawk-nosed man stuck his head out. He spotted Nox and flung the door open wide. "Bring him in. No time to waste."

"Coming." Ryon spun to the cottage. "Be right back, Violet." Then he left her crying in the road, his heart breaking.

"You owe me," he whispered to Nox's unconscious body. "And if I find out you hurt Mariun, I'll murder you myself."

Heartsong

V iolet slid off Gwen's back and paced away from the healer's cottage. She should probably go in and stay with her uncle, but she just couldn't. Instead, she sank down on the cobblestones in the village square, cradling her head in her hands.

Golden wings fluttered, landing beside her. *"Are you all right, child?"*

"No. I'm not." Violet sobbed. *"Nox is hurt. I tried so hard to heal him, but I couldn't."*

"The hardest battles in life are the ones that must be fought alone."

"What's that supposed to mean?" Violet scrubbed her eyes with her sleeve.

Orry tucked her long legs beneath her and settled beside Violet. *"Have you ever considered that the reason you can't access the magic within you is that it's needed for a greater purpose?"*

"What greater purpose?" She threw an arm back to the cottage. *"Nox could die. Isn't healing him great enough?"*

"Healing one strong man who will eventually heal on his own? No. Not when the alternative is so much more."

Violet scoffed. *"More. More riddles. I swear, I'm sick of them. Could you speak plainly for once?"*

"I could speak all you'd like, but nothing will change until you learn to listen."

She stared at Orry, her eyes round. *"Listen... listen to what?"*

"Your heartsong, child. It's time."

Sitting up straight, she drew a deep breath. *"And that will help? Will it heal Nox?"*

"No. But it will allow you to see the greater picture." Orry cocked her head. *"Please, humor an old bird and try."*

"Fine," Violet said grudgingly. *"What do I need to do?"*

"It's as easy as breathing once you know how. When you're focused on another, you will find it helps to look deep into their eyes. But for yourself, you must focus on your mind's eye."

"How do I do that?"

"Close your eyes and look within. Find the quiet center of your soul and listen with your heart. You'll hear it, Violet. You'll hear the song."

She stared at Orry, frowning. *"That's all?"*

"Yes, child. Now stop putting it off with your questions and disbelief. This is not the same as before, with those little scraps of magic you're trying to clutch. You will hear the song. I promise."

Violet's stomach twisted. That was exactly what she'd been doing. Putting it off out of fear. What if she tried and failed? She'd failed at so much already that it wouldn't be that big of a reach. But Orry was right. She'd never know if she didn't try.

Her eyes fluttered closed. She sat on the cold ground, the icy breeze chilling her cheeks. The clatter of footsteps echoed somewhere behind her. A peel of laughter rode on the wind. The quiet sounds of village life continued onward, heedless of the broken man inside the healer's cottage. But that wasn't what she needed to listen to.

Violet shoved her worries for her uncle aside. She ignored the soft sounds of the community and delved deep down into herself.

"That's it, child. Deep breaths. Focus," Orry whispered.

She obeyed, taking a huge lungful of crisp air into her chest. She listened to it rush in and out. In and out. After a few repetitions, the quiet whoosh morphed, ringing out in her mind like a trumpet's blare. It startled her so much she jolted.

"That's it," Orry instructed, her quiet voice brimming with excitement. *"Keep listening."*

She delved deeper within, listening to the steady thrum of her pulse in her ears. Within a few beats, that changed, too, the *pitter-patter* of drums and the *chime* of cymbals exploding in her mind.

Violet gasped.

"What did I tell you, child? Listen. The song will show you what you need to see if you listen closely."

Excitement hummed through her blood, warming her limbs even with the icy chill of the cobbles under her. She sat still, concentrating. The longer she listened, the richer the song grew. The sweet notes of a flute and the merry *twang* of a lute joined in. Even more instruments piled on, some familiar and others she couldn't recognize, until the song in her mind wasn't merely a song. It was a grand symphony ringing through her bones and making the most joyous smile spread across her face.

Even so, she had seen nothing. She'd been concentrating so much on the sounds that the canvas in her mind's eye was a blank slate. And when she lingered over it, the song faded. Orry had said the song would show her something... there must be more.

As she listened, she stopped just idly enjoying the glorious tune. She knew instinctively this gift wouldn't be handed to her without her putting in the work. She needed to do her part, too.

It was all about intuition, wasn't it? That was the key.

Violet listened with a new goal in mind. She let her intuition guide her. As soon as she focused on that goal, she heard it. Something was off in the song. A single note out of melody with the rest. As she focused on it, an image finally coalesced, swimming in the black nothing behind her eyes.

It was a harp—the lone instrument out of tune. And though she'd never played it—had only ever seen one mounted on the wall at Kings Keep but never dared touch it—somehow, she found herself beside it, plucking the strings. The notes thrummed through her chest, and the strings' light vibrations tickled her fingers.

But while she played, all the notes stayed in perfect pitch with all the rest. Where was the note she'd heard before? If she kept playing, would it return?

What did she need to see?

As the question formed in her mind, her fingers plucked the wrong note. The image of her playing washed away, and a new image flashed. Bright and clear and utterly unmistakable.

Violet's eyes snapped open. "*The ring.*"

"*You've seen it before, yes? Been there in the flesh. The odyssey ring. That is where you must return. Where your magic will be needed.*"

Violet frowned. "*I thought I was just drawn to it because of my wish...*"

"*What wish?*" Orry asked.

"*When Ryon and I wished for the ability to breathe water as well as air. Wasn't that the consequence?*" Her pulse thrummed, picking up speed. If she'd been wrong about that, then what else was she wrong about?

Orry scoffed. "*Why would you think that?*" She shook her head. "*Consequences are not guaranteed with wishes. And I'm sure you can see now that your connection to the ring did not begin with the wish you made.*"

Violet rubbed her temple, a bud of hope blooming in her chest. "*So, Ryon. He's not drawn to me too? Because he wished to understand me?*"

Orry lifted from where she sat and flew into Violet's face, smacking her in the cheek with a golden wing.

"*Hey!*" She leaned back, wiping her face. "*What was that for?*"

"*Someone needed to slap some sense into you.*" Orry landed gracefully and pinned Violet with a hard glare. "*Are you so blind you cannot see that man is in love with you?*"

Her heart pounded. She stared at her lap, twisting her hands together. "*I-I thought it was the wish—*"

"*And so what if it was? Love should always be treasured regardless of how it began. Especially if you return the feeling.*"

Everything Orry said made perfect sense. Still, the thought of Ryon being in love with her without magic in play made her hands tremble. If only she could enjoy the feeling for more than a heartbeat without grief rising to wash it away.

How could she revel in love when Nox lay in there with one foot in death's door? And Mariun. She hadn't even stopped to fully consider that Mariun was gone. It didn't feel real. They'd just spoken that morning on the bridge. How could she be dead?

The mystery of what exactly happened ate at her. Who injured Nox? Was it Mariun or someone else?

She sensed from the disgusted looks Brother Pip had thrown Nox's way while jogging into the village that he blamed her uncle. Pip was wrong. Nox would've fought to protect Mariun. Someone else must have been involved. If the masked were still camped down below, then maybe someone in the village. Some cruel man who saw Mariun dancing around the bonfire and wanted her for himself.

It wasn't fair. After everything Mariun had been forced to endure, she deserved a true chance at happiness. She should be returning with them to Dracwood, far away from Jurdan's clutches, where she could start a new life. Not at the bottom of a cliff, her body broken and her spirit gone for good.

Violet couldn't help it. She burst into tears.

"Oh, child. It's all right. Things are not always as dark as they seem."

But Orry's reassurances weren't enough to stem the tears. Not by a long shot.

The healer's cottage door snapped open. Ryon emerged, heaving a weary sigh. "Violet." He brushed off his weariness and jogged over, gathering her in his arms. "I'm glad you're still here. I have good news. The healer says Nox will live."

She lifted her tearstained face and met his eyes. "He will?"

Ryon gently brushed the moisture off her cheeks. "It might be days before Nox wakes, but the healer's certain he will."

"That is good news." Violet stood. Gwen lay in the village square, staring at the healer's cottage, her head on her forelegs and big green wings wrapped around her body. Violet strode over to her and patted her neck soothingly. "He's going to be all right, Gwen. You did well, bringing him here so swiftly."

When Gwen did nothing more than huff out a sigh, Violet gave up. She wished she could do more for her, but without Nox, no one could speak to the hatchlings.

How would they continue to train them? Surely they couldn't just give up teaching the hatchlings to fly. Especially not now, when she had a new reason to leave this mountain.

She turned to Ryon and, at the same time, spoke in her mind to include Orry. "Do you think the dragons will be ready for more training tomorrow? Can the silvers help them again? I wager the best thing we can do while Nox is recuperating is continue helping them learn to fly."

"*The silvers will help*," Orry declared, both whistling for Ryon and speaking in her mind.

"I'll help, too," Ryon offered. "Whatever you need."

Violet sucked in a deep breath, her pulse thudding madly. "Once they've mastered flying, I'm leaving. Now that you've healed Rovan—"

Ryon didn't let her finish. "I'm coming with you."

Her eyes widened. "Just like that? You don't even want to hear where I'm planning to go?"

"Yes. I'd follow you anywhere." He smiled crookedly. "If you don't mind me tagging along?"

"Don't mind? Are you kidding?" She threw her arms around him, hugging him tightly. Warmth spread through her chest, and she had to fight back the urge to squeal.

Ryon chuckled lightly, returning her embrace. "Just for curiosity's sake, where are we going?"

Violet pulled away and nodded to Orry. "While you were in there with Nox, Orry taught me how to use my boon. I heard my heart-song."

"So now we follow it." Ryon grinned. "Do you know where it's leading you?"

"The ring." She bit her lip. "I need to return there."

"Huh. I suppose I could stand another swim."

Violet smiled, but all too soon it faded. Her gaze fell on the cottage where her uncle rested. "I'm not leaving without Nox. I have to know he's better. I need to see it with my own eyes."

"I understand." Ryon grabbed her hand and squeezed. "Let me check on him again, and then we can get some rest. I'll rise bright and early to work with the dragons. Sound good?"

"Yeah." She had to admit, after finding Orry last night, and with all the excitement and worry today, she was more than ready to rest. She had a feeling sleep would claim her as soon as her head hit the pillow.

Ryon disappeared into the healer's cottage, closing the door lightly behind him. Violet almost followed him, but really, what would be the point? She couldn't understand what the healer said, anyway. And she didn't think she could bear to look at Nox all bruised and covered in blood without bursting into tears yet again.

She wandered over to Gwen instead. Was there some way to convince her to return to the barn and rest? It would be hard, no doubt, but—

Violet stalled, the back of her neck erupting with prickles. She spun sideways, her gaze narrowing on a small corridor between the healer's cottage and the house next to it. She jogged over, unable to deny the urge. The creepy sensation of eyes on her back demanded she investigate.

But when she reached the narrow opening, the space was empty. Rubbish bins overflowing with kitchen scraps and other refuse crowded the gap. She leaned in, certain someone would leap at her from behind them.

She gasped, clutching her chest as a black bird darted into the sky. "Blazes!"

"*What is it, child?*" Orry asked.

"*Nothing. I could've sworn someone was back there, spying on me. But it was just a bird snacking on the rubbish.*" She backed away from the corridor, waving a hand. "*One of those silly black hat birds.*"

"*Hat bird?*" Orry laughed, the sweet melody of her giggles setting Violet's heart at ease. "*What in the world is a hat bird?*"

Violet shook her head. "*It's not important.*" The door opened again, and Ryon stepped out. "*Do you mind if I tell you later? I'm beyond ready for this day to end.*"

"*Of course. Go. Rest. I'll stay with Gwen tonight. We can keep watch over her bondmate together.*"

Violet smiled softly. "*Really? You don't mind?*"

"*It's no trouble at all. I'll see you in the morning.*"

Ryon reached her side. "Nox is still doing fine. The healer promised to keep watch over him all night. You ready to get some rest?"

"Yeah. Let's go." Violet let him lead her away. She'd done all she could for today. If only Nox would wake... but she could wait. She would wait as long as it took.

Gliding

"That's it," Quill whistled, "get those big wings flapping!"

Ryon chuckled, shading his eyes from the morning sun. Ari perched atop a stone bluff, mimicking the silver orecoln's movements. Quill stood just in front of the massive dragon, wings flicking like mad as he attempted to teach the lumbering hatchling to fly.

This was the third morning they'd woken at daybreak, made the trek to the barn, and collected the dragons for training. The first day had been the hardest. He'd almost given up after an hour of shoving, cajoling, and bribes hadn't been enough to persuade the hatchlings to exit the barn. But then Gwen arrived.

She was with them now—her shoulders slumped and her head hanging low—but she was here. She'd arrived every morning since and was the first to subject herself to whatever odd "lessons" the orecolns dreamed up. Then, every evening when they called it quits, she wandered back to the village square to hold vigil outside the healer's cottage.

Nox still hadn't woken. With each day that passed, Ryon's stomach ached a little more. The healer insisted he would recover. That Nox's many bruises and cuts were healing well with the aid of his poultices and potions. Still, the amount of time he'd spent unconscious was concerning. A part of Ryon wondered if the healer had it wrong. Would Nox ever wake?

They'd seen no sign of Mariun. Dozens of villagers had pored over the river, braving the sharp rocks and cold water. But despite wading the waterway's full length, they'd not discovered any trace of her. It appeared more and more likely that she'd been dragged back into the mountain and her body would never be recovered.

They were no closer to discovering the cause of her fall, either. No one had come forward with clues, and with Nox still unconscious, all they had to go on were those mysterious bootprints in the barn. Any evidence outside had been washed away in the storm. Yet, he couldn't shake the thought that someone else had been involved. But who? And why?

The masked were still camped at the mountain's base. Brother Tham's men had kept a constant watch. They'd alerted him when the masked rigged a pair of men with crude climbing gear and struggled to scale the base. But after that sad attempt ended with one man injured, they'd given up quickly.

If he could judge by the amount of building they'd undertaken since, they'd decided to starve them out. It seemed the masked wrongly believed the mountain was a barren peak. They weren't aware of the lengths his people had gone through to survive up here. Sure, they enjoyed occasionally hunting the tritusks down below, but Avion had more than enough grain, fish, and eggs to keep the village fed indefinitely.

Ryon sighed. All the more reason to get the hatchlings flying. Once they flew away—flying low enough to give the masked a perfect view of them retreating—then they'd abandon their foolish siege.

"Yes, that's it!" Quill bent down. "Now leap." He launched off the rock, lifting into the air gracefully.

Ari bent his knees, his gaze glued to Quill, and jumped into the air. Ryon winced, readying himself for the slam that would surely come next.

"Ha! What did I tell you?" Quill shouted triumphantly.

Ryon's jaw dropped. Ari hadn't fallen! With his blue wings flapping furiously, he circled the air overhead before gliding down and landing hard on his feet. The ground trembled slightly, but Ryon barely registered the tiny rumble beneath his boots. It was nothing compared to the hundreds of slams he'd witnessed.

"I can't believe it..." he murmured under his breath. Then, swallowing his reaction, he threw a fist into the air and whooped. "Ari, you big, beautiful beast! You did it!"

He raced over, wanting to slap his rump to celebrate, but backed away when the other hatchlings barreled into Ari, all of them jostling and bumping their brother playfully. Even Gwen seemed to be in higher spirits after watching Ari's successful glide.

What was even more miraculous was that seeing Ari's success somehow became the catalyst that the others needed to have success of their own. Within a few tries, each of them glided successfully as well.

Quill landed beside Ryon as Mena, the last of the siblings to figure out gliding, swooped down. "I'm ready for your thank you now." He puffed out his chest, clearly pleased.

"And you have it. Who would've known? Quill, teacher of dragons!"

"I'm a bird of many talents." Quill bowed, doing a fair imitation of the human act.

"That you are. I can't wait to tell Violet about this."

"Why don't you fetch her?" Quill asked. "I'll keep the dragons practicing until you return."

Ryon eyed the sun's position. It was still a long time before they needed to break for lunch. "You sure you don't mind?"

"No. Go get your sweetheart. I'm sure she'll be mighty thankful to you, too."

He cocked a brow and pursed his lips but refrained from replying. He was too excited about showing Violet the dragon's progress to strike up an argument with the silly orecoln. "All right. I'll be back."

Ryon jogged away from the practice site behind the Aviary and made his way across the bridge into the village. He didn't have to guess where Violet would be. She'd become as much a creature of habit as he had the last few days. Every morning when he left to train the dragons, she went to sit with her uncle.

Soon he'd made it through the village and stopped in front of the healer's cottage. He took a few deep breaths and straightened his clothes and hair. Then he knocked gently on the door.

"Come in," the healer called.

Ryon entered, nodding to the healer before heading straight for his guest room. Violet perched on an old rocking chair beside the lone cot. Her hands were busy, working on a feather trinket.

Ryon smiled, recalling the way his family had come to help her. Ma brought her lunch each day, and Rovan sat with Violet most afternoons. It wasn't long before he'd offered to teach her how to craft the feathered-and-beaded trinkets. Now he found her working on them more often than not. He was certainly glad she'd found something to help her through this challenging time.

But Nox... he still looked just the same. It was hard to keep coming here day after day and finding him in the same state. He couldn't imagine what kind of toll it was having on Violet. Here in Avion, Nox was her only family. He could tell from the way she watched over him she loved him dearly.

"How's Nox doing today?" Ryon asked quietly.

Violet peeked up from the golden feather on her lap. "The same." She sighed, and then her brow furrowed, and she shot a glance out the window. "You're here rather early today."

"I have good news. The hatchlings are finally making progress. I don't think it will be long before they're flying fully."

"Really?" Violet's face brightened. "That's wonderful news."

"I thought you'd like to come see?" He reached out a hand, intending to help her out of the rocker.

Violet stared at his hand and frowned. "I-I don't know. What about Nox?"

"He's not going anywhere. And if he does wake, he'll be right here when we get back."

Her gaze flitted around the room, landing on Nox, then the window, then his hand.

"Surely you deserve a little break. And some sunshine? We don't need to stay long if you don't want to."

With a big sigh, she grabbed his hand. She stuffed the feather into her skirt pocket and rose from the rocker. "Just for a little while. They're really flying?"

"Well, I'd say gliding is more accurate, but yeah. It's a pleasant change from all the slamming down they've been doing so far."

Violet chuckled. "It's lucky they're such resilient creatures."

"It is." Ryon tucked her arm into his elbow, and together they left the healer's cottage and started the long walk back to where the dragons trained. "Where's Orry? I'm surprised she wasn't at Nox's bedside with you."

"She went for a visit at the Aviary." A tiny smile lit her lips, and Ryon was instantly glad he'd convinced her to tag along. "I think sometimes she misses bossing the silvers around."

Ryon grinned. "It's nice she has a chance to teach the new Mother Orea her secrets. I'm glad to learn they're all on good terms. That first night when the silvers looked away from her after she fell"—he shivered involuntarily—"was so eerie to watch."

"It was. But I suppose this is new territory for them. They were expecting her to die..." Her voice trailed off, and Ryon scrambled to think of a less morose topic.

"It's a beautiful day for a visit, at least. So warm." He cringed internally. The weather? Really?

"It is a lovely day." Violet lifted her face to the sun. "I almost can't believe it was sleeting a few days ago."

He shrugged, thankful she hadn't scoffed at his pitiful change of subject. "Weather in Avion can change very quickly. You get used to it after a while."

"What I don't understand is how you grow crops if it can snow during the summer?" Violet's brow furrowed, and her fingers tightened on his sleeve as they began crossing the bridge. "I've loved sampling the delicious breads your mother makes. You must be growing that grain somewhere."

"You're right. I'm sure you've noticed we're not using just the one mountain peak. There's a whole string of mountains connected with the river flowing between them. There's a valley a few peaks over where we do most of our planting. It's low enough that the freak summer storms don't affect the crops."

"Huh." Violet blew out a deep breath as they finished crossing the bridge. "There's so much more to your island than I realized."

Ryon nodded. "Yeah, I guess you could say—"

He jolted, shoving her behind him as a masked man jumped into their path. Ryon's pulse galloped wildly in his veins. This shouldn't be happening. How had the masked made it up here? Brother Tham's watch should have warned them long before any of them reached this height.

But as the fiend stalked closer, brandishing a shining blade in one hand and a short pole in the other, Ryon shoved the questions aside. There would be time for that later if he and Violet escaped unscathed.

He bit back a gasp as he tore his gaze away from the weapons and it landed on the man's mask. It was the spider! The same man who'd followed Mariun around like a hound throughout Thalassia. The same one Jurdan had surely ordered to chase Mariun and wouldn't rest until he found her. What would he do when he learned Mariun was no longer with them?

And how was he going to protect Violet? Ryon had come out here relatively unarmed, thinking no one would dare hurt him in his home. Any other day, he'd be correct in that assumption. His stomach churned as he realized the small crafting blade he wore on his belt was the only weapon he had at his disposal.

Heart pounding out of control, Ryon did the only thing he could think of. He yelled, "What do you want?" Maybe if he got him talking, they had a chance. If he distracted the spider enough, Violet might even be able to run back across the bridge and find help.

"The diva. Where is she?" the spider asked gruffly.

Ryon flinched. He'd been expecting him to ask for Mariun, not Lark. "I don't know where she is. She's not here."

He turned, trying to communicate with his eyes to Violet. He looked at her pointedly, then darted a glance at the bridge behind them. But when he finished and glanced back at Violet, he couldn't stop the frown that overtook his face.

What was she doing? She hadn't looked at him once. Not a single muscle in her face had moved to confirm she grasped his silent plan. Instead, she stared at the spider, frozen in place, almost as if she were in a trance.

Guano. What now? It seemed he was on his own. His fingers twitched, ready to dive for the tiny blade on his belt that wouldn't be a match for the huge curved blade shining at the spider's side.

The spider stood just as stiffly as Violet, but he was much harder to read with that fearsome mask in place. Still, Ryon had a feeling if he made a single move, the spider would be on him in a heartbeat.

He kept still, holding his breath. What would the fiend ask for next?

"Give me a feather."

"What?" Ryon barked.

"I've been watching you." Spider waved a gloved hand at Avion laid out behind them. "The whole lot of you. I've heard what those feathers can do. And I've seen that silver bird following you around. Call for it. Now."

Ryon bristled. "I don't know what you're talking about." No way was he calling for Quill. He refused to subject his friend to the spider. He'd likely try to steal a feather by force.

"Lies. Call for the bird," Spider demanded, waving his blade menacingly.

The spider wasn't as knowledgeable as he professed to be, or he'd have known about the feathers hidden in his hair. Still, that he'd learned about the orecolns at all was impressive. Spider had been watching them… for how long? How long had that monster been creeping through their village, spying on them?

Violet nudged his side, startling Ryon so much he almost yelped. "Give him a feather."

He glanced at her, his jaw dropping and his brows pinched. "What? You can't mean that—"

"I do." She peered at him, eyes shining. Then she turned back to the spider and stared. "Don't you trust me, Ryon?"

"Yes. Of course I do." But what she was asking… he couldn't just hand over one of his precious wishes to this villain, could he? Spider could wish for anything. The power to kill them on the spot.

"If you've ever trusted me, then you'll do this now. Give the spider a feather," Violet said calmly, her gaze never wavering from the spider's mask.

Ryon's fingers shook. He couldn't do what she was asking. There was no way. She reached for his hand and squeezed. He met her eyes.

"Please, Ryon. Trust me," she pleaded.

As he looked into her eyes, the decision was suddenly perfectly clear. He grabbed his belt knife and, with a few deft flicks, pulled a silver feather out of one of his dreads. Ryon gulped. He handed the knife to Violet, then walked to the spider. When he was a few paces away, he halted and held out the feather.

The spider cocked his head but made no move to reach for the feather.

What was Spider doing? He'd asked for a feather and now refused to take it. Was he waiting for an explanation of how to use it?

Ryon cleared his throat. "Think of what you'd like to wish for. Make sure the wording is clear and precise. Then add a drop of blood and make your wish."

Still, the spider stood frozen.

"Go on," Violet called from behind him. "Take it."

Spider grabbed the feather, plucking it out of Ryon's hand with two gloved fingers. Ryon backed away slowly, his heart beating madly.

Please tell me I didn't just make the worst mistake of my life...

Awake

Nox groaned, a dull ache in his limbs pulling him out of sleep. His eyes fluttered open, and he frowned at the unfamiliar room.

"*Where am I?*"

When only silence greeted him, he gasped and bolted up, shoving the sheets off his legs.

The block. Pain. Snatches of memories flooded back to him, all jumbled up like a puzzle it would take ages to solve.

What happened? He couldn't be sure. But as he reached for his bondmates, one thing was obvious. The block in his mind remained.

Nox sucked in a deep breath and concentrated. Within a few heartbeats, he'd torn it down. Even before he said a word, a sense of belonging stole over him as he connected to his bondmates.

"*Gwen? Flint?*"

"*Nox!*" Flint replied.

"*You're back!*" Gwen shrieked in his mind, making him wince. "*Never do that again!*"

"All right, all right. As long as you promise not to yell at me." Nox pressed his fingers into his temples, then shook out his limbs. Except for the ringing in his head from Gwen's screaming, he was all in one piece. A little sore in a few spots, and so parched he immediately downed the cup of water he found on the table beside him, but nothing serious. If only he could shake the fuzzy edges off his memory, then everything would be normal. *"Can someone explain what happened? I just woke, and I'm having trouble remembering."*

"You almost died." Flint's voice was grim. *"Ryon found you on a cliffside beaten and unconscious, left for dead in the middle of a sleet storm."*

"How strange. Why can't I remember...?" Nox rubbed the back of his neck and stilled when he brushed a tiny bump with his fingers. *"The masked. They're here!"*

"We know. They've been camped at the mountain base for days now," Gwen replied.

"No. Not down there. They were up here! That's why I can't remember." Nox flipped his hand over and stared at a second bump in his palm. *"Those rotting darts."* He gasped. *"Mariun. They had her. They took her."*

"Are you sure?" Flint asked.

"Yes... I think." Nox scrunched his brow, fighting to make sense of the scattered fragments of his memory. *"Where is she? Where's Mariun?"*

"No one's seen her since you went missing. I saw the villagers searching the river, looking for her. But I haven't seen any masked in Avion." Gwen added, *"Believe me, I'd remember."*

The river... why would they be searching the river? Unless they thought she'd fallen. Rot and decay. He was the only one who knew she was missing, wasn't he?

Nox shook his head. *"I'll admit, my memory is cloudy. But it would be if they'd drugged me."* He swung his legs over the bed's edge and scanned the small room for his boots. There. He snatched them off the floor and shoved his feet inside. *"Where am I?"*

"You're in the village. They brought you to a healer," Gwen explained.

Flint cut in. *"You've been asleep for three days."*

Nox's stomach sank. Three days? That meant the masked had Mariun for all that time, with no one looking for her. She could be anywhere by now. Even back in Jurdan's clutches. He had to find her.

"Where are you?" he asked.

Gwen's voice brimmed with excitement. *"Training out behind the Aviary."*

"You kept training without me?"

"Yep. And you're not gonna believe it! We're finally getting somewhere."

"Really?" Nox finished lacing his boots, choking down the flash of disappointment that he'd missed it. *"Don't move. I'm coming to find you. I need to see this for myself."*

Perhaps his luck wasn't as awful as he'd first expected. If Gwen was ready to fly, then maybe he could catch Mariun before the masked returned her to Jurdan. It wasn't much of a plan, but it was something.

He quietly creeped out of his room, scanning the house. He spotted a hawk-nosed man, his mouth hanging open as he dozed in a kitchen chair. The healer, he was guessing. Nox inched toward the door. At least no one would stop him.

Images bombarded him as he tiptoed out of the healer's cottage and strode into the bright daylight. Mariun perched on his lap in the barn, tracing the scar on his neck. Her fierce confession. The smile on her lips as she lay beside him in the stall.

Nox might not remember clearly what happened after, but the time he'd spent with Mariun was engrained in his mind. It had been unlike anything he'd experienced. The connection they had transcended the physical. When they'd come together, a light had sparked deep in his soul.

Mariun had been so trusting. So blissfully sweet. And then after, she'd opened up and shared her secret.

Nox gasped. Kayda. He was still the only one who knew about the danger his sister faced. Three days... He scrambled to do the math. When was the Harvest Festival? Had they missed it already?

He was so wrapped up in calculations, he barely noticed that he'd reached the village's edge. It wasn't until his boots smacked down on the hard stone of the bridge that he lifted his gaze ahead of him.

"Rot and decay!" Nox broke into a sprint, his feet moving without thought.

"*Gwen! The bridge. Run!*" He wasn't taking another chance of being left without his bondmate. Not ever again if he could help it.

"*What is it?*" Flint demanded.

"*I'm coming!*" Gwen's panicked voice made his stomach clench. But he couldn't afford to calm her. Not when his own panic was a living, breathing monster ready to swallow him whole.

"*The masked have Violet! It's the spider. Hurry!*"

Violet and Ryon stood just beyond the bridge's edge. Spider hovered ahead of them, a gleaming curved blade in one hand. What were they doing? He couldn't quite make it out from so far away, but it was clear they weren't engaged in battle.

It surprised Nox none of them had noticed him running. He'd not called out, but he'd made no effort to disguise the slap of his footfalls, either. Yet Ryon and Violet didn't turn to see who was coming. Even the spider, who stood facing him, paid no attention to Nox as he rushed across the bridge.

No, they were all staring at the same thing. Spider's hand.

Spider held one hand at eye level. His fist clenched around something. Nox gasped at the flash of silver he finally spotted. Was that a bloodfeather?

Before he could do anything other than widen his eyes in disbelief, the spider lifted his curved blade and sliced his palm. Blood splattered the feather.

"No!" Nox skidded to a stop beside Violet. "What have you done?"

Violet grabbed his arm. "Nox! You're awake."

A shadow darkened the horizon, and Nox's jaw dropped. "Gwen!" She was flying!

His heart skipped a beat as he stared at the majestic spread of her wings. She soared over the boulders at Spider's back and slammed into the ground beside him, spewing a stream of earth at his head. Spider fell to one knee, covering his mask with his hands to protect himself from the onslaught.

"No!" Violet shook Nox violently. "Make her stop. Tell Gwen to stop!"

Nox shied away from the steel in her tone. What was happening? The spider was already half covered. He wasn't a threat—for the moment. "*Gwen. Stop. Violet says to stop.*"

Gwen cut off the earth, but not before her magic buried the Spider in a massive mound of dirt and rock. Violet raced forward, quickly working to shove the larger stones away.

Nox shared a look with Ryon, who shrugged before rushing to help Violet. He, at least, kicked the spider's blade far out of reach before joining her, knocking the spider loose.

"*What are they doing?*" Flint asked. "*I thought he had Violet?*"

"*So did I.*" Nox finally caught his breath from the run. "*Don't worry. I'll get to the bottom of this.*"

"*I need to go back to the others.*" Gwen winced. "*They're flipping out over me leaving.*"

"*Go. Calm them down. I'll explain as soon as I can.*"

"I—" Violet began, but Nox held up a hand, stopping her.

Spider's head broke free from the rubble. Nox stepped forward, his hand outstretched. "You." His voice dripped with rancor. "I know who you are." He ripped the mask off Spider's face, revealing a middle-aged bald man with dark-brown skin and dark shadows rimming his eyes.

But the man's expression was all wrong... Nox had been sure he'd be met with a sneer, or maybe a frown. Even a groan of agony from the pain of being pummeled with hundreds of stones and partially buried. Not this... Spider beamed. His face was lit with the smile of a man who'd just been handed his wildest dream on a platter.

"I do, too." He met Nox's eyes, his dark-brown orbs swimming with unshed tears. "I finally remember."

Violet grinned, brushing more dirt off Spider's shoulder. "I knew it. I could *hear* it. He needed that wish. He deserved it."

"Wait. Did Lark tell you, too?" Nox asked.

"Tell me what?" Violet peered at him, her face the picture of curiosity.

It seemed either way, the secret was out now. "That the spider is Jayan. The man Kayda sent searching for Druturion's eggs twenty years ago."

"Kayda..." Spider—Jayan—jerked first one arm, then the next out of the pile of earth. But the dreamy wonder painting his face when Jayan uttered his sister's name made Nox want to bury him all over again.

"How could you work for that fiend? Kayda trusted you." Nox barely buried the urge to scream. "Do you know what Jurdan's planning to do at her wedding?"

That wiped the stupid smile off Jayan's face.

Violet gasped. "Jurdan's planning something at Aunt Kayda's wedding?"

"Aye." Jayan shoved dirt away from his torso. "You're right. The filthy dust eater. I've been such a fool."

"Wait. I'm not following half of this." Ryon tore away a rock wedged behind Jayan's back.

"What day is it?" Jayan's gaze flitted around wildly. "There's still time, isn't there? We have to warn her."

"I'm not letting you anywhere near her!" Nox sneered. Anger rose, furious and hot. His fists burned and claws burst free. He leaped forward, shoving Jayan down, wrapping his hands around his lying neck. "You bastard. Where is she? Where's Mariun?"

Violet lurched forward, grabbing his elbow, her voice quivering as much as her fingers. "Wait. Mariun fell. S-she's dead."

"No, she isn't," Nox bit out, his fingers tightening. "Tell her."

"He's right." Jayan struggled to force the words out until Nox released a bit of the pressure on his neck. "Mariun's with the masked. I sent her with a few of my men on the second boat. They have orders to bring her back to Thalassia."

It was Ryon's turn to gasp. "That's impossible. How did they climb up the mountain? And why are the men still camped down below?"

Jayan choked out, "My orders again. A diversion so you wouldn't suspect we'd used the hidden passage Jurdan had built in this mountain long ago."

"Hidden passage?" Ryon's jaw dropped. "Guano."

"Why?" Nox demanded. "Why should we believe any of your lies after what you've done? All the years you spent working for that monster. How can we believe a rotting word that comes out of your mouth?"

"Please..." Jayan winced as one of Nox's claws drew blood. The little bead of red slid down his neck and soaked the black collar of his tunic. "Let me explain."

Violet spoke up in his defense yet again. "Uncle. Let him explain."

Nox didn't want to. He kept picturing Mariun, scared and alone, out on a boat with only those rough masked for company. He held the man responsible in his grasp. He could end him here and now. Slice through his neck and watch him bleed out.

But what would that solve? He still wouldn't be any closer to saving Mariun. And he'd never learn why. What could drive a man, who'd become so beloved and trusted by his queen, to betray her to his enemy?

"Speak." Nox withdrew his hands and backed away, willing his anger to fade, though he doubted it would disappear easily.

Jayan coughed and rubbed his neck. "Twenty years ago, I was in an accident that nearly killed me. Knowing what I do now, I suspect it was a shipwreck. But for years, all I knew was what I learned after I woke. The memories of my youth were lost to me until the moment I made my wish on that feather."

Violet pressed a hand over her heart. "So, you're saying you didn't remember Kayda when you started following Jurdan?"

Jayan nodded. "I didn't remember any of it. My entire past was a mystery. I couldn't even remember my own name."

That, at least, was a blessing in disguise. It seemed Spider had shared none of Jayan's secrets with Jurdan. He'd have no way to spill details about Kayda, Dracwood, or anything back home if he couldn't remember it.

Yet, it didn't justify what he'd done in Jurdan's name. Mariun's tale replayed in Nox's mind. Spider had been there that day. He'd watched Jurdan slaughter those innocent people. Women and children. He was likely complicit in so much more; they'd barely scratched the surface of his crimes.

"And you think that's a good excuse?" Nox scoffed. "Couldn't you see what a villain he was? You still followed him, served him, for twenty years."

"I had my reasons." Jayan shuddered. "And I can't say I don't have my regrets. But what's done is done. All I can hope now is to do better in the future. That starts with saving my queen."

Ryon crossed his arms. "How can we trust you? You just spent weeks chasing us on Jurdan's command. What if this is another trick to steal the dragons?"

"Jurdan didn't want the dragons. All he wanted was Mariun."

Nox froze. Anger boiled in his veins. Jurdan couldn't have her. He wouldn't allow it.

Violet frowned. "It doesn't make sense. Why did he have the map to the eggs in the first place? Why allow us to escape?"

Jayan's lips thinned. "I don't know. But I know all he cared about was getting Mariun back. That was his only order. I stayed behind to hunt for the diva. When she loosened my mask, I thought she recognized me. I'd hoped she could tell me about my past."

"Is that why you knocked her out back in Thalassia?" Violet asked.

Nox's stomach buckled. That act of violence he'd witnessed with his own eyes. The sickening thud of Lark's head on the wall replayed in his ears, making the rage smoldering in his gut reignite.

"Yes," Jayan admitted, his voice filled with remorse, though he didn't utter an apology. "You can send men to check the boats in the harbor if you don't believe me. And I can lead you to the passage. But please, after you've confirmed my story, let me come with you. I owe it to Kayda to be the one to warn her."

Violet met Nox's gaze and shrugged. He could sense she wanted to give Jayan a chance. "He's bound to know things that could be useful."

Jayan lifted his chin. "I do. Countless things, I'd wager. I'll spill them all. But only if I can save my queen."

Nox grabbed Violet's arm and tugged her aside. "I don't like it, but I suppose it makes sense to bring him back to Dracwood with you." He sucked in a few deep breaths, concentrating on Violet's face. As his temper cooled, the burn in his fingers faded. "What do you think?"

She sent him a slight smile. "I don't think he's a threat any longer. I didn't have time to tell you yet, but my boon is increased intuition." She turned, staring at Jayan. "He's changed. I can *feel* it."

Nox knew more than anyone that boons could be powerful things. If hers was telling her to trust Jayan, then that meant something. "All right. Let him warn Kayda. She can decide what to do with him."

Violet nodded, then frowned. "Wait. You said bring him back with *you*. Aren't you coming too?"

Nox shook his head. "No. I have to find her." Violet peered at him, compassion filling her eyes. "Gwen and I will save Mariun."

He waited for Violet to argue, but she surprised him. She reached into her tunic and tugged out a string. He cocked his head as she slowly pulled, revealing more of the necklace.

"Has anyone told you about the difference between silver and gold bloodfeathers before?" She finished tugging the long string, revealing a brilliant golden feather embroidered with intricate black beadwork.

Nox squinted, trying to make out the tiny picture. "No. What has that got to do with anything?"

Violet gathered the string and lifted it off her neck. "I spent a lot of time sitting with you while you recuperated. It gave me plenty of opportunities to listen."

He quirked a brow. She thrust the necklace toward him, dangling it in front of his face, and his gaze caught on the shape again. A black cat.

"You made this for me?" The cat wasn't an example of expert craftsmanship by any means, but it still put a tiny smile on his face. The little reminder of Flint made his heart clench.

She jiggled it until he grabbed the soft feather out of her fingers. "Golden bloodfeathers let you change one thing about someone else. But make sure the wish you ask for is worth a lifetime of sacrifice. You only get one."

Nox gaped at Violet. "This is a real bloodfeather?"

"Yes. I had Orry give me one. When I listened to your heartsong, I knew you'd need it one day. And that you'd suffered enough already to be worthy of it." She flashed a lopsided grin. "I just didn't realize I'd be giving it to you quite so soon."

"Wow." He pulled the necklace over his head and tucked it inside his tunic. "Thanks, Squirt."

For once, the old nickname didn't earn him a scowl. She thudded into his chest and wrapped her arms around him. "Do what it takes to find Mariun. As soon as we finish warning Kayda, we'll return for you. All three of you."

"I will." Nox hugged her back. "It's a good plan. The dragons can communicate over far distances. They'll lead you back to Gwen."

"Maybe you should take one of the others. Ari or—"

"No. There are three of you. One for each dragon. We're already taking a chance they can make it across the ocean. No need to tax them even more." He glanced sideways. "Ryon's going with you, right?"

Violet nodded against his chest. Nox pulled back and shared a soft smile with his niece. It felt strange to be making plans to leave her. After all, they'd spent so long traveling together, and he'd vowed to protect her.

But she had Ryon now. From the wary way he'd stationed himself between Jayan and his niece, he was protecting her even now.

More than that, Violet had grown into her own. She'd proven with the spider that her judgment had profoundly changed in such a unique way. And from watching her over the course of their journey, he had no doubt that she'd stand up to whatever challenges came her way.

"I guess this is goodbye, for now." He pulled her close for one last hug. "I'm leaving as soon as I gather supplies. There's no time to waste."

"You won't catch her." Jayan stood, brushing the dirt off his black pants. "That boat is our fastest. Two days and nights of fair winds will have seen it back to Thalassia."

Nox cocked his head. "Guess I better prepare for a swim." He leaned down and lifted the spider mask out of the dirt. "Think this might come in handy?"

"Keep it," Jayan said gruffly. "I never want to see that thing again."

"Good luck." Ryon clasped Nox's shoulder.

"You'll find her. I know you will." Violet threaded her arm through his. "Let's return to the village and gather supplies."

Gwen spoke up. "*We're back in the barn. Everyone is calmed down for the moment, resting. Can you tell me what's going on now?*"

Where to begin? So much had changed in the last few moments. They'd gained an ally—of sorts. Made plans to part ways. Now, he had to tell Gwen she was about to be separated from her siblings. That he was taking her on a dangerous journey. Back to the place where he'd been held prisoner. Where Flint had died.

But there was no other choice. If he didn't go after Mariun, he'd never be able to live with himself. Gwen would understand. She had to.

Best to rip the bandage off. "*Time for practice is over. Tell the others we're leaving.*"

Dracwood

Wind rushed through her hair. Violet clutched Mena's neck, peering at the landscape below her. The first hints of yellow, orange, and red painted the trees of her homeland. But while autumn's arrival had always brought a smile to her face—and a few more sneezes to her nose—now the sight only made her stomach sink.

"*I hope we're not too late,*" she confessed to Orry.

"*You won't be.*" Her bondmate snuggled tighter against her belly. Orry started the journey flying, but it hadn't been long before she'd tired and seated herself with Violet atop Mena. "*I've seen it.*"

Violet ought to be comforted by Orry's claims. After all, not everyone was granted a bondmate who glimpsed the future. And yet, her stomach still wouldn't settle. She had a feeling it would take seeing Kayda in the flesh before she felt at ease once more.

At least the sight of her home brought a small measure of comfort to her soul. She couldn't wait to see her family again. With any luck, they'd be at the castle, eager to celebrate with Kayda. Her father's leg was bound to have healed by now. And Lark wouldn't miss the chance to reunite with the Wandering Bards. It was a rare occasion when they missed performing at Flamesmoat's premier feast.

Even without a royal wedding, the Harvest Festival was the grandest event held in Dracwood. From their calculations, they expected to arrive the day before it began.

Excitement welled in her belly. She'd been so certain she'd miss it this year. It would be a crime to miss her aunt's wedding, but she'd told herself that finding the dragon eggs would make up for it. Now she got to do both. It was more than she could've hoped for.

And she couldn't wait to introduce Ryon to her home. Of course, they couldn't stay long. Not if they intended to keep their promise to return to help Nox. But the dragons would need to rest after such a long journey. It would be enough time to introduce him to the people she loved most and show him a small bit of the country she grew up in. He deserved as much after the hospitality he'd shown her in Avion.

Still, a part of her rejected the happiness fighting to infect her. Mariun was gone. In the short time they'd known each other, they'd become friends. When she'd gone missing, Violet's fear for her uncle had overshadowed her worry for Mariun. Then the news of her death had unleashed a wave of grief. Grief that had been replaced with regret. If only they'd searched harder after that storm, not just assumed Mariun had fallen...

What were they supposed to think, with all that blood and no sign of her? Now they knew what really happened.

Before they'd left, Jayan had led them to the hidden entrance to the secret passage. The blood belonged to one of the masked Nox had killed while trying to rescue Mariun. During the struggle, the masked hit Mariun with a dart and Nox with a second. Spider ordered his men to take her and stayed behind. He threw the body into the river to remove the evidence and hid Nox where Ryon found him.

She could tell the story stunned Ryon. After all, it would've been simple to toss Nox down with the corpse. But Violet wasn't surprised. It was proof that even after losing his memory and serving a monster, deep down, Jayan was good at heart. The type of man who wouldn't murder an unconscious man. Or who'd save a little girl who'd just used a power she barely understood for a heartbreaking reason.

Her stomach turned. She still couldn't believe Jurdan had Mariun. He could be doing anything to her.

But leaving the dragons baffled her. He could've easily ordered his men to take the dragons, too. With the passage giving them access to Avion, they could have infiltrated the city by force. Maybe they'd have even caught them unawares and captured everyone with enough of those darts. Why had he only wanted Mariun?

Who knew what lengths it would take for Nox to save her? Ryon had given him a silver feather before he left, which Nox used to learn Thalassian. She only hoped that with Spider's mask and without the language barrier, he'd be able to pull off a rescue easily.

As Violet spotted the first hint of blue lingering on the horizon, she pushed her thoughts aside. They'd flown long and far, passing over the Salt Sea, the Orddon Ocean, and most of Dracwood. Now, they'd almost reached the Eprora Ocean. Dracwood's capital, Flamesmoat, was nestled on the coast. It wouldn't be long now before they arrived.

Violet smiled as the trees thinned beneath them. Soon they flew over the great ring of fields surrounding the city. During the spring and summer, the land ripened with crops. Every year after they'd been harvested, those same fields were used to host the traveling performers and citizens who flocked to the capital for the annual Harvest Festival.

Thousands of tents and wagons crowded the massive fields. More than she'd ever seen. But it wasn't every year that the queen married.

Surely everyone who could had made the trip to be a part of such a momentous occasion.

Despite the crowds already gathered, the spread of tables closest to Dracwood was unoccupied. Violet's heart lifted. It seemed their calculations were correct. The feast, and wedding, hadn't begun yet.

"Are we landing here?" Ryon yelled from his perch on Ari's back.

Violet shook her head. "No. Let's head to Kings Keep." It didn't make sense to land outside the city when the person they'd come to see was likely at home.

She kicked Mena's side, directing her to fly toward the castle perched in the Northmoat section of Flamesmoat. Screams and shouts rang out, and she spared a glance for the people below her.

For the most part, they'd flown high enough that she was sure few people noticed them. Especially with the thick forests that dominated Dracwood blocking the sky. She couldn't say the same for Magehaven, or now for Flamesmoat. Everyone out and about stopped what they were doing to gape at the sky and watch them pass.

If she were in their place, she'd have likely done the same. No country in the world revered dragons like Dracwood. They had the Church of the Dragon to prove it. But after the battle in the Abandoned Lands, everyone assumed they were extinct. It must be the shock of a lifetime to see three of the majestic creatures flying overhead.

She could count on one person to not be surprised. Kayda knew about the eggs. Violet's insides buzzed. She was about to bring her aunt—her queen—the thing that had eluded her for twenty years. Talk about a great wedding present. Surely no one would offer anything better.

Mena flew over the deep moat surrounding the city, which no longer housed the flames that gave the city its name. Then the well-kept homes and shops of the city's prosperous Northmoat section slid beneath them.

To the north, the coast was home to Kings Keep. The castle and surrounding grounds stood out starkly from up above. The old stone mansion and gorgeous manicured lawn would have seemed more at home in the countryside instead of within such a large city.

Still, the sight of their destination made Violet's smile widen. She was beyond ready to set foot on solid land. Dragon riding was exhilarating, but after hours of clutching Mena's back, every muscle in her body ached.

Violet nudged Mena again, guiding her to land on the castle grounds. Mena angled for the lawn, landing between the old stone tower and the castle. Crys and Ari thumped onto the ground beside her.

Jayan hopped off immediately. He shook out his limbs, and the pallor Violet had first spotted when he'd mounted Crys' back finally lifted. "If I never have to do that again, I'll die a happy man," he grumbled.

Ryon jumped off Ari. "What are you talking about? That was amazing." A brilliant grin lit his face as he circled Ari and approached Mena.

Violet handed Orry to Ryon when he offered her a hand. He cocked an eyebrow but didn't hesitate to cradle her bondmate in his arms while Violet slid off Mena's back.

"*I'm quite capable of walking,*" Orry said, but from the amusement in her tone, she wasn't too upset at being helped.

"*And here I thought you were used to having all your needs seen to by humans.*" Violet adjusted the straps on her pack.

A door slammed. Men carrying weapons streamed out of the tower. Violet's stomach dropped. How did she forget the tower was home to the Castle Guard? Within moments, they were surrounded, staring down countless blades and arrows.

"Stay back," one of them shouted.

"Defend the kingdom," another man cried.

Blazes! Violet held up her hands in surrender. "We're here to see—"

"Silence invaders!" A guard pushed forward, waving a battle axe in the air.

Mena tensed and cracked open her jaw. Several of the guards gasped, their eyes widening as they stared at the light spilling out from the fire burning in her belly. Ari and Crys cocked their heads, their gazes darting between each other and the guards.

Violet worried her lip with her teeth and backed up, leaning against Mena's hide, hoping to calm her. Without Nox, no one could talk to the hatchlings. He'd instructed them what to expect before leaving with Gwen, but who knew what they'd do if they felt threatened?

Violet spotted Ryon fingering one of his dreads. He'd offered to make a wish to talk to the dragons, but she'd advised him against it. They had no idea what challenges they'd face when they returned to the ring, so she thought it wise to save them. Now she sensed he was regretting listening to her.

What were they going to do? Tension curled through the air. She held her breath, trying to calm her racing heart and think of a solution.

An overweight older man elbowed his way through the crowd of guardsmen, sweat beading on his brow despite the cool afternoon. "What is the meaning of this?" He halted, his gaze roving over first the dragons and then landing on her before she recognized him. "Violet?" His eyes widened. "Is that...?" He clasped his chest and his jaw dropped. "Jayan? It can't be!"

"Aye, it is." Jayan strode forward, heedless of the men still pointing blades in his direction, and shook hands with Guard Captain Gawain.

"At ease," Gawain barked. The men lowered their weapons, but none appeared eager to disperse. Most stared unabashedly at the dragons, and many began to point and whisper among themselves.

Still, Violet sighed as Mena's jaw snapped shut and the tension in her frame faded. That could have ended disastrously if not for the Guard Captain recognizing them.

"Hundreds of folks have arrived for the wedding tomorrow, but none of them have made an entrance like that." Gawain chuckled.

Violet strode over as the men broke apart, nodding for Ryon to follow. "Thank you for stepping in, Guard Captain. My apologies for landing so close to the castle without warning, but I must have a word with my aunt. It's urgent and of the utmost importance."

"Of course." Gawain frowned. "They're hosting dinner in the Great Hall. I'll bring you immediately. Follow me." He leaned sideways. "The dragons will need to stay out here. No room inside." He raised his voice. "No one will bother them. You have my word."

Violet paced back to Mena. She stopped in front of her and motioned with her hands while speaking. First, she indicated herself and her companions. "We need to go inside." She ended by pointing to the castle. Then she pointed at each hatchling and down at the ground. "You three, stay here, please."

She wasn't sure if Mena understood or if she'd comply. Especially when Mena's gaze returned to the castle after Violet finished waving her arms. The white dragon stared at the building for a long moment with narrowed eyes. She nodded once, folded her wings neatly, and seated herself on the lawn. The other hatchlings followed suit. Violet loosed a sigh, then turned on her heel.

The walk to the castle passed in a daze. Guard Captain Gawain kept up a steady commentary, mostly chatting about the wedding and inquiring about Jayan's whereabouts. But though she certainly noticed how it unsettled Jayan, who only provided short, clipped answers, she couldn't concentrate on their conversation.

Violet was awash with stress. The words she planned to say ran unbidden repeatedly through her mind. She barely even noted the castle's splendor as they entered.

The servants had outdone themselves, making the halls and common rooms sparkle. Flowers overflowed in decorative vases on nearly every side table. The fresh aroma smacked her in the nose, though the effect was wasted on her.

She shouldn't be so nervous. Kayda was family, after all. Much of what she had to share would surely leave her elated.

But her aunt was also queen. It was hard to not be unsettled when she needed to tell Kayda her life was in danger. Not just the immediate danger at the wedding, either. Violet wouldn't stop until she'd shared all of it. Jurdan was a threat they couldn't afford to ignore.

The murmur of voices bled through the door to the Great Hall. Gawain eased it open, revealing a crowd unlike any Violet had seen within. The Great Hall usually comfortably seated all the merchants and local officials important enough to have the ear of the queen during the Harvest Festival. Today, the room was stuffed with foreigners as well.

Several tables had been added to accommodate everyone. Thick-bearded blonds and redheads from Doln brushed elbows with scantily clad dark-haired Raimish. Jorian traders in their brightly dyed spider silk tunics and even brighter dyed hair chatted with Sul warriors wearing orange clothes and fierce expressions.

The conversations continued, and no one paid much attention to their group as they entered. Gawain shuffled sideways, leading them away from the door and through a thin aisle between the crowded tables. Even though it was more packed than usual, the space hadn't escaped the servants' frenzy. The enormous chamber shone with light from spotless stained-glass windows, and the brilliant tapestries decorating the walls looked freshly laundered.

Violet's breath caught as she spotted her aunt. Kayda sat on a raised platform at the far end of the Great Hall, next to her intended. They were decked out in finery for the occasion. Taul wore a perfectly tailored suit, and Kayda a beautiful gown, in matching shades of plum.

But their clothing was about all Violet could see for the moment. The Great Hall was huge, and with how crowded it was, they were forced to move at a snail's pace. Gawain certainly hadn't been kidding when he'd claimed there was no room for the dragons.

Before they'd passed the first set of tables, Taul stood. He lifted his glass and tapped it repeatedly with a fork. As everyone spotted him, their conversations halted.

"I'd like to make a toast," Taul declared, his deep voice ringing out and echoing off the walls.

Violet had half a mind to interrupt in the silence that followed. She ignored the impulse. Sure, she had important news, but that didn't mean she should be rude. With any luck, they'd arrive at the front of the room, at Kayda's side, after Taul finished his toast.

"I'd like to thank you for coming to the Harvest Festival this year. I'm sure I speak for Queen Kayda as well when I say how honored we are to have so many friends here to celebrate our impending wedding."

Kayda tilted her head sideways, and though her red eyes didn't quite land on Taul, she nodded and smiled, lifting her glass.

"Doln and Dracwood haven't always been the closest allies. The battle with the Unseen revealed how foolish we'd been to let trivial differences divide our people. That day, we learned that our countries—our people—are far stronger together than apart."

Clapping rang out, and a few people shouted, "Hear, hear," and, "Rightly so." Violet dodged the arm an enthusiastic Dolnman thrust into the aisle.

Taul spun his cup in his hands. "Most of all, I'm eternally grateful to Queen Kayda for agreeing to have me as a husband." He turned to Kayda, and his voice softened. "I shall endeavor to prove to you we are better united as well."

Jayan stiffened beside her and stopped walking. Violet cleared her throat quietly and nudged him forward.

"Let us drink to unity!" Taul shouted, lifting his glass high.

"To unity," the crowd echoed. The room erupted, shouted cheers and well wishes competing with the *clink* of glassware.

Violet strode through the sea of waving arms and sloshing cups. They'd passed most of the tables during Taul's speech but still needed to navigate past two more to reach Kayda.

Taul and Kayda were still oblivious to their presence. The pair held their cups above their heads, clearly waiting for the cheering to die down before they drank. Finally, Taul sat and clinked his glass gently against Kayda's. She smiled in his direction and lifted her glass to her lips.

Crash!

Glass exploded, raining down from one of the massive stained-glass windows. The cheers flooding the room morphed into screams. A few people leaped out of their seats, either diving to protect loved ones or reaching for weapons.

Violet gasped as a white blur darted through the hole and landed directly behind Kayda. Guards rushed forward immediately, but none were quick enough to stop Mena from knocking the cup out of Kayda's hand with a single whip of her long tail.

"Stop!" Kayda's voice cut through the din. She jolted out of her chair, toppling it over. She spun to the guards advancing on Mena. "No one harm her!"

Guard Captain Gawain burst past the last table, moving faster than Violet would've thought possible for a man his size, even shoving a few guests out of the way unapologetically. He knocked an old man directly into her path, blocking her, Ryon, and Jayan from joining him as he flew toward the high table. "My queen. Are you hurt?"

Kayda brushed her hands through her long auburn curls, knocking a few shards of glass loose. "I'm quite all right. My new bondmate just saved my life."

Gasps sounded, flying out of mouths left and right. Violet leaned down, helping the old man to his feet. The man barely spared her a glance. He was too busy gaping at the scene unfolding.

"Your life, my queen?" Gawain arrived at her side and scanned the table like a dagger might be hidden upon it. Violet cursed inwardly and urged the old man to return to his seat.

"That cup was poisoned. Had I drunk from it, I'd be dead by morning."

The gasps that had sounded mere moments ago paled in comparison to the cacophony that filled the room then. Violet spotted more than one head whip to Taul and heard a woman whisper, "That was Dolnish wine."

A drop of sweat dripped down Gawain's temple. "Guards! Secure the queen. This room will be locked, and no one shall leave until we have questioned everyone present."

Excited chatter broke out as Violet finally worked her way to the front of the room. But guards rushed into the gap, blocking the high table. She fumed and opened her mouth, prepared to yell her head off to secure a word with her aunt, but at that moment, Kayda's voice rang out once more.

"Please, friends! Be seated. Eat. Celebrate. This will be sorted out swiftly, I promise." She snapped her fingers at one of her attendants. "See to it that fresh wine is brought up from the cellars." Then Kayda's head spun to stare at her, and Violet almost wondered if her aunt could see again, her aim was so true. "Captain Gawain. Bring my niece and her companions with us."

The guard allowed them to step forward. Mena leaped into the air and flew out the broken window, causing more shouts and screams. Violet's head spun as she followed Gawain's retreating back toward the same door he ushered Kayda through.

What the blazes was that? It all happened so fast... Was that the danger they'd come to warn Kayda about? Mena had saved Kayda right before her eyes, but she could still barely grasp it, even though she'd seen it unfold.

And were they truly bonded? The long look Mena had given the castle earlier flickered in Violet's mind. Had Mena sensed even then that her bondmate was inside and in danger?

She spared one last look at the scene. Servants bustled around, removing the broken glass. Guards mingled among the guests, and a pair appeared to be questioning Taul already.

The door shut behind them, enclosing them in a formal sitting room decorated in warm, sunny tones. Richly upholstered settees and chaises sat in a loose circle in the room's center.

Kayda didn't sit on any of them. She turned as soon as the door closed and threw her arms open wide. "Violet, come here. I've missed you."

Violet rushed forward and folded herself into Kayda's embrace. "I've missed you, too, Auntie."

"Thank you. For everything," Kayda said in her ear, her voice thick with sincerity. "I can't thank you enough for helping me fulfill the last promise I made to Dru."

"What promise?" Violet asked.

"I promised to find his eggs. To find his young." Her voice caught. "I never imagined I'd bond with his daughter." Kayda pulled back with tears shining in her eyes and a brilliant smile lighting her face. She raised her voice. "Gawain, would you mind throwing open the windows?"

Gawain pushed off his spot stationed at the door and strode swiftly across the room. Violet giggled when Mena popped her head inside the opening as soon as she was able. Gawain backed away, eyeing the white dragon nervously.

"It's quite all right, Gawain." Kayda chuckled. "I'm afraid you and your men will need to get used to seeing dragons around Kings Keep again."

Behind her, a throat cleared. Jayan stood beside Ryon, his patience clearly at a breaking point.

"Auntie. There's someone here—"

"Princess," Jayan cut in huskily.

Kayda gasped. "Jayan?"

"Aye," he replied.

Kayda stepped forward. Jayan met her step for step until they collided. Tears fell, and sobs escaped.

Violet backed away, sensing she should give them a moment of privacy but unable to peel her eyes away from the touching reunion.

Twenty years. They'd been apart for so long. Jayan had no idea what he'd left behind, but clearly Kayda hadn't forgotten him.

She pulled out of his arms, tears staining her freckled cheeks. "I'm so sorry. I wish I'd never asked you to leave."

"It's over now. I'm home." He cradled her face, wiping away her tears.

Ryon's hand slipped into Violet's. She squeezed his palm but didn't stop watching.

Kayda slid her hands up Jayan's arms and traced his face. "I missed you so much." She sighed deeply. "If only I could see you."

"*It's beautiful, isn't it? I can't look away.*" Orry's voice in her mind finally broke Violet out of her stare. She darted a quick glance at her bondmate still cradled comfortably in the crook of Ryon's arm. "*If only love could heal the blind,*" Orry mused. "*Perhaps for them, it shall, hm?*"

Violet's nose scrunched. "*What's that supposed to mean?*"

Orry cocked her head, turning to face her. "*Don't ask me.*" She spun back to watch Kayda slowly trace Jayan's face, tears silently spilling down her cheeks. "*Stop looking and listen.*"

Listen... Their heartsongs.

Violet closed her eyes briefly, then snapped them open. She concentrated, calling on the part within that she'd only learned to use once she'd bonded to Orry. Her inner ears opened wide, picking out the first hint of a beautiful melody in the air.

She focused on Kayda, thinking the gorgeous notes must be coming from her aunt. But when she did, the tune faded.

How strange. She turned to Jayan and bit back a gasp.

Violet had listened to Jayan's heartsong before. The melancholy dirge she remembered had pulled at her heartstrings. But this... "*It's different,*" she confessed to Orry. "*How is it so different now from when I listened to him in Avion?*" His song was a grand ballad that sank into Violet's skin, wrapped around her chest, and brought tears to her eyes.

"*Love,*" Orry replied. "*It changes everything.*"

Suddenly, she knew. "What if you could, Auntie?" she blurted.

Kayda startled, seeming to have forgotten anyone else was present. "Hmm?" Her hand stilled on Jayan's face, then dropped to her side. "What if I could what?"

"What if you could see again?" Violet turned to Orry, who nodded and plucked a golden feather off her chest.

"Violet, it's all right. I've made peace with the loss of my sight. There's nothing to be done." Kayda smiled wanly.

Violet dropped Ryon's hand and lifted the soft feather out of her bondmate's beak. Ryon grinned crookedly and handed her his blade.

She strode over to Jayan, the items held in her outstretched hands. "You came here to save your queen, but Mena beat you to it. How would you like to heal her instead?"

Jayan took the feather and blade without hesitation. "What do I do?"

"Exactly what you did with the silver feather. Only this time, you can only change one thing about someone *else* with your wish," Violet instructed.

"A wish? No!" Kayda jerked forward, her hands flailing, searching the spot beside her. Jayan dodged, stepping aside and weaving to face the window. "I won't have anyone else sacrificing themselves for me. Please!" Kayda's gown fanned out around her as she collapsed to the floor, cradling her face in her hands.

Violet stilled, her brow pinching until she recalled the story of Druturion's death. He'd used a golden feather to bring Kayda back to life. "Jayan won't die. Trust me, Auntie."

Whether Kayda would have agreed, they'd never know. Jayan spun back around, the golden feather clutched in one fist and a blood-stained blade in the other. "It's done," he announced. "Open your eyes, Princess."

Kayda lifted her face out of her hands. Her body trembled and her eyes remained tightly closed. It was as if she was too afraid to open them and discover the bloodfeather had failed to heal her, like everything else she'd tried.

"You're still here?" she whispered. "Jayan?"

"Aye." The blade clattered to the floor. Jayan kneeled in front of Kayda and grasped her hand. "Right here where I belong."

Slowly, Kayda's eyes fluttered open. Violet frowned. She'd been expecting the odd red color that her aunt alone possessed to be gone, yet it wasn't.

Jayan smiled. "Did it work? Can you see me?"

Kayda blinked furiously. "Yes, but"—her head darted around, flicking to Mena and back to Jayan—"not like before. I'm looking through new eyes." She grabbed Jayan's hand and stood, tugging him to his feet with her. She led him across the room and directed him toward the open window. Toward Mena.

"Did I say it wrong?" Jayan stared at the bloodstained feather he still held in one hand.

Violet glanced at Orry. "*What happened?*"

"No." Kayda spoke up before Orry answered. "You've given me a great gift, Jayan. Now let me look at you." They both stopped in front of Mena. Kayda faced Jayan, but when he moved to do the same, she said, "Not yet. I'm not through."

"*I don't understand...*" Violet quirked a brow. "*I thought the feather would heal her? Why is she looking through Mena's eyes?*"

Orry twisted her neck, angling for a better view of the trio at the window. "*Wishes are fickle things. The consequences are not always what we first pictured. Often there is knowledge in our blood that transcends our desires and gives one what they truly need instead.*"

"*I won't pretend to know what that means.*"

"*A wise decision*," Orry replied, laughter in her voice. "*Don't fret. Listen again.*"

Violet shook her head but obeyed, using her boon to listen. This time, she didn't hear just Jayan's song. Another tune played in concert, the melodies entwining with each other so perfectly she couldn't hold back her gasp.

Ryon slipped his hand back into hers. "Everything all right?"

"Yeah." Violet nodded and wiped her burning eyes. "It's wonderful."

Sure, that wasn't entirely true. A host of problems awaited them. She had a friend to save and a journey to embark on. But for once in her life, she refused to worry.

Her mother had promised her before she'd left home that the choices she made would change the world. And sure, maybe there was more to come, but right here and now, the proof of her mother's claims stared back at her.

A soft smile lit her face. She didn't have to wonder anymore. She *had* made a difference.

Violet squeezed Ryon's hand, closed her eyes, and listened.

Epilogue

The charcoal scratched on the parchment as Ereni signed her name. She folded the page neatly, all while her body hummed with worry.

If this letter didn't arrive on time... No. It would. It must.

She'd always known fate had special plans for her. For her family. Long ago, she'd tried to escape it. But no longer. This trip was just more evidence of fate's heavy hand guiding her steps.

A knock drew her from her reverie. She stood, tucked the letter into the pocket of her pale-pink dress, and quickly crossed the inn bedchamber's wooden floor.

She swung the door open to reveal a stranger. He was perfectly ordinary in every way, with average looks and height. The only thing that stood out was the badge on his tunic—a rolled parchment held in the mouth of a dove.

A courier. How convenient when that was exactly what she needed. You might even say—fated. But she supposed she needed to see what he'd come for first.

"Hello. What can I do for you?" She fought to keep the impatience out of her tone, but a smidge bled into her voice.

"Ma'am." The man cleared his throat and thrust a sealed parchment toward her. "I have a delivery for Conall of Greenvale. Is he within?"

Ereni shook her head, making her dark-brown ponytail bob across her shoulders. "Not presently. I will make certain my husband receives it." She unfolded a hand, holding it out expectantly.

The courier handed her the letter but made no move to leave. Waiting for a tip, no doubt. Ereni twisted the parchment in her hands, catching a whiff of something odd on the paper. Was that fish?

"Who is it from?" she asked casually.

"I didn't catch her name, I'm afraid." He leaned in close. "'Twas a lovely blonde. Quite fetching."

Ereni stiffened. She tore open the wax seal, her gaze quickly darting across the page.

The courier cleared his throat. Ereni glanced up, only to find him offering her a second letter. "She said the woman who answered would read it, and to give you this once ya had." He chuckled nervously. "I honestly didn't believe her."

Ereni snagged the second letter and tore it open. A cursory scan revealed it to be a duplicate of the last, except for who was addressed in the greeting.

"Well, if that'll be all..." The courier stepped back.

"Just a moment." Ereni fished out her coin purse and withdrew a coin. "For your trouble."

The man's eyes gleamed. "Thank you."

Ereni offered him five more. "I need a letter sent by dove. Can you make certain it flies with due haste?"

"That won't be any trouble, ma'am. What's the destination?"

Ereni pulled the letter out of her pocket and handed it over. "Kings Keep."

The courier nodded and began strolling down the hall. Ereni rolled her eyes and cleared her throat. "One more thing."

"What's that?" The man turned, cocking a brow.

"I wasn't kidding when I said haste." Ereni tossed him another coin, which he caught in midair. "Run."

The courier pocketed the coin and took off at a jog.

Conall appeared at the top of the stairs just as the courier barreled past him. He jumped aside, clutching a laden pack to his chest. "Blazes. Is he trying to break my other leg?"

Ereni stood in the doorway, watching her husband hurry down the hall. His bondmate, Shadow, trailed behind, his gray tail swaying happily when he spotted her. Both of them shone with a bright-red aura to her seer eyes.

"Did you find everything?" she asked.

Conall jiggled the pack in his arms. "Took a bit more coin than I'd expected, but it's all here." He nodded backward. "Who was that?"

Ereni lifted the letters. "We've been summoned to the docks."

The pack thudded on the wooden floor. Conall leaned over, planted a kiss on her cheek, and snagged one of the letters.

Ereni smiled softly as he pulled away, a twinkle in his hazel eyes. But once he'd scanned the page, the twinkle faded. "Any clue who sent this?"

"The courier didn't give a name. He did say she was a fetching blonde. And of course, there's the odor."

Conall sniffed the page. "No." He dragged a hand through his gray hair. "What would she be doing this far south?"

Ereni shrugged. "I suppose we should go find out."

"All right. We can stop there on the way out of town." Conall hefted the pack and dumped it on the bed. After quickly separating the supplies into two packs, they left the room and headed down the stairs.

Ereni shifted on her feet while she waited for Conall to speak to the innkeeper. The common room was abuzz this morning. And far more crowded than the last few days they'd breakfasted in the sunny wood-paneled tavern. But she supposed it was to be expected after what the town witnessed earlier.

"Can you believe it?" a man declared, slamming his mug into the table behind her. "I thought they were dead for good."

"Seems like a bad omen, if you ask me," a woman answered.

"Bad omen? Are you daft? 'Tis a blessing."

The woman scoffed. "Remember what happened last time? Why else are they returning if not to fight something worse?"

Conall appeared at her side. "We're all set. Ready?"

They exited the inn, stepping into the bright sunshine. Shadow loped along beside them, earning a few stares from the people of Magehaven. Soon, they'd passed the willow in the town square and turned for the docks. A mass of rocks clattered inside Ereni's stomach the closer they came to the water.

"I forgot to tell you," Conall said. "I didn't secure the horses yet. The stables closest to the inn didn't have any available. We'll need to try the one on the outskirts of town."

Ereni nodded absently. They'd decided to head back to Greenvale. After this morning, there was no reason to stay.

Her mind flashed back to the spectacle they'd observed. They'd heard shouting and stepped onto the inn's balcony. She'd been so sure some fool would be up to no good on the road. But the townsfolk were looking at the sky instead. No one watching would have recognized who flew above them. She couldn't make out faces on the tiny figures from where she stood. But she had one advantage no one else possessed.

The violet glow surrounding the person riding the white dragon was slightly redder than she recalled, but nonetheless unmistakable. Ereni's breath had caught as she made the connection, pride swelling in her chest.

But then she'd spotted the glow around the second figure. Silver. Most people were dull, with no glow at all. Blue used to surround the few with elemental magic in their veins. These days, she rarely saw it. But silver... In all her years, she'd never seen an aura that shade.

And the third, Ereni shuddered. After the battle in the Abandoned Lands, she'd prayed to never see that color wreathed around someone again. Until this morning, she hadn't.

Conall sighed heavily. "What a waste of time this was."

She grabbed his hand and squeezed. "No, it wasn't. I needed to see. It will make a difference. I know it."

"You could've seen it just the same if we were at the festival."

"I suppose we'll never know." Ereni grinned. "At least we got to relive old times, camping in the woods."

Conall smirked. "That was rather fun, wasn't it?"

They turned down a side road and spotted the docks. Ereni tugged a letter from her pocket. "Here," she declared, pointing to the center berth. They trailed to the very end and found a tiny craft moored to the spot they'd been directed to. A man sat in the rowboat, humming and whittling a rough piece of wood.

"Hello," Conall called.

The sailor looked up and set his craft and knife down. "You the ones I'm waiting for, I take it?"

Ereni held up the letter. "Yes."

"Hop in. I'll take you to her."

Shadow had to be coaxed, but soon they'd piled inside. The sailor kept up his humming as he rowed them across the shallow bay to a huge-sailed vessel anchored offshore. A sign on the side dubbed the vessel *Laumarle's Triumph*.

They clambered on board and followed the sailor below deck. He knocked three times on a door. "Come in," a woman called from within.

Conall twisted the knob and pushed the door open. Ereni walked through, her gaze immediately falling on the curly-haired blonde perched on the edge of a small cot in the tiny cabin. A woman she instantly recognized.

"Halynn. To what do we owe the pleasure?" Ereni asked. The years had been kind to the Winter Witch of the North. It had been more than two decades since Ereni last saw her, but she looked like she'd barely aged. The same bright-green glow Ereni had only spotted on Halynn and her predecessor was still wreathed around her shoulders.

Halynn's blue eyes flashed, scanning them quickly before a wide grin spread across her face. She stood, digging in the pocket of her simple black dress. "I've come a long way to find you two." She stretched out her hand, revealing three tiny glass vials filled with green fluid. "I hope you're up for a swim. There's something you need to see."

Mariun groaned. Her head pounded incessantly, and her body swayed. Her shoulders and back ached, and though she tried to move to relieve the pressure on them, she couldn't manage the task.

Where was she? What was that awful noise?

Squinting, she cracked open her eyes and spotted a gull perched beside her. It opened its mouth and cawed loudly. Her eyes widened as she stared beyond the ugly bird. Endless blue blanketed the horizon, a cloudless sky above and the sea below.

It all came rushing back. The masked abducting her. Nox sprawled out on a cliff, covered in blood. The constant prick of darts in her skin, and confusion blanketing her every time she crawled out from under the sleeping tonic's lull. After the first time she'd woken and attacked the man closest to her, they'd taken to keeping her drugged constantly.

She flinched, her gaze darting away from the annoying gull.

Were the masked watching her now? Was someone about to drag her under with another dart?

If only she were back in Avion. She hadn't wanted to leave. It was the last thing she'd wanted to do. But they'd threatened to sack the village if she didn't go quietly. To kill her friends and the innocent men, women, and children who'd shown them so much kindness in their time of need. To murder Nox while he lay unconscious at her feet. What was she supposed to choose?

What Mariun spotted next made the hair on her neck stand on end and her stomach roil. A murder of crows descended, landing on board the ship. The gull took off, and one last caw pierced her ears.

The thump of boots rang out moments later. Mariun stilled, then tugged on her arms again. The sting in her wrists confirmed her fear. It wasn't the darts that were keeping her from moving. She was bound where she sat, arms pulled back behind her and secured to the mast.

"Hello, Mariun."

The familiar voice chilled her blood. Mariun slowly turned her head, cursing her rotten luck.

"Jurdan." She sneered.

"That's Father to you." Jurdan the Supreme kneeled in front of her, his long purple robes pooling on the deck at his feet. He set his black eyes on her, and Mariun shivered.

"Didn't you get the message when I left? I want nothing to do with you. Can't you just let me go?"

He stood, circling behind her slowly. "I'm afraid not. I had to bring you back. I have something to show you." He sliced through her bindings, and the pressure on her shoulders finally eased. "And of course, I need to thank you as well."

"Thank me?" she asked incredulously. "For what?"

"Come. This way." He strolled away, heading to the bow railing.

Mariun rubbed her shoulders, following him cautiously. She scanned the boat. Masked men were about, but none seemed to pay any attention to her or Jurdan. A few stood on the aft deck, working together to drag a heavy load of fish on board. When it thumped down, they dug through the pile, tossing the smaller brightly colored fish overboard and keeping the few fat silver ones with big bulging eyes.

This could be her chance! She could race to the side rail, grab something heavy, and disappear beneath the waves.

It wasn't the first time she'd contemplated ending things. With Jurdan there pulling the strings of her existence, it often felt like it might be her only escape.

But the idea didn't bring her comfort any longer. Not when she knew what she was missing. Her life had changed so much since she'd left Thalassia. She'd made friends. Found someone who saw her and who proved that good men still existed. She'd *lived*. Mariun couldn't bear the thought of taking the coward's way out when there was still a chance to get that back.

Besides, she couldn't deny the need to witness the rest of this story unfold. What did Jurdan want to show her in the middle of the ocean? And what could he possibly want to thank her for? Frankly, she'd been expecting him to scream and berate her for daring to leave.

So she followed. He stopped at the railing and offered her a spyglass. Mariun frowned but plucked it out of his fingers.

She squinted at the horizon. "Where do I look?"

Jurdan pointed. She followed his direction and stared through the glass.

Was that a bird? No. Mariun gasped.

"The champion returns." Jurdan chuckled. "I wasn't sure if you'd make him fall in love with you, but I suppose you must've."

Mariun's heart pounded. "I-I..." The spyglass clattered and rolled when her shaking fingers dropped it.

"You what? You didn't realize I'd been counting on your foolish lover to come save you?" Jurdan smirked, flicking his long black hair over one shoulder. "I'm not surprised. You may have inherited my gift, but the gullibility comes from your mother."

Relief pulsed through her, nearly making her lightheaded. Nox was alive! She's been so afraid his attempt to save her had led to his death. But chills quickly chased away the warmth blooming in her heart. "I don't understand..."

"It's simple. Once the fool is captured, his bondmate will call the rest of the dragons to come save him. And I'll have them exactly where I want them with the leverage to make them obey." Jurdan's smile spread, his eyes lit with a cruel glint. "I truly can't thank you enough, Daughter. You played your role to perfection."

Mariun backed away. "But what do you want with the dragons? If you think you can make them fight a war for you just to save one man, I don't think—"

"Ha." He laughed caustically. "You have it all wrong. Why would I bother taking over one continent when I can take it all?"

What was that supposed to mean? She threw out a hand, pointing at one of the crows. "The dragons aren't dimwitted birds. They won't follow your orders."

"No? Are you so sure?" Jurdan stared off the bow, a sneer curling his lips. "Trust me. Grief can cause even the smartest among us to make terrible choices."

Mariun's stomach sank. "What are you talking about?"

"Did you know Queen Kayda can bond dragons? How much do you want to bet that once she dies, they won't be willing to watch another one of their siblings lose a bondmate?"

If that was true... But wait. A slow smile creeped across Mariun's face.

"It won't work. I told Nox what you were planning. They'll save the queen from whatever foul mischief you've arranged at her wedding." Mariun's confession didn't achieve the effect she'd expected.

Jurdan met her gaze calmly and grinned. "You're wrong again. Do you know why?" He didn't pause to let her answer. "Because I learned this lesson long ago. Never trust anyone. Especially family."

Mariun's mind raced. He couldn't mean... Had he planned for her to betray him?

"I see you're getting it. The first attempt—the one I allowed you to overhear—was merely a distraction. But don't worry. The real threat is in place, right under her nose." Jurdan chuckled. "I'm afraid there will be no wedding at the Harvest Festival. Perhaps they can turn the celebration into a funeral?"

No. Nox would be devastated. He spoke so fondly of his sister Kayda. She didn't deserve to be murdered, caught in the midst of the sinister plans of an evil man she'd never even met.

And here she was, just as stuck as those poor fish squirming on the deck. When Mariun had escaped, she'd told herself that she'd never go back. Her life in Thalassia was miserable. She'd been led around like a puppet, without choice.

Never again. When she'd escaped, she'd vowed her decisions would always be her own. So was this. Jurdan wouldn't succeed. She refused to allow it. For all the people he'd killed. The lives he'd destroyed. Whatever he was planning, she would find a way to thwart it.

Forget the coward's way. She would be his slayer, and if death was her reward, then so be it.

Also by

Binge the complete Palisade Trilogy now. An epic fantasy adventure,
full of unique magic, animal companions, dragons, betrayal, and a
quest to save the world.

Shadows That Bind Us — Palisade Trilogy 1
Muses That Align Us — Palisade Trilogy 2
Lines That Drew Us — Palisade Trilogy 3

Sign up for my newsletter for a free standalone prequel novella that
tells the story of how the Palisade was built centuries ago.
You'll find the link on my website amberlwerner.com

Standalone Short Story
Somewhere In Between

The Blood Song Trilogy
The Odyssey Ring – A Blood Song Trilogy Prequel

Bloodfeather Lullaby — Blood Song Trilogy 1

Bloodfeather Heartsong — Blood Song Trilogy 2

Bloodfeather Symphony — Blood Song Trilogy 3
(Expected Release — Fall 2024)

About the Author

Amber L. Werner loves to write about magic, monsters and mythical creatures. She lives in Norristown, PA with her husband and two children. Read more of her work in the Blood Song Trilogy, and The Palisade Trilogy, her complete debut series.

Follow her Facebook page Amber L. Werner
Or Instagram amberlwerner

Sign up for her newsletter and receive a free novella.
Find it here amberlwerner.com

www.ingramcontent.com/pod-product-compliance
Lightning Source LLC
Chambersburg PA
CBHW022256310726
48973CB00001B/96